LADDER
MEDIA

A
British
Crash

Roger Harper

This is Roger Harper's first novel.
Roger is a Priest of the Church of England
and a regular contributor to *Christianity* magazine.

Ladder Media Limited

a Christian Equitable Company
www.abritishcrash.co.uk

First published in Great Britain by
Ladder Media 2009

This paperback edition
1

Cover design by Russell Wallis, © Ladder Media Ltd. 2009

"Millennium" words and music by John Barry and Leslie Bricusse and Guy Chambers and Robert Peter Williams © 1998, reproduced by permission of EMI Virgin Music Ltd and EMI United Partnership Ltd, London W8 5SW Published also by Kobalt Music Publishing Ltd.

A catalogue record of this book is available from the British Library
ISBN: 978-0-9561848-0-1

Printed and bound in Great Britain by CPI Antony Rowe Ltd.

For my mother,
with thanks for all the encouragement and support
over the years.

Saturday Night

'Tariq! No!' A young woman's scream tore through the air. Her anguished and terrified voice echoed around the car, ricocheting off the blue interior.

Tariq, at the wheel, was paralysed. His mind filled with the piercing wail, rooting him to his seat, clamping his arms.

'Do something Tariq!' The girl threw her face towards him, her golden hair following frantically.

Tariq saw the rush of gold at the corner of his eye while his eyes were mesmerised by the concrete wall in front of them. With a great jerk he wrenched the steering wheel to the right, terrified that the car would still hit the wall on the left, the girl's side. For a fraction of a second he hoped that the solid old Japanese car would be tough enough to withstand the bruising smash that seemed inevitable.

Nothing happened. The nightmare continued. The steering wheel could go no further and had made no difference to the car. The wall was still rushing towards them, a monstrous grey slab, indiscriminately able to crush metal, glass, flesh and bone.

Lizzie's scream ran down Tariq's back like a bolt of lightening. His mouth gaped wide, his wide eyes darting from the wall to the wheel, to the wall to the girl, to the wall.

Suddenly her head leapt towards him. As her body jerked, her hand shot out and grabbed the hand brake. A fraction of a second before the car smashed into the wall it lurched to the right.

The left corner of the bumper folded into the pale blue body of the car and jammed the wheel. The headlight burst into a thousand shards as it was engulfed by the putty-like body metal.

Inside it all seemed so quiet, even her scream lunging at him from a distance now. 'This is it' flashed calmly through his mind. 'The end.'

The engine block began to give way before the voracious wall, crashing through the inner body of the car onto the flimsy legs inside. Then, as it compacted itself, it began to resist, and suddenly held firm. Bodies and metal collided.

Black silence exploded in his head, claiming everything.

Why write at all? The events of the last eighteen months have been so extraordinary that I need to write them out. My place in it all has been extraordinary too; no-one else could have been involved as I was. I was like a little dinghy suddenly caught up in a flotilla of ships, all looking to me in some way. So no-one could write the story in the way that I can. And it needs to be written. The ramifications of what happened are extensive for all of us here. That's another reason to write, to try to see what it all means.

Paul, our vicar, is often encouraging us to write, to write a record before God of what has happened and what we have thought and felt, a journal he calls it. A couple of years ago on a church weekend he had us all writing like this for half an hour each day. It was odd at first but made me see and understand what had been happening in a clearer light. It was like going to the gym. You have to make yourself do it, but you feel better afterwards.

Since then I've been writing from time to time, enjoying the flow of pen on paper, glad to be able to stand back half a step from life. (It's certainly better than staring at a screen at work and fumbling with four fingers on a keyboard). Without that weekend I wouldn't have ever thought of writing this all out. Things do come together, work together. Sometimes it's definitely right to write.

David Jeffery

Sunday

The first I heard was when I asked Will after church how Jason was. Jason had been pretty low all year since his engagement to Lizzie had been broken off. I'd hoped that over the summer he'd have picked up a bit, perhaps met a good girl at the youth camp where he was a leader.

'He was looking a lot brighter,' said Will, 'until he heard about Lizzie's accident.'

'Nothing serious, I hope.' I tend to fall easily into banal comment.

'Very serious. She was out with her new man on Friday. He smashed up the car. Smashed up Lizzie as well. She's in a pretty bad way. In intensive care at Queens.' Will was almost spitting.

'Grief. Jason'll be worried sick.' I didn't want to make any comment about Lizzie's new boyfriend. That would be too dangerous.

'He doesn't know whether to visit her or not. You know Lizzie's Mum was pretty glad she'd dumped Jason.' Will paused for me to confirm this. I kept as non-committal as I could. Jane and I had always thought this was Will's way of coping with losing the future daughter-in-law he had set his heart on. 'He doesn't expect they'll welcome him to her bedside. But he can't keep away either.'

'Poor Jason' I said. 'Tell him Jane and I will pray for Lizzie and for him.' That sounded a bit pious for me, but I couldn't think of anything else to say and we were in church. 'We'd love to see Jason again if he could come round some time? Perhaps talking about the summer would take his mind off it a bit.' I took a deep breath as curiosity got the better of me. 'How's Lizzie's new man - I can't remember his name?'

'Tariq,' Will said distastefully. Losing his future daughter-in-law to an Asian lad had been a hard blow for Will, his racism untouched by his faith. Jane railed at him that she couldn't see how he could be a Christian and say the things he did. I thought Will did it partly for effect.

'They're both in intensive care, stable but barely conscious. The car was a complete mess. That Tariq totally lost it on Queensway and smashed into the walls of the underpass. God, he must have been going it. Took two hours to cut them out of the car. Not much that wasn't broken on either of them. Careless bastard.' Will always speaks his mind even if it includes casual blasphemy. He's not our best witness. He's like a likeable alcoholic who keeps trying and slipping back. Today was not a day to tell him to dry up.

'Look, Will, if there's anything I can do, let me know.' I said. It's funny the way we always say that and most of the time expect and hope that there will never be anything we can do .

Will went off to try and catch Paul who was once again stuck listening to the other Jayne, the one with a 'y', usually a 'Why me?'. I tried to see my Jane but she'd walked home early again, rather than face more questions about what she was 'up to' these days.

I was really bothered about Jason, knowing how much Lizzie still meant to him and how he could burst into the hospital and goad Lizzie's mother, perhaps without intending to. I liked Lizzie too, although I hadn't seen her for nearly two years. She used to stand in church with Jason, her long blond hair and orange jacket shining out in all the dark wood of the pews, swaying to the music of the band. As I looked to the front of the church again, I saw Beryl sitting on her own in the old Lady Chapel, sitting in case someone had a concern to pray about. She smiled at me and, with nothing better to do, I went to keep her company.

'I've just heard about Jason Jennings' ex'. I explained to Beryl. 'She's in intensive care after a car accident.'

'Oh dear' said Beryl in her soft West Country accent. 'And that's what you want to pray about?' She said this with a slightly questioning rise in her voice at the end, just a bit, not enough to merit a full question mark. We sat quiet together for a moment and then Beryl prayed for them all, managing to say all I would have wanted to say. I felt that my problem had been at least halved by being shared with God, said thank you to Beryl and started to stand up. 'Oh,' she said in an encouraging but 'please don't disappoint me' tone, like a good girl who's been told that it's nearly time to leave playing with her best friend down the road.

'Let's pray for you and see if the Lord has anything for you.' I had been warned about this and my experience was that the only things 'the Lord' ever had for anyone from Beryl were sweet nothings of the 'good boy' kind. But I didn't have any reason to go - needing to pick up a green cup and saucer with lukewarm 'good for the poor farmers' coffee before it was tipped away wouldn't sound a good enough excuse. Beryl sat quietly again with her hands on her blue floral skirted lap. I closed my eyes and said something like 'Please help me to do the best I can for my family, for others, and for you.' It felt good, quiet and restful, the old stone around us a haven thick enough and wise enough to keep away petulant storms and insinuating frosts. 'I see you with a helmet,' said Beryl, 'a tall medieval helmet with a long nose guard. It's your helmet for you to put on.' 'Thank you,' I said wondering what on earth that was about and if she'd been taking her grandchildren round Warwick Castle recently.

Jane was not impressed when I told her about Will's attitude to the accident. 'Couldn't he find even an ounce of sympathy for the poor boyfriend? God he's even accusing him of murder.'

'Come off it Jane. How would you feel if one of ours had a friend in a car accident?'

'That's just it. I wouldn't go jumping to conclusions blaming people. You Christians are so quick to say you're so right all the time.' She shook her head snorting like she was cold as well as angry.

I was riled and didn't mind showing it. 'And where were you this morning? What were you doing sitting in church, Little Miss Criticism?'

'What? Can't I even go to church without people taking me as a bigot too?' Jane was narked. 'You don't become a car by visiting in a garage. Or haven't you heard that one before?'

'What I mean, as you know very well, is that you can't criticise people for not being perfect Christians when you yourself aren't even trying!' That was too much. I shouldn't have gone that far and regretted it immediately.

'Oh, ppohhh!' Jane sounded like a steam engine ready to explode. She ran out of the kitchen door slamming it behind her.

I was shocked. There was no lunch to be had, it seemed, only an eerie silence. Jane's angry waves felt odd in this place that was meant to be so calm. Why was she so upset? Is this what my helmet was for? But it wasn't the first time that we'd lost it on a Sunday. Somehow church seemed to bring out the worst in us. We had married quickly after realising we were the only ones in the youth group who weren't interested in holding back on sex much longer. Or at least that's how it seemed. But the marriage had lasted and borne fruit. We each valued our independence highly and argued more now than ever. Some people just do, don't they? Anyway it was time to go and see when the rugby was on. Australia thumping England soundly would give me something else to be miserable about.

In the sitting room the windows were streaked with rain and the fire was off. The children were away at a friend's party or at least helping with the party. One of their godparents had four younger children and another on the way and ours were delighted to go and set up the birthday party for the seven-year-old. Why had I chosen this time to argue with Jane? Or wasn't it her arguing with me? She had started it with that nasty jibe at Will. Easy target but still my friend.

Why do we Christians act so badly to each other? There's enough aggro from other people who just think we're soft in the head. 'Oh yes,' they say politely, 'how nice for you to have faith,' as though faith is like a cosy holiday cottage which only the privileged can retreat to, while real people have to struggle through in the grimy city. But living with ideals and standards doesn't make life easier. It's hard to live knowing that you aren't measuring up to the habits, the suit of clothes, you really want to. Other people can just choose their habits to fit them perfectly, no discrepancy, no baggy collars or tight waists to worry about. Just chose the values that suit you as you are. We Christians have our ideal habits which can't change. We have to fit ourselves to them. And we never seem to make it. What a life! Maybe I should just go out to the pub for a few pints, then come back and carry on the argument with more venom. That's what I wanted to do.

The television was filling time with another political discussion about the Millennium Dome. 'What a waste of money,' said one worthy in an orangey-brown jacket. 'What a great way to celebrate Britain,' said the sober Party man. It reminded me of the Britannia Park theme park near Nottingham. A British theme park! Wonderful idea. One newspaper reviewer had said that many of the displays would do credit to a Sunday School class. A year later the place was revamped and reopened as 'The American Adventure'. Why do we 'celebrate' Britain in such a worthy, numbingly boring way?

I was about to watch people from the other side of the world come and play a game invented in England. Admittedly they were descendants of the English. But what about that other English invention, football? Everywhere, except for the deepest recesses of rebellious America, men and boys play our game. Skiing began as a crazy English sport. Where do we celebrate this great contribution to world culture? The Establishment had better things on their minds, conquering the world for Civilisation, Commerce, and Christianity, politely but brutally. But the ordinary Englishman has always been more interested in a game of something. Why can't we celebrate this?

Back in the kitchen cutting a couple of thick slices of home made bread, and a chunk of cheddar, I felt more annoyed. The television had been supposed to calm me down, but it just filled my head with more stupidity to be annoyed at. I couldn't say any of this to Jane as she would only goad me into speaking up, to the authority concerned, or shutting up. Most people could pontificate happily without being expected actually to do anything, but not if Jane was around. The pub seemed even more enticing. Maybe I could watch the match there, on a decent big screen. Cheered by the thought of beer for pudding, I ate more happily. On the way out I shouted to Jane where I was going.

'On no you're bloody not!' Jane came purposefully down the stairs with cleaning cloth in hand. 'You stay here. Don't skulk off.'

'But it's just to have a good view of the match,' I lied.

'You can bloody well use that television you insisted on buying.' Jane was not keen on television and the whole family had had to work hard on her for our twenty-four inch screen.

'And if I shout a bit you'll whinge again. For God's sake just give us some freedom.'

'Seriously David, why are we arguing? Come on let's at least try and sort this out.' My threat to go out had brought her downstairs. I couldn't refuse a flag of truce.

'Look I'll make a coffee and a funny tea. The match doesn't start for a while yet.' Jane looked at me daggers but still clutching her cloth, went to the sitting room.

We sat in silence for a while.

'Go on then,' I said provocatively

Jane took a deep breath, closed her eyes briefly, and spoke like a measured bereavement counsellor. 'I know you like Will and I do respect you for sticking with him, but can't you see that he's dangerous sometimes?'

'What's the danger in wanting to protect his son and think the best of him?' I wanted to hold onto my grumpiness a little longer.

'The danger, as you jolly well know, is that he lashes out at anyone who criticises his little darling.' Jane was sparking again. 'Jason can do no wrong. Ever. It's unreal, unchristian, dangerous.' Jane had spoken often about parents who were indignant at any discipline she, as teacher, tried to give their children.

'Stop exaggerating. Give him some space. That's all.' I paused and Jane didn't leap back at me. Her cheeks pulled her mouth into a very brief grin. 'OK he may be a bit partisan as far as Jason is concerned. But you could be more sympathetic.'

Jane went quiet and put down her cloth. She opened her arms and smiled at me. I smiled back, stood up and went to her. Standing over her I took her hand to shake it. She slipped her hand away at the last minute and grabbed my trousers.

'So you're interested in my tackle too,' I challenged, slipping down onto the settee bedside her.

'The children, they are flown,' Jane said huskily. 'And the Jews they say that making lurve on the Sabbath has double blessing.'

'I should threaten the pub more often,' I smiled, not sure if I had pushed it too far. 'Come on, let's ruffle some sheets.'

England scored early as well, but then had to cope with the unfamiliar feeling of not coming from behind. It was needlessly nail-biting, but they just managed to hold out the yellow peril. There are advantages to a slow beginning.

I was relieved but drained. Needing a blast of fresh air I took the Rover out to fetch the children and we had a tray of left-over sausages on sticks, cherry tomatoes, and French stick for supper. I was glad that children today are still trusted with wooden spears. The Health and Safety Pharisees haven't caught up yet. A&E departments are clearly not swamped with children clasping punctured eyeballs or screaming in pain from sticks up their fingernails, despite lurid imaginations provoked by the innocuous sounding words 'Risk Assessment'. Is this what I needed my helmet for?

The children had eaten all day so it was only Jane and I in the kitchen.

'What did happen with that car crash?' Jane asked.

'Just going too fast in the underpass. An accident,' I said blithely. Little did we know. If I could have known then, I might have gone on holiday for a fortnight.

'Strange though isn't it? Moslem boy and English girl. Not a popular combination with some people.' I couldn't tell how serious she was.

'Come on, Jane. Accidents happen. Who's jumping to conclusions now? Slowly does it.' It felt good to have the last word. Jane stuck out her tongue at me.

It did all build pretty slowly, like a party which doesn't get going until most of the guests have arrived. Except it wasn't a party, but a funeral.

Monday

Next day, I thought about putting on my Dad's old flat cap for work, it being the only hat or helmet I had, but Jane said she'd throw it in the wheelie bin if I wore it for anything other than gardening. I did wonder what might come crashing down on my head.

Work was steady, occasionally fraught but not dangerous. Solicitors have been around long enough to have built up intricate but robust systems of, mostly mutual, protection. We fight for the rule of law to protect rich and poor alike (or at least some of us do still) but we don't put ourselves or our families at any risk. My workload was the old-fashioned mix of divorce and conveyancing (often linked, good for solicitors if no-one else), minor criminal work and wills (not linked thank goodness, although one partner did once drunkenly suggest we extend our partnership to include a detective agency and undertaker for the complete service). It was a good varied life, which meant I had to use my brain, usually in similar ways to previously, and meet a variety of people about whom I learnt interesting things very few others did.

One client was Mohammed Khan, local chip shop magnate, who was buying a flat for his elderly aunt and, I believe, wanted to use this as an opportunity to try out a new firm of solicitors. A fellow parent at his girl's school had recommended us to them. It seemed like a simple conveyancing job but one in which we had to impress.

Mohammed and I worked well together - not just because I was making a special effort. We shared a common attitude to his aunt, respectful admiration with occasional bursts of extreme impatience. She had liked the first flat the estate agents had found and we had begun to prepare contracts but then she had decided that a ground floor flat wasn't at all secure. Mohammed, or Philippa his sumptuous PA, didn't take long to find a lovely third floor flat with a good view towards Sutton Park. This was the home of her dreams for long enough to set up a full chain of five people before she decided that she couldn't live her last years without being able to walk straight out onto God's earth as he had intended.

Last Friday she was being taken for the second time to see a ground floor flat in a block where, apparently, there had not been a burglary for twenty-two years. That burglar had been a chivalrous son reclaiming for his divorced mother a family photo album grabbed by the father. Mohammed's aunt had promised the imam that they could have her terraced home next month for a couple of students, over from Pakistan for a year, and there was no way she could break a promise to God and live. So she had to move into her flat or lodge with Mohammed, which would cause his wife to need to visit her aunt in Bradford until Mohammed's aunt left. I had promised Mohammed to be ready this Monday to do all the paperwork necessary to push through the purchase of the flat. Mohammed was determined his aunt was going to like this flat and agree to it, and, on balance, I thought he would succeed, being the more desperate party.

Sure enough, at 8.50 a.m. the phone rang and I could hear Rose saying that I was expecting a call and I would be delighted to speak to Mohammed's P.A.

'Morning, Philippa,' I almost shouted breezily. 'Who's won the contest - the wily lady from Lahore or Birmingham's own Prince of Plaice?'

'Very funny David. Mr. Khan would like you to proceed with utmost urgency with all the necessary work for the purchase of 16 Sandringham Gardens.' Philippa's classy voice had a peeved edge, but she had called me by my Christian name which made up for it.

'Certainly Phil.' I felt like pushing the familiarity a little. It always helps to establish a close rapport with a client's secretary. 'Please congratulate Mohammed for me and say I'd be delighted to treat him to a celebration lunch at the Press, alcohol-free of course. You sound a bit serious this morning, dear Phil? Had a bad fall from the horse yesterday?'

'Not very funny David, in fact not at all funny.' I thought at first Philippa was putting on a show of crossness but she continued even more sharply. 'Mr. Khan's son Tariq was involved in a terrible car accident on Friday night. Mr. Khan is trying to contact the police, handle the Press and get some sense out of the doctors, so he doesn't need your limp humour.' Philippa's voice suddenly started to waver. 'He's bearing up but it's just so...' She was fighting back tears and didn't want me to hear the anguish. She put down the phone. My heart went out to her, concerned and guilty.

I had put my foot in it, not good behaviour for a respectable solicitor. When I stop acting carefully, I can swing to acting childishly. Tariq Khan in a bad accident - that must have been with Lizzie. Were they a pair? I hadn't seen any local news over the weekend. I dashed next door.

'Rose, did you see the *Birmingham Express* on Saturday? Was there anything in it about a bad car accident in Queensway?'

'Oh yes.' Rose is charming but she can be slow in speaking.

'And..?' I said, hoping I came across more encouraging than impatient.

'Yes.' Rose nodded slowly. 'An Asian boy and a white girl were nearly killed. The paper said it could be suspicious. Is Mr. Khan connected with that boy then?' She beamed a concerned smile.

'It's his son, and I'm connected through church with the girl as well. You don't have the paper do you?' Suddenly I wished I paid more attention to the local press. It's the one thing that divides those born locally from those who move in. Even after twenty-five years in Birmingham, local papers and local politics aren't important to me, but I don't let on to true locals.

'Don't worry. I'll enjoy having a walk round to see what I can find,' said Rose, putting down her glasses and smiling sweetly at me. I didn't think I had told her I was worrying and I was sure that the last thing she wanted was to disturb her routine so early in the day, but Rose's offers were not to be refused.

'CAR SMASH CHAOS.' The early edition of the *Birmingham Express* had the story of the accident on page 2. Queensway had been closed all Saturday and most of Sunday. The City Council were assuring people that it was now safe to drive through the underpass – as if there was any reasonable alternative for most people. Lizzie was described as a bright junior reporter on the Post and Tariq as her companion. 'The police are investigating every possibility,' the piece ended, hinting at dark motives, probably to entice readers to buy the next edition. People lose control of their cars all the time, although not usually in such a prominent place.

I wondered what to do now, whether to send a card to Mohammed, and, if so, what kind. It seemed too serious for a 'hope you're soon better' card. A card wouldn't touch Philippa, though, and I felt an impulse to make things better with her. Having brought her to the edge of tears, I could at least go and offer her a hankie or something stronger. But what? A card and a hankie seemed feeble. 'Flowers! Of course,' flashed through my relieved mind. 'Flowers for the lady in distress.' Immediately, I headed for the door of the office, ignoring Rose's matronly voice, 'But David..?'

A couple of corners away stood a flower stall where I had bought softeners for Jane a couple of times. Philippa felt different, classier. It meant a longer walk to 'Pheme', the florist with lots of tasteful space between expensively contorted pots and silver buckets of flawless tall flowers. The assistant also looked like she had stepped out of *Harper's Bazaar*, and even had an American accent to go with it. I explained that I needed a small token for a dear friend recently bereaved, quashing the nagging voice which called this an unwarranted exaggeration. 'Pheme' isn't the place for gifts for the servant class. Her selection of pink and white looked stunning in clear cellophane. The price was also momentarily stunning. I expected, with a raffish smile, that Philippa would recognise the quality of the message.

Walking through the streets towards Mohammed's, I might have liked to meet an acquaintance to show them that David Jeffery wasn't the unimaginative suit that people often wanted him to be. The stirrings of youth had not died away. But, more strongly, I would not want to have to explain the detail. I walked fast to avoid recognising anyone. Round the last corner, I slowed down. 'The card for Mohammed!' How had I forgotten the main thing?

Another headlong march to Carrs Lane Church and Bookshop, where I arrived grateful for no interruptions. The flowers seemed out of place in the Christian simplicity of Bibles and wholesome children's books. I found a tasteful 'Sorry to hear about your difficult time, our prayers are with you' card, to which I just added 'Please let me know if there is anything I can do to help' and headed back to Mohammed's office. It was good to know that, as a man of faith himself, he wouldn't be embarrassed by my mentioning prayer and God.

Mohammed Khan's office didn't look much from the outside, just a doorway on Temple Alley. Inside it was all panelled oak and high ceilings and crimson carpets with the smartest and youngest secretaries in Birmingham. Philippa wasn't one of the young ones but she was always smart with her short light brown hair pushed back from her forehead in a hair band, showing off her brown eyes and immaculate deep red lips.

'Hello David,' she said with a warm edge to her voice, as though she saw me as a friend from school more than a business contact.

'Good morning, Philippa. I'm sorry I put my foot in it earlier.' I smiled and raised my eyebrows. Philippa smiled, pursed her lips and raised her eyebrows too. She fiddled with her necklace. She was not in dragon mood. 'I hadn't realised it was Tariq in the car crash. These are for you.'

Philippa looked bemused. 'I really am sorry about putting my foot in it.' I explained earnestly.

'For me?' Philippa looked open-eyed at me. 'They're not for Raisa, I mean, Mrs Khan?'

'Well, I haven't put my foot in it with her, at least not yet.'

My attempt at light-heartedness was also met with a blank look.

'Look, it is important to me that I don't go around upsetting people I work with. Here…' She had made me stop and think. It hadn't been her son who had died. What was I doing? Embarrassed, I stood back while holding out the flowers.

'Oh Mr. Jeffery,' Philippa's suddenly soft voice reached out first as she stood to come and take the flowers. 'Well. What can I say?'

What happened next had far more significance than I realized at the time. It still left me feeling stirred up and bemused. Philippa came forward to take the flowers in her right hand, and kept coming. Her left hand reached out round my shoulder and drew me to her. Her soft lips pressed briefly into my cheek. As I allowed myself to be drawn into this unaccustomed embrace, Philippa sobbed slightly, apparently overwhelmed by the emotion. She leant into me. Suddenly out of my depth, I couldn't callously draw back. I put my arm comfortingly on her shoulder, which seemed an inadequate response. Briefly I rubbed my hand gently down and up her back. Philippa sniffed back her tears, and also leant into me. I could feel her soft breasts on my chest. Her whole body was pressed against me, with a slight pocket of warmth against my thigh. I recoiled but kept my hand patting the top of her shoulder. I felt a very inadequate comforter. Philippa sniffed again, with more determination to not cry, and looked me in the eye. I fumbled in my jacket pocket for a handkerchief, glad to have a less intimate way of expressing sympathy.

Philippa shook her head, breathed deeply, and walked away towards her desk. 'I'll just keep this in the kitchen,' she said, 'in case anyone gets the wrong idea.'

When Philippa returned, she strode confidently into the room, hair glistening slightly above her immaculate face. 'I will tell Mr Khan you came to express your condolences?' There was only a hint of a question in her voice and slightly raised eyebrow.

'Oh yes. That's, erm, that's what I, err, came for, of course.' I handed her the card. 'Thank you. Thank you so much.' I wasn't sure what I was thanking her for. I left, feeling that somehow my attempt at sympathetic making amends had gone awry. I walked away relieved to be heading back to my depth and my office again.

'A Will Jennings phoned' said Rose letting her curiosity show around her professional coolness like my daughter Emily does when she brings me the post. 'He was quite agitated. He wants you to ring him straight away at home.' I knew the number by heart.

'David, it's serious.' No pleasantries from Will, as usual. 'You asked yesterday if there was anything you could do? Well, Jason's got to go and talk to the police.'

'Yes...' I was trying to slow Will down

'To do with his Lizzie's accident. Could you go with us, sort of professionally?' Will sounded frantic but controlled. It was too early for his whisky.

'I'm more than happy to do what I can, Will.' I stressed the last part to alert Will that he might be asking for the impossible. The 'sort of professionally' request, could mean any amount of work with no clear boundaries and a good chance of falling out with my friend. 'Tell me more, when do they want to see Jason?'

'4.30 p.m. at Central Police Station.'

'Is that tomorrow?'

'Look, if you're busy today...' Will wasn't expecting to have to say anything else

'No, it's just that I'm not sure I'm the most appropriate person for you. Why don't you come round and we'll talk it through?' That would give me a little time to compose my response to Will's request.

'All of us?'

'Jennifer, Jason and yourself. I think that'll be enough.' I pushed my voice up playfully. Will kept quiet.

'When can you be here?'

'Don't go anywhere, we'll be straight round.'

'Jason's OK is he?'

'A bag of nerves. That's why we thought you should be there. In case he says something stupid.'

'Any news of Lizzie?'

'Haven't heard anything. Doesn't sound good. Don't tell Jason. Thanks, David.' The line went dead.

I was afraid that Will, typically, hadn't picked up my hints about not being able to do exactly what he wanted, but I couldn't just say 'No.' This was not just because we were old friends. It wasn't only Rose who was curious about how this would all work out and I wanted to be near the centre of it all.

Jason was a bright and eager young teenager when I came to know him properly in our days leading Pathfinders at church. He was respected in the group as someone who could and always would mend or embellish your bike for you. Never the first to crack a joke or take on a leader if things were becoming boring, he wasn't too far behind. He wasn't the first to drift away from Church, nor to go out seriously with a girl either, but these two great marks of adolescence came together, as they usually do, when he started going out with Lizzie shortly before he was seventeen. We never lost contact completely, hearing about him through Will and Jennifer and seeing him occasionally in church or at the shops. Jason had developed into a pretty good mechanic and he helped out at Paul the grease's little garage on Saturdays and in his holidays. I saw him there occasionally when the Rover needed some work.

Will and Jennifer were worried that Jason would lose Lizzie when she went to Lancaster to study, while Jason stayed at home with his engineering at U.C.E. But they stayed together. Lizzie became a Christian at Lancaster and we began to see more of them in church in the holidays. After Lancaster, Lizzie started working as a reporter on the *Birmingham Express*. We noticed for a while that they weren't around at church, and thought they were probably going somewhere else with more people their own age. But then we heard that they'd split up and Jason was devastated, dejected, and pretty angry. He gave up his new technical job at Longbridge and spent most of his time at Pete's garage, or so Will and Jennifer said. Jennifer could hardly talk about anything else for a while.

Jason was hunched and hesitant when he came in, ushered manfully by Will. You would have thought our office was the police station. Neither wanted a drink so we sat round the coffee table. There wasn't much to say.

'So the police have asked you to go and see them?' I said as matter-of-factly as possible.

'God knows why,' said Will. 'Jason's not seen the girl for months.' Jason winced, his floppy hair trembling.

'What are you worried about?' I asked, looking at Jason.

'We're worried the police will make more of this than they need. We're worried they'll bully Jason. Look.' Will slapped the early evening edition of the *Birmingham Express* down on the table.

'Attempted Murder?' was the headline. They were going to make as much of this as they could with Lizzie working for them. I read it quickly as Will carried on. 'That boy's father is claiming foul play. Can't believe his son could have been so stupid. Pissed out of his head.' Mohammed had been saying the car must have been tampered with. I tried to calm Will down.

'That's just the Press blowing it up. It'll settle down in a few days. These wild allegations never come to anything. Life is always more boring than you think from watching the television.' Little did I know then. 'Don't be afraid of the police. They're firm but mostly polite and careful with it. There's no bonus for more or quicker convictions. But they probably have people onto them demanding they do something, and questioning a few people fits the bill. Pardon the pun.' They didn't laugh.

Instead Will just became more insistent and louder. 'No respect for white boys. They'll do anything to avoid antagonising the darkies.'

'Will! That's enough.' I wished I didn't have to be the schoolmaster to his bullying schoolboy. 'Stop acting like you believe everything the *Sun* tells you, for God's sake.'

Will shut up but glared at me.

'You'll be fine, Jason. I can come with you, but unfortunately I can't act for you professionally.' I made the most of the silence. 'For one thing I know you too well, and for another I know the boy's father too. You won't believe this, but I've actually been helping him buy a flat for his aunt. If you're really worried, contact another solicitor.'

'We're not going in there without some kind of proper support,' said Will, looking at me with half an angry sneer. 'I'll get in touch with the fellow who helped me when my father died. He seemed a tough nut.' Will stared at me, waiting for me to take up his challenge to stop being a weakling. The bully was still in him even after being a Christian for years.

Thankfully I managed to keep calm. 'That was John Strutt, wasn't it? He'll stand up to the police all right but he can put their backs up as well.'

'Better than someone too soft.' Will wasn't giving up without a fight.

I couldn't help smiling, even though I knew it would make Will even more angry, seeing me sneer back at him in my own polite way. 'Please let me know how it goes.' Part of me did want to be kept in touch, but this was also patronising – satisfying to me but annoying to Will.

Will snorted. 'Come on!' he snapped at Jason and Jennifer. As they left, I hoped Will would let Jason do the talking in future, as he would have to.

I had to concentrate on the paperwork for the aunt's flat and a couple of other houses but it wasn't easy. Had I just ended a good friendship? The desire to stay friends in some way, and my curiosity, grew through the day.

As soon as I was home I phoned Will. Jennifer put him on. 'Look, can I come round and talk? I'm bloody furious. Jen can't handle me. Says we must pray about it. For God's sake! Wants me to talk to Paul, poor bloke. You know more about this sort of thing. Can I come and fill you in?' I thought this would be better than Will 'filling in' anyone else. I'd seen him seethe at the Church Council and even rage when we had the churchyard business. He needed someone to let off steam with, so once again I postponed an evening walk with Jane and the three of us were soon sitting down with some of Jane's rose hip tea.

'It couldn't have started worse. The bully boy in blue launched in with "Jason Jennings, where were you last Friday, from morning till evening?" Before we had a chance Jason pitched in with "Not playing with Tariq Khan's car, if that's what you mean." The uniformed git should have calmed him down. He just shouted back "Answer the question." Mr. Clueless Strutt sat there and said nothing. I tried to put a bit of reason into this. I politely asked if they could tell us why Jason was being interrogated. They police prat then turned on me and ordered me out. They were in there for ages. Jason came out trembling. Mr. Strutt just followed him saying nothing. Jason ran into the street and has hardly said a word since.'

'Poor lad,' I said, partly for the need to slip a word into Will's torrent.

'I asked Mr. Strutt what on earth had gone on in there. All he said was Jason had not been co-operating. No blooming wonder. Strutt-brain eventually asked to end the interview. The pathetic plod wants to see Jason again. They'll let him know when, could be any time. It's inhuman to put pressure on a lad like that.' Will sat back and looked glum. He had been rehearsing his tirade and now didn't know what to do.

Jane was sympathetic. 'Poor Jason and poor you. You do seem to have had a bad deal with that man. Whenever we've had police in the school they've been brilliant with the kids, calming everything down.'

'He'd probably had too much to drink at lunchtime - it's CID tradition' I said, immediately regretting giving Will more ammunition.

'Oh, great!' said Will. 'Drunk policemen throwing their weight around.' Will calmed down, I was glad to see. Maybe I had assured him that I was on his side. 'Look, David, couldn't you do something about all this - have a word with someone at the police station? Get them to go easy on Jason. You know him; he's all worked up. But he'd never do anything nasty. Couldn't ever get him to stick up for himself at school. Or maybe have a word with that boy's father, get him to see sense?'

'I had been thinking of trying to see Mohammed when I could,' I said.

'Yes David,' said Jane perkily, 'be the mediator, the investigator - it's just you. No-one else could.' I couldn't tell if she was being 100% serious but I couldn't argue with two of them. I did want to help Will and couldn't let him down by refusing. It seemed to work as well, for Jane managed fairly soon to get Will talking about the new Villa manager and he left a calmer man.

Jane's encouragement had surprised and cheered me. For herself, Jane was unsettled, knowing that she could soon take on more than a couple of days supply teaching a week, but not at all sure that was what she wanted. She felt trapped in teaching, occasionally talking of art courses, or doing a theology degree, enjoying being a mother, but impelled somehow to do something more with her life. Some people, especially at school, couldn't understand what her problem was, but I could see it. She had been too good a girl as a teenager and ended up in a life that didn't fulfil her enough. She was a 1990s woman. The media were shouting at her that she could make more of her life, that she had to find satisfaction in everything. It all made her moodier than before, but I didn't feel threatened. At worst I was exasperated with her gloomier times of indecision, but it was also exciting to think I might become husband to a renowned local artist or even to a radical vicar. The children shared the frustration and excitement; a little wistful for 'proper' Sunday lunches but proud of the new hairstyle and occasionally new hair colour their mother would be seen in. And her new 'out of the mainstream' perspective made her sometimes say things refreshingly unexpected. I smiled at myself as The Investigator, with my good woman looking on admiringly.

Tuesday

Phil Wittle was the someone in the police station I could talk to. We hadn't met through work but had found ourselves sharing a jacuzzi at Spring Harvest Christian convention earlier in the year. I'd been a bit wary of going back to Butlins after the cold March of four years ago and I vowed to have a soak in the hot bubbles at least once a day. Some of the teaching had been as crude as the accommodation, but the atmosphere had given us all a boost for the whole year. I thought Jane needed a lift and perhaps some direction. It was good, and, after singing until my lungs hurt one evening, I thought I'd keep my vow with the jacuzzi. Phil was there already luxuriating in all his six foot seven inches, welcoming me with 'How do you tell a buffalo from a bison?' before shouting the answer - between gulps of Brummie laughter - 'Yer can't wash yer 'ands in a buffalo', and splashing his enormous hands in the water. He couldn't believe that I was from Brum too, with my accent.

When I had cajoled him to move over, we settled down happily and went around together for the next couple of days. He claimed he went to the seminars for *Guardian* readers before teaming up with me, but I didn't remember seeing him there. Since then we'd met up for lunch a few times and had prayed together in the Cathedral once when he'd been in the middle of a paedophile investigation. He had said he felt so contaminated by the evil in people that he needed to pray, and I'd said I'd come with him. He was a member of a strong Methodist church in Shirley and, more importantly, worked at the Central Police Station.

I rang Phil and asked him if he was free for lunch. He asked me what trouble I was in and didn't believe me when I told him it was about a friend's son.

I didn't know whether to ring Mohammed or not, feeling nervous about talking to him. When I thought of talking with Philippa again I wanted keenly to reply to the local Law Society summer tea party invitation. I recognised this as my usual ploy to veer away from the urgent, important and nerve-racking into the not urgent, not important and easily achievable. (At least I know some of the theory of efficient working.) I breathed a quick prayer and then thought it could be easier to call in later at Mohammed's office, especially as the sun was shining despite the miserable forecast

Over lunch at the top of the Palisades, Phil asked 'what's up with your friend's son then?' making quotation marks in the air and winking with the words 'your friend's'.

'Honestly,' I said, emphasising the words, 'my friend's son Jason has been questioned about the car accident involving Mohammed Khan's son and his girlfriend.' Phil looked up and now looked serious. 'Jason used to go out with the girl, Lizzie. According to his Dad, Jason's been treated a bit roughly and he's asked me, to ask you, to go easier on him.' Phil is too sharp for playing games.

'You've come to the right man,' said Phil. 'I was put on it today, one of a posse. Yes siree. And we gun-toting modern sheriffs like nothing more than blasting our pistols at the floor to make them darn suspects dance.'

'Phil,' I said gently and slowly, appealing to his friendship. 'You know I am not someone who thinks you lot are forever taking the law into your own hands, whatever the media impression.'

'OK. Fair cop!' It was good to see Phil smile cheekily again. 'I just think we are like teachers today, you know they can't come down on any naughty child without a nannying parent complaining about their poor Johnny.'

'I know all too well. You should talk to Jane. Yes, I know there's asking hard questions which is what you are meant to do.'

Phil nodded slowly. 'And asking Jason Jennings hard questions is all we've done. OK?' He looked at me steadily.

'Thanks Phil, you're one of the good guys.' My mission to Will completed, I relaxed, ready to change the topic.

Phil leaned forward. 'I can tell you now, because you'll hear it tonight, that it's not looking like an accident at all.'

'OK…' I replied slowly, 'so..?'

'So he wasn't driving that fast either.' Phil leant back again and looked up at me, half challenging.

'Not reckless driving, but something else?' It was like encouraging a witness to speak in their own words.

'Something crocked, by someone who knows his spanners.' Phil folded his arms in a challenge.

I winced and sighed inside. But there was a challenge inside too. 'Just keep looking, Phil, beyond the end of your nose. OK?'

'OK...' It was Phil's turn to nod slowly. I couldn't tell if he was accepting a fair challenge, or telling me to leave him alone to do his work.

I wanted to keep to the subject but not challenge too much more. 'There's quite a few of you on the case then?'

'Oh yeah. Top priority now. And everyone wants to get in on it. Birmingham crime's not usually so spicy.'

'Or so juicy for the media. Part of me wishes I wasn't so involved.' And part of me was surprised at myself insisting that I wasn't just one of Phil's 'everyone.'

Phil smiled and shook his head. 'Field day or what? *The Birmingham Express*'ll make hay for a whole year.'

'And the nationals – unless there's a royal tiff, so the poor journalists don't have to leave London.' We happily moved on to bemoaning the Londo-centricity of the nation, and to comparing our newspaper and reading preferences. At Spring Harvest we had both rashly signed up subscriptions to *Christianity* magazine, and were surprised to be both still looking forward to the next edition. The magazine says it's about 'Real life. Real faith. In the Real World.' The story we were engaged in didn't feel altogether real.

With one of my pledges to Will fulfilled so painlessly, I decided to go for the second straight away. Walking up Temple Alley, I didn't know what to think. Avoiding Philippa would be best, maybe I should have tried to visit in her lunch hour? Our encounter yesterday had left me feeling stirred up, like having eaten a hot curry when I was expecting lamb stew. But maybe she was feeling the same, and it wouldn't be right at least to try to put things right. A helping of cool yoghurt was what both of us needed. I smiled at the thought of me acting cool and smooth and caring.

'Ah, Mr. Jeffery!' Philippa's voice was confident and bright and expectant. 'Twice in two days.' She raised her eyebrows. 'You've come to see..?' She put her hands down on her desk, sat upright, and focused her brown eyes at mine. Her red lips pushed forward a little, shaking her head slightly as she waited for my reply to her question.

'Yes, erm,' I cleared my throat and tried to make my voice deeper and cooler than usual. 'Yes, erm, both of you, of course. It would be good to touch base with Mr. Khan – and ... also with you.' I returned her smile and looked her in the eye. I told myself that I was being brave.

Philippa touched her necklace. 'Well, in that case, I'll just give Mr. Khan a little buzz to let him know you're here, and, while we're waiting, you can fill me in too. You intrigue me Mr. Jeffery.' She motioned to me to sit on a gold settee while she rang through to Mohammed. I sat down, near one end of the settee and, nervously, smoothed the seat next to me.

Philippa stood up, ran her hands down the back of her skirt to unruffle it, and came and sat on the settee. There was an uncomfortably short gap between us; she turned to look towards me. Surprised, I wanted to withdraw my hand from the settee next to her, but didn't want to offend. Nor did I want to let her know how nervous of her I was.

'You know,' Philippa said, putting her hand on the settee near mine, 'those flowers really touched me. It's not every man who notices a secretary, let alone thinks about her feelings.'

'Well,' I said, still trying to keep cool and smooth, 'I'm not every man, and you're not every secretary. You touched me. You brought something out of me. I didn't want to just leave you high and dry.' I felt I was a film star floundering with a bad script. Philippa just looked at me, encouraging me to continue. 'I mean, I realised that you were upset, rightly so, and I thought the least I could do was soothe you in some way.'

'Well, you succeeded, masterfully,' Philippa replied, touching her fingers onto my hand lightly in what I took as thanksgiving.

'Erm, yes,' I cleared my throat again, 'And today I just thought I could carry on where I left off yesterday. Let you know it wasn't just a one off. If we're going to be seeing each other more, I wanted you to know that I'm serious about getting on with you, so to speak, as best we can.' Why I didn't say anything about this being a business relationship, I don't know.

'Thank you, David,' she said, giving my hand a warm squeeze. 'You've really bowled me over again. Two lovely surprises. I'm more than happy to, as you say, get on with you more.' She squeezed my hand again briefly and then lifted her hand to her hair. She brushed over her ear and shook her head a little, looking at me all the time.

I felt puzzled and it must have shown, for she, in return, looked playfully puzzled at me. I tried again to look cool, looking at her and nodding seriously. 'Who knows how much we'll be seeing of each other?' I paused feeling that that wasn't quite the right comment. 'Depending on Mohammed entirely, of course.' Maybe a little joke was needed. 'He may not want to be solicited by me?'

'Rest assured,' said Philippa as she stood up to answer the phone, 'that we are both more than happy with your services so far. You're the lawyer with the little extra which counts for a lot.' She went behind her desk and, picking up the phone, leant forward towards me.

I was glad that Mohammed was free to see me. I told myself that maybe she had noticed the extra kindness which was supposed to be our Christian witness, but this didn't feel quite right.

'David,' Mohammed smiled bravely. 'Thank you for your card, so thoughtful. May God hear our prayers, and may I introduce you to Frank Gatley, an old friend.' His arm directed me to a man with thick grey hair, a thin muscular face and green tweedy clothes. Mohammed was as usual very smart, in pinstripe dark blue with one of his striking ties, a slightly more sober one today than some days.

'Thank you for coming, David,' said Mohammed. 'It is good to see a trustworthy man in these difficult times. I trust that you and your family are well, and that my dear aunt will soon be able to have her beautiful flat. She needs to find some peace.'

'It's good to see you too, Mohammed. Please reassure your aunt that she will soon be able to have a home where she can be herself. We should be exchanging contracts in two weeks. But I wanted to come and say how sorry I was to hear about Tariq and Lizzie. It must have been terrible for you all.' Mohammed bowed briefly. 'How are they? Do you have any news from the hospital?'

'The hospital hardly tell us anything. My son and his fiancée are in intensive care, fighting for their lives, and the doctors won't talk to us until tomorrow. They won't even let us see them properly.' Mohammed's voice was even but deeply determined.

This was a bit much to take in all at once. Was Lizzie really engaged to Mohammed's son? Were the doctors really trying to keep him at arm's length? Mohammed was certainly angry, while managing to appear pleasantly polite.

'I am sorry to hear that the hospital aren't being as helpful as they could. It must make it worse for you. Of course you want to be with your son but intensive care do have strict visiting times.'

'Thank you for your understanding, David. We all want to be with Tariq and with Elizabeth. The nurses are very kind and hard-working, but they don't know him as we do. He needs his family now, to speak to him, to remind him of happy times, to sing his songs, to pray for him.' Mohammed looked straight at me with sad, moist eyes. I admired the way he could bring emotion and argument together: a well-integrated man. I just looked back nodding a little, seriously. After a moment Mohammed continued. 'You here don't have everything right, but I can say this to you, David. Other people aren't always so sympathetic.'

I wondered if he glanced at Frank then, and then wondered if Frank had been trying to 'talk sense' to him about not kicking up a fuss with the hospital. Frank looked at bit cross himself, and I thought I'd better try to have a word with him if I could, to help him to go easy on Mohammed.

'You're right, Mohammed, we do tend to leave things to other people too much. Even praying with people in hospital we leave mostly to the clergy.'

'Healing isn't all about strangers doing things to people's bodies. We also need our family to bring peace to our soul while we fight for life.' Mohammed was a surprisingly poetic businessman.

'And the doctors too often treat family as ignorant people who are almost irrelevant. We're at the receiving end of that sort of attitude too - and we put up with it too much.' Mohammed bowed slightly again. 'I expect Lizzie's parents are going through much the same as you. You must have met them now - especially as you say Tariq and Elizabeth are engaged.' I wanted to say that I knew Lizzie but thought it better to wait a bit for Mohammed to get a bit more off his chest

'Elizabeth's mother is a good woman. But they don't see things in the same way as we do, and they don't have the same pressure that we have. Too many people are accusing us of terrible things, of Tariq being drunk. He never drank alcohol. The way of Islam meant too much to him for that.' Again Mohammed wasn't pretending that he wasn't deeply sad and angry. But he still spoke in a measured and gentle way. 'These were two good young people celebrating their engagement and attacked by a jealous lover. The car was sabotaged, it must have been.' He raised his head and looked me in the eye again.

'I know what you're talking about, and...' I drew a long breath. 'This may come as a surprise to you, I know who you're talking about. Elizabeth's old boyfriend is the son of some friends of ours at church. He used to bring her to church sometimes. I've known Jason for years. He's not the sort to take revenge like that.'

To my surprise Mohammed smiled. 'Allah be praised!' His ways are all good. Here we have a good man of the law who is at the centre of all this. I pray that you will be able to bear the truth when it comes out.' He paused, maybe wanting to let the implications of this sink in. This did not seem to be the time to challenge his assumption and I could not think of anything to say.

Mohammed continued. 'But it is a comfort to know that you know all these people. Have you been to the hospital? No, of course not.' He looked down and then raised his head to face me with a winsome smile. 'David, please go. Go with your priest. Pray for these good young people who have been so cruelly attacked. You see if they will tell you that Tariq had no alcohol in him at all. Maybe God will be merciful and give us strength to fight all our enemies.'

I thought this was bit extreme, but it occurred to me that the real 'enemies' were death, and everything that stood in the way of the truth - as he saw it. I was about to say that hospital visiting was not my forte, having only seen the inside of the Nuffield as a patient, briefly, four years ago. But something told me not to be so reluctant. Perhaps I could find out something about the drinking? Goodness knows how but, despite Mohammed, it might help Jason.

'Mohammed, I will pray, and if it's OK with you, I would like to see them in hospital with Paul, our vicar. We will pray for their recovery and for us all to be guided to the truth.' I paused to draw strength as I felt that now I needed to look Mohammed in the eye. 'Tariq can't have been drunk, I understand that. I don't think Jason can have had a hand in it either. We'll pray for you and all your family too.'

Mohammed bowed his head slowly, recognising the seriousness of what I had said. 'You please take your priest. I think you said at some time that he has some power in this way. And if Tariq knows that your priest has had a hand in his improvement maybe he won't be so extreme. David, thank you for coming. I will remember what you have said. Please let me know how you find them.'

'I'll be in touch.' We embraced and I smiled at Frank as I turned to go, half inviting him to come with me.

Frank stood up and went up to Mohammed, with an outstretched arm. 'Goodbye, old boy. Good will come out of this some way, mark my words. I'll be thinking of you.' They shook hands and Frank left with me.

I persuaded Frank to have a cup of coffee at one of the many American-Italian coffee shops that seemed to have suddenly opened in every street in the centre of Birmingham. In some ways these places are a strange throw-back to the old coffee houses of history. They also seem to mark a certain point of modern prosperity - when people are happy to pay good money for a good cup of coffee. I'm in between the generation who find it hard to spend so much and the generation who relishes at last being able to drink well in nice surroundings, with newspapers and settees. Frank didn't quite fit into the place, the bright colours made his clothes seem almost mouldy. But he seemed happy to talk.

I asked him how he came to know Mohammed. He said he'd known Mohammed from when he was born as he had met his father in the army. He'd helped the family come to this country. He spoke warmly of Mohammed's father as a 'character' who had 'got into trouble with some old customs' and needed to leave for the 'safety of a civilised country'. Mohammed's father had been proud to be British, said Frank, and wanted his children to be proudly British too. Frank seemed to have had a part in this, or at least he thought he did. He also told me more about what had happened.

Tariq and Lizzie really had got engaged. The Khans had known about it for a month, and, before it went public, the couple went out for a celebration meal. They had come out of the restaurant in a playful mood, with Tariq swooning and laughing, so that people thought he was drunk. Frank didn't think so, 'too proper to enjoy his booze, not like his grandfather…' Then the car had crashed.

'It could have been the car failing - these Japanese cars aren't all they're cracked up to be.' Frank spoke with distaste. Then he raised his forehead looking as though a new thought had suddenly struck him. 'Or could it have been that jealous young man, the one who's an expert mechanic?'

I wondered if Frank had heard me say that Jason was a family friend or if he was choosing to ignore it. He gave me a card as we left, asking me to get in touch if there was any way he could help 'old Mohammed'. I watched him walk stiffly away and thought that Mohammed was kind to keep up with this old friend of his father's. What I couldn't believe was that Tariq and Lizzie hadn't been drinking. Lizzie could let her hair down and get tanked up like a good modern girl. 'Temperance' isn't in their vocabulary. Tariq must have been well inducted into beer at his public school. If it wasn't alcohol, it must have been something less legal.

Back at the office Rose greeted me warmly and primly. Rose is a thin woman with outsize glasses, short grey hair and a gift for efficient filing and Sunday School teaching. Her memory is phenomenal, she likes things to be right, and she can see the child in everyone. This means she can disarm hardened criminals and patronise self-important estate agents. Rose has been our secretary for sixteen years. She was well established when I arrived twelve years ago, so that I have always treated her with friendly respect.

'You've had phone calls.' Rose could still make it sound almost like I was such a lucky boy. At least now she used sticky notes like everyone else, instead of just remembering as she used to.

'First, the lawyer acting for the vendor of Mr Khan's aunt's flat wants to talk about a problem that has cropped up.' I sighed. 'Second, Will Jennings asked you to ring him at work. Third, Paul phoned just to say you were on his mind. Fourth, Mrs Bright wants to go over the divorce proposals again as she has been talking with her friends and they have advised her to make sure her position is secure.' This meant that she had been thinking for herself and wanted more money. 'Fifth, a Mr Smithson would like to know if he can talk to you about creating you a website. And I really need to tell Paperbiz today what we want to do with the photocopier.'

That made five things which needed me to think hard. I decided to go for the other one, the most intriguing one. I rang Paul, with the excuse that as a vicar he would probably be out later.

'Paul, thank you for ringing. Would you believe I was talking about you this morning? Yes, you probably would, you're used to this sort of thing.' One of Paul's habits is to say nothing when you expect him to say something. Sometimes he can also say something when you think he would say nothing – a habit which has led him into trouble a few times. But for now the only response I had was a slight, interested 'Ummm.' I continued. 'Could you come with me to the QE some time today please? I want to go and see Jason's ex, Lizzie, and her new man in intensive care.' Another pause for a response that did not come. 'I know the boy's father through work. We were talking this morning and he encouraged me to go and to take you with me. He's a good Moslem, open to other possibilities too.'

Now Paul spoke without hesitation. 'That's why I had to phone you. I wondered why. And I have to come with you to the QE. Can we meet there at five o'clock? I'll ring IT first so they're expecting us.'

For once I did then tackle the job I least wanted to, and rang Ryan Hollings, my oppo for the aunt's flat. Ryan is young, breezy and remarkably successful, a bright star in the Birmingham law scene, according to some.

'My client finds herself in an awkward position.' Ryan sounded like he was in court. 'One of her neighbours in Sandringham Gardens has a cousin who is now on his own and he's just decided he would like to live in Sandringham Gardens himself. He's in a bit of a state after his wife's death, and my client's neighbour is quite desperate to arrange a move for him. My client naturally wants to help her neighbour who she has known well for a number of years. She's very sorry that she didn't know about this before putting the flat on the market, but she really does want to sell to the neighbour to help him and his cousin. It's not a question of money or anything else, as I'm sure you understand, but we will have to withdraw from our negotiations with your purchaser. Isn't it frustrating how things work out sometimes?'

'Oh yes, Ryan,' I said through clenched teeth. 'Thank you for letting me know. I'll await your confirmation in writing. Goodbye.'

I might have believed young Ryan if I hadn't heard this kind of story before, and if he hadn't mentioned 'money or anything else'. His fake reassurance pointed me to what I suspected was really going on. The neighbours had got wind that the flat was being sold to an Asian woman, who then whipped themselves up into a frenzy of fear, much helped by them all being *Daily Mail* readers. They would be telling each other how this alien would probably have her enormous family visiting at all hours, including several illegal immigrants sleeping on her floor, and would cook enormous pots of fierce curry that would defeat any air freshener in any of the nine flats. They had banded together against this appalling threat to their entire way of life and young Ryan had found them a way to fend off this enemy. Once Mohammed's aunt was off the scene the 'cousin' would suddenly change his mind ('you know how important it is for people in bereavement not to make hasty decisions') and the flat would reappear on the market looking for a nice white buyer.

The law can't really do any more than indicate what should be done - people will usually find a way round it if they want to. I wondered what I should tell Mohammed. He was enough of a friend for me to want to tell him what I was thinking but I wasn't sure it would do him any good. The only way of proving this would be to hire a detective to try and find this supposed cousin - but that wouldn't prove enough. Mohammed was valiant or stubborn enough to give it a try but I couldn't see him achieving anything.

Mrs Bright made me feel uneasy. She wanted me to advise her according to her own ideas of what she was entitled to, but unfortunately these ideas were unrealistic. I wanted to tell her to stop being so selfish and accept that life would never now be what she had hoped it would be with a rich husband, but I was acting for her and had to try at least to follow her instructions. I steeled myself, phoned her and said that if she wanted to consider changing the details which we were beginning to agree with her former husband we would have to meet and go through it all properly, which could, of course, add to her total costs. I left it for her to contact me if she did want a thorough review, suspecting that she was mean enough not to want to pay me any more.

I then held off the photocopier salesman, asked Rose to find two comparable quotes and wondered what I would do now that the scheduled work on the flat was unnecessary. I phoned Philippa and arranged to see Mohammed the following day because of the problem that had arisen with the flat purchase. I also asked her to let Mohammed know that Paul and I were going to the hospital later. I decided to ignore Mr Smithson. That left only Will.

'Thank God you've phoned, David.' More drama. It's not easy being Will's friend. 'It's Jason again. Don't know where he is. Paul's not seen him today. Went out this morning with that little rucksack looking full. But his lunch was still on the table. Where's he gone? Look could you pray for him? Could you tell Ginnie for the Prayer Circle - I don't know what to say.'

Not many people would ring a solicitor at work to ask them to pray. That's what warms me to Will. I told him I'd come round later with Jane if she was free, and then I did actually pray. The sun was shining low across the room, making it look bigger. I thought of Beryl's helmet and asked God to keep my mind clear and free as I seemed to be in the centre of all this. I couldn't think of what else to say so I just thought of them all and said the Lord's Prayer.

Parking at the QE Hospital is always a nightmare so I took the train. Paul was already at the door to intensive care but said he hadn't been there long. It was good to see him wearing a dog collar for a change, although I wondered if bringing his large Bible with him would be a bit threatening to some people. He buzzed and explained and a nurse came out to see us.

'Mr Khan and Miss Edwards are in a very serious condition,' she said. 'They have members of their families with them now, so I'm afraid it's not convenient for you to come in.'

'That's a shame,' said Paul. 'Do you know how long they will be here? We could wait a while?'

'Tariq Khan's father specifically asked us to come today,' I said. 'I'm afraid the family will be a bit put out if we can't see them. Please could you go and ask the Khans if we could have a word with them?' The nurse grimaced a little and then smiled and went to talk with them.

'That's rather hard-headed of you,' said Paul approvingly, as though he was seeing a side of me he hadn't registered before.

Tariq's mother came out with two of Tariq's sisters. She was a large woman in a bright green sari and extensive jewellery, with two very slim girls in smart suits. 'You must be David Jeffery. I'm very pleased to meet you. Let me introduce myself - Raisa Khan. And you must be David's vicar - pleased to meet you.' Raisa spoke in perfect Home Counties English with a hint of a plum in the far corner of her mouth. Paul shook her hand, looking a bit bowled over by this determined friendliness. 'Mohammed has so much wanted you to visit,' Raisa continued. 'He'll want you to come in and pray with poor Tariq - and Lizzie too. This place can be so soulless.'

Raisa ushered us into the unit past the helpless nurse. It was spacious and open-plan with fewer beds than I had expected, each with a small crowd of attendant equipment. Tariq was lying on his back with his muscled brown chest uncovered except for the heart monitor pads and wires. His face looked calm and still.

Raisa looked tenderly at him. 'He's not giving up' she said. 'Sometimes he smiles like he used to when he was very little, sleeping on the sofa when he had German Measles. Often he's striving. He's trying, you know, trying to stay with me.' The girls hugged each other gently. 'Please will you pray for him?' This was all easier than I had expected, and certainly better than my memory of visiting a couple of home group members in hospital before. The routine then seemed to be half an hour of awkward chat followed by an offer of prayer which felt something of an intrusion.

'Yes, of course,' said Paul. 'When we pray for people we usually like to talk with them a little beforehand so that we agree what we're praying for. Obviously I can't talk with Tariq himself, so is it all right if I ask you a question?' My heart sank a little, as I wished Paul would just get on and pray. He was the professional after all. I had heard that there was a new 'model' of prayer ministry on which he was keen and which involved some cross-questioning. I hoped that Raisa could cope with this, despite her appearance of powerful competence. She agreed readily.

'How do you need God to come to Tariq?' Paul asked. 'What is it that Tariq needs now and how could you imagine God coming to meet that need? Maybe you could put it in a picture somehow, imagining God coming and doing just what you want him to do?'

Raisa was not thrown by this cross-questioning, but was soon in full flow. 'Oh when Tariq was little I used to cuddle him and warm him whenever he was ill. He was such a skinny little boy, so full of energy and life. But when he was poorly he just lay still, very still, and he shivered - even with duvets and blankets he still shivered. I used to hold him in my arms until I could feel him going warm again, until he could move his legs or his arms a little, and then I knew he would be fine. That's what I want to do for him now. I want to hug him and make him feel loved and warm, but I can't even put one arm around his chest without the nurse coming and asking me to keep away.'

Raisa paused and looked round. Paul nodded, again in his 'say nothing' mode. So it was up to Raisa to continue. 'They're very good and kind and I suppose they're right. I don't want to smother him, but sometimes I wish he didn't have all these wires and machines and I could just hug him. But maybe God can do that for me now? I have been to the Mosque and made special offerings for my Tariq. My family are going every day with special gifts. Perhaps God will come and make Tariq warm again? Could you ask God to come and do that for him?'

'Yes, we can all ask,' said Paul, 'and we will ask. We'll ask God to come and be mother to Tariq, to wrap his arms around Tariq and make him feel warm and safe. We'll just ask. We don't make offerings for our progress. Jesus told us just to ask. God doesn't come because we pay him to come. He just comes because he loves us, but he does wait to be asked. I'll ask him to come and be mother to Tariq - and do you think you could ask too?'

Paul paused and looked at Raisa who seemed to be going along with what he was saying. I wished Paul would look at me so he could see signals for him to stop this rigmarole and get on with the prayer. But he carried on his way. 'What I'd like is, if I say a short prayer first, and then you ask, out loud, for God to come as you have said, to do for your Tariq what you can't do for him. I'll then agree with you. Then we'll wait a little, and stay quiet and wait for God to come. Sometimes we need to give God that time for him to work in. As we're praying quietly, if you're aware of anything, please let me know. If something comes into your mind or you feel something somewhere, please let me know and we can welcome whatever it is that God is doing. Is that OK?'

Raisa looked straight at Paul with large moist eyes. She looked uncomfortable, but couldn't refuse. 'Yes,' she said. 'I'm sure you know best'

'Thank you,' said Paul. 'Let's pray.'

I closed my eyes and listened to Paul inviting the Holy Spirit to come and guide us, not knowing what Raisa and her daughters would make of this. Then Raisa did pray, a lovely mother's prayer to God the Merciful and then Paul prayed with tenderness, asking God to be mother to Tariq. This seemed a strange mixture - could Allah ever be thought of a mother? Then there was a silence. All I could hear were the bleeps from the machines, several all at once, quite soon after Paul's prayer, which seemed worrying, but, as no one came to do anything, I assumed it was all OK. I did take a peek at the machines, just to check, and thought I could see Paul looking at them too, but I quickly shut my eyes again and tried to concentrate.

'Shash kial a ho, no rana ka.' Paul was praying quietly, or rather singing quietly in tongues. My heart sank again. Why couldn't he just stick to English, here of all places? He actually sounded quite good for Paul, and he didn't go on too long thank goodness. I hoped Raisa would just think of it as some ancient mystical chant. There was another silence punctuated with bleeps and some fidgeting from the sisters. 'Thank you, dear God, for coming to Tariq. Thank you for his fingers relaxing. Please keep coming and keep warming him.'

I wondered what sort of imagination Paul had and opened my eyes to check if anything was moving. Paul was just looking at Tariq and smiling sort of wistfully. And Tariq's fingers were moving gently, backwards and forwards in a contented sort of way. Then his right leg stretched out a little and Paul thanked God for that. Then he smiled a little and Paul thanked God for that. Raisa was looking at Tariq now with a little stream of tears down one side of her face. 'Let's just pray and thank God for coming as we asked,' said Paul, and we did.

'Thank you so much,' said Raisa. 'How can we ever repay you? God has heard your prayer, I'm sure. Thank you.'

'Sometimes when we pray God shows us things.' said Paul. 'What was it like for you when we were praying quietly?'

'I don't know if I was imagining it or not,' Raisa sniffed a little and drew breath, 'but I thought I saw an angel standing behind Tariq. He was right behind him over his head, learning forward with his wings stretched out. It was bright and lovely, but probably wishful thinking.'

'No' said Paul. 'That was real. That was for you. That's a picture God has given you to help you to pray for Tariq. When you pray, remember that angel and ask the angel to be there with Tariq, and bless him. The angel's wings will do for him what you cannot do now.'

'Yes,' said Raisa quietly, almost whispering, 'yes.' Then she brightened up. 'Now you must pray for our poor Lizzie too.' She took Paul's arm and led him to the other side of the room. I followed. Raisa bustled over to the opposite side of the spacious room and clasped the hand of a strained, stiff, middle-aged woman in a blue woollen suit. Next to her was a young woman with bright orange hair and a nose stud.

'Patricia, my dear,' Raisa effused, 'This is Paul, a wonderful man of prayer who has come to bless our dear children.' Patricia pulled her hand away and looked warily and suspiciously at Paul.

'Hello' said Paul. 'I'm Paul Cooper, the vicar at St Luke's Braydon. David here knows Mr Khan, Tariq's father, and he asked us to come and pray. I don't think I've met you before but I have met Lizzie. She came to St Luke's a few times with Jason Jennings.

'Oh, that boy's church,' said Patricia. 'Religion's never done her any good.'

Something made me speak up. 'We do understand your concern for Elizabeth, Mrs Edwards. She was such a bright and talented girl. We couldn't imagine her staying long at St Luke's - or with Jason Jennings. This must be such a trial for you and your daughter.'

Patricia dabbed her eye with a little white handkerchief, sniffed and said 'Yes, well...'

'I'm Meg, and I am her daughter, Liz's sister. Hello.' Meg offered me a handshake, thrusting out an arm, with several bangles, in a rough mint coloured striped jumper.

'Pleased to meet you,' I said, and then looked at Paul, not certain what to do next.

Raisa smiled enthusiastically 'Come, let us pray for our dear Lizzie.' Mrs Edwards winced and Meg said she was just about to go off and get a drink. She picked up a shoulder bag and left.

'I'm sorry if this is an intrusion, Mrs Edwards,' said Paul. 'We can just pray for Elizabeth in church if you would prefer. But I think it could help you too if we were able to pray here.' Patricia nodded and looked around.

'Thank you, Mrs Edwards' I said. 'We know this is a very hard time for you.'

'When we pray with people,' said Paul 'we usually talk with them first to work out how we're going to pray.' Patricia raised her eyebrows. 'Could I ask you a question please?' She just looked at him blankly. She too wanted him just to get on with it and get it over. 'How do you need God to come to Elizabeth?'

Patricia burst into tears. 'Oh God!' she said, 'How am I supposed to know? You pray for her, vicar.'

Paul looked taken aback by this sudden emotion. 'That's fine. I'll say a prayer for her, asking God to come and touch her with the hand of Jesus. Then we'll pray quietly for a while and I'll round it off when it seems right.'

He turned to Lizzie, her oxygen-masked face framed by fine blond hair, lying perfectly still. I closed my eyes and listened again to Paul praying, wondering what Patricia Edwards was making of all this. Paul did pray that God would come and touch this daughter of his with the hand of Jesus. Then there was a silence in which I could hear Mrs Edwards rustling in her handbag.

'O God the Merciful, the All Seeing, the All-Knowing,' Raisa broke the silence with an impassioned prayer 'Give us help, we pray. Send your angels of mercy and light to dear Lizzie, O God, O God.' Mrs Edwards started coughing and spluttering. The machines started bleeping more and a nurse ran in to look at them.

'Please! Could you just give the patient some space?' She stared at us, her jaw set angrily. 'I'm going to have to ask you to leave.' She turned to Patricia and put a hand gently on her arm. 'Just for a minute or two.'

Meg was sitting out in the corridor turning a necklace around in her hands. She looked up at us. 'You were quick, not much you could do for her then?'

Mrs Edwards smiled at her daughter. I felt accused by her. Raisa walked with us to the hospital entrance, thanking Paul again, and making excuses for Mrs Edwards.

Paul offered to drive me back into town to pick up my car. I very much wanted to talk with him. I was worried about all this prayer for God to hold Tariq in his arms and to send his angels. It sounded like he was going to die. I thought too that we had put Mrs Edwards' back up seriously and couldn't see what to do about it.

Paul was phlegmatic. 'I can see what you mean about Tariq,' he said. 'And I can't say you're wrong. I don't know whether he is going to die or not. We just ask God to come and he does what's best. But when Tariq's hand started moving I thought personally that he wasn't going to die. And Mrs Edwards must have a history somewhere - perhaps some awful institutional religion. That's put her right off. We'll keep praying for her and trust she'll soften. Perhaps if Lizzie gets better she'll think better of God. This could be God's way of drawing her to himself.'

'Unlikely,' I thought, but all I said was 'Let's hope so. That daughter's a hard nut.' Paul just replied 'Mmmm.'

Jane wanted to know all about what had happened at the hospital. It was nice to have her so interested, as the fascination of conveyancing had long since died in her. She looked bright, perky even, and had made a nice meal of salmon and mashed potato just for us. I didn't ask if this was the special offer of the week, although it probably was. Emily and Nicola were out at a Youth Fellowship evening planning for the autumn house-party and Peter was staying with a friend. We had candles over dinner and looked forward to a summer night's stroll afterwards.

I had reached the end of us praying with Tariq, and our plates were half empty when the telephone rang. Jane wanted to me leave it but I couldn't. It was Mohammed.

'David, please forgive me for interrupting you at home. I needed to say "Thank you so much" for taking your priest to pray with Tariq and Lizzie. Raisa has told me all about it. It is so good to see her hopeful again. I don't understand about these things but I know how much it has meant to her, and seeing her so comforted and positive again means a lot to me. I am so grateful, David.'

I was a bit taken aback by the rush of gratitude, and didn't quite know what to say. 'Oh Mohammed, it was good to meet your lovely wife, it was good to pray with her. We try to believe that they are in God's hand now and he will do what is best for them.' I didn't want them thinking that Tariq was healed now but I couldn't exactly say I thought he might well die.

'We trust that the doctors will do what is best too. Did they say anything about alcohol in his blood? They won't tell me a thing - they only say that's a matter for the police. I don't mind them talking to the police but I need them too to talk to me. I am his father.'

'I'm sorry Mohammed, we didn't have a chance to talk with them. But I'm pretty sure I know what the answer is. I don't know why I didn't say earlier.' I had hoped not to have to talk about this so soon.

'You don't sound very positive.'

'No. The truth is that very probably no-one will ever know. To have a blood test for alcohol the person has to give their consent, which Tariq clearly couldn't do.'

Mohammed exploded. 'But… but surely the police can ask for this kind of testing. The hospital have to do what the police tell them. It is a critical piece of evidence. Don't tell me that no policeman even thought of asking. That would be too much.' I was glad that I had not heard Mohammed angry before.

'In this country, Mohammed, the police can't order the hospital to do anything. The hospital will only take a blood test when the patient gives their consent.' I was also glad now that I wasn't experiencing his wrath face to face.

'But they knew as soon as I saw them in the morning that a blood test was vitally important. We are his parents for goodness sake. They could have taken a test then.'

'Even you cannot give permission on behalf of a next of kin. They still needed Tariq to agree for himself. It's the law.'

'No wonder your papers are full of criminals who go unpunished. Even the innocent cannot justify themselves according to your law. It is a miracle your policemen ever get anyone to do anything if they always need their permission first!' Although he was still fighting, his voice wasn't as biting as before.

'It's a complicated balance of authority and freedom and it's not perfect by any means.' I tried to speak gently. 'In this instance it would have been better to test him, I can see that.' I paused, hoping that would be the end of it.

'Yes indeed. No proof. We just have to find other ways of proving his innocence. I know you can't solve everything David. Thank you again for going with your priest man. At least Raisa is now at home and more settled. Thank you for that.'

Jane understood my dilemma. I didn't want to encourage Mohammed too much, as I still thought, mostly, that Tariq was going to die, maybe with Jesus somehow, but still die. I couldn't even reassure Mohammed that he'd be 'all right', for that probably meant he was going to live. What if he didn't? What would Mohammed think of our God then? Yet I couldn't dismiss the real sense that we all had that God had come close to Tariq, and that did make a difference. Jane assured me that I had said the right things, and we were soon talking about the children and what we could do at half term. Our bowls were half empty of summer pudding when the telephone rang again.

Will was frantic. 'David, I need someone to talk to. You've got to save Jason. He's taken it all on himself, tried to kill himself and left a damn silly note. It's a mess, a complete mess.' Jane had come to stand with me by the telephone: she told me to go, with a kiss on my cheek. Driving through the rain I couldn't believe what Will had said. If Jason had attempted suicide it made him look guilty. They say most murders are committed by someone the victim knows. But not Jason the floppy. However hard I tried, that idea just wouldn't fit into my head.

This time it was City Road hospital. The A&E reception had a sprinkling of people sitting in little huddles. Will was the only one pacing up and down, near the doors to the treatment rooms. The receptionist was keeping an eye on him. Will turned to me crushed, hardly able to look at me. He slumped into a chair.

'It can't be, it can't be Jason, it can't be.' What could I say to that? He bowed his head as though the effort of believing what he wanted to believe was too great.

'Tell me what happened, Will,' I said as gently as I could.

'Jason was off on his own again. Not at work - you know. Turns out he went down to Pond Wood on his own. Hose through the window. God!' Will turned towards the wall stiffening his lips. For a moment neither of us could speak.

I breathed deeply and dared to ask 'What happened?'

Will breathed deeply too and shut his eyes. 'An old couple saw a hose going along the side of the car and pulled the door open. He hadn't locked it. Can't have been serious. You think?' His bloodshot eyes appealed to me.

'He always was sensitive.' It seemed pretty serious to me. Suddenly I saw an opportunity to lighten Will's mood. 'God knows where he gets it from.' If Jane had been there I wouldn't have said it. Later, Will enjoyed telling people it was nearly the end of our friendship. Now he shuddered and then carried on.

'And God knows what they were doing there - something to do with their dog running off. Anyway, they called the ambulance. The worst is, they found this on the seat by him.' Will handed me a white paper with Jason's spidery writing.

There's nothing left for me here now. I can't live thinking about Lizzie and how I drove her to him, and into the hands of those mad, harsh people. If only I could have loved her better, stronger - but I don't feel I can love anyone. I just don't have it in me. I caused all this. I just wanted her to get frightened and back away. But now she's damaged and it's all down to me. I can't bear it and it mustn't ever happen again.

'He was more distraught than we thought,' I said.

'How can he think it was all down to him?' wailed Will. 'He's just made it look like he was responsible for her crash, but he can't have been.' Will was wringing his hands and then clenching them and pinching his knees. 'Stupid boy. We've just got to make sure the police don't see this. They'll stitch him up for attempted murder, crime of passion or whatever. That'll please the paki business man - which is all they're after.'

'Will,' I said, trying to look him in the face. Will's prejudice shocked even me and all I wanted was to get him to turn his mind to something else. 'Calm down, you've had a bad shock. This note doesn't say that Jason had anything directly to do with the car crash. You have to concentrate on loving and supporting Jason now, not trying to have a go at other people. It's not what I would usually say but we need to pray. Come on Will. That's something we can do for Jason. Let's go to the chapel - there must be one here somewhere. I'll go and tell them what we're doing.' To my surprise he let me lead him away.

The chapel's dark brown wood was a shock after the polished greys of the rest of the hospital. It felt churchy and medical at the same time, remarkably quiet. I just sat Will down to one side on one of the cushioned wooden chairs, sat next to him and, with an apology that this really wasn't my thing, just asked God out loud to help Jason. I don't really approve of people putting across a point to other people through prayer, but this time I felt I had to. 'Lord, please help Will to realise that he needs to call on you to help Jason, to look for your help and follow your ways.' I didn't think I could quite add 'ways of kindness and forgiveness' but that's what I thought.

Will grunted and slumped and let out a few tears. 'Thanks, David,' he sniffed. 'You will keep praying won't you? I can't think straight.' Will was a bit calmer as we walked back to Casualty, but straightened his back tensely as we sat waiting again. Quite soon Jennifer came out, almost as confident and calm as ever, but with one side of her hair tousled and dark bags and tired wrinkles by her eyes. Will rushed up to her and they hugged and talked. Then Jennifer came over to me.

'Thank you so much for coming, David. They think he's going to be OK.' She smiled a brave smile.

'That's a relief.'

'He's still in a coma, but the convulsions have stopped and his heart seems to be strong.' I could hear the nurse's words in hers. 'He's breathing fine with the oxygen and he looks OK, not at all pale or strained. The doctor said that someone his age and fitness should recover from this without complications, thank God. I think it's all right for Will to come in now. Thank you so much, David.'

I knew when I was being dismissed, and grateful to think only of white cotton sheets and a firm mattress, rest for my body and mind which had had enough. It was good to be able to share with Jane my pleasure that I did seem to have been a help to Will also. She had been praying for us too, and had been baking a cake for Will and myself. It was a good sleep that night.

Wednesday

At 6.30 in the morning Jane had to thump me to wake up for the telephone. I had hoped for a calm day but Raisa's voice was far from calm.

'David, David, I am so sorry to disturb you but you need to know, and your priest needs to know. Mohammed didn't want me to call so early, but he doesn't understand fully about these things. He did trace your phone number for me, but he wants to apologise for the early hour. I am sorry, David, but Lizzie is dead. Please will you tell your priest? You must pray for her now too.'

'Oh, Raisa,' I leant back heavily. 'What happened?'

'She just slipped away, I think. I don't know the details. I just phoned to ask about them both and they told me. You will pray for her won't you?' Not being a Roman Catholic it wasn't easy to answer this one straight. Thankfully lawyers have a lot of experience in using not the whole truth.

'Raisa, we'll certainly pray, and I will contact Paul.' That seemed to be enough for her and I put the phone down. 'Oh God!' I breathed out heavily. My mind raced round what this would mean for Jason, Jennifer and Will and I shuddered. I didn't want to phone Paul so early, but Jane encouraged me (or was it told me?) to get shaved and washed and then ring him. It turned out that he was off to some diocesan meeting, leaving early, so I caught him in time. I could tell he was concerned and saddened but not shocked.

'Do we pray for Lizzie now or is to too late?'

'What harm can it do? They've asked you to pray, so pray. Just tell him what you're thinking and he'll sort it out. I sometimes feel it does make a difference to pray with someone who's died either just before or just after. It's as though the prayer stops anything nasty getting in at the crucial time when people are raw. I don't understand it, but I know that it does make a difference for good. There's no chance you could go and pray with the family? I'm sure Will and Jennifer know where they live.'

'Me! That's your thing Paul.'

'OK, don't worry. I'll have time in the car to pray. You just sit down with Jane. She does know about all this doesn't she?'

'Yes, of course,' I said, wondering why he needed to ask.

Jane wanted to do what Raisa had asked. We sat quietly together for a while. I wondered if she was waiting for me to say something in prayer, take the lead like a good evangelical man, but nothing came. It felt like one of those awkward times at the home group when everyone is waiting for someone else to say something and is thinking that the others are all close to heaven in silent ecstasy instead of just thinking about what the time is and how long the awkwardness is going to last. Eventually Jane spoke. She managed to put into words nearly everything I would have wanted to say. I was very grateful for her and told her so.

'And who does Paul think I am, his curate? Visiting the newly bereaved? Lawyer and scribe is my limit.'

Jane thrust her head forward, her eyes bright. 'Nonsense' she said. 'Paul suggested it. He's your vicar, your leader. He must have had a reason to say that. You don't have to do any work on the flat now, and I'm sure the rest can wait - everyone knows solicitors work to their own timetable. I'll drive. You ring Will.' Was she a braver woman than I, or one treading beyond the step of angels?

I find it hard to say 'No' to Jane and I did have a sneaking feeling that she was right despite the jibe about us solicitors doing things in our own time. I would rather Jane had rung Will at this hour with this bad news but they were more my friends than Jane's. In the end we both went round to see them. We couldn't do this on the telephone.

Will opened the door unshaven and bleary 'David - and Jane - thanks for coming. We've had a fairly calm night, all things considered.' Jason had slept peacefully, with no more convulsions, and was breathing well. We went into the front room and sat down. Will drew back the patio window curtains to let in a flood of light. Looking at the long neat lawn, rose beds and tall trees cutting us off from the rest of the world, it was hard to believe we were in a deadly crisis.

When we all had some tea (and I had asked for sugar in case Will needed it in a while) and were sitting down I told Will about the phone call this morning. He went white, and put his head in his hands. 'Oh no. Now it's murder. Those stupid one-track policemen.'

'The police are slow sometimes but they're not out to get Jason,' I said, unsure about trying to take Will in hand.

'Jason's getting better,' said Jane warmly, 'and soon he'll be able to explain everything. He'll live, you'll see. David did have a word with a policeman friend and they will treat him carefully. Jason will be OK. It's Lizzie and her family that we need to be worried about.' Will seemed able to take this for a while.

'But they'll think Jason killed her. Never liked him anyway. Wasn't good enough for her mother, and that sister always seemed to have it in for him. She really got to him. Thank God she wasn't around much.'

'They may be tempted to think like that,' said Jane soothingly, 'but they'll not know what to think now poor things. I know this may seem strange, but we'd really like to go and see them. Paul suggested it and I think he may be right.' Jane's forthrightness and thinking surprised me again. 'If we go and see them we may be able to help and we'll be showing them that we're not afraid of them - or of what they might be thinking.'

Will soon told us where the family lived and we left him to wash and work out how to tell Jennifer. Thankfully Jason wasn't coming round properly yet so no one needed to say anything to him. They just had to make sure there were no newspapers around him when he did come to.

Jane had us stop at the shops for flowers and a card. She found a bright one with poppies and no message inside, wrote 'With our love and prayers for you all' and gave it to me to sign as we sat on the road outside the large half-rendered house with its long drive and apple trees.

'What are we doing here?' I asked.

'We're visiting the parents of a girl we know a little who has just died. We're trying to do what Paul suggested and what Mohammed's wife asked for. I'm nervous too but they won't attack us, people aren't like that. Good God, go before us, go with us, we need you, good God'. I recognised the last bit from a Celtic prayer book Jane had read when the home group was at our house a month ago or so. I thought again of my helmet with its nose piece, although it was more my stomach that needed protecting or untying from all its knots.

We walked up the drive carrying the flowers and reached the steps of the front door. The door flew open and Meg charged out fiercely muttering, 'stupid woman, stupid woman...'

We just watched her go, small and intense with her orange hair and purple jacket. Patricia Edwards stood at the door with a telephone in her hand. She looked at us and tears flowed. She dropped the telephone and just kept looking at us and the flowers. She knew that we knew - why else would we have flowers? Jane went up to her, put her arm around her and led her inside. I followed, not sure whether to shut the door or leave it open for Meg. I closed it for Patricia's safety, picked up the telephone and followed them into the kitchen.

Patricia was sitting at the table picking at the flowers that lay in front of her. Jane was putting the kettle on. The kitchen was big with tasteful blue and white tiles and a sturdy modern wooden table. Patricia was in an old shiny pink quilted dressing gown which reached to the floor.

'She seemed to be getting better.' Patricia broke the silence. 'After you left it all went peaceful. The nurses looked calmer too. We stayed late, until early this morning, but there was nothing to do. It was all so calm and Elizabeth was breathing better. I was so sleepy and Meg kept saying there wasn't much point in us being there. The nurse even started reading a book. So we went. Why did we go? Why did we go?'

'It must be so hard for you, Mrs Edwards,' cut in Jane like she was used to comforting widows. 'How would you like your tea - one or two sugars?'

'I usually have my saccharine,' Patricia replied dreamily.

'I'll put in two.' said Jane. 'It's what you need now to give you energy.'

'How did you hear?' I asked and then felt ashamed for my curiosity.

'I couldn't sleep until half past five. The hospital phoned when I was asleep and Margaret let me sleep longer before telling me. Goodness knows what she did, but she burst in to my bedroom saying "It's over, it's over. She's free now. A free spirit like Dad."'

Patricia looked up and around, bewildered, her face wet with tears.

Jane said something soothing and Patricia continued, her face turned to her mug. 'I didn't know what she meant at first and then she told me that Elizabeth was dead. That's not quite what she said but I gathered that's what it was.' Patricia bit her lip to hold back even more tears. She kept talking, glancing at Jane from time to time.

'Then she wanted us to go to the hospital for something - the freeing I think she called it. I had no idea what she was talking about. I just wanted to talk to them but she said we had to go to the hospital straight away. I don't understand what's happening?' Patricia looked at Jane and Jane looked at me.

Jane braved the silence. 'Elizabeth has died this morning. I'm so sorry. We heard from Tariq's parents and we just wanted to come and be with you. We don't know any more than you do. Let's phone the hospital shall we?... David?'

I went off to find the number. Eventually I reached intensive care and brought the telephone back to the kitchen where Jane was now sitting at the table with Patricia. Jane smiled at me and said 'thanks' and I was relieved to be able to leave. I sat in the hall - another large space with black and white floor tiles and a staircase rising to a large window where it turned back towards the upstairs rooms. The sun was bright in that tall window. I wondered why it was so bright on such an awful day. 'Oh God, what do we do now?' My head was in my hands. I couldn't think straight and just imagined driving out in the sunshine past tall trees and sturdy houses. I felt in my pocket for the keys to the Rover and felt reassured. I wondered if I should just leave them to it and take myself for a drive to calm down, but that didn't seem fair. I went back into the kitchen.

Jane was standing up drying mugs with a tea towel. 'Here's our chauffeur,' she said, smiling at me. 'As soon as Patricia's dressed we're off to the hospital. I'll just put these flowers in some water. David, you say a prayer for us. You'd like that, Patricia, wouldn't you?'

I couldn't help thinking of yesterday in the hospital and how uncomfortable Patricia had been with Paul praying. I did assure her that we didn't have to pray. I could cope with the driving but was way out of my depth otherwise. Patricia looked at Jane and Jane smiled and said it would be fine - bother her. She then turned to the sink and left me to it!

'Yes... er, well. We'll pray. How about the Lord's prayer?' We got through that and then I managed to carry on a little, thanking God for being Father, asking Him to do the best for Lizzie and for Patricia and Margaret, and bring them through this difficult time. When I opened my eyes Patricia was crying more and, as Jane went up to her, she just shook and sobbed. I felt awful, as though I had twisted a knife in a wound that should have been left alone but Jane smiled again and thanked me, and Patricia looked at me and tried to smile through her tears.

The drive to the hospital was quiet, helped by the sunshine dappled by leaves. We parked in a disabled space for once, which gave me something to occupy my mind - constructing arguments for intense grief being a disability even without an orange card. Intensive care seemed even quieter. Even Raisa, who was there already with Tariq, just looked at us as we came in. Lizzie, or her body, was lying with her head turned a little to her left, her golden hair making the pillow beautiful. All the wires and tubes had gone. She was still and empty. I left the women and went to Raisa.

'Thank you for phoning, Raisa.' I said, suddenly feeling a little tearful myself, in front of this large brightly-dressed, kind woman. Raisa smiled and said nothing. She just looked at Lizzie's bed where Patricia was stroking her dead daughter's hair. We both had tears in our eyes.

'It's good that you're here,' said Raisa, and she turned back to Tariq who was twitching a little uncomfortably, although still unconscious.

Jane beckoned me to come over to them and she asked me to contact the chaplain. With relief at something to do I went to talk with the nurses who offered to use the bleep but I said I'd go to the chapel office first I didn't wait for them to try to change my mind but just headed out into the hospital corridors asking directions from the first hospital-secretary-looking woman I came across. The chapel was brighter and newer than at City Road and there was a little service going on, just three or four people, and what I took to be the chaplain at the front - a small woman with short thick brown hair and a blue dog-collar blouse. I didn't know what I had expected but it wasn't this. These extraordinary few days were teaching me to be more used to going with whatever the flow brought with it.

After the service was over I introduced myself and explained to Jane (not another one!) the chaplain that we would like her to go and see Patricia. She went into her office and came back with a little bag and a book. On the way back to ITU I wondered about phoning the office briefly, but I though I'd better at least introduce her to the others.

Patricia was sitting quietly by the bed holding Lizzie's hand. The chaplain went up to her and put a hand on her shoulder, speaking with warmth and authority. My Jane explained a bit more of what had happened and then chaplain Jane said how hard it was that there had been nothing that we could have done for Elizabeth, but now we could express in prayer and symbolically how much we had wanted to do for her. She then invited us to put some oil on Elizabeth's forehead, perhaps making the sign of the cross, to show how much we love her and also as a sign of how much God loves her. This all seemed to me a bit strange and Catholic, but Patricia again just looked at chaplain Jane and went along with her. She prayed a couple of prayers from her book, or a psalm and a prayer, and then thanked God for Elizabeth. She took a little silver thimble from her case, unscrewed the lid, laid her thumb in the thimble and reached out to Lizzie's forehead. As she made the sign of the cross, she left a thin shining film behind. 'May the Cross of Jesus be ever before you, to comfort you; may the Cross of Jesus be ever beside you, to forgive you; may the Cross of Jesus be ever behind you, to reassure you; may Jesus of the Cross welcome you and lead you on, now and always.'

I was glad that Lizzie had been a Christian, that I could remember her singing with us, and that she would be with Jesus now. Chaplain Jane handed Patricia the thimble. Patricia's hands shook and she spilt a little oil but she did reach out to her daughter's head and touched her with oil. 'My Elizabeth, my Elizabeth, my Elizabeth...' Patricia just stood there with her hand moving gently across the shining forehead.

Suddenly there was a loud cough next to us. Meg was standing there, looking angry still, clenching her fists. A youngish man with long hair was standing behind her, hands in the pockets of his long shaggy coat. I felt had I had to say something.

'Meg, I'm so sorry, we could have brought you too. This is my wife Jane and the hospital chaplain Jane Slater. We're just praying and anointing Elizabeth. It's so good that you are here.'

Chaplain Jane tried to include Meg and her man but Meg just shook her orange head and stiffened her shoulders. My Jane did her anointing and I thought that was plenty for Meg to cope with so I declined. Later I regretted that I hadn't been bolder.

Meg put her hand out to the man behind her and he took out a little drawstring black pouch. He poured a few shiny stones out into his hand and gave them to Meg. We just stood and watched as Meg pulled back the cover (Patricia trembled) and put the stones on Elizabeth's belly button. Her body was so white and vulnerable, marbled with bruising, her skin so thin. The stones rested oddly. Meg then pulled the covers up over the body again and smiled. She relaxed a little and went up to touch the side of Elizabeth's head 'It's OK now, sis. It's all OK. He says it's OK, you'll live free now.' Then she turned and looked round, trying to smile at us. 'Who's coming to have a drink with us?' Jane and Jane looked blankly at her while Patricia smiled at her fondly. 'Celebrate the passing. Glasses raised to the spirit. There's no point in looking back. We've freed her.' Meg took the hand of her man and walked swiftly out of the room. I breathed heavily, not realising how tense I had been.

'Margaret's always been a character' said Patricia. 'The ways of her young people are different, but there's something to be said for them. They're not stuck in a rut.' She looked round for our support. Revd Jane said that it was good that they had both been able to do what was right for them. Would she like to stay there longer or would she like some tea back in her office while they worked out what to do next? Patricia looked at my Jane who said that tea seemed nice.

Out in the corridor I decided that it was high time I made contact with the office. Jane said that I could leave them to it now, so I gave them the car keys, Jane having promised to pick me up after work. Watching the three of them walk off down the corridor I felt relieved and a bit drained. I turned back towards the train station and found Raisa waiting to say something.

'I am glad you were here. She was such a lovely girl, and what you did was so good again. But why did you allow that sister her pagan rites? Can't we go and take those crystals off her? It's not right.' Raisa seemed quite distressed but I assured her that it was harmless and that everyone has a right to grieve in their own way. Later I wasn't sure if that was right or just dangerous. We wouldn't allow people to cut off an arm to keep with them because this was their way to grieve. But who says what's acceptable?

On the train I wondered about Meg. Why was she so positive about her sister dying? She seemed to think that it was all meant to happen. I longed to cross-question her about just what motive she had for seeing her sister dead.

Occasionally some people at church would make a comment about 'the days of New Age thinking' but it all seemed simply the old witchcraft coming back with a vengeance. Was Meg's attitude just part of her paganism? I couldn't remember her shedding any tears.

Rose smiled at me as I came through the door. 'Ah, David...' She put her pen down and looked at me. I sat in the chair by her desk and tried to explain everything. I really didn't know what to do next. Rose went and brought a cup of proper tea and a piece of cake from somewhere. That improved my energy levels and I began to think a bit more clearly. There was work to do - I still hadn't told Mohammed about the flat purchase falling through, and dear Mrs Bright wanted to talk with me again. But Will was my priority.

Rose agreed to explain to Philippa and to put off Mrs Bright and anyone else who called on me. We decided that I was involved in a 'very serious investigation' and that I wouldn't be available until after next week. We hoped that people wouldn't be exasperated by a solicitor arranging things at his own convenience but impressed by knowing that their affairs were being handled by an important man in great demand. 'Fat chance,' I thought, but couldn't see any other option.

I phoned Will, who was out. Reluctantly I dragged myself off to hospital again. City Road this time. I was even beginning to long for the inside of a court or a police station. Eventually, after much asking, I found the long old-fashioned ward where Jason was, with Will and Jennifer by him. Jason was sleeping.

Will and I left Jennifer and went outside. The sun was still shining on the little patch of grass. 'It gets worse,' said Will, staring at the earth. 'They'll want him for murder now. How was Mrs Edwards?' I told him briefly about Patricia and Meg. 'Mad girl,' Will said reflectively, but I didn't ask what he was remembering. Jason was improving slowly, still very sleepy, and had had a couple of quite bad nightmares. I reassured Will that Jason had nothing to fear. I was sure that he didn't have it in him to plan such sabotage, even if he did know about cars. I asked if the police had been informed, and Will said that was the last thing he would want to do. I tried to explain that the more open and forthcoming he was with the police the less suspicious they would be. I offered to have a word with Phil Wittle, to explain what Jason was like, before explaining about the note. Eventually Will put the note in my hand and told me to take it before he changed his mind, but to make sure they had it back. I think he was glad to be rid of it. I could imagine him re-reading it and failing to make any sense of it.

Phil was in and we agreed to have lunch again. I needed somewhere nice and calm with good simple food so he agreed to meet at the Metropolitan, as long as I paid. I appreciated the thick carpets, well upholstered chairs and the muffled quiet even if it was a bit gloomy. Phil stood tall in front of me and put a hand on my shoulder. 'It must be pretty bad - for you to be spending your firm's money on me.' He winked. 'I'll make sure you have what you're looking for, know what I mean?' he continued in a fake cockney accent. I wondered if he was a bit nervous about being seen to be maybe taking a bribe. Why couldn't friends just meet up for lunch any more?

Phil was his usual bright self at the table, praising the bottled water and detecting tones of cowslip with a slight bouquet of sheep spit. It was good to relax with him. He read the note and suddenly became quite serious. 'We have to find out where Jason was on that day,' he said. He assured me that he believed me about Jason's character but didn't think that would make any difference to the others on the investigation. They'd have to wait a while before questioning him again. I suggested that in the meantime they talk with Paul the grease, as Jason had probably been with him. 'There's no other place to look for a murderer,' Phil said. 'And it was murder. Keep this quiet but we've now found a hose from the power steering. It was broken off in the impact but it had been cut through. We were lucky to find it. It's only small but it would explain the car going out of control when it did.' I shivered and thought of Will and Jennifer and Jason.

I asked Phil why they hadn't told Mohammed about there being no way of determining the alcohol in Tariq's blood. 'As it's murder we like to keep things just as the murderer wants - that way they're more likely to relax and let something slip. They think we're blaming it on the booze and won't think we're suspecting them. When we do have a suspect - or two,' he said hastily, 'we can make sure they hear the truth when someone's watching so we know their reaction. At least that's what the boss says. We wonder if he thinks his middle name is Hercule.'

'But Mohammed's just getting more and more cross. People are pointing the finger at his son.'

'Look, David, do you want your lad to be the only suspect or what? You can't have it both ways.' Phil was giving me a glimpse of his hard side. It didn't put him off his pudding. I have never seen a man eat so much custard. Before he left, he checked that I wouldn't end his career by publicising the details, but he knew that I couldn't afford to make enemies of the whole of the West Midlands Police Force. They have perfected closing ranks beautifully.

I knew Rose would make a good job of dealing with my clients, better than I could, so I thought I should go and see if Mohammed was in. Frank was sitting by Philippa's desk and from the warmth with which Philippa greeted me, I gathered that she had been finding him something of a trial. She gave me a lovely wide-eyed smile which made me wish I was ten years younger and had put on some smarter clothes, and she asked me to come and tell her all the news. Rose had already explained about the flat and I told her what I thought was really going on. 'How awful,' she said. 'I hope they end up with a young party animal who keeps them awake all hours. What a strong and sharp mind you must have, as well, to see all that!'

Frank wasn't so quick to condemn. 'Our generation need to be reassured. We know how different some people are. They're not all as likeable as Mohammed and his Dad, by any means.'

I asked Frank more about his background in the North-West Frontier with the British Army. Surely he had made friends with more locals than just Mohammed's father? 'A few friends and plenty of enemies,' he replied. 'Most of them are too touchy. They're just looking for a reason to have a go at you. As soon as you say anything, even in good humour, that could be remotely hard, that's it. They're after you. Mohammed's father got the sharp end of it, believe me. He warned me about them. "No forgiveness," he used to say. They end up fighting everyone and they never give up. It's just a good thing we had the decent weapons and they didn't.'

Philippa looked up in mock despair. I guessed that she had heard all this before. I asked her about Mohammed and whether he was free. 'Not yet I'm afraid. He has to see to someone first, but I expect he'll be delighted to see you in half an hour. Why don't you and Frank find somewhere to talk man to man for a while?' Philippa raised her eyebrows and almost pouted. Philippa's combination of husky voice and sweet determination was irresistible, so I found myself on the street again with Frank.

I didn't want another coffee and couldn't face the sight of Frank in his mouldy tweeds sitting on an orange sofa, so I suggested we have a look in the Cathedral. Frank said he'd never been in before, so I dragged him in to look at the ironwork and the Burne-Jones pictures. Frank didn't look so out of place there; the building looked lovely and clean in the bright sunshine.

We sat in a pew and looked at the strange East window. Frank said it was all right as far as churches went but he'd be more comfortable in the British Legion without any men wandering around in dresses. A verger or chaplain or someone was pinning paper meticulously onto a notice board by the entrance.

'Frank, it's good the way you stick by Mohammed, you must have been very close to his father?'

'Pash was a good laugh, he was. The first time we met, there were three or four of us making merry, having a grand time, singing our heads off. Then this enormous big brown woman comes storming out at us with a broom, jabbering something about quiet. She was so mad one of the lads even took out his pistol just to calm her down a bit.'

I recoiled and raised my eyebrows at this bullying but Frank didn't seem to notice.

'Then Pash appeared out of nowhere, smiling and laughing. He just put an arm around my shoulder and led us on straight past the old cow, who just stood with her mouth open.'

Frank chuckled in a spluttery way, and put his hand on mine. I took that as a sign that he wanted to continue as soon as he had the breath. 'It turns out that she was the bossy-boots local midwife who didn't want 'her' babies being born with so much hilarity going on around them. Pash said she was always a miserable sod, never able to have children of her own. But apparently all that was a great insult to the family, which meant about half of the town, and Pash, who was just trying to help and calm things down, wasn't wanted any more.'

Loud-mouthed foreign soldiers scaring pregnant women were bound to antagonise. I blinked and shook my head, wondering how Frank couldn't see this. He probably took my gesture as agreement that the townsfolk overreacted. 'Yes,' I commented, 'I can see he was choosing whose side he was on! But what future could he have then?'

Frank was blithely unconcerned. 'We found him a job in our stores and that was that.'

'So he sort of became British while still in India,' I nodded.

Frank smiled, showing a few more dark yellow teeth. 'More British than the British, good lad! We soon taught him how to enjoy himself and he enjoyed having a bit of money behind him for a change.'

I blinked a bit at this definition of the essence of Britishness – enjoying booze and being proud of wealth. 'With that sort of life, he really couldn't stay in India, could he? Was it long before he emigrated?'

Frank didn't reply directly. 'When he came over here he was one of the first, we soon got him into the Legion - war service of course, just like Gurkhas,' Frank winked, 'and a job at Dunlop. He sent a fair bit of money home but they never seemed to appreciate it really.'

'You kept up with him, then?'

'He used to help out at the Legion, so we never lost touch.'

I had a glimpse of this bewildered immigrant behind the bar, looking out at the circle of friends he had hoped to join. 'He was pretty much on his own, then?'

'Oh he tried to get together with one of our girls but they never quite took to him. Eventually he married a young woman not long over from Pakistan, and that's how Mohammed came about.' Frank had completely missed what I meant. It reminded me of divorce cases where each side has a very different view of reality.

'So Pash had to go back to his old home, in some way...' I mused. 'And he gave his son an 'old home' name.'

Frank grimaced. 'He wasn't called Mohammed at first, but Thomas. At least Pash called him Thomas and his mother called him Mohammed.' Frank's face softened. 'He poured all he had into that lad, gave him the best education money could buy, worked all hours, you know.'

I wondered if Pash would have worked so hard if he'd had more real friends to spend his evenings with. 'You were friends, then?' I asked.

'I always promised I'd look after him, make sure he fitted in here. Got him the job at the Legion. Put him right about our ways.'

Inwardly I shuddered at Frank haranguing Pash not to upset the drunken customers. I wondered if Pash ever regretted his impulsive kindness with the drunken soldiers. 'A bit of a sad life, though,' I said, wondering if Frank would object to my implied criticism.

'The sad part was that Pash didn't really see his boy grown up. I always thought it was up to me to keep an eye on him for Pash. Stop him going back to the old ways.' Frank snorted. 'His mother's family never seemed to want to live like us.'

I felt a lot of sympathy for Mohammed's mother and her family. If Pash the Anglophile rebel hadn't been truly accepted, what hope was there for them? 'I can understand Mohammed being close to his mother. Did she help him find Raisa?'

'Help him?' Frank looked at me, frowning. 'Bloody arranged it. Pash would have wanted him to marry one of us but somehow she only wanted a dark'un. The woman's all right of course, but her family are a rum lot too. There's plenty of them and some of them are just what Pash warned us about.'

I raised my eyebrows, not sure if I wanted to know the details of Frank's xenophobia. 'So you're a sort of counter-balance?'

'I promised Pash I'd make sure they were safe, and I've kept my promise. He knew the dangers and we've tried to make sure they at least are safe.' Frank looked at me intently, and then looked down. 'It's a battle, still. Maybe more so.' He shook his head and went quiet.

It didn't seem right to interrupt the quiet in the Cathedral. In the silence I wondered about this old man with his longstanding 'friendship.' At least he'd made one good contact beyond his immediate culture, which was perhaps all that you could expect from someone of his generation. But part of me wanted to shake him out of his blind prejudice.

There was more I wanted to know. 'Frank what about Tariq? What's he like?'

'He was a serious lad.' Frank sighed. 'Didn't have the playfulness of his grandfather in him. Not much laughter even as a baby. He was always looking for something else.'

'That seems sort of like his grandfather in some way?' Looking for real friends, for a home, was what I was thinking but didn't dare say.

Frank shook his head with rapid short movements and breathed in, almost in anger. 'Not at all. Quite the opposite. He got mixed up with some religious types from the mosque. He changed. Even more serious, moody even.'

'That would have bothered you,' I said concealing my irony.

'I didn't see much of him, but his Dad was worried about some of the people he was mixing with. There were men from Pakistan always at the mosque. He used to say that Tariq was becoming an angry young man. That's why he was glad when he got together with that girl. It reassured old Mohammed no end, though I wasn't sure.'

'Did Tariq make any enemies, do you think? You don't think he was drunk do you?'

'Well I suppose he could have changed. Perhaps he did have more of his grandfather in him than we realised?' Frank smiled hopefully. 'But with that lot he was mixing with it wasn't hard to make enemies. Some of them seem to be looking for enemies to make, just like Pash said.' Frank fell silent and then slapped his thighs, stood up and led me out into the sunshine. He seemed to have had his say and it was time to move on. There wasn't much more I could take in either. I was glad to feel the warmth of the sun and to hear a few birds singing again.

Philippa told us that Mohammed was waiting for us, so we went into his panelled office. 'David, how good that you are here with Mr Gatley. Our two champions of everything English! Do sit down.' Nothing seemed to quell Mohammed's cheerful flattery.

'Thank you for coming, David, and thank you for going to the hospital with our Lizzie's parents. I hear that you had some trouble with the sister.' He raised an eyebrow, glanced at Frank and carried on. 'But you brought with you a holy woman this time - you have good connections, Mr Jeffery! A holy woman for a grieving women - how good. And now you have come to console me about my aunt's flat. These things happen, but it is in the will of God.' He glanced at Frank again. 'My aunt is a very understanding woman and I am not her only nephew. She will find a good home temporarily until we can find her a good welcoming place, maybe with some nice Asian neighbours?' I nodded emphatically. 'There are more important matters to deal with here. We must find out who killed my son's fiancée, and we must see that Tariq recovers well. He is stable now, thank God, responding a little more since yesterday.' It was amazing how Mohammed seemed to be up to date on everything. No wonder he was such a good business tycoon.

'Thank you for calling us, Mohammed. It was the best thing to do, although I must admit it didn't feel like that at the time.

And I am so pleased that Tariq is showing signs of recovery. That must make it a little easier for you all.' I felt that I had to both choose my words carefully and maintain a good flow.

Mohammed acknowledged me with a polite bowing smile. He then spoke in a lower, quieter, more serious voice. 'What would make it easier for us would be for the police to soon stop thinking that this was an accident.'

'I am sure they don't think that at all,' I said as emphatically as I could. 'I know a number of officers in the CID, professionally of course, and I know that they are far too clear-sighted to be put off by a silly suspicion like that. Tariq was known as a committed Moslem by his own choice. Alcohol doesn't come into it. The police are probably hoping to lull the murderer into a false sense of security.' This felt like sailing close to the wind, but within the boundaries.

'You're saying it's murder then,' said Frank quickly. 'What makes you think that?' he frowned and held his head back tensely.

'If there was no alcohol, or anything else, in Tariq's blood, then there must have been some other reason for the car to crash. It was probably tampered with.'

This time Mohammed just looked at me, as though wondering what I knew. 'But accidents happen all the time,' said Frank stiffly. 'They can't all be murders.'

'Not like this accident. That's all I can say at the moment.'

'Well I hope they don't waste time and drag it all out needlessly. The family need to be able to put this behind them.' Frank seemed even more concerned than ever but I wasn't sure that Mohammed entirely welcomed this concern.

'Thank you for trying to convey the truth, David,' said Mohammed who had clearly grasped all I had wanted to say.

'I seem to be caught up in the middle of all this,' I said 'and I can't make sense of it. Why would anyone want to try to kill Tariq? He didn't have any enemies did he?'

'David, you are too close to it all. Perhaps you had better leave it to the police to handle the suspect.' Mohammed did not seem to want to talk much further. I realised then that he was still convinced that Jason had had a hand in this and there was no way I could change his mind. At least he would be a little reassured of Tariq's innocence. It was time for me to go, so I left him to talk with Frank.

Jane picked me up from the office. It was strange following the familiar route with her at the wheel. I asked her if she would like to be a chauffeur for a while, but she just said that the grey uniform didn't suit her.

Jane had stayed with Patricia until the afternoon, when her brother had come over from Nottingham and taken things in hand. Patricia had asked if Paul would do the funeral at St Luke's as it was the only local church Lizzie had ever gone to, and Jane had assured her that this would probably be fine. We just had to talk with Paul when he was back from his day course.

I wanted to know more about mad Meg. Jane didn't like me calling her that, but she was just as curious as I was and had found out a lot during the day. Meg, or Margaret as Patricia called her, lived in a kind of commune near Newtown in Wales. She had always been interested in spiritual things and as a child had been to the local Catholic Church with a friend and her family. Five years ago Mr Edwards had died of cancer. While he was very ill Meg had read about spiritual healing and found someone in Birmingham who could channel healing energy to people. The healer seemed nice enough and Meg's father had gone with her to see him. Mrs Edwards said that he was touched by her concern and didn't want to disappoint her. Patricia herself had stayed away, not being at all religious in any way, as she put it.

Derek, Mr Edwards, had seemed to improve for a while and Meg was overjoyed. But when the symptoms returned he didn't want to go back again, and Meg had blamed Lizzie. Apparently Lizzie was at that time coming to our church and told her father that she didn't think this healer was as harmless as he seemed. Meg still kept going to see him and was soon involved in a weekly 'healing channel' group. When Derek did die Meg surprisingly carried on, and it wasn't long before she began to say that she had had messages from her father saying that he was OK and was watching over them all. Patricia had found it a comfort, but Lizzie hadn't wanted to know and there had been quite a rift. Lizzie became a Christian which made Meg deeply angry. Poor Patricia found herself in the middle, not really able to comfort either grieving daughter.

The more involved each of them became in their religion, as Patricia put it, the more arguments there were. Meg made nasty remarks at Jason, and Lizzie would criticise Meg's new friends. Meg went off to live in Wales to make a new beginning. Then all of a sudden everything changed. Lizzie came back from university and didn't know what to do. She went to see Meg in Wales and somehow they made it up and became close again. This had lasted for a while, until Lizzie met up with Tariq. If Meg had not liked Jason, then it seems she hated Tariq. Once again they had rows and doors slamming whenever Meg came to visit. Patricia had tried to reassure Meg that Tariq was only a boyfriend but Meg seemed to see him as a great threat and another rival.

'Patricia really didn't know quite what was going on,' said Jane, 'but she was worried. She said that she was afraid how Meg would react if she ever thought Lizzie and Tariq were engaged. I don't know if she knew they were or not. She said that Meg could be so jealous.'

It was that simple comment that made me sit up. 'The police think she was killed. Was it Tariq who was the target? Did the police have the wrong jealous lover?'

Jane thought this was all far-fetched. But once the thought was there I couldn't shake it out. I needed somehow to find out more about Meg and her friends, but how?

Jane went off to ring Paul while I just turned over in my mind all that had happened since Sunday - and it was only Wednesday evening! Here I was turning myself into some kind of detective when I didn't have a clue where to start.

Peter and Nicola came in and wanted to know what was going on. Peter was at the grammar school, his passion for his saxophone not taking over too much from schoolwork. Nicola was developing a keen interest in formula one motor racing, perhaps the most pointless and wasteful of all 'sports' but not destined to lead her into deep iniquity. Emily, our youngest, was still keen on animals - the smaller and cuddlier the better. The girls' school reports were satisfying (or should that be satisfactory) with the occasional glow from a favourite teacher.

'Why are you and Mum talking so much?' asked Nicola.

'And why are you home so early?' asked Peter. 'Is it to do with that Moslem's car crash?' He'd been reading the papers and watching *Midlands Today*. 'They're all arguing about whether he was drunk or not, and *The Birmingham Express* are really hyping it up with all stuff about "our new angel, the brightest young reporter we have ever had at the prestigious *Birmingham Express*." A candle with a unique scent, cruelly snuffed out. It's all a bit much.'

'Yeah,' said Nicola, 'and they're almost having to close Queensway for all the flowers. That's the paper making too much of it as well and encouraging people to go silly. How fast was he going - that's what I want to know? He must have been going it to have smashed them both up so badly.'

'Come on Dad, tell us the solicitor's story,' said Peter clearing his throat. 'Yes, Mr Jeffery, please can you tell the truth, the whole truth and nothing but the truth?'

'Oh I wish I could!' I sighed and they realised how serious it was. 'The girl's Lizzie - you may remember her with Jason Jennings in church. The police think the car was tampered with and they think Jason did it.' Even Peter was stunned and lost for words.

'Jason!' said Nicola. 'He's no murderer. He doesn't have narrow eyes or bad breath or anything. Oh - but he does know a lot about cars.'

Peter asked me quietly what I thought. I told him I was sure Jason hadn't done it. By now I was only about 80% sure but I didn't tell that part of the whole truth. I was also trying to think who else could have done it.

'Someone else who knows a lot about cars,' said Nicola. 'Who hated Lizzie's new man and knows about cars? Keep looking until you find him, Dad.' She went off to the kitchen.

Peter looked quietly at me. 'That's not a simple thing to do is it? Was there anyone else who might have wanted him dead - or maybe just wanted to give him a scare for some reason?'

Reluctantly, and swearing to secrecy, I told him about Meg. 'Murders are usually committed by someone who knows the victim well, even a family member.' It was another indiscretion I later came to regret.

'Are you sure you've not got it in for her because she's a New Ager? They're not known for being violent, you know, except when trees are at stake or world leaders …' We both thought of the scenes in Birmingham when the G8 meeting had been here last year – cars set alight in Centenary Square while police were pelted venomously. It had been all the more sickening as earlier in the day the anti-debt protest had gone so calmly. Peter had gone with a group from another church. Jane had gone too while I stayed and caught up with some paperwork. They both came back enthusing about the warmth of the sunshine, the friendliness of everybody. Thousands of people, mainly Christians, had filled up Birmingham and then made a continuous chain for miles around the city centre. Jane said it had been the happiest gathering she had ever been in, with no hint of trouble. Peter was delighted that he had actually waved at a minibus full of world leaders who had secretly toured the route of the chain a while after it had dispersed. I must admit a point had been made and people in this country seemed to have taken it in. Whether that would make any difference to anywhere else in the world, I doubted. But by the evening of that very day the focus of the Press had been on the few hundred violent eco-protesters and not the thousands of friendly Christians. Those people did seem capable of violent outbursts of anger, when they had what they considered a legitimate target.

Peter fell silent again. The clock ticked slowly in the background and a van rumbled by on the road, its white top just visible above our front hedge. I certainly didn't know what to say next.

'Perhaps,' said Peter reflectively, 'If they thought he was part of the enemy. Perhaps…'

'Well it certainly wasn't Jason. And it could have been a mad maverick. How would anyone know?' If Peter could see the possibility then I reckoned it must be worth pursuing.

'Perhaps,' said Peter tentatively, 'perhaps you could go and find out more about this Meg woman. You could go and see where she lives and talk to some people.'

'But how? It isn't as easy as that – walking into a New Age commune somewhere in my best office suit and asking questions. They're not going to want to talk with me.'

'But you never know.' Peter suddenly became more animated. 'Perhaps you could go there with Paul! He's going to be taking the funeral isn't he? He could make a point of seeing Meg at home. Why don't you persuade him to go and to take you along for the drive? While he's talking with Meg you could see what you could find out from anyone else around.'

I laughed quietly. It seemed so unlikely that Paul would talk to these pagans. 'I don't think Meg will be there. She'll be with her mother at home. Even New Agers know they are needed at home at times like this. But if she has taken herself back to Wales, who knows?' It was all so unlikely that I just smiled and said 'Maybe … maybe…'

Then Jane came back in and said that Paul had agreed to take Lizzie's funeral as long as it wasn't on Wednesday as he had to talk to a group in Cambridge about a project in which he was involved in India. He said that it was unlikely to be so soon anyway. Jane was going to tell Patricia or her brother. I thought that maybe my son had come up with an unlikely solution to my impasse.

'OK Peter. I'll talk with Paul tomorrow. Thanks for your help, mate.'

Thursday

The following morning I talked with Paul and agreed to see him for coffee. This was good of him, as I knew that he had a strict pattern of deskwork in the mornings and people work in the afternoons. Paul is tall and, dare I say it, handsome. He has a larger group of admiring women than any other vicar we have had; even a couple of ladies who were very keen on the great Mike Channing now seem to have switched their admiration to Paul. He has a deep fruity voice and a deceptively languid manner for someone so highly time-managing.

Paul invited me into his large study where his computer was humming in the corner displaying a screensaver of angels flying past with various messages of encouragement from the Bible. There were a couple of blue armchairs and a small brown settee that all looked bright and clean, but on closer inspection were of a good age indeed. Jill brought us both a rather nice coffee. I was not surprised when Paul began by saying, with apologies, that he had promised to make a phone call in forty minutes' time. He then prayed briefly out loud. He sat back with his mug in his hands and waited for me to speak.

'It's about the awful business with Jason and Lizzie and Tariq Khan. You know that I'm involved in it all up to my neck

… It's amazing how I seem to know everyone involved. Anyway you must know that Jason is the prime suspect as far as the police are concerned…' Paul nodded. 'But that's got to be nonsense. He couldn't have done something as nasty as that.' Paul just said 'Mmm…,' which wasn't enough of a questioning of my certainty to give me reason for challenging him, but was a bit disturbing. Maybe Paul didn't see Jason as so innocent? But maybe he was just being the professional, rather more detached than I was? It's amazing how thoughts or impressions go so quickly through your head and take so long to write down.

'Anyway,' I continued quickly, 'I don't think Jason is the one. There's Lizzie's mad sister, called Margaret or Meg, you remember her being shirty about us praying with Lizzie? It seems to me much more likely that she had something to do with it.' Paul raised his eyebrows and said 'Yes?' in a gently 'you cannot be serious' kind of way. 'Someone had tampered with the car, a pipe in the power steering was cut. Jason wasn't the only one jealous of Tariq.' I tried to be my court persona, calm and reasonable.

'You think Meg sabotaged Tariq's car?' Paul was quizzical now, less openly sceptical.

'Not necessarily Meg herself. One of her friends who knows a bit more about cars.' Paul encouraged me to continue. 'Her mother said that she's not got over the death of her father five years ago, and that she was incredibly jealous of any man who went out with Lizzie. She's the most likely jealous lover here.' I let that sink in before continuing.

'And you should know that there's no love lost between New Agers and radical Moslems. If any two groups are natural enemies, it's those two. Put Meg's jealousy together with someone wanting to have a go at a rising hard line Moslem leader – that's a pretty strong motive. And look at Meg's behaviour. She hasn't cried for her sister. She gives the impression she was somehow ready for this. She's clearly unstable, capable of strange, even violent actions.' Again I paused as Paul sat with his hands clasped against his lips, his eyes fixed on me almost in a stare.

'You will think this is unlikely. It does seem hardly possible. But knowing Jason as I do, I am sure that his having a hand in this is even more unlikely. I just need to know more.' It was time to let Paul have a say.

'There's a lot here.' said Paul, nodding his head slowly. He spoke calmly with a hint of questioning. 'You've come to me because you think Meg could have arranged the accident…?'

'Yes, and because I think you can help me get more information on Meg. You'll see the family won't you? You couldn't possibly go to see Meg at her home could you – she lives in a kind of commune near Newtown in Wales – and take me with you? I know that she might not be there at the moment, which would make it all go wrong. But if she has gone back to Wales, could we go and see her there? If she is back in Wales it might be pretty suspicious too – it would make me think she couldn't cope with being around here, perhaps because of the part she had in it. She certainly doesn't seem to care much for her mother.'

Paul breathed deeply. 'Let me see if I have this right,' he said slowly and carefully. 'You want me to arrange to go to Wales to see Lizzie's sister about the funeral so that you can go and sleuth around?' I nodded. 'Well there's a quick answer to that: No. David, I can't.'

'Why ever not? This is serious. Jason's in danger. Will and Jennifer are going frantic. We have to do something to help.'

'What you're asking me to do, David, is fundamentally dishonest. You are asking me to pretend to do something, which I wouldn't normally do, for your ulterior motive. Now your motive may be very good, but that doesn't mean it's right to be dishonest.' Paul paused and I looked at the floor. He continued warmly. 'I can see that the situation is serious, but it's not that urgent. No one can sort it out quickly, however frantic Will and Jennifer are. It's a big mess and a terrible tangle, but it has to be untangled the right way and that takes time.'

Unfortunately for me I could see what Paul meant. I felt like an enthusiastic teenager being put right by a kindly but strict uncle. I sank into silence and then asked more quietly 'Well, what can I do?'

'David, you've already done a lot.' Paul smiled broadly and threw his hands in the air. 'You went to see Lizzie's mother and you even prayed with her, despite telling me that you wouldn't. You have done a lot.'

'But that doesn't help Jason! And it was going to see Patricia that made me meet Meg again. Perhaps that's what God wanted me to do all along and maybe he now wants me to pursue it further.'

'I'm not sure about rushing around – that doesn't sound like God's way to me. If there's something more that he wants you to do, he'll let you know. He's more likely to get through to you when you're calmer than you are now. If Jason is innocent, God will bring it out.' Paul smiled a slightly false, slightly patronising smile.

This was like a red rag to a bull, or at least stepping on a professional lawyer's toes. 'Do you think I've never seen an innocent man sent down? God doesn't just protect the innocent on His own. He needs a bit of help. And you don't understand that once an investigation has begun moving down a certain track, the pressure is on to reach that destination however scanty the evidence is.' I was trying to control my temper but seething inside at the other-worldly platitudes that Paul dared to dump on me.

Paul stopped smiling which was good as I would have wanted to hit him if he hadn't. He leant forward and looked me in the eye calmly. 'You are desperately concerned about Jason and rightly so. It's just not right to charge into anything, especially if it means deceiving.' He kept looking at me.

I felt hot and looked at the floor again. A browny-orange flecked carpet, newer than I expected. Paul leant back a little and spoke more warmly. 'And, David, surely there are alternatives? It looks, from what you say, as if someone was trying to harm Tariq. What do you know about him? Meg's a strange girl, but she clearly cares enough for her mother. She couldn't do that and harm her sister so badly…'

Paul wasn't going to cooperate with me but he wasn't going to change my mind either. I cleared my throat and it was my turn to put on a smile. 'Of course, Paul, I am open to all possibilities. I just want to give something to the police to help them see other possibilities too.'

Paul nodded. 'What do you know about Tariq?'

It would have been rude to refuse to go down this track. I shrugged and spoke with a little frown. 'Not a great deal. There's a friend of his father I've talked to a couple of times this week. He just gave the impression that he's a good Moslem, not a drinker.'

Paul leaned back and relaxed. 'What does Jane think of all this and what you should be doing in it all?'

The change of track surprised me. 'She's quite keen for me to be involved. It was Jane who dragged us along to Patricia's yesterday. She seems to think I do have a special role to play here.'

Paul was quiet for a moment, rubbing his chin. 'Well perhaps you should go back and talk with her about what to do next. But you're right to be worried about Will and Jennifer and Jason. It's good you're so concerned for them. Let's pray for them, shall we?'

Again I could hardly say 'No.' Vicars have this way of ending things where they want them to end. Maybe it comes from all those sermons. We did just pray for them and for me, and Paul prayed for himself too with all that the funeral would mean. He prayed a simple prayer, covering a lot, and I did feel relieved. It made me realise that he had a lot on his plate too in all this. Rather ashamed, I thanked him for his time. 'It's really good of you to give me this time, Paul. It must be hard for you too. Not a normal funeral.'

'No, I've never taken a big media funeral before. The phone call I need to make today is to the Diocesan Press Officer who's going to be in London until Tuesday and I need her advice about what we are all to do. It is quite daunting, but I'm pleased that Mrs Edwards wants us to be involved. I didn't think that would happen after Tuesday. Let's keep praying for each other, shall we?'

And with that Paul stood up. I followed and went out into another sunny day. The Vicarage front lawn was cut neatly but thickly and the blue and white border flowers had a few dandelions and buttercups poking up among them. No doubt gardening had been pushed even further down Paul's 'To Do' list this month, poor man.

Jane was making herself an early lunch so that she could call round at Patricia's early in the afternoon. She had collected a key and agreed to take her dogs for their mid-day walk to free Patricia and her brother to go to the registrar and the undertaker without worrying about the time.

Jane asked me what Paul had said and smiled when I told her. I could see that she agreed with him.

'So what do I do now?' I said. 'I can't just leave Jason and Will to worry themselves to death.'

Jane looked at me again with a wry frown; another faux pas. 'Go for walk,' ordered Jane forthrightly. 'Paul's right. You need to take time to calm down and think clearly. It's a lovely day again. Go out an enjoy it and maybe your head will be calmer after that. I know! 'Jane smiled brightly 'Why don't you take the dogs for a walk while I cook something for Will and Jennifer?' I groaned. 'I bet they're not getting any proper food at the moment. I'll cook a toad-in-the-hole for Will and some almond biscuits for Jenny.'

Part of me wished that I had never asked Jane, but I didn't have any energy to argue with her. Part of me also could see that what she said made perfect sense. I couldn't cook for Will without making him pull a face, but she could. I was even glad that Jane was taking such an interest in my friends, despite the way they kept asking her about 'what she was up to these days?'

Jane made us each an egg toasted sandwich and I finished off the ginger cake. The sun was still shining as I set off for Patricia's, but Jane advised me to take a coat as rain was forecast. I drove up to the house along the gravel drive and back to the steps down which Meg had rushed yesterday morning.

I wondered where she was now. I couldn't imagine her in the sober offices of the registrar or the undertaker. (I guessed that they would use Bentons with their Rolls Royces.) Why then couldn't she take the dogs out – unless she had gone back to Wales with something of a guilty conscience?

The dogs were yelping as I opened the door, but didn't appear. I looked around wondering what to do now, when I saw a little note addressed to Jane. In it Patricia explained that the dogs were in the kitchen and the leads were on the back of the kitchen door. With only a little wrestling, we were ready to go. They pulled at my arms down the drive and veered to the left as soon as we were onto the pavement. At least I didn't have to choose which way to go. I guessed that this was their usual walk, and who was I to disturb the habits of two creatures who were probably 'in their own way' deeply traumatised, despite giving the impression that Christmas day had come in mid-summer.

The dogs' decision to turn left could also have been due to an aversion to the man hovering to the right of the drive, an aversion that I shared. This was a young man, slightly taller than average with neatly cut light brown hair and a pale grey suit. Despite our obvious desire to walk as quickly as possible away from him, he jogged up to us and started talking.

'You must be a friend of poor Mrs Edwards,' he said. 'How is she?' I nearly said something like 'bearing up but busy at the moment' but stopped and asked him who he was, waiting in ambush. He smiled and introduced himself as Alan Hogan from the *Daily News*. 'I'm so sorry to have talked without introductions,' he said, 'but it's been a very long morning standing out here. Please can we have a talk?' I warmed to the man surprisingly quickly. He did seem genuinely sorry and his direct question was disarming. Either that or he was a very good professional indeed.

'Well, I'm just the dog walker, I'm afraid, but you're welcome to keep me company.' At least that would mean that he couldn't pester anyone else for a while. I was also intrigued by the prospect of talking with a journalist, rather like a mouse keeping a cat at a 'safe' distance.

'There's a park along this way, before you come to the railway,' Alan said. It turned out he was a local who had moved to the area when he was a teenager and had occasionally seen Lizzie about at bus stops. He knew now that she was Lizzie Edwards of the *Birmingham Express*. As he had contacts here and it was difficult for the *News* to learn anything except what the *Birmingham Express* told them, the editor had told him to come up and find out what he could. He was afraid someone would recognise him and think badly of him for pressurising people to say something, but he didn't think he had a choice. 'People nowadays treat us as the enemy. You can see them clam up as soon as you say who you are. They're more than happy to read as many personal details as they can, but they won't want to think that they've told anyone anything.'

I couldn't work out if this was genuine innocent frustration or a clever attempt to open me up. I asked him what he knew. He pulled out a copy of the *Birmingham Express*. There was a large photo of Lizzie with a dazzling smile amid her long blond hair and a headline: 'City Mourns Angel.' 'They say how wonderful she was as a reporter and a daughter, a friend and a campaigner for turtles.'

'Turtles?' I asked with surprise.

'Yes, apparently she went on holiday a couple of years ago to some island in the Indian Ocean where she saw a turtle being bludgeoned to death by a couple of locals who wanted its shell as an aphrodisiac. She started her own campaign to publicise the plight of the turtles. That's how she met her boyfriend, or fiancé depending on who you believe. You didn't know about the turtles?'

I explained that I was really the friend of a friend, that it was my wife who had me walking the dogs because I had nothing better to do, and that I knew very little about it all. I did wince inside a little at this 'not the whole truth' but carried it off, I thought. Whatever happened, I wasn't going to give my name. I left it to Alan the reporter to make the running.

'So there's not much point in talking to you!' said Alan cheerfully. 'Have you seen Mrs Edwards since Liz died?' I had to admit that I had. 'How was she?'

'Shocked, as you would expect,' I said warily.

'Would you say that she was distraught?'

Now it was my turn for a cheerful rebuke: 'Don't go putting words into my mouth. If I want to give you a quote I'll make up my own, not one of your second hand ones.'

'Sound like you've had dealings with us before?' Alan fished around trying to find out more about me.

I still wasn't co-operating. 'Afraid so!' I said with as winsome a smile as I could manage. 'I really don't know the family much at all.' But Alan had managed to touch my curiosity just where it was looking. 'You say that Lizzie met her boyfriend through the turtles. How was that then? He's from an Asian family isn't he, quite a successful one by all accounts? I didn't know they were interested in saving animals.'

Alan took out his notebook and wrote something in. I didn't dare ask what it was. I couldn't see anything noteworthy in what I had just said. We paused to cross the last road before the park. We were at the narrow end of a large triangle of grass with some wonderful tall horse chestnut trees. The railway line went along the far side of the triangle, the road ran straight off up to our left forming the near side. We couldn't see the bottom of this triangle for the trees and bushes ahead. The dogs jumped up and down next to me. I suspected that they were used to being let off the lead here, but I wasn't taking any chances.

'Tariq Khan was interested in Liz. Apparently she approached him to support her campaign and he quickly lent his support as a good Moslem. They've written it up like a Mills and Boon.' Alan scanned the paper a short while and then read out. ' "Tariq smiled, showing his bright even teeth. 'Islam is always wanting to help people to see the error of primitive pagan ways, and to live in peace under God, the creator of all life.' Liz recognised strength and integrity when she saw it, as she later said, and, from that moment on, they were destined to be a couple." It sounds good doesn't it?'

'You think it's not all so lovely?' returning question for question. Alan looked me in the eye. 'Well it looks as though the car was tampered with, and that means that someone wanted to do some damage, probably to Tariq. There are all sorts of suspicions that you wouldn't dare print.'

'But the dogs have promised not to sell their story,' I said wryly. My heart was beating fast. As long as I didn't foolishly agree with anything he said, I thought it would be safe to find out more. It felt like a God-given opportunity to further my investigations. 'You're welcome to share those suspicions with me. It might connect with something I know…'

Alan couldn't help looking round before he spoke. 'Tariq, or Ali to some, hung around with some pretty hard characters in the Moslem world. Some people say that he was the acceptable front of what was basically a revolutionary organisation. Maybe some rival group had it in for him. Or maybe one of his own didn't like him becoming too friendly with this English girl. It's not the sort of thing you could print, not until it's been said in court, but it's what they're saying in London. Any connections?' Alan smiled as the dogs saw a squirrel and yanked at the leads and my arm.

'It sounds like a London story, not a Birmingham one. London's the place for those sorts of groups.'

'Well, no longer, I'm afraid. There are a few of these extreme Islamic groups around the country and not everyone's happy about that. But then we could be making too much of it all like the French. You know what they say about Islam in France?'

'No, though I imagine it's pretty strong there with all the Algerian and Moroccan connections.'

'They say that Islam is now the second strongest religion in France. What do they say the strongest is? The fear of Islam.' Alan chuckled a little. I could see that it was a witty thing to say but somehow it didn't make me want to laugh.

We walked on in silence for a bit, before I was rudely pulled back by a dog deciding to poo under a bush. Patricia had thoughtfully provided a couple of little plastic bags and a small yellow plastic beach spade to use as a scoop. Alan agreed to hold the dogs while I crawled half under the bush to reach the warm mess. 'You could have just left it there,' he said. 'It was out of the way.' I looked at him seriously, and went to a rubbish bin to dump the suspicious-looking plastic bag. He obviously didn't have children who sometimes ran through bushes.

Canine bowel movements were a signal of mission accomplished. We turned round, the sun now shining strongly on the right side of our faces. I kept wondering how I could find out more from this unexpected source without having to say more than I wanted to. I decided to keep up the challenge. 'It's still a bit far-fetched for Birmingham isn't it? Just the sort of drama that Londoners would come up with.'

'There's more of this about than you think,' said Alan. 'Why not Birmingham? You have a strongish Pakistani community, and it's probably easier for them to organise themselves here, without the police or other groups looking out for them as they would in London. I bet that's where the real story is, among the Moslems, but there's no way I'd be able to go poking around there. I'll have to keep to this side of it for the moment.' Alan shrugged and mimed holding a microphone in front of my mouth. 'As a family friend would you say that this young woman had it coming to her for associating with such suspicious characters?'

I played along pretending to be a broad Brummie 'Of course not. It were great that Lizzie had such a fine relationship with a youngster from the Asian community. We was all delighted for her. You're not going to print that are you?' I added, suddenly worried

'Well you said it,' replied Alan cheerfully. 'But it doesn't amount to very much does it? I don't suppose you know anything about the funeral yet?' He sounded so plaintive that I did tell him that it would be at St Luke's, taken by Paul Cooper. As he eagerly took out his notebook again, I felt guilty, as though I had given away someone else's secret. But I knew it would be public very soon so I couldn't see any harm in telling the poor young man now.

The sky was grey when we reached the house again. Alan took up his station behind the hedge and I returned the dogs to their home, still with as much energy, or at least with as much noise, as when I had taken them out.

I drove back home pensively. I had begun the day with a mission to prove that Meg was the suspect the police should be concentrating on, and now I wasn't so sure. She could be the one, but I had to admit that there were other possibilities. There were two groups of people I very much wanted to know more about, Meg's commune and Tariq's friends. What Alan the reporter had said had set off echoes of other people's comments; his suspicions couldn't be dismissed. How do you find out more about these groups at the edges of 'normal' life? The truth must be somewhere in one of them.

Fragrant smells of home baking greeted me, and, although it wasn't for me to eat, I was almost moved to tears. Jane and I had a mug of tea (why do people still say a 'cup of tea' when no one ever drinks from a cup?) as we talked over what had happened. She thought the suspicions of some extreme Moslem jealousy or rivalry far-fetched. She was more interested in whether and how I would be mentioned in the paper the following day and she thought I had been silly to give him those details about the funeral. 'Patricia won't like it if she thinks that people have been talking behind her back. You'd better ring her later and explain before she reads about it in the paper and wonders who this big mouth is. Do you want to take this round?' she said pointing at the dish wrapped in tin foil and the old green biscuit tin lying on the table.

I could see that it probably was right for me to take it round but I did want Jane to come as well. So we waited a while for the children to come home from school, and Jane rang Jennifer to say that we'd be round shortly.

Peter made a show of being upset that I was still around and not 'snooping around some barns in Wales with a false moustache,' and Nicola had brought home the same edition of the *Birmingham Express* that the reporter had showed me. Jane told her to look out for me in the *Daily News* the following day and she looked up at me with wonder.

'Everyone at school's talking about it. I'll tell them that you're in the centre of it all.' Emily was quieter and more thoughtful. She looked straight up at me and gently and deliberately asked, 'Dad, is Jason going to be arrested?' I told her with a bit of a lump in my throat that I was doing all I could to make sure he wasn't, whereupon Peter shouted 'Go Dad Go!' until Jane told him to keep quiet.

We left them watching some very dubious programme on television about a teenage witch. 'Should they be watching that sort of thing?' I asked with some indignation. 'Doesn't it give the impression that witchcraft is a good thing? We don't allow Halloween, so why should we allow that sort of thing?'

'Oh go back to your office!' said Jane brightly, but with a hint of exasperation. 'If I stopped them from watching that 'sort of thing' as you call it, there wouldn't be much they could watch. At least half the programmes have witches or ghosts or violent heroes who don't act like saints. You know what it's like. You used to watch *Bewitched* when you were young didn't you? It's just television. That's how it is.' There wasn't any arguing with that, both because Jane wasn't in the mood for a debate, and because I couldn't mount a detailed response, either then or, probably, ever.

'Sorry,' I said quietly (she would probably call it muttering). I did wonder what kind of world we were bringing our children up in. Even the television trailers turned me off now; short snippets of people raging at each other or cars exploding in great orange balls of flame. Nightmares, but they call it entertainment. I could begin to understand why some people want to have nothing to do with this 'culture' and become very angry about its complacent dominance. I wondered what television Meg or Tariq's friends watched.

Will and Jennifer looked worn out. Jennifer's hair was as immaculate as usual at the front, but as she turned from the door the back of her head looked straggly, trailing a few wisps down her neck. Will managed a big smile for Jane as she carried in her dish.

'That isn't ... it can't be ... Oh Jane, not Jewish burgers in the desert? The true manna!' I can't remember why he always called Jane's toad-in-the-hole such a stupid name, but this wasn't the time to try to politically correct Will. A few people had tried, on various issues, but Will just found these attempts highly amusing and 'Carried On' regardless.

Jennifer thanked Jane for her kindness and went with her to put the food in the kitchen and make some tea. Will and I went into the sitting room and Will stood by the patio doors looking out. It had begun raining lightly. 'That'll be good for the beans,' he said. 'But I've hardly noticed them this week. They're probably shrivelled. The wind's already had a few of the leaves. Still there's more to life than beans.' He breathed in a couple of short deep breaths and turned to me. 'How's Lizzie's Mum?'

I told him what I could, and said how good it had been to be with her yesterday thanks to them. I didn't want to talk much about what had happened in case it made him think about Jason being so near to death himself. As soon as I could, I asked him how Jason was.

'He's on a proper ward now. Doing fine they say. The convulsions have stopped and they think he's out of danger with his heart. He's talked a bit, wild things mostly about trees and snakes. Has calm times too.' Will looked up at my face. 'He's got a policeman not far all the time now. A copper in the ward! As if that's going to help anyone get better. They ought to be out looking for the real culprit not wasting time with a harmless young man who can hardly breathe. The other visitors keep looking at us. Must have us down as a mafia family.'

Jane and Jennifer came in with tea and we all sat down silently. 'So Jason's improving,' said Jane after a pause. 'That's some good news. David's been trying to find out as much as he can, haven't you?'

I told them how sure I was that Jason hadn't mucked around with the car, and that I was trying to convince the police to look elsewhere.

'Yes, but where?' said Will gloomily. I told them about the rumours of Tariq's extreme Moslem connections.

'Mad lot and dangerous with it,' said Will with conviction, although I had never thought of him as knowing anything about people of other faiths, as the polite expression is. 'Jason met a few at U.C.E. Tried to disrupt the Christian Union, put him off completely. What with them shouting slogans and some Christian idiots shouting back in tongues, Jason just took himself off and never went again.' This scenario seemed highly unlikely, but then there may have been some history behind it, as well as a degree of Willish exaggeration.

This time I wasn't going to let Will get away with it. 'Students! They're always ready to shout about something.' Jane looked sharply at me as though I had farted in front of the headmistress.

'Oh no,' said Jennifer unexpectedly. 'Jason tried to look into it a bit more, to get behind the shouting. He's like that, he has to know what's going on.'

'Sorry Jen. What did he find out? Go on.' I relaxed and tried to look as innocuous as I could. Jane relaxed too as the floor was left to Jennifer.

'He had someone he knew from lectures who was a Moslem. This lad explained that just as there are Christian mission agencies, with some rather extreme people, so there are Moslem sort of mission agencies, 'jihad' I think they call them, and some of these attract fanatics.' Jennifer was leaning forward with both hands lifted in front of her and shaking with passion.

'God knows I told him to leave it alone. But then he looked at some lurid web sites. Now these really were scary. All death to the infidels. Moslems rise up in defence under the bloody assault of American imperialism! That sort of crazy thing. We played it down - just like us singing "Onward Christian Soldiers." But he wouldn't leave it at that. Then when Lizzie started going out with Tariq, it just made him worse. Of course he was broken hearted, but he couldn't cope with the sort of people she was mixing with.'

'But, Jen, Tariq is no fanatic. I know his father, as you know. He's very much part of things here.' I wanted both to reassure her and to find out more.

'Yes, but Jason saw Tariq hanging about with a couple of the extremists he had known from U.C.E. They were at that grand turtle thing where it all went wrong. Jason was working so hard to put it all on, behind the scenes mostly. He didn't take much notice of Lizzie talking to Tariq and that bunch, until she ditched him.'

'Worst thing he could have done, taking her on that holiday. Not that he could afford it…' Will interjected.

My heart sank. 'Has Jason told anyone else about all this?' I couldn't even hope that he had just kept it between himself and his mother, but I had to ask. Now the police had not only a jealous lover but a man afraid of Islamic extremists as well. No wonder they had a guard on his bed. Where else did they need to look? Will and Jennifer looked at each other gloomily.

In desperation I reached for my earlier suspicion. 'At least I've now met Lizzie's sister. She's strange character isn't she? I suppose you met her over the years?'

'Only a few times,' said Jennifer. 'She was never comfortable with Jason somehow. Jason thought she was jealous of him. Even Lizzie used to call her her green-eyed little big sister.'

'Lizzie was the younger one,' said Jane. 'You'd never think that, seeing them together. Meg looks so naïve somehow compared to sophisticated Lizzie.'

'Mad Meg, he used to call her,' said Will grumpily, although he seemed a little pleased to be thinking of something else. 'Once she locked them out of the car. Just threw the keys down a drain and told them to walk. And here she just walked in, and sniffed, "Do you know what it says on a can of air freshener?" - as if we were trying to kill her!'

Jane laughed. 'Well what does it say on a can of air freshener?'

'Little strop just looked at Jenny. Shouted, "'Don't inhale.' I'm not staying here to be poisoned. You destroy the air if you want, but leave me out!" Off she went. I ask you!'

'Does it really? Did you ever check?' Jane was curious.

'Don't be soft' said Will. 'How could it? Everyone uses it. You need it when people like her come round.'

'Well, I did actually go and look,' Jennifer said tentatively, looking at Will, 'but I can't remember what it said in detail.' Jane encouraged her to go and fetch a can. Anything to take the attention somewhere different, she was probably thinking. Jennifer read out 'Shake well. Spray lightly into the air. Do not spray on or near food.'

'As if anyone would,' snorted Will. 'What's the fuss about?'

Jane reached for the aerosol. 'Can I see please?' she added, looking at Will. 'There's this bit in the special box too: "Deliberately inhaling this product may kill. Use only as directed." If it kills you when you sniff it directly what does it do in little bits when you're breathing it all the time? I don't think she's as mad as all that.' Jane now looked at me. 'I sometimes wonder who is mad.'

This was just the sort of vague guilt-inducing comment that put Will and Jennifer's back up. You can't have a go at people for just living normally, and certainly not in their front room. I looked at my watch. 'It must be nearly visiting time,' I said, and moved to the edge of the chair. 'Do give our love to Jason won't you. We will be praying for you all.'

Will asked us to go to the hospital with them, but I wasn't keen and thought that they maybe wouldn't appreciate Jane being there. I promised to go and see him tomorrow, with some grapes or something, and after finding out when visiting hours were we left rather hurriedly.

I tried to talk reasonably to Jane, but she quickly started having a go at me. 'You make comments about the children watching rubbish on the television, but you're not bothered about any old rubbish that people spray into the air. Isn't it the same – it's all sweet rubbish that makes us feel nice for a while but isn't real and ends up poisoning us. At least television doesn't pollute the same air that animals breathe, and leave a residue to go through the earth's system for ever.'

Sometimes I wonder why Jane didn't become a barrister. She could turn any argument around, and she left me, a mere solicitor, struggling to think so quickly. She also didn't invite any real response, ending on so definite a note. Perhaps teachers and barristers have that in common - the confidence of knowing they have the conclusive arguments? I apologised meekly.

'And please don't forget to ring poor Patricia,' Jane added sweetly. She enjoys winning a round or two with me. I wondered later why I didn't use her own argument against her.

'It's just air freshener. That's all. That's how it is.' The trouble is that both of us know that it's not right just to settle for what is – that's not the Kingdom of God. But what do you do about television and air-freshener and all that this mad modern world throws at us?

Cordless phones, I think, are comparatively harmless, and I was glad to be able to choose a quiet corner of the bedroom for my uncomfortable phone call to Patricia Edwards. I told her that I had walked her dogs instead of Jane and been accosted by a journalist. She went quiet when I said that, so I quickly told her that I had only told him one thing, the church where the funeral was to be, and that I thought she needed to know who had said what in case it was in the papers the following day. She thanked me very quickly for phoning and said that she hoped to see Jane soon.

That started me thinking about the funeral and my mind boggled. Would everyone be there? Jason might be well enough, although Tariq probably wouldn't, but his friends might represent him. Mohammed and Raisa wouldn't miss it no matter how much the English tried gently and indirectly to put them off. What would mad Meg do? I couldn't imagine her sitting quietly through a Church of England funeral service. I prayed with real feeling for Paul, having to lead such an unpredictable service, with all the media present too.

Back in the sitting room, Jane had not forgotten the extra motive, the extra suspicion of Jason. 'Do you think he really was worked up about those Moslem fanatics?'

Glumly, I was ready to concede a little. 'Jason's too level headed, quiet but basically stable. He'll have been concerned, no more.' I surprised myself by being so definite.

Jane looked at me with a hint of challenge in her eyes. 'Well I don't see how anyone makes a fuss about these so-called extremists. They're just kids playing up against the "marvellous" Christian empire which has ruined their countries and their lives. They all grow out of it.'

I wasn't sure if she was supporting them or playing them down. 'Well they're still strong enough to worry more than a few politicians. It's like the Communists. Lenin and co may have been angry young men, but they still managed to attack where it hurts – and ruin millions of lives.'

'Oh come on, David. Stop the melodrama. That's just an image they like to portray. For goodness sake don't take them seriously!' Jane was sitting forward in her chair, her head and hair swaying with the vehemence.

I wasn't at all sure that this time she was being too liberal. 'Just don't forget the history of Islam. You remember that speaker from the "Provide for the Persecuted" people? It could be more than just words.'

'It's people like that who just make things worse, make people more afraid.' She had at the time been fairly quiet, not keen on the large donation the church had made. 'They just stress one side, leaving out all the good peaceful people. You wouldn't want someone talking only of the Christians who supported the Nazis, would you? As if they were typical!'

'Well I don't think these extremists, as you call them, are so untypical, given what's happening in places like Indonesia and Sudan.'

'That's because you have never met a real Moslem, have you? You're only beginning to know Mohammed. You remember Susha? I bet she's far more typical.'

Susha had worked with Jane as a classroom assistant, the best one she ever had.

'Go on, then,' I said wearily. 'What's so special about Susha?'

'David!' snapped Jane, rising to my bait. 'She's not special, that's the point! Do you really want to know about Moslems?'

'I want to know anything that will help me understand this awful mess,' I said and meant it.

I had actually met Susha on a couple of school social occasions, but only registered bright Indian clothes, long shiny dark hair, and a whiff of spices. Jane, Susha, and a couple of the others at the school had palled up and gone out for meals together, alternating between curry and Italian. Apparently Jane had really enjoyed coming to know Susha, who had more guts in her than appeared from her demure exterior.

'Susha,' said Jane, 'used to say that Islam is quite clear that we will all be judged by God, and that means that it's not up to us to take the judging into our own hands. Those who do impose 'judgement', especially with violence, are simply being unfaithful to the Qu'ran.'

'I've not heard that interpretation before,' I said with a hint of challenge.

'It's about time you did then,' responded Jane firmly. 'It's what the ordinary Moslems think.'

'Yes,' I said eager to please teacher Jane, 'it would be good for them to be more restrained.'

'Them more restrained!' Jane nearly exploded. 'Our media choose to make a huge deal of every poor fellow who has had enough and tries to hit back, but makes nothing of the thousands, millions, who simply put up with being treated as second class by the mighty Christian empire! Restraint! They could teach all of us a thing or two about restraint! They know it's a good thing, they're taught it's a good thing. You might not believe me, but it's true.'

'Sorry. It's just that we don't hear much about that. We do hear more about the 'kill your way into heaven' sort.' I wasn't ready to give in completely.

'And all the millions of others simply waiting for the reward of a good life in heaven, don't they count?' Jane stared hard at me. 'Why do you always choose to focus on the worst? They know they have to lead a good life to get into heaven. It's not as easy for them as it is for us. And they know that a good life means being good to people. For God's sake, it's simple! Just think about it.'

'OK!' Perhaps it was now time to give in. I smiled at Jane like a schoolboy who has been caught swearing, but knows the teacher likes him really. 'I'm interested, I really am. Replace my ignorance.'

'Look, imagine what you would feel like if you knew that you had an angel on each shoulder recording everything you did and said and thought, and you knew those angels would present their report on you when you died, and you need the good one to have more to say than the bad one? Wouldn't that make you stop and think before being nasty to anyone? Why should you be any different to them?' Again I thought that Jane really should have been a barrister. I just nodded.

'And imagine,' Jane was in full flow, 'what you would feel like if you knew that God was all-powerful and merciful and his blessing is more powerful than any prosperity you might sweat for or grab yourself? Even getting even with people who have done a dirty on you doesn't bring you anything like a fraction of what God's blessing can give you. Wouldn't that make you stop and wait for the blessing from God rather than the revenge or whatever you feel you need now?'

'It's another view of Islam that sounds much closer to what we believe.' I was still resisting seeing Jane's view as the only true view of Islam.

'It's the ordinary common sense, undramatic, get-on-with-your-life-being-kind-to-people view of most Moslems!' Jane had her arms up, her hands open like a voluble Italian talking about their football team. 'It's the way they are brought up. It's what they're taught on Fridays. Being good to people, no matter who they are. God made them all, you'll be judged for how you treat them all. And how you treat animals as well, by the way. All the other stuff about not drinking and fasting and going to Mecca, that's just the shell. The core is simply being good to people because if you don't you're going to have to answer for it one day.'

I was impressed. I had never heard such a passionate advocate of Islam before. But even Jane couldn't quite remove all my sense that Islam is actually quite different from Christianity. 'The other stuff seems pretty important. And I thought they were the pillars? They're the main thing, without which it all collapses?'

'Oh for goodness sake!' Jane was even crosser now. 'That's like saying that going to church on Sundays or reading your Bible is the main thing. Those things are pillars. They support the building. Not for the sake of the wretched building but for what's inside. You need a shell, a structure, to support the core, the spiritual centre of it all. We go to church, have Lent, all sorts of things. They do their own stuff, but we all know that the core is what we actually do, how we live, not ignoring God and our responsibilities to other people. You have to have some structure to it all, but, David, don't make out that it's the be-all and end-all.'

She was, as usual, winning the argument. 'I suppose it's like with us, the mullahs, or whoever, make out that going to the Mosque and keeping to the rules is pretty important or else they'd be out of a job.'

'You know how seriously a normal Moslem takes that? Susha told me once that the family was all ready for the big celebrations at the end of Ramadan, but there was some uncertainty about which day was the proper day.'

I frowned, puzzled.

'It's all to do with the moon,' Jane continued, more teacher than barrister now. 'Ramadan ends when the next new moon can be seen. That year people weren't sure when the new moon would be visible here, either on a Thursday or a Friday I think. But for Susha's family Thursday was much better. They had everything prepared on the day and Susha's brother went to the Mosque to check that it was OK to break the fast The Imam had other ideas and told them to wait. He hadn't seen the new moon. Susha's brother argued that the Imams in Saudi Arabia had seen the new moon and it was the same moon wasn't it? Still the Imam wouldn't budge. Susha's brother was annoyed. His parting words were "Well the Americans have landed on the moon, and we can't even see it!" And when do you think they had their party?'

'Sounds like they ignored the Imam,' I conceded. 'Bet that didn't go down too well.'

'Do you do all that Paul tells you? Do all the Catholics do everything the priest tells them? Look, David, just get it into your head that these people are just the same as you! Stop being such a prejudiced bigot!'

That ultimatum was unanswerable, at least with Jane in this mood. I still wasn't convinced that the religions were 'just the same', or even had that much in common. The lives of Jesus and Mohammed were poles apart. But it was high time to lighten the mood. 'Of course I would follow every word that our esteemed vicar says, to the letter. But it would make him uncomfortable.'

Jane raised her eyebrows and opened her eyes wide. 'Try it!' she said, smiling.

'Mind you, I wouldn't want his job, especially not the funerals. You can't exactly ask for an adjournment if you're not ready, can you?'

Jane and I then finished the day running through various awful funeral scenarios in our imaginations. None of them even remotely came up to the actual extraordinary day

Friday

I was awake early on Friday morning, again thinking of Paul and the funeral. As soon as I thought it a decent hour I rang him.

'Paul, it's David. I'm so sorry I burdened you yesterday with my silly ideas. I know you have a really difficult role to play in all this, with the funeral coming up. Please tell me: is there anything I can do? I really do mean it this time; I need to be able to help you in some way.'

Paul took this outpouring in his customary stride. 'David, that's kind of you. Thank you. It was good to see you yesterday. What did Jane say about your investigating the sister?'

'She told me to go for a walk, and then she gave me some dogs to walk with – Mrs Edwards' dogs would you believe?' I told him about the walk and the journalist and the new suspicions. 'But, wait a minute, Paul, I've rung you because I want to help you, not for you to listen to me! What needs to be done for the funeral? Can I take your dogs out for a walk, or do anything else to help?'

'Thank you for offering so persistently,' Paul said cheerfully. 'I don't know myself all that's needed. Perhaps you could help on the practical side?'

Feeling vaguely challenged by the word 'practical', I responded slowly, 'Ye-es. I could try.'

'I think we may need the service relayed outside, but I'm not sure. St Luke's holds 400 at a push.' I didn't leap to volunteer for that level of the technically 'practical' so Paul continued. 'Other than that, there may be music and words to sort out. You never know with this kind of service. People nowadays want to personalise it all.'

'Paperwork I can do, and a bit of organising for the PA if you want.' My boldness surprised myself again.

Paul cheered up a bit. 'How about if you come with me when I go and see Mrs Edwards and if there's anything practical that needs taking care of you can pick that up? It'll be good to have a friend alongside too.'

I hadn't envisaged myself talking with Patricia about her daughter's funeral, but as I had done such a lot with her already, despite not knowing her, I couldn't refuse. Paul's taking me as a friend was heart-warming too, although maybe a bit of flattery. I agreed readily. Paul said that tomorrow was his day off so he wanted to try and see the Edwards' that day and he would ring me back when he had more details.

It felt odd not going into the office. I couldn't resist ringing Rose just to see what was happening. She wasn't pleased. 'Now what have you been doing talking to the Press, David?' I asked her what she meant and she said that I was mentioned in the *Daily News* as a close friend of the family who also knew Elizabeth's previous boyfriend. They said I was very interested in trying to find out more about her current boyfriend as I was suspicious of him.

I was flabbergasted. 'Where on earth did he get all that from? I didn't tell him who I was. I hardly told him anything.'

'Well he must have worked it out somehow; these people don't just ask one person you know, they keep asking until they get some answers.' Rose paused sternly for a moment and then brightened her voice to indicate that that was enough. 'Anyway we've had three reporters on the phone already and I think there's someone outside as well. You're too popular, David Jeffery!'

I was very glad that I hadn't gone into the office, but, beyond that, I didn't know what to think. 'Just fend them off, Rose, please. Tell them that I don't have any more to say – it seems like I've said too much already. I don't suppose there are any other crises with our clients?'

'They're all very understanding, except Mrs Bright. She doesn't see why there's such a fuss about a girl dying in a car crash, and why she has to be kept waiting.'

I sighed. 'What a woman!'

'I just sympathised with her, David, and told her that she was your highest priority as soon as you had some time to attend to her. Then she said that she's off soon on a Rhine cruise, so it can't be that urgent! No, David,' Rose said sweetly, 'don't worry about the people here, you have more important people to give your attention to now.'

As usual, I didn't argue with Rose. Being a media celebrity was something I hadn't anticipated. Most of me was appalled, but there was a little part that was intrigued with the idea of speaking to such a huge audience and wanted to try and make a good job of it. I was talking about this new development with

Jane when the telephone rang. We stopped short, looked at it and at each other and then Jane said, 'I'll get it.'

I followed her into the hall. 'O hello Mohammed,' she said stressing the name. I nodded and she soon put me on to talk with him.

'Good morning David.' Mohammed spoke calmly and warmly. 'I am sorry to ring you at home so early again.' I said that that was fine. 'The newspaper tells me that you are now a friend of the Edwards family too and that you are wanting to know more about my Tariq and his friends. I thought I could save you a lot of trouble and offer to answer any questions you may have about him. Unless the newspaper has it all wrong of course; you never know what to trust in your media.'

My poor brain was having to work hard again, in ways that it had never done before. 'Mohammed, I'm terribly sorry about that. I've only just heard myself. I did talk to a reporter yesterday but I didn't tell him half the things that he's written. I don't know where he got them from. But I would like to have a chat with you, Mohammed, if that's OK How is Tariq doing now? Is he out of intensive care?'

'You obviously don't read your papers, David. Tariq is fine and recovering well now. We'll be able to talk with him soon, and then the police will talk with him, and then things will be clearer for all concerned. I would like to reassure you about him, David. Could we meet tomorrow, say at 11 a.m. at my office? Perhaps you could meet Philippa at New Street at the top of the escalator and she'll show you the back way. I'm sure you'll understand. Thank you, David.'

Today was turning out no different from the previous days, full of the unexpected. I had thought that maybe it would all

quieten down for us between now and the funeral but, again, I
was wrong.

Jane asked me what Mohammed had wanted, and seemed
very concerned when I told her. I had to admit that I had
probably lost my chance of impressing him professionally, or
rather blown my chance, but there were other things to think
about. My allegiance was firstly to Will and Jennifer and Jason.
Jane said that doing the right thing for Mohammed was just as
important, but I left it at that and asked what we were going to
do now.

'You'll wait for Paul to call you, find out what it's like to be
kept waiting,' Jane smiled. 'I'll do some baking. Do you think
Mohammed and Raisa would like a cake as well as everyone
else? You can come and help me if you like.'

I don't think I had helped make cakes since I was about eight
years old and the memory of our kitchen in Shaw Lane with the
green Formica-topped table and the airing rack suspended from
the ceiling came back vividly, along with the smells and the
yearning to taste the mixture at every stage. The only
differences were that we had an electric mixer and I was forty-
six years old. Jane had Radio 4 on, waiting for the morning
service, so we listened a bit, talked a bit and mostly I just sat and
watched. It was comforting to be together.

After the news we heard the lovely but few voices singing
'O for a thousand tongues to sing' (it was the feast of the
Wesleys apparently, an anomaly which probably had them
turning in their graves – except that they were, no doubt, firmly
in heaven and had better things to do than worry about their
reputations here). I was just plucking up courage to join in when
the telephone rang. Jane went off to answer it, stopping with a

withering schoolteacher look my half-formed protests at how it would be better for me to go without sticky hands.

She came back with the cordless and stood in the door telling Paul that I was just here and would be right with him. Paul said that he had been talking with Mrs Edwards' brother. As they needed to go out and talk to the *Enquirer* this afternoon, he had agreed to go very soon, this morning, and would that be all right with me? With a bit of an intake of breath with the mention of the Press, I agreed and Paul said he'd collect me so that I could show him the way.

In the car we had a little time for me to tell him what I knew about the family, including what had happened on Wednesday, and we were then approaching the drive. Alan Hogan the Press Rat, was outside again. I felt like doing a Will and shouting 'Bastard' at him as we drove in, but he just smiled, waved and took out his reporter's notebook again.

'Is that the man who interviewed you for the *Daily News*?' asked Paul. 'He rang our house yesterday too and talked to Louise. He didn't say who he was, just started asking questions about the Edwards family and what I was doing with them. Thankfully she didn't have a clue what he was talking about and was sensible enough to call for her mother, but it scared her a bit.'

'Trying to wheedle information out of a child is just the thing he would do!' I didn't feel very forgiving.

'The Press Officer suggests very strongly that we prepare a Press Release with the family to be handed out before the funeral, and leave most of our communication to that. *Midlands Today* are coming to interview me later, and I have agreed to be interviewed by a local Asian radio station too, but we don't have to talk to every reporter.'

'Thanks Paul. Sorry to land you all in that.' Another dimension of my loose tongue which I hadn't realised. Once again I felt sick at my lack of caution.

Paul rang the doorbell and the dogs started yapping. I wished I could offer to take them out for a walk and leave Paul to it, as long as that reporter kept his distance. This was all new to me.

Patricia opened the door, looking quite calm for someone who was going through the trauma of losing the second of the three people most dear to her in her life. She was dressed in blue again, a close-fitting dress with a flower-type brooch on her left shoulder.

She invited us in with a smile which showed a few wrinkles around her eyes, and introduced us to her brother Bill who was standing behind her in the hall. He was a short man with clipped dark brown hair combed across the top of his head, a fawn jumper and light trousers.

Patricia offered us a drink, which Paul accepted. He had once said that that he had been trained to keep a note of all the available public loos in the parish because the clergy end up drinking at every visit. We turned away from the kitchen this time into a long rectangular room with a large deep three-piece suite, a white stucco fireplace with a mantelpiece full of cards and a large modern television. In the armchair by the television, sitting sideways with her legs draped over one arm of the chair, was Meg. She waved at us as we came in but said nothing. She was wearing a baggy jumper in various shades of brown, purple leggings and sandals.

'You've met Margaret I believe,' said Bill. She smiled at us again as we said hello and sat down to wait for Patricia. Paul took out of his pocket a small Bible and a couple of folded cards with some pictures and writing. When Patricia had given us all our drinks, and Meg had gone to fetch the biscuits, which she offered round, Paul made a start.

'It's good of you to see us today Mrs Edwards. You must be very busy at the moment. It's so awful that this has happened. You must be in shock and find it hard to believe.' Paul ended his sentence with a little note of enquiry in his voice, almost a question.

Patricia said nothing and took a sip from her drink.

Paul plunged in again. 'Thank you for asking me to take the service for Elizabeth. It really is a privilege to be asked to help in this way. I remember her in St Luke's, she stood out against our dark pews, taller than most of the others there. She certainly seemed to enjoy singing, and not only the modern songs. She could lift her head, and her voice probably, for a good old hymn too.'

'She always liked singing,' said Patricia, 'from being in the school choir. Not that she had a great voice,' Patricia looked at Meg, 'but she did enjoy it sometimes. What she lacked in tunefulness she made up for in enthusiasm – that's what her teacher once said of her and it's true.'

Paul had managed to start Patricia talking and all we did then for a while was listen as she told us about Lizzie with a few comments from Bill and silence from Meg. She had been a bright schoolgirl, finding the work easy, and enjoying her clarinet and later saxophone. She had been a keen Brownie but didn't take to Guides. She enjoyed reading and swimming and had three good pen pals, one in America, one in Portugal and one in Singapore. She enjoyed travelling and only lately had become so involved with the poor turtles. She had done wonderfully well in raising an awful lot of money and making some very important people take notice. She had been a little disappointed when her 'A' levels weren't as good as everyone had hoped, but she had had a super time at University, travelling with the University Band. I had the impression that Patricia had long found great pleasure in talking about her daughter and I was surprised how easily she could still do it.

Paul thanked her for talking so fully about Lizzie, as it was important to feel that you really understood the person, and he asked if there was anyone who would like to speak about her at the service. At this they all looked at each other, not having thought of this at all. Paul suggested they give it some thought.

'But we haven't arranged when the service will be yet.' Paul became quite businesslike. 'I understand that the police will almost certainly release Elizabeth's body after the weekend, so I don't think we need to hold back from making arrangements. I'm sure you don't want there to be too long an interval, probably not another weekend before the service? So let's work on next Thursday shall we? How does that seem to you?'

Bill spoke up, 'We didn't think it could be so quick. Of course if that's possible, it would be a relief in some ways.' Patricia nodded. Paul reassured them that it was almost certainly possible and suggested midday. They were too shocked to do anything but agree, grateful that someone who knew what they were talking about was taking the initiative.

'The service itself will be a Christian service of course,' said Paul looking at Patricia but, I expected, thinking of Meg. 'we'll have a Bible reading. I'm happy to choose that if you wish, but if you'd like to think of that as well, please do.' Patricia nodded again.

'And if there's any one who you'd like to read a reading, a colleague or an old friend perhaps, do let me know. It's a hard thing to do if you've known someone very closely, but it may be good to involve someone in this way. Nowadays people sometimes like to have another reading or two as well. Unfortunately there are some readings which don't fit in with what the Bible says about death, so they wouldn't be appropriate, I'm afraid.' I wondered what on earth he was talking about, probably just making sure that Meg didn't take it over for some New Age rite of 'freeing' or whatever. Meg just smiled and Patricia nodded again.

'So if you would like another reading do let me see it. I expect it'll be fine, but it's worth being clear about this. The same goes for music. I don't expect you've chosen anything yet. We usually have two or three hymns or songs for everyone to sing, ones that people generally know. Then there's music as we come in and go out, either on the organ or on a tape or CD. You have a think about what would be best and we'll talk about it another time. It's good to make it as personal as you can for everyone's sake. But don't let it be a burden to you. If you want just to leave it until we meet again that's fine.'

Patricia nodded, dropped her head a little in thought and, after a pause, she spoke up. 'Will we be able to have the coffin open in the church?' Stunned, I rocked back in the chair and closed my eyes. This must have come from Meg – a first thrust at paganising the whole thing. Paul was not going to like this.

Patricia carried on, sensing the need to justify her odd request 'Margaret thinks it's so much better than having her all shut up and I can't help thinking that these young people have a point. We shouldn't cover up death as though it's not quite real. Would that be all right in the church?'

Paul looked at her and at Meg. 'Yes, of course. It's a good part of the Christian tradition in many places, just not usually in the Church of England. No there shouldn't be any problem with that. Were you thinking of anything else to do with having the coffin open?' Again he looked at Patricia but I was looking at Meg. She was smiling faintly and looking at her mother.

'Well I'm not quite sure. Maybe Meg's friends will have some ideas about that. They're quite sensitive you know, and spiritual, so I'm sure it'll be fine.'

'Why don't you have a talk about it all and then when we meet again we can see what you've thought and how best to fit it all in. Have you thought about when you'd like the coffin lid put on?' Patricia looked blank. 'We'll talk about that too another time,' said Paul warmly. This wasn't going to be easy for him, with television cameras recording it all. 'Is there anything else you want to ask?'

Bill spoke up curtly from his corner. 'I think you've given us plenty to be going on with, thank you.'

Paul didn't seem to notice the slight rebuke in Bill's tone. 'So when shall we meet again?'

There seemed to be a lot to talk about so we arranged to meet on Monday afternoon, Paul checking that this was all right with me, and explaining again that I would be involved. I gathered that he had explained my role before. Paul also explained that it would be good to have a short biography of

Lizzie for the press, despite it all having been in the *Birmingham Express* already, as well as a copy of what people said at the service.

'David can vouch for this,' Paul said, and I wondered what he was calling on my support for. 'Our Press Officer says that we have to be very careful about what we say because there may be a trial and we mustn't affect that in any way. So everything that's said had probably better be checked legally. David can do that if that's OK with you? It's a bit of an intrusion, but it'll make us all prepare thoroughly and the service will probably be the better because of it.'

No one said anything, a silence that we took for consent. Paul then said how good it had been to be together and asked, rather brazenly, if they would like to pray while we were all together. Meg stood up, picked up the biscuits and walked out of the room. Patricia stared ahead. 'Some people prefer to leave it for the service to pray,' Paul said quietly, 'and I know that it must be hard for you, maybe, remembering the last time we prayed together...' Patricia nodded.

Paul looked up at me. I leapt in. 'It's all right Mrs Edwards. We don't have to pray now. Thank you so much for spending time with us. It has been good to hear more of what a super girl Lizzie was.'

Patricia shivered a fraction and looked at Paul. She spoke softly. 'Yes please, would you pray for her please?' and she then bowed her head with eyes closed. Paul prayed quite a long prayer thanking God for Elizabeth, thanking him for Jesus coming to each of us with his offer to guide us through life and death, and asking for his Spirit to be very much present with us at the service.

I wondered what other spirits he might be thinking about. I didn't think we had prayed for Lizzie as such, but when Paul had finished, there was a comfortable sort of peace for a few moments as Patricia dabbed her eyes with a tissue. She then said 'Thank you. That was lovely.'

Paul went on to explain how good it is to have someone to pray to who has himself died, not because he needed to, but because he wanted to share everything we go through. He even shared the punishment that we all deserve so that he can be right there to bring us God's forgiveness.

I was taken aback by this mini sermon in the sitting room, thinking that Patricia and Bill probably had many other things to think about, but Paul did put it well. I wondered if this was something he said to everyone or whether he had composed it especially for Patricia.

Back in the car I commented on how well he had come across. Paul laughed a little. 'When you've been doing this for as long as I have, you know what to say.'

'But surely you had to be different this time with Meg around. I thought you were being a bit hard about the pagan readings she'd want to have, but it needed to be said. Good for you.'

'That's something I say every time,' said Paul smiling with a hint of the conspirator. 'Nowadays there are so many strange verses passed around that I have to warn everyone that I won't just accept everything. In fact all I said today is much the same as always. People need to hear the same things.'

'Do you pray and preach Jesus each time?' I hoped he didn't think I was criticising him. 'I'm sorry about nearly putting her off. I really thought that she didn't want to pray but couldn't quite say so.'

'I wasn't sure, but most people do want it. It's usually the ones who are acting brighter and more competent that don't. The vicar who trained me told me to pray with everyone I visit whether they ask or not, as it's what we clergy are for. It's a good habit, but I do tend to ask now. You should try it more often, David!'

'No, I'll leave that to you. But maybe you could have a little space in our office. You could hear confessions and then we could work out how to get people let off. A complete service of releasing sinners.' Paul didn't seem to be amused. He just thanked me for coming and asked me to make a few enquiries about having the P.A. relayed outside St Luke's on Thursday.

Jane and I had another de-brief in the bake-house kitchen over lunch. There were Madeira cakes on wire racks next to the cooker and a couple of fruit cakes in the oven. Jane seemed quite happy, wearing a green sweatshirt and jeans with her blue apron over the top. She had a tape on in the background, classical guitar versions of some old worship songs. It took me back a few years to when guitars in church seemed daring.

I had to deal with the P.A., about which I knew nothing, but I knew a man who could do most things electrical, Pete Hardy. I left a message on his answering machine and went back to talk with Jane.

I still didn't know what to make of Meg. She had sat quietly and seemed to accept us being there happily enough. But she didn't show much obvious sign of grief and I had a feeling that she was pulling strings behind her mother. I expected that she had a definite idea of what she wanted to do in church with her sister's open coffin, but she wasn't telling anyone. I could imagine her bringing six strange friends with smoking torches and circling the coffin with a slow dirge-like chant, before dropping the torches into the coffin and running cackling out of the church.

Jane thought I needed to go for another walk, well away from it all this time, to calm my imagination which was clearly out of control. 'Solicitors aren't supposed to have imaginations like that,' she said. But she did smile. I thought she was quite pleased, as a teacher who has just been presented with a weird and colourful picture from a child who up until then had just made little marks on the edge of the paper.

It was too early to go visiting the hospital. It wasn't raining and looked as though it could brighten up or darken over more. I wondered about where I could go for a walk and didn't want to drive too far, especially if it might rain. Then I remembered the Botanical Gardens. It was a long time since I had been there – not since the children were little and my father had been staying with us. We had had a great summer afternoon there, with Peter rolling down the grass slope until he was sick and Emily talking with the famously coarse-mouthed mynah bird in the large glass house and refusing to come and join the rest of us. Dad had enjoyed the stroll through the gardens; it made a nice change from the promenade at Bridlington, which he had come to know intimately. He had treated us to a wonderful tea, ordering cakes until we could eat no more. Jane wasn't too happy when no one wanted to eat the casserole she had made, so Dad had had to take it back with him. From then on it was a family warning – 'Behave or it'll be casserole for you!'

The Botanical Gardens seemed the place to go, not too far, and I could then go straight on to City Road and see Jason as I had promised. Jane gave me a madeira cake for the Jennings, hoping that Jason could manage a little himself. I put it carefully in the boot of the Rover and set off.

The car park at the Gardens was fairly empty and the sky was going darker, so I was glad to go inside. The entrance fee seemed a lot for a short visit and I did hesitate a little before bringing out my wallet. Why I still have this impulse to meanness, goodness only knows.

The glass house was lovely and warm, the tall dark green palm fronds and the sound of trickling water filling the space. I wandered round, expecting to hear a bird squawk out, but there was nothing. I thought about asking someone but didn't want to bother the thin man bending over weeding the beds. Outside it was still cloudy. The grass sloped away down to some beautiful bushes with coloured leaves, but looked too wet to run down. Not that I would have anyway; I am a 46-year-old solicitor.

I turned right and walked down through the different gardens. The roses weren't as full as earlier in the summer but still made a glorious sight. There was one big yellow rose spread out against the wall like a bright curtain gathered at the centre. I enjoyed the rowan trees too, with their vivid red berries. They reminded me of the first summer I had been at work, walking to the office in Sutton, enjoying not being a student any more, beginning real work at last

For most of the walk round there was no one with me, and then a couple of old ladies one of them poking at the plants and labels with her stick. They talked knowledgeably and constantly as old friends.

Back at the top I did feel refreshed, and wondered why I didn't do this sort of thing more often. On the way out I looked to see if they had a kind of season ticket with which I could come at lunchtime once a month or so. The woman behind the counter asked me what I was looking for and gave me a leaflet about a yearly pass. It seemed reckless to pay for it without thinking more and talking with Jane. It was probably too late for a Family Pass; I couldn't see Peter or Nicola rushing to come out and see the plants and Emily would only want to see the bird again. I asked where the talking bird was and was told that it had died happily shouting 'Bugger Off' to someone offering it a peanut, before grabbing the nut, almost with the child's finger, and choking on the nut.

A policeman was sitting on a chair outside the door to the ward reading a newspaper. A short nurse in a light brown stripy uniform brought me to where Jason was, sitting up in bed at the end of his bay looking out of a window. It was now raining outside. He was alone. His hair fell down over his eyes as he looked up at me with only a half-hearted shake of his head to shift the curtain.

Jason said hello to me quietly and calmly as though I had been around all day and was just returning with a cup of coffee. I gave him the cake as a present from Jane, hoping that he'd be able to eat it before his Dad fell on it. He smiled and I pulled up a chair.

'Where are they then, your Mum and Dad?' I asked, not wanting to pry but not knowing what else to say either. I didn't think that asking 'How are you?' or anything about him was much of a good idea. What do you say to a failed attempted suicide?

'They've gone to see the doctor.' Jason looked out of the window again. I sat awkwardly still, not knowing what to say. 'David, thanks for the cake, and thanks for coming to see me.' Jason was talking slowly as though through a fog in his mind. 'Mum says you saw Lizzie just after she died. Tell me.., what did she look like?' He had a couple of tears in his eyes.

'She was as beautiful as ever, and very calm. She looked at peace, and her hair was bright next to her slightly pale face. Do you want me to tell you what happened?' He nodded, so I told him all about it, all about the chaplain and Meg and her friend. He smiled when I talked about Meg. At the end he said it was a good story; someone ought to write it down.

I carried on telling him everything that had happened. Sometimes he looked at me and sometimes he looked out of the window with a far-away look. I even told him about the open coffin. We sat again in silence. Talking of the chaplain at the QE reminded me of going to the chapel here at City Road too, so I asked Jason if he'd maybe like the chaplain to call. I said that I was sure that Paul would want to come and see him but he was very busy with the funeral and everything.

Jason thought for a while and said 'Yeah. OK.' I thought it could be a help to talk to someone outside it all, maybe get off his chest what had led him to try and kill himself.

Will and Jennifer came up the ward with a short Asian doctor with a large full beard. His white coat reached down well below his knees. The coat was unbuttoned and his pockets were bulging with thick books and a trailing stethoscope. Above his black beard was a wide forehead and large brown eyes that twinkled. Will seemed very comfortable with him and introduced me to him as he would an old friend of the family.

Dr. Rahid smiled at Jason and said, 'You're looking better, Jason, maybe ready for some good hospital food. We'll keep you here until you've tried everything on our delicious menu. The nurses won't let a handsome young man like you go without a fight. Just be careful when they try to wash you. I think you'll be better off doing it yourself. Was there anything you want to ask me?' Jason shook his head.

'Well I've told your Mum and Dad that you should be fine in a little while. It's a good thing you're not older and fatter than you are. You may be a bit shaky for a while and have trouble remembering things, but that'll calm down fairly soon. Keep me up to date with those transfers at the Blues won't you?' He then shook hands with everyone and bounced off up the ward.

'You know who he reminds me of?' asked Will. 'Try and guess.' I searched my slow mind for anyone resembling this bright little doctor. 'Dr. Kildare?' It was the only thing that came to mind.

'No,' Will said impatiently. 'Who's short and fat with a long beard?' 'Roger Platt?' I said thinking of an elderly former churchwarden at St Luke's. 'No his beard's nothing like as long. It's Father Christmas! An Asian Santa! Just make his hair grey and his skin pink and he's just the part isn't he?' Will looked round for encouragement to Jason and Jennifer who had probably been told this likeness before. I had to admit that, although it would never have occurred to me, the doctor did look like and act like Father Christmas. I wanted to say how good it was that Will thought so highly of an Asian doctor, but thought that comment had better wait for another time.

I told him about Jane's cake for Jason, and apologised for Jane's inappropriate forthrightness the previous evening. Will said he didn't know what I was talking about and told me to thank Jane for her wonderful dish, and its contents of course. Jason seemed curious about what all this was about, so I told him it was another story, and left Will and Jennifer to explain.

It did occur to me that a good Christian would probably pray with them all, but I was going to ask the Chaplain to be involved and I was sure that he or she would do a better job of it than I ever could. The Chaplain's office was shut, but there was some paper for messages. I wrote quite a long note, trying to explain all that seemed necessary, and giving my name and telephone number for any queries.

The traffic was becoming crowded as I made my way home under the dark rainy sky. The cloud cleared a little as I came out of the centre of town. As I waited at traffic lights, the sky ahead was a dense slate grey but the sun was streaming golden from behind. The trees, with a few red leaves already, stood out brightly against the heavy background. It was a lovely picture and I hoped that it would be true for Lizzie's funeral, that in that deep grey darkness there would also be a golden light, not taking the darkness away or even dispelling it a little, but somehow making it beautiful and right.

Jane was pleased to hear about Jason, and shared my amazement at Will being so friendly with an Asian doctor. She said that it was kind of him to keep Jason in as long as possible; probably to keep him away from the police for a while. It hadn't occurred to me that that was what it was about, but, knowing what Will thought about the police, it would partly explain his affection for Dr. Rahid.

The sky was clearer now and the children were occupied with telephone calls, homework and rubbish on the television, sometimes all together. We went out for the walk we had been trying to have since Monday. We only strolled around the streets admiring roses and denigrating gnomes, and then, to my surprise, Jane agreed to try out the new non-smoking corner of the Coach and Horses. She said that I had earned a pint of Guinness this week, as long as I gave her permission to hold my nose if it made me snore in the night.

We had just sat down at a small round table when a couple of men from the church came over. I had forgotten that this was where they drank. Bill Woosnam and Bert Cord were both old divorcees who had found a place in Paul's Men's Group. They had been so relieved to find that beer was allowed after the Bible Studies, and that they both shared a taste for obscure bitters, that they didn't stop telling people. It wasn't the kind of life-changing testimony that people shared in books or sermons, but they told it as though it was the most significant thing that had happened to them for years.

They were quite sober this evening, holding full pints and saying what a terrible thing it was that had happened to Jason. They asked how Jason was and seemed to want to know more, so I invited them to sit with us and told them all about the visit that afternoon.

'That doctor sounds just like the one who noticed the fracture in our Katie's wrist She'd fallen at the riding school and it was hurting a lot so we took her to Casualty and the first doctor, a big South African he was, said it wasn't broken, but a little one with a huge beard looked at it more carefully and said that it was. We were already on the way out and I'd just stopped to go to the loo. When I came out, there he was asking us to come back in and look at the x-rays again. Katie wasn't too pleased, as she had to have her arm in plaster, with no riding for weeks, but I reckon he did a good job; saved the hospital from a bad mistake. I wonder if it's the same one?' We all thought that it couldn't be the same one, unless the NHS was so desperate that it was cloning doctors without telling anyone.

I asked Bill and Bert what they were doing on Thursday and if they could help out with the funeral, in the car park or something. They were happy to be asked. We then left, saying we'd see each other on Sunday. 'That'll be a full church I should think,' said Bert, 'with all the women wanting to know the details.' I thought he had a good streak of curiosity himself, but held back from saying it. Jane didn't. 'You seem pretty nosy yourself, Bert. Enjoy your beer and chat. See you soon.'

Saturday

Jane was still asleep beside me when I woke the following morning, so I assumed that I hadn't driven her downstairs with my snoring. It wasn't long before she followed me into the kitchen and we had breakfast together. Saturday mornings had become the main time for us to chat. We had lost our late evenings to ourselves a long time ago, when Peter started going to bed later than Jane. We had found ourselves having a go at each other more than usual before we realised that we just hadn't caught up with what was going on with each other. A visiting couple had spoken at church one day about relationships and had said that Saturday mornings were the only time they had on their own together away from the teenage children. Jane now tried to make it a time for us to talk too.

'You didn't ask me what happened to the cakes,' said Jane. I realised again how wrapped up I was with my side of the case, or the drama. I apologised and asked her what had happened to them, hoping that there was one for us as well.

'I took one round to Patricia's yesterday. There were a couple of neighbours there worrying about that man from the *Daily News* who was still there. Eventually I went and told him how all the neighbours were looking on him with great suspicion and that he had better move away.'

'Good for you,' I said vehemently.

'Patricia had said that she had had a good long interview with the *Enquirer* and didn't want to talk with anyone else. When I left about thirty minutes later, he had gone.' There's nothing like a schoolteacher for moving people on.

'Was Meg there too?' I asked.

'I know your interest in that girl, David Jeffery,' said Jane cheerfully. 'Well, yes, she was, with a friend of hers, a nice girl with long black hair and plenty of make-up. No, she didn't have a pointed hat as well, before you ask.'

I waved my hands in a mock gesture of innocence. 'Tell me more.'

'They were upstairs talking while we were downstairs, but they did both thank me for the cake. That's all.'

I put on a disappointed look. 'How was Patricia?'

'She showed me some of the cards she had been sent. They were really lovely, even one from the staff at the restaurant they had been in, saying what a lovely couple they had been, so happy despite not tasting any of their 'superb wine' as they put it. She showed me one which had a verse on it about death not being the end, which she said she really liked, and found a great comfort. She may want to have it read at the funeral.'

'I hope Paul will approve.' Jane seemed not to notice my warning.

'She's really a lovely gentle character, Patricia I mean, and she did seem to appreciate Paul although she was worried that he thought her rude. I told her that he was used to dealing with people going through such a hard time as she was, and I was sure he didn't think her rude at all. I'll give you a cake to take to Mohammed and Raisa too,' Jane added quickly.

I was a bit taken aback by the change of subject. 'Well, that's nice, but It seems an odd thing to be bringing to a businessman's office.'

'Oh nonsense,' said Jane. 'I expect they give each other food at times like this. When I was teaching and your father died, three of the Asian children came in with sweets from their mothers. It can't do any harm. Take it. And you can have one for your tea, too, to build you up after you've been taken down a peg or two.'

'Thanks, Miss,' I said, and went up to shave.

Pete Hardy phoned while I was in the bathroom. I phoned him back and explained what was needed with the P.A. for Thursday. 'Leave it to me. I'll see if I can get a day off work. If I explain what it's for, I expect it won't be a problem. They owe me a favour.' Pete was the sort of person who kept doing favours for people. He had fixed our computer when the fan had started making an awful death-whine, and repaired the wiper on Will's Honda to save him buying a whole new unit. I imagined that he was equally popular at work. What Brenda, his wife, thought of all this helpfulness was another matter. She was always happy to pass messages on to Pete, but their house did look as though it hadn't been painted for thirty years.

I made sure I was early at New Street. Once there, seeing all the shoppers in their casual clothes, I wondered if I had been wrong to put on a tie and jacket. This wasn't work but it wasn't a simple friendly meeting either. Standing there with a cake wrapped in tin foil, made me feel like a schoolboy and I nearly went to buy something useless just to have a carrier bag to hide it in. I wondered why I had ever talked to that stupid reporter.

At 10.58 Philippa walked purposefully round the corner, people making way for her noisy heels. She slowed when she saw that I had seen her and waited as I jogged up to her. 'Good morning David,' she said efficiently but warmly. 'Let's go.' I tried to ask her how Mohammed was today, and Tariq, and just had the swift pleasant answer 'Fine' each time. I settled for a silent walk, there being no other option. Philippa walked quite close to me, occasionally brushing my arm. Her perfume was spicier than anything Jane used.

We went in past a large wheelie bin, through a grey door, up some steep stairs and past a small kitchen before another door led onto the familiar landing with thick maroon carpet and dark panelling. Philippa rang through to say that I was here, and I went in, holding tightly onto the fruit cake in my right hand.

'Ah, David, it is good to see you.' Mohammed beamed his usual smile. This time he wasn't wearing a tie but a black polo-neck top. I wanted to make my quick prepared apology and leave as soon as I could.

'I'm so sorry about the piece in the *News*, Mohammed. I still don't know how he pieced that together.' Mohammed seemed calm, so I sped on. 'Somehow he put two and two together and came up with five and a half. Please be assured that I just want to do what I can to help everybody involved and to bring out the truth. You know I know the Jennings too and I just can't believe that Jason had anything to do with this.'

'David, it is good to see you. I know how involved you are with everybody in this business, and that's good.' Mohammed's beaming continued. 'Don't you remember me saying how good it is to have a man of justice involved?'

'Yes, of course,' I replied warily.

'I want you to help make plain what happened and who is responsible. I want to help you with your enquiries, David.' Mohammed held open his hands towards me. 'And Raisa is still so grateful that you and your minister came to pray for Tariq. He is so much better now and we don't have to worry so much about his recovery. Do put down your package and tell me what you want to drink.'

'Oh, this is for you, for Raisa and you, just a little gift for you at this terrible time.' I held out the cake.

'Ah sweet gifts, from your good wife no doubt, who is a sweet lady herself? Thank you so much.' He took the cake and then handed it to Philippa when she came in with the drinks. I couldn't tell if he was pleased or not.

'Now please do ask me what I can tell you about Tariq and his group.'

I said that I didn't know much at all, only what I had heard from Frank and from a friend of Lizzie who had recognised a couple of Tariq's friends as colleagues at University. Mohammed raised an eyebrow and smiled. I suddenly decided to plunge in.

'This friend said that Tariq's friends had been part of an extreme Moslem group at U.C.E., very disruptive to the Christian Union and making all sorts of threats of terrorist action. They had been trying to raise money for the Palestinians, and their leaflets seemed to be supporting people like Hamas.' Mohammed raised his eyebrows but sat calmly, his hands together in front of him. 'I suppose with our wariness of the I.R.A. and our disgust at Americans who support them financially, we're a bit sensitive to potential supporters of terrorism. If Tariq has been mixing with these kinds of people, then goodness knows what enemies he could have picked up. It's not very likely, I'm sure, but it would be good to hear more about these people.'

Mohammed looked very relaxed. 'I don't know exactly who you're talking about, of course,' he said, 'but I know a lot of students who like radical theories until they have to face the real world.'

'And some of us have been there!' I tried as hard as I could to show I was not against Mohammed.

'Tariq is a keen Moslem; that's true. But not every Moslem is a terrorist, as I'm sure you know, David.' Mohammed paused for me to nod and then continued confidently. 'Tariq has had a good British education and he can see serious faults in this country. I don't have to tell you, David, that there's selfishness and immorality everywhere, although sometimes it's hidden under niceness and respectability. I'm sure Tariq loves Britain and wants the best for it, and at the moment he thinks that Islam will be better for everyone. None of us want Great Britain to return to the ways of the jungle!'

I remembered hearing a sermon saying much the same thing, just with a different religion, and continued nodding enthusiastically.

'Even one of your leaders said recently that Christianity has failed here, didn't he?' I stopped my nodding and responded with a non-committal 'Umm…'

Mohammed continued with graceful purpose. 'Well, Tariq thinks that it's time we all tried seriously living a better way, and he's not alone. There are many young people like him, who want to live a pure life, not as rotten as ours. I trust that doesn't offend you?'

'Oh no. Not at all.' I spoke quickly to reassure Mohammed. 'We do often compromise too readily.'

'Of course among the young, as always, there are a few hot-heads.' Mohammed looked at me with a little more urgency. 'But I'm sure it's all mostly talk. You know, I'm becoming tired of the prejudice against Moslems that keeps coming up everywhere. I'm sure you understand things better, David. I'm sorry you can't ask me anything more specific. Perhaps if that friend of yours can remember an actual name or two we could talk some more, but this kind of general talk doesn't help anyone does it?'

I had the impression that some of what Mohammed said was a prepared speech, although no less heart-felt for it. And he certainly ended with a challenge. He seemed to think that was the end of the matter, but I was worried. If Mohammed had to admit that some of Tariq's friends were 'hot-heads' there probably was something worth investigating. I decided that I had to go and talk more to Jason. But it wasn't worth saying any more at the moment. I just had to come back with the names I had been challenged to produce.

'Have you encountered much prejudice yourself, Mohammed?' I asked.

'There's always some!' Mohammed relaxed again. 'My father was disappointed in this country. I think he thought he could really become one of those care-free Tommies he met when he was young and penniless, but it didn't work out. Most English people will welcome you so far but no further.'

'Yes I've heard others say that too.' I thought of Brigitte, the Belgian wife of a solicitor colleague.

Mohammed shook his head gently as he thought of his father. 'He was then left abandoned in this cold wet island. We have found it better to live our own life here with our own people. Yes, there's prejudice, but we can live with it.' Mohammed smiled, 'especially if the natives allow us to trade with them and bring us presents from time to time.'

I couldn't work out if that was just a clever parody of British imperialism or also an awkward reference to our fruit cake. 'Well this native is very glad that you're here and looks forward to seeing more of you and your lovely wife. How is she? And how is Tariq now?'

'Raisa is bearing up. She is at the hospital most of the time and is delighted that Tariq is able to sit up and take some home cooking now.'

'Oh good' I hadn't expected him to be eating curry so soon.

'Raisa is still a bit wary of my aunt,' continued Mohammed, smiling over the sharper turn his words were taking, 'but I have reassured her that we will find somewhere permanent for her as soon as we can. I hear that you have been taking a break from work?'

'Yes, I've found myself so involved in all this that it seemed the best thing to do.' An unapologetic response seemed best 'I now find that I'm chief location engineer for the funeral on Thursday. You have heard that it's almost certainly on Thursday haven't you?'

'Yes, thank you. So your minister will be conducting the ceremony. Raisa will be pleased. I wonder...' Mohammed paused and shook his head a little, 'would it be possible for us to have word with him about that? I'm sure that Tariq would want to make some expression of his love for Lizzie. I don't think he'll be well enough to be there, but could I have a word with your man, Paul, isn't it?'

This was another surprise. I couldn't imagine what they could want included, and thought it a bit odd. But I had to be welcoming. 'I'll gladly give you his number – Paul Cooper it is. He's already told Lizzie's family to let him know what they would like included, as long as it doesn't conflict with Christianity that is. I expect he was thinking of Lizzie's sister Margaret.' I hoped that Paul would understand and forgive me for adding yet another complication to his awful job. I told Mohammed the vicarage number.

I then thanked Mohammed for his hospitality and said that if I talked with the friend who had recognised Tariq's friends I would be in touch. I said that we all hoped Tariq would make a speedy recovery, and stood up to go, both relieved that the interview was over and worried about the unexpected developments. Mohammed though had another surprise for me, a pleasant one this time.

'Before you go, David, I want to give you something to show our appreciation of all that you are doing, for all of us. You were most kind with my aunt to begin with, and have continued to be a help and encouragement to us. This has not been an easy time for you either.' I had no idea what this was all leading to. 'So please will you accept this from us with our thanks.' Mohammed turned to his desk and brought out a bottle of wine wrapped in tissue paper.

I guessed that it was no ordinary supermarket bottle, and indeed it turned out to be a good Macon a few years old.

'Mohammed, someone's been talking about my vices,' I said. 'Thank you so much. This is really very kind of you. A true native's gift!'

We both smiled and shook hands and walked out to Philippa's desk. She wasn't there so Mohammed took me through to the back door and stood watching me go. It seemed a good exchange – fruit cake for a bottle of wine – and I was very glad I hadn't gone empty-handed. I decided to call in at Thorntons for a few lemon truffles to show Jane how much I appreciated her.

Driving home I was thinking about Paul again and how he would manage the funeral. I had to warn him of Mohammed's desire to add to his complications. Then I wondered when I would go and talk with Jason about those friends of Tariq that Jennifer said he had recognised. I was glad that it was Saturday afternoon with time to be with the children. Suddenly I saw again the policeman outside the ward, and imagined Jason in custody. I would have to talk with him while he was still in the friendly confines of the hospital and not yet becoming acquainted with the harsh side of the judicial system. 'Another trip to hospital,' I thought. 'I'm subsidising the N.H.S. in car park fees.'

I told Jane how brilliant it had been to take Mohammed a cake and left her to open the chocolates while I phoned Paul. The answering machine apologised for being itself and invited me to leave a message; the multiple beeps told me that I wasn't the first I stumbled and repeated myself but I trusted that Paul could understand that he would soon be troubled by a telephone call from Mohammed – unless Mohammed had rung already. That businessman kept his fingers on things very deftly; he wasn't the sort to put off what could be done straight away. At least he too would only have encountered the machine.

Jane thanked me for the Thorntons, but it was more of a nod of acknowledgement than a gush of gratitude. She then told me that Will had rung. Jason was better again today, and could I give him a ring please. 'And seeing as it's such a nice day, perhaps you could also make an appointment with the lawn?' It was a couple of weeks since the last cut and the grass was beginning to look more like a field for silage.

I thought I could try and persuade Peter, or maybe Nicola, to help. They needed paying for this kind of simple house help and the rates kept going up. Last time for the car washing I had put my foot down and refused to offer any more – but all this meant was that I had to do it myself. If only there were other quick and easy rewards instead of money.

Will was out when I phoned. To tackle Peter or Jason first? I knew I should do the more difficult, challenging and open-ended task first, but suddenly the faint prospect of rain later made it essential that I sort out the lawn firSt Over a quick lunch I mentioned to Peter that the lawn needed cutting and that I was willing to put my hand in my pocket to encourage family work-sharing.

Peter only wanted to talk amounts. We agreed on £10 for the lawn and the Rover. Later on, Nicola was indignant. She needed money for a trip to the N.E.C. for some car event and would have done it for less, a lot more cheerfully. I told Jane that I was going out to see Jason again and that Peter was the man for the lawn.

A policewoman was sitting outside the ward this time, chatting to a friend. Jason was sitting up next to his bed looking perfectly well, his long hair falling over the side collar of his pyjamas under his ear. He was listening to the radio and switched it of with reluctance.

'Jason, it's pretty important,' I warned him cheekily, 'more important than the Blues' annual flirtation with the higher realms of football.' Jason just looked at me, not quite sullenly, ready to indulge this old man for a short time. I decided I needed to come straight to the point.

'Jason, you know that Tariq Khan's car was tampered with, and that the police think it was your doing?' He shrugged. 'Well I don't think you did do anything like that and I'm determined to point the police in other directions.' Jason kept looking at me. 'Your mother says that you recognised a couple of his friends as people you knew from U.C.E. She was talking about some fund-raising do for turtles that Lizzie organised and you helped with.' Jason shrugged. 'It seems to me that that sort of person is far more likely to want to attack Tariq, thinking he wasn't doing the right thing or mixing with the right people, whatever that might mean to them. So all I want to know is: did you know if any of Tariq's friends were caught up in some extreme Islamic organisation and could you tell me any names, please?'

Jason looked away out of the window, and smiled to himself. 'That's why Mum and Dad wanted me to have a quiet afternoon to myself - or so they said - so I could answer your questions.' He pulled up his nose with a bit of a sneer. 'Well I can't see that it'll do any good.., but yeah, I did know some of the people who hang around with that Tariq.' He paused pensively. 'I wanted to keep them away from Lizzie, and now look what's happened.' Tears came to Jason's eyes and he punched his fist hard down on the arm of the chair in front of him. The men in the beds opposite looked up at us.

I waited to allow them to look away again, and entreated Jason gently. 'Please just tell me what you know and then leave it to me. I know Lizzie has suffered, which is why I want to see her killer brought to justice. Someone was responsible for all this and I'm going to help find out who it was. Just tell me what you know, and I'll leave you in peace.'

Jason looked down at his hands. 'There was Yusuf Iqbal and Fahid Masoof. They were with Tariq that day. And there was Peter Strang; he was the worst of the lot, except that he didn't call himself Peter Strang, but Yusuf Maloud.'

I relaxed. 'That gives me something to work on. Thanks. Anything else?'

'Peter.' Jason spat out the name. 'He converted to Islam in the second year. He'd been into the drug scene before, dealing in hash a bit. One of the public school types; arrogant, looking down on anyone he considered naff or naïve. He'd spit when someone he didn't like walked past him.' I raised my eyebrows, but then corrected myself. I wanted Jason to think I believed him. Jason continued, spurred on by occasional encouragements. 'Well, at the beginning of the second year he suddenly started hanging around with these Moslem groups. He stopped all the drugs and told everyone he'd found a better way. He became sort of super-fit and started coming to lectures, sitting at the front with his new friends. He kept away from women, at least in public, and wanted them sitting behind him. Once one of his old girl customers came and stroked his hair and tried to sit on his lap for a joke but he just whacked her hard across her cheek and threw her to the floor. You should have seen the smile on his face when he turned to his new friends after that. Sickening. He was there with Tariq Khan at Lizzie's reception, him and a few others. Bastards.' Jason had been speaking loudly, with passion, but he ended quietly.

'Thanks, Jason. Your Dad said that some people once tried to break up a Christian Union meeting. Were these the people who did that?'

Jason nodded. 'It wasn't just once. They would stand outside and stare at the people who went in, making a list of names. Then sometimes a couple of them would come into meetings and keep asking awkward questions.'

'What sort of questions?' I kept having to prompt Jason to continue, nodding and gesturing when he seemed like stopping.

'About terrible stuff some leading Christians had done, and how they had been allowed to get away with things... And when we tried to have a time of worship they just sat there staring at us as though we were mad, coughing and yawning, and in the prayers they spoke long passages of Arabic or something, probably bits of the Koran, but who knows? One or two of the Christians would then pray in tongues, which sort of fitted, but sometimes it was just a battleground, with people shouting each other down. There were these West Indians lads with pretty loud voices.' Jason smiled. 'It wasn't all the time. They tried to change the meetings so that they couldn't come and disrupt but then the Moslems complained to the University that the C.U. was holding secret religious gatherings and acting like a sect. They really had it in for the C.U... I went to the chaplaincy once at lunchtime, but no one talked to me and all they seemed to do was want to arrange get-togethers with Sikhs and Hindus...' Jason tailed off.

I wanted to know still more. 'This kind of disruption is pretty sick, but it sounds almost childish. They sound like they needed to grow up rather than like a major threat to anyone.' Jason shrugged. 'Was there something about web sites too?'

Jason looked at me and nodded. 'Yeah. There was this nice Moslem I knew and he told me what some of the organisations Peter was getting into were about.'

'Which was..?'

'A couple of the C.U. lads were trying to find out more about that lot and they came up with some names which appeared on a few posters. They knew I was mates with Haroun so they asked me to ask him what they were all about. He showed me some web sites and they were pretty scary... There was loads of stuff about how Moslems were mistreated in all sorts of ways and how right they were to fight back to defend themselves. There were these gruesome pictures of Tony Blair and Bill Clinton being shot and screaming in agony as the bullets exploded in their bodies. It was scary.'

'I can understand that being more nasty. But that could be just childish spite too. It's only what happens to most villains in modern films, except there it's political leaders rather than drug barons or whoever. Isn't it all just propaganda?'

Jason spun his head around to face me. Suddenly he leaned forward and his eyes blazed. His voice dropped in tone and he spoke with twice the passion he had shown so far. 'That's not what Haroun said. He said they were always after money for something or other, and if the ordinary Moslems didn't pay, people would know how disloyal they were. "These people have been to Afghanistan," he used to say, "and that's what they want to do here." They're not just University students; it's far wider than that. That's what I was trying to protect Lizzie from.' Jason threw himself back against his chair and stared fixedly out of the window.

I couldn't just let this go. Without thinking, I pressed on after him. 'Jason, I want to help you. I'm sure it wasn't your doing. But you seem to want to think that you had a hand in all this.' Now it was my turn to speak with passion. I wanted to grab him and shake him. 'What did you do? How were you trying to protect Lizzie?'

Jason jerked round again, stared and me, and then turned suddenly back to the window. 'I'll talk to the police,' he said, vehemently.

'But they'll just think you've got all the reasons to want Tariq dead and the ability to do it!' I was trying to control myself, but the men opposite were by now staring at me. I suddenly felt ashamed. 'Sorry Jason, it's just that you're all such good friends.'

'Yeah. That's it,' said Jason. 'Just leave me to talk to the police and everything'll be fine. OK?' He switched his radio back on.

In some ways I had found out what I wanted, although it didn't seem to amount to much. Back at the desk in the centre of the ward Dr Rahid was chatting to a couple of nurses. He looked as relaxed as the previous day. He recognised me as one of Jason's visitors, and took me off to one side for a chat.

'I'm glad to have seen you,' he said. 'Jason's parents have been here rather a lot, you know. He's not that ill, and I'm not sure that it's helping him to have to be talking with them so much.' He smiled and his teeth showed a lovely white amid the luxuriant beard. 'Young men don't often have much to say to their parents. I'm sure he's fine with them and he knows how much they care for him, but perhaps they need to allow him a bit more time to think by himself. And, unfortunately,' he paused and looked serious, 'we can't keep him in here indefinitely, however much the nurses would love to see more of

him.' He smiled briefly again. 'We'll probably be discharging him early next week. I'm not sure how much his parents can cope with that.'

'It's been good of you to take such good care of Jason, and of his parents. Thank you.' I wasn't sure there was much I could do to curb Will especially, and I could see that Jason moving from hospital to police custody would raise Will's blood pressure considerably, especially if Jason was as obstinate with them as he had been with me. 'I'll try and have word with them. Mr Jennings is a bit emotional, but he does have some good friends. We'll support him. You just do what's best for Jason medically. You've done a lot already.'

Dr. Rahid thanked me and turned to go away. 'Can I just ask you a strange question?' He turned and nodded. 'I was talking about Jason to a friend last night and mentioned you. He said that he'd seen a doctor very like you in Casualty a few weeks ago. Do you have a brother or something here?' He laughed a deep Father Christmas laugh. 'No that was probably me too. I'm on G.P. training and we rotate around. You never know where I might appear!' And with that he went off into the ward.

I watched him go, his white coat tails flapping below his knees and I thought warmly that I would like to know this doctor better. And perhaps he could give me another view on the British Moslem world, which was beyond my experience, but suddenly seemed so important. The fragments I knew now made me want to see it all more clearly.

I walked slowly out of the ward and ambled along the corridor, enjoying the brightness where the sunshine lit up patches of floor and made them shine. Suddenly, charging towards me, I saw Will and Jennifer. My heart sank for Jason who would have so little time to himself. I armed myself with my strongest smile, usually used for magistrates, and set off to meet them.

'Will, Jennifer, it's good to see you. You phoned earlier. I phoned back but you were out. Let's go for a coffee and you can ask me what you wanted to this morning. I'm dry; and I'd love to have a chat, just us.' I thought that even Will at his most bull-like wouldn't be able to carry on to the ward against that.

'David! What on earth are you doing here? Not seen Jason have you? Got to keep things quiet for him, give him space. He's not supposed to have visitors, that's what I was ringing about. Oh for goodness sake!'

I was glad that I knew Will well. Otherwise he might have put me in Casualty. I pressed on. 'Well, he's had me for a little while and he's now listening to the football. Come and have a drink and tell me what else they've said.' I shot off another smile, this time the one usually used on people in cells who didn't want to talk.

Will looked at Jennifer, who smiled at me but didn't say anything. She was quite happy for the men to fight this one out. I waited half a moment to work out what to do next, and Will cut in. 'Look, we could have a chat, David. What drove you to come back here so soon? But there's no time. Give us a ring tomorrow. OK?' With that last shot he set his sights on the corridor again and moved off briskly. My rugby tackle days are over, especially on such a public hard floor, so I had to watch them go, crossing the patches of light and shade, Jennifer just keeping up with Will.

Back at home, the grass was waving at me in a friendly way and Peter was watching the television. Unlike a good Christian parent, I tried to sting him into action. 'You said you'd cut the lawn. I think this means no pay and money off your pocket money unless you do it now!'

'Wey! Hang on, that's not on! I said I'll do it and I will do it. You didn't say when it had to be. If you're so bothered do it yourself! Stupid.' The last word was thankfully spoken softly, as if to himself, so I could choose to ignore it. I was on the point of ordering him out away from the stupid television, but it was rugby he was watching and then Jane appeared and looked at me with raised eyebrows. 'David. Come and have a drink. I'm sure Peter will do the grass later when it's fully dry.'

She did make me a drink and heard about Jason and Will and Jennifer. 'I wonder why he didn't just tell me?' she asked but I think we both, sadly, knew. Will did not see Jane as his fiend.

It was half time in the rugby match then and I joined Peter with an apology. It was a good match, for a change, England attacking with some style and actually winning by three points. At the end I still felt cheated somehow; the game hadn't lived up to its unspoken promise, as 'entertainment' which we all paid for, to pick me up, make me feel good. I now quite wanted to spend some time outside, and dragged Peter out into the garden with me. It felt good to be working together, and I even enjoyed a short time of weeding and cutting things back. So many people say gardening makes them feel close to God. Blooming tidy gardens are great, but I wonder why on earth he made weeds to be so persistent.

Washing hands in the kitchen afterwards, Peter asked me what was happening about going off to Wales. I had to think what he was talking about for a while, and then explained that Paul hadn't wanted to play our game. 'I'd still like to find out more about that Meg, though. But she's not the only one who could have been out to get Tariq. By all accounts he has some pretty mad Moslem friends.'

Peter promptly ticked me off. 'That's prejudice, that is. That wouldn't be allowed in school, Mr Jeffery.'

'OK, fair cop. He has some pretty extreme Moslem friends. Is that better?'

'Better but still a bit dodgy. The paper said you were trying to blame it on the Moslems. I've been telling people that's nonsense and there's someone else completely you have your eye on.' Peter put on an aggrieved look.

'Paper? Me?' My heart sank. 'What paper?' Peter fitted my criterion of having been born locally so he kept up to date with the *Birmingham Express*. He looked up to heaven and shook his head as he dried his hands, returning with the paper before I had finished scraping the earth out of my fingernails.

'ANGEL MURDER – New Suspicions Attention today has been turning to a feud between rival groups of young Moslems in which Tariq Khan might have been involved. The police were making no comment, but it was being taken as a serious possibility by David Jeffery, leading Birmingham lawyer.' They didn't have the cheek to make up a quote, but most people wouldn't notice that and would take it as read that this was my opinion.

'So what are you going to do now?' asked Peter with sympathy.

'I don't want to blame anyone, I just know that Jason didn't do it, that's all. I don't know what I'm going to do. I can find out a bit more about Tariq's friends from his father; at least he's still speaking to me. But goodness knows how I find out anything about Meg now.' It wasn't something I had thought about for a while.

'Mum knows them too doesn't she? I thought she went there today again.' I had to admit that I didn't know what Jane had done today.

After dinner we did sit down and I asked her. It turned out that Patricia's brother had phoned up and asked if she could help with the dogs again. They had had enough attention from the media and from friends and she wanted just to get away to Wales for the weekend. Patricia was staying in a bed and breakfast near Meg's commune and Bill was going home. Apparently the bed and breakfast place was somewhere Patricia had stayed a lot, and the owners had become friends, so Patricia felt that it would be a good comforting place to go.

I couldn't help saying, 'I hope they don't use air freshener.' Jane didn't think it was funny. 'I wonder if there's any way we could go over, perhaps if one of the dogs suddenly went off her food completely?' I said hopefully, with a hint of a wicked grin.

Jane lunged back at me: 'Patricia has gone to be away from everything. Especially from insensitive men tramping around asking awful questions. Leave it to the police.' She was right and sensible but I still wanted to know more about this sister who seemed almost happy that Lizzie was now 'free.' I kept quiet.

Jane wondered what church would be like the following day, as it was Battle of Britain Sunday again. I was horrified. 'Oh no. Poor Paul, having that to contend with as well at the moment.' Our part of Birmingham was not distinguished by very much, except by an unusually active section of the Royal Air Force Association, who had 'always' paraded in church once a year to mark out their independence from the lowly earth-bound men of the British Legion. It was always a tension between the visitors who thought that we were privileged to have them to help mark this tremendously significant day, and the regulars who weren't happy to have their Christian worship taken over by these presumptuous visitors. Mike Channing had managed happily to accommodate both groups and had welcomed the veterans by draping their flag on the altar when it was presented to him at the beginning of the service. On his first Battle of Britain Sunday, Paul had leaned the standard against the side wall where it could hardly be seen, and I know he had been taken to task for that. Then, the following year, he had invited one of our most left-leaning church members to lead prayers in the service and there had been too many prayers for our enemies for the liking of the boys in blue. By the third year Paul had changed his policy on robes and didn't wear them any more, not even a dog collar. The traditionalists took this as a further snub to them and to their dear padre, Father Harrison, who had drunk with them through the war and only died four weeks before the service at the blessed age of 93. There was certainly a battle every time and it seemed worse each year, although it was a bit much to call it the Battle of Britain. I did 'say one for Paul' before I went to sleep, glad that he seemed such a calm and capable man.

Sunday

Peter was still asleep when it was time to leave for church. Emily was watching television curled up with three teddies. She knew it was different this week and wanted a Sunday off. Only Nicola, who was now interested in joining the Air Cadets herself, wanted to come along.

A dark morning made the church look lighter inside. The new entrance area was warm, with its green carpet and bright spotlights shining on the notice boards. Helen Baxter was welcoming us with service booklets, and this week's 'Know This' notice sheet. She was looking very smart in a light green trouser suit, a long top coming down below her knees, and a fawn scarf lying tastefully across her shoulders.

Through the doors into the main worship area the space opened up wonderfully, soaring to the old roof, now with the beam-ends red, green and gold to match the decorative bands on the white pillars. There were already quite a few people milling around, more at the sides than at the front, where the first two rows had been reserved for the RAF. The voices made a pleasant quiet hubbub, muffled by the new carpet and embraced by some quiet worship songs from the speakers on the pillars. Just before 10.30 the trickle coming through the door turned into a stream, and we were all ready at half past. It seems to be an unspoken rule of English church life that you have to start on time, as precisely as the BBC.

Paul welcomed everyone and gave the notices. He pointed us to where Lizzie's funeral was mentioned in the 'This Week' section, asked us to pray for that service, and for him, and to come and help with the practical arrangements. He said how glad he was once again to have the opportunity to focus on our national life before God, coming to him not just as individuals but as a nation with a common history in which God has been much involved. After a brief prayer we sang 'O God our help in ages past' and the old men marched in behind their standard. Most of them seemed quite short, dressed in jackets of various blues, with medals making a splash of colour under their grey heads. The standard bearer, with white gauntlets, was younger, marching stiffly down the aisle. The rest walked smartly, but it wasn't a march all in step, more of a relaxed progress. Two or three clearly found even this quite a struggle. Quite a few looked around the building as they walked down, not familiar with the new look. They seemed very ordinary, less stiff than my own father, men who would make good grandfathers. It made me wonder what they had been like sixty years previously. Their relaxed yet orderly manner was impressive and comforting in itself, so different from the goose-stepping regimentation against which they had fought.

We then had the children's slot: a couple of 8-year-olds had to come to the front and play 'Name That Temptation' answering questions about different situations and what exactly people were being tempted to do, before we all had to sing 'I'm in the Lord's army' which, somewhat to my surprise, seemed to have everyone singing along together happily. The children then left for their groups and we sang some worship songs led by our band. Beryl Davis led the prayers with warmth and gentleness, and we then sang 'Amazing Grace' accompanied by the organ. The reading was Jesus' temptation in the wilderness.

Paul stood up to preach, standing in his usual place on the steps in front of the chairs.

There has been so much said about this sermon that I made a point of securing a copy of the tape to record what Paul actually said. Paul's words are written out at the end of today's entry.

Paul's initial comments about London not looking very Christian made me think about the place from a new angle. The boys in blue began to grow restless when he went on a bit about us not being Christian. He didn't actually say this in so many words but they weren't entirely comfortable. Paul does tend to go on a bit sometimes, so I was glad when he started pulling people out of the congregation to liven things up. This was another new departure for Battle of Britain Sunday. Percy was chosen to be the poor man in debt, in Third World Sutton of all places. Percy Bottomley is in his early thirties with three young daughters already. He always looks very smart in a casual way, with perfectly matching jeans and cotton shirts, and he exudes confidence. He has probably had to develop it with a name like his. Mel, his wife, is calmly stunning, with short dark brown hair and deep hazel eyes. He was an obvious choice for the first character up at the front. He sat by the vicar's reading desk, looking dejected.

Bert and Bill played the other characters well, Bill taking a bit more coaxing to the front than Bert. When I realized that Bill was to be the Jesus character all I could think of was him standing with a pint of beer in his hand at the Coach and Horses. He stood fairly still while Bert seemed to enjoy himself more, wandering around trying to act out a little what Paul said his character was doing. I was pretty sure that Paul had primed them beforehand, and was wondering who he had lined up for the next character when he was introduced. There's not that many men whom he could count on to do this sort of thing.

When he looked straight at me and called my name my heart dropped ten feet. But there was no getting out of it and I had to play the devil character, respectable but opposed to Jesus. 'Is this how he sees me?' crossed my mind. Paul had seemed pleased to be the first to tell me the joke about the devil moving the boundary markers of hell stealthily until one day Gabriel takes him to task and tells him to put them back. The Devil pleads innocence, that the boundaries were there all the time and that, if Gabriel doesn't apologise, he'll put his lawyer onto him straight away. Gabriel stands his ground, or his cloud, and says he'll find a lawyer too. The devil laughs and counters 'And where will you find a lawyer on your side then?'

The sermon ending was quite powerful. Everyone seemed quite sombre as we prayed. Paul invited anyone who thought that something at all significant had happened in prayer to talk to him or to come to our next Alpha course. Once again that made my conscience twinge that I hadn't asked anyone to Alpha, and I wished Paul didn't keep going on about it. I hoped he didn't mention it at the funeral. We then sang 'O Jesus I have promised' as the visiting veterans marched out.

With a few more people in church, I thought I'd help with the coffee; this also meant that I could avoid talking to anyone who had seen me mentioned in the paper. Jane was a bit surprised by this burst of domesticity, but agreed readily to walk home with Nicola. Margaret and Tim Pryce were on the rota that morning and it was a pleasure to rub shoulders with them, chatting about their grandchildren and Margaret's Spanish lessons.

Time passed very quickly and when we came out of the kitchen, only Paul was there, chatting with Christine Williams, the warden. She was concerned about the arrangements for Thursday, and Paul reassured her loudly that I was a fine right hand man. 'See you tomorrow at Patricia Edwards's house,' Paul said cheerfully. 'It'll be good to have a chat then. I just have a couple of things I need to discuss with Christine now. See you later.'

Paul was being his usual friendly organising self - no wonder the church seemed to purr around him. Even the formidable Christine Williams, whom no one ever called 'Chris', widow of Dr Williams who had died two weeks into retirement, had readily agreed to be church warden at Paul's suggestion. The two of them fitted well together, with Christine treating Paul as a fond younger brother, and he treating her as a reliable aunt with whom he could joke when he wanted to. They stayed in the church entrance as I walked out into light rain and drove home.

Lunch that Sunday was a bit mad, with Nicola regaling Peter and Emily with my dramatic exploits of the morning, saying she thought I looked really serious, and probably cross, a scary devil.

'I didn't think you had it in you,' said Emily.

'We'll have you in the Pantomime next year,' shouted Peter.

'Oh, no, you won't!' I couldn't help retorting.

'Oh, yes, you will if you go on like that,' said Jane, springing the trap shut with a triumphant smile.

'Then we can all be in it,' said Emily with a degree of wonder not usually associated with a twelve-year-old.

Jane had been wanting me to join in the church pantomime for a couple of years, but I had always said that I was part of enough play acting at work and never wanted to do this in my spare time as well. Last year I had enjoyed painting in a few trees for Sherwood Forest, after someone else had done the outline; painting by numbers being the full extent of my theatrical ambitions.

After lunch I tried to read the paper but Nicola had the latest Grand Prix on the television and my eyes were struggling to compete with the attraction of the commentator's excited drawl and make sense of the lines on the paper. Jane suggested a short walk with Patricia's dogs, so we strolled off together again, this time in the opposite direction to yesterday.

Jane was concerned by what Paul had said this morning. 'Do you think he really means that about lightning striking Britain - not literally but metaphorically?' she asked.

'I don't know, you'll have to ask him. I don't suppose he expects anything awful. He's probably just making a point.'

'But it's not the first time he's said things like that. I think he really believes it somehow.' Jane wasn't going to be put off by my reluctance.

'People have been saying for years that we need to be more committed as Christians. That's all Paul's saying, he's just dressing it up a bit for people who have heard it before.' I also wasn't interested in talking much theology.

'He's said before that he thinks life will become much harder for us all than it is now, harder for Christians and harder for everyone.' Jane continued regardless of my calling to the dogs. 'I've heard him say that's why we hear so much about the Holy Spirit coming really close to people these days, so that we're prepared and strengthened for the hard times soon to come.'

'Yes, but the point of it all is to be more open to the Holy Spirit and to live as better Christians. It's the same point as it has always been, just with a slightly different introduction.' I wasn't going to be put off and I wanted to think about roses and children playing on a Sunday afternoon, and not about sermons.

'I think it's more than that,' Jane persisted, 'these are really odd times, not just with all the hype about the end of a millennium and the beginning of a new one. It's as though there's something unreal about things, sort of shimmery and flimsy, as though soon we'll all find that we've been living in a film set and not in the real world.'

'These dogs look pretty real to me. Did you bring a plastic bag?'

Jane was not to be put off. 'It's like that film, *The Truman Show*, except that it's not just one man with everyone else watching; it's al of us with no one watching. And you know what marks the beginning of the end of the lie that Truman's living in? It's when something falls out of the false sky and almost kills him. Something dropping out of the sky like lightning.'

'Not a sermon? Aren't sermons supposed to change lives?' I was becoming impatient.

Jane looked at me scornfully. 'It's a film. Truman doesn't realise what it is at first, but it sets him thinking and questioning until he finds out that his world isn't real at all. That's what it feels like now. We're waiting for something to puncture a hole in our false world somehow.'

All I could reply was 'Mmm....' Not very constructive, but when Jane was in one of these questioning moods I couldn't keep up with her. I was worried about something else far more imminent. 'I feel as though I've had my world punctured already, punctured and somehow expanded at the same time, by Lizzie's death.'

Jane responded with gentle sympathy. 'It's been a strange week'

'I can't believe it's only a week ago that it all happened. And here I am about to go and talk to a bereaved mother about her daughter's funeral.'

'Doesn't it make a nice change from wives in dead marriages?' Jane could be sympathetic and cutting at the same time.

'How did all this happen? And what is mad Meg going to want to do with the open coffin?' Somehow that had stuck in my head like an arrow. 'What do New Age people do at funerals?'

'They probably do some rather lovely symbolic things like putting a bay leaf in the mouth of the person who's died.'

I gave Jane my 'you cannot want me to take you seriously as a witness' look.

She answered the question in my face calmly. 'That's what a girl at school said they did for her grandmother when she died. It seemed really nice. All we ever do is talk, and then we delegate that to a vicar usually. What are you worried about?'

I repeated my fear of druids circling incantations in thick incense. Jane was not sympathetic. 'What's wrong with incense, there's plenty of it in the Bible, mostly from the East?' She said 'the East' with great dramatic emphasis, a bit of fun at people who might think that anything Eastern came with great suspicion and danger.

'You know what I mean,' I said with more than a little exasperation. 'I don't know what they could do, but it could be subtly weird, maybe seeming all nice and symbolic and spiritual but in the wrong way. It could be an invitation to God knows what.'

'Don't be so paranoid,' said Jane firmly. 'The Holy Spirit can cope with some unusual goings on better than you can. She's probably seen it in other parts of the world and loves to have a touch of colour in a British funeral for a change. And if you're so bothered why not try to find out. You know, forewarned is forearmed and that sort of thing. You can probably find something on the web. They're probably pretty clued up about computer communication.'

That seemed a brilliant idea to me; at least I'd know what sort of things they do and could tell Paul. We would then have time to think about a possible response before we went to see them. I was so taken with this idea that I forgot about Jane slipping in another reference to the female Holy Spirit. When we were almost back at the house, Jane pointed out my lapse. 'The Holy Spirit's been guiding us all along. Isn't she good?' 'You've been working that one out carefully,' I accused harmlessly. 'Yes he is. All the time, for good measure.'

Peter was on the computer and made me wait to the end of his game before I could log on. He quizzed me hard about what it was that was so urgent and when I finally told him he immediately closed down his game breathing, 'Oh so coo—ool!,' just what I had feared. We typed in 'funeral rites New Age' and had a great list of different sites. Peter clicked on the second name on the list and the screen went black. I wasn't quite sure what was going on and the hairs on the back of my head began to tingle. A devilishly red script began to appear near the top of the screen. There can't have been any sulphurous smoke wafting across the screen but it felt like that. A red face like a Halloween mask started to appear, and my nerve ran out. I cleared my throat, very lawyer like, and said quickly, 'I don't think I really need to see all this. It's getting late anyway. I think I'll talk with Paul first You can turn it off, Peter.'

'Oh but this looks wicked! You go and change and I'll tell you what weird ceremonies they get up to.' I put my foot down as best as I know how, with all the force of a marshmallow. 'Well I really don't think I'll have time, you know, and I don't think this sort of thing is really very good to look at. No, just turn it off and go back to your game or something.'

'Well … OK,' said Peter with disappointment, making me feel surprised to be effective for once. 'But thanks for showing me the site. I'll look at it another time.'

'You dare!' I replied hoping this was a joke. 'You bet?' was his cheeky reply.

Thinking about it, I really did need a cup of tea and would be reassured to talk with Paul first. It was becoming late, and Paul would soon be taken up with the evening service so I promised myself a teacake with my tea if I rang Paul first. Paul answered me quizzically. 'What can I do for you on a Sunday afternoon, David?'

'Paul I just wanted to talk about what we might say tomorrow, or, I mean, what you might say.' Having not prepared what to say meant I just blurted on. 'I mean about Meg and the open coffin. I thought about finding out what sort of things these New Agers get up to – at funerals of course – but I left it rather late, I'm afraid. And this is such a heavy day for you, with this morning as well. That was great this morning; it certainly struck home with Jane. So what do you think?'

'Calm down!' said Paul with half a laugh. 'I don't think we need to do any special research. We don't know what they want, and it's not worth trying to speculate.'

'But we'll have to give them an answer straight away.'

'We'll just go and listen and pray and do what they ask us to, unless it's really way out, just like we always do.' Paul's reminder that he was an old hand made me stop and listen more. 'You'll be surprised what ordinary English people ask for sometimes nowadays. I'm glad Jane gained something from this morning. It's not easy for church members but it is an opportunity to think about national issues - which we don't often do.'

'I thought you did really well, although you could have chosen someone else for the up front bit.' I didn't want to become the vicar's automatic extra actor as well as funeral sidekick. 'Look, this is a really heavy day isn't it, that sermon must have taken a long time to write. And you don't want any more opposition from the, err, the older members of the wider community, so to speak.'

Paul exhaled breezily, like a swimmer surfacing. 'I had most of that written a few weeks ago. It's like Christmas. You know it's coming round, so your mind thinks of it automatically. I just hope some of them were listening. See you tomorrow.'

I went sheepishly into the kitchen for my reward, hoping that no one would ask me what Paul had said. Emily was playing the piano in the dining room, Nicola was upstairs, phoning a friend again or something, and Peter carried on with his game, charging through some medieval landscape randomly feeding or decapitating peasants and knights. Jane and I settled down with the *Observer*, and a Beethoven symphony on CD.

The rain came down, lightly but steadily washing grey even the geraniums in the garden. Our terracotta and gold curtains came into their own, brightening our substantial nest With the lights on and, later, even the gas fire, we were grateful to survey the world, as the *Observer* showed it to us and invited us to think about it, from such a place of warmth and security.

Page 5 had a piece about the investigation in Birmingham, with the 'news' that a man was about to be charged. The *Observer* gave prominence to a City Councillor who apparently said, 'It's stupid how some people will twist anything to do with Moslems. Here is a young man who has clearly been the victim of a terrible accident and some people want to blame his friends. It's just racist prejudice, nothing else.' I turned hastily on.

I can't remember what else we read about, probably twenty different interesting pieces about people and policies. We felt that we cared enough to know and think a little about all these things, some even quite distressing. Whether this benign interest made any difference to our lives, or, more importantly, to theirs, I doubt. But in some way the newspapers help to make us the people we are, compassionate and informed, we hope, but maybe not always active.

A little later we had Songs of Praise on, with Emily joining us, before a late tea in the sitting room with some of Jane's cake, for us this time - at last! Peter and Nicola ate quickly, complaining at having had to suffer such boring and cheesy music in their house. I knew they were only jokingly turning the tables on us and what they inflict on us every other day of the week. Peter had just begun his engagement with heavy rock and Nicola loved to turn Robbie Williams up loud and sing along even louder.

I decided to fight back. 'It's better than that daft song you have on every day. Millennium, millennium. That's all he seems to be singing. He's just cashing in on the hype. I don't blame him, everyone's trying to do it, but he could be a bit more subtle.'

'Dad you don't know what you're talking about, as usual.' Peter was his forthright self.

'I don't suppose you've ever bothered to listen to the words have you?' zoomed in Nicola sharply.

I carried on, with a little less confidence. 'I can hear Millennium, millennium on and on. I don't suppose the rest of the words, if I could hear them, are any better. "The end of a thousand years, the beginning of many new years," something like that?'

Peter threatened to go and get it there and then, but Nicola and Emily both immediately said 'Oh, please!' with brutal annoyance.

'OK, Mr Judge-all,' Nicola was away on her high horse, 'if you bothered to listen, you would hear. *'We're praying it's not too late 'cause we know we're falling from grace. Millennium.'* How about that for a pretty important comment on where the world is at the moment?'

Peter charged in too. 'I haven't heard Cliff Richard or even the Archbishop of Canterbury saying anything as bang on as that!'

Once again I was silenced. 'Sorry, Nic. I didn't realise that's what it said. Makes you think. What else does it say?'

Nicola, bless her, gave up this great opportunity to smirk and simply sang: '*Some say that we are players, Some say that we are pawns. But we've been making money since the day that we were born. Got to slow down, 'Cause well low down.*'

'So Dad,' challenged Peter with relish, 'is that just like rubbish about a country that's zooming round in circles and won't like slow down because it's all about making money?'

'Well, hands up, you win.' I said as gracefully as I could. 'And there's more?'

'*Live for liposuction, Detox for your rents. Overdose for Christmas and give it up for Lent. My friends are all so cynical refuse to keep the faith. We all enjoy the madness 'cause we know we're gonna fade away.*' Nicola sounded good, albeit slightly breathless. Then the others joined in, chanting, '*We've got stars directing our fate, and we're praying it's not too late, cause we know we're falling from grace. Millennium.*' It did make me think, and the rest of the meal was somewhat sombre.

The weather was dark and nasty as I took Peter and Nicola to Youth Fellowship, picking up Gemma Maldon. I was grateful that Nick Maldon was bringing them home. Back in the snug, we watched the Sunday evening television: the usual slightly more pleasant, less violent or lusty stories for the Lord's Day. We explored the green and pleasant land of Ireland in *Ballykissangel* and the crude foibles of Cockney women in *Birds of a Feather* (again) before the news brought us a taste of real life, with an interesting twist at the end.

I reflected again on how friendly the media were being to Christian clergy. Dawn French's *Vicar of Dibley* was a good-hearted heroine, with all the failings of 90s women, but nice with them, aiming to be nicer yet and sometimes succeeding. The priest in Ballyk. was similar, very nice if a little naive, trying to put into practice modern ideals of tolerance and community spirit. The media seemed suddenly fond of the church, or at least of the clergy.

Peter had told me that one of the breakfast programmes had a regular slot for 'Vicars with Attitude', or something like that. Even *Eastenders* had a young and attractive vicar. It was good to see young trendy vicars instead of the stereotype old doddery ones, and I hoped that sooner or later we would have an ordinary Christian featuring somewhere in mainstream television, as attractive and sympathetic as these media clergy, struggling as they do with modern life, but with a foundation of integrity. All the committed church members I had ever seen in television fiction turned out sooner or later to be more hypocritical than anything else, giving in to temptation and their weaker side. Perhaps script writers and editors find the idea of an ordinary lay Christian making a go of living out their faith too threatening, although *Songs of Praise,* in its own way, showed examples every week.

I did wonder too if this sudden fondness for the clergy was something of a farewell gesture. A visiting speaker had preached at church about modern culture being like small ships sailing away from a homeland of which it was bored, looking back wistfully on the land being left behind, while knowing that they had chosen to leave for the open seas – guided by the stars, both astrological and commercial. This seemed to me a good picture, and worrying, but it was nice for those of us on the shrinking mainland to have some warm and friendly waves from the captains leaving us behind.

This week's episode from Ireland had its usual two strands. The races were coming soon and the priest was being asked to bless some local gambling and feeding of beer-sodden grain to a rival horse, with his presence and financial investment as well as his prayer. This would cement his ties to the local community, show that he was one with them, and not with the village in the valley next door, and make a good contribution to the church project for providing holidays to inner city kids. All this was going on in the context of the funeral of a crabby old woman, which just seemed to provide endless opportunities for the people to come together and talk, at first by the open coffin and then, after the Mass, in a drunken carousing in which the priest rashly found himself committed to the local shenanigans.

I wondered what Paul 'Battle of Britain' Cooper would make of it all. It was just my luck to watch an unusual funeral on television this week and I tried not to think of Thursday. I still managed to sleep well enough that night.

Paul Cooper's sermon, Battle of Britain Sunday 2000

'Have you ever looked at this country through the eyes of a foreigner? Last year I had the great privilege of showing a dear Indian Christian friend around London. He was thrilled to hear the chimes of Big Ben for himself. He said his father had loved that sound on the radio and as a child in the village he too had wondered what it was that made such deep music.

As we went around and I showed him the monuments, it suddenly struck me that there was nothing really Christian to show him. We saw the great churches, Westminster Abbey and St Paul's, but outside of these there was nothing to show that this was a Christian nation. The monuments had Roman gods and legends in plenty, but where were the Christian symbols? Where could we see a statue of David defeating Goliath as a tribute to our own soldiers who had fought against overwhelming odds? Where was there a depiction of the King saying to his servant, 'Well done, good and faithful one, enter into the joy of your master', as a tribute to a great politician who had made the most of the talents that God had given to him, for the benefit of the nation. It's not that there aren't the Christian images that could have been used. It's that no one, it seems, thought of using them, preferring to keep with the old pagan Roman gods and their stories. How then can we say that this has been a Christian nation?

When you say to most people in Britain that they are not Christian they take it as a great insult, as though you were saying that they were purely mean and selfish. This is not what I mean. I am pleased and proud to belong to a country with a lot of good in it, a country which has done good things in the world. I know my Indian friends are mostly grateful that they had the British ruling over them rather than anyone else in Europe or in Asia. This country has developed commerce and democracy and science and sport, and shared them across the world. This nation has had a great part to play in the spreading of the Gospel across the world. But we have still used the Roman gods in our public statues.

Jesus and the Bible have a respected place among us. We have kept them alongside us over the years, mostly as a comfort when needed and sometimes as a guide when puzzled. We have kept Jesus alongside us as we have made our way in the world, and we have made a better way in the world than many because of it. But is that what being a Christian is about?

Is it about having Jesus alongside us to help us make our way in the world? It sounds good. Is it, as Frank Sinatra crooned, doing it my way, with His help of course? That doesn't sound so good. Or is being a Christian more about doing it His way? That sounds more like it. Is it about having Jesus not alongside us, but in front us so that our minds are fixed only on him, and not on where we want our lives to go?

Can you see the difference? Jesus alongside us, Jesus in front of us; Jesus as a companion on our way, Jesus the director on His way? To be fully Christian we need Jesus in front of us, Jesus the one on whom our eyes are fixed from beginning to end. The struggle and the battle of the Christian life is precisely this, for us to keep Jesus in front of us, for us to keep our eyes fixed firstly on Him, for us to live His way, with Him as Lord. The battle is to keep to His way, when we would rather go our way.

All of us who are Christians are engaged fully in this struggle. We don't always succeed. We fail to live Jesus' narrow way. We listen to other voices, we are drawn into other ways. But we keep trying. We acknowledge Jesus as Lord. We know that in practice He doesn't influence the whole of our lives. But we know that He should, we state with our minds and our wills, as much as we are able, that He is the boss, and we are wanting to follow Him more and more.

For, it is not only Jesus who claims our loyalty. Jesus' enemy, and his minions, call to us too. We have had pride and selfishness alongside us on our way, lust and sloth as our friends too from time to time, envy and greed as companions to spice up our lives. We have made Mammon our goal, happy to do almost anything, allow almost anything, in the cause of profit. Every day we battle between these two claims on us. Are we going to have that conservatory? Are we going to watch that film? Are we going to phone that member of our family? Are we going to apologise?

You can see the battle, can't you? You know the battle – it's the battle of every Christian, every day until we reach heaven. And what is true of our individual Christian lives is true of our life as a nation. As a nation we are engaged in the same battle between Jesus the Lord and his enemy who likes to be called the prince of this world. The Battle of Britain, the battle to follow Jesus.

Not only as individuals, but also as a nation, we have had Jesus alongside us, and we have also had pride and selfishness alongside us on our way, lust and sloth as our friends too from time to time, envy and greed as companions to spice up our lives. We have made Mammon our goal, happy to do almost anything, allow almost anything in the cause of profit. Every day we battle between these two claims on us. Are we going to build that new stadium? Are we going to allow that film on television? Are we going to ignore that dictator who sells us so much oil? Are we going to apologise and pay for the damage we have done?

You know the battle – it's the Battle of Britain. It's the battle between the influence of Jesus on our nation and the influence of his enemy. On one side are faith, hope and love. On the other side, are greed, idolatry, pride, revenge and a whole host of other attractive options. The continual Battle of Britain, the battle to follow Jesus.

This country has never won the battle against Mammon and greed. Often we have not even tried to fight that battle. This country has never won the battle against idolatry or revenge, or pride and a host of other enemies of Jesus. Above all, this country has never won the battle against selfishness and pride.

Instead of winning the battle, we have reached a truce, a British compromise. We managed to keep our hold on the gods of gold and selfishness and pride, while at the same time holding onto Jesus as well. We walked our way, with Jesus on one side, and his enemies on the other side. All the time Jesus has been gently calling us to let go of the other side and come fully over to His way. And all the time greed and selfishness and pride have been calling us too, to follow their way. We cannot go on for ever. The two claims on us become stronger and stronger. We come to places where we have to choose. It is no longer possible to hold onto both sides. We have to choose. The truce is over. The real battle is on. The Battle of Britain. The battle to follow Jesus.

As a nation today we are owed many millions of pounds by poor countries who cannot ever pay back those debts. In simple terms, a few years ago we gave these countries generous mortgages to build new European-style farms and factories. But there were problems with the new farms and factories and there were a few years when nothing was paid back. The debt mounted up. Then the new farms and factories started producing, but prices had fallen dramatically so that the income just about covered the interest payments on the mortgage, but didn't reduce the capital. Even to keep paying the interest, these countries have had to cut back to the bare essentials – no hospital care, no schools.

Can you see the dilemma? Percy come up here a moment will you? Imagine that Percy here has bought a decent house in Sutton with a mortgage from his friendly helpful bank. He then lost his job and had to take a new one earning half as much. He is completely unable to sell the house and buy another one. He is unable to declare himself bankrupt. (Countries don't have either of these options.)

All he can do is to turn off the central heating, sell the furniture, and eat only the potatoes he grows in his garden, while at the same time paying the interest on his mortgage. And he knows that he will never be able to pay off the mortgage. He'll just have to keep scraping along.

Bert, please will you come up as well? Now imagine that Bert's the bank manager. He has given this mortgage which seemed like such a good idea at the time. He knows that it's turned out harder than he thought. He looks to see if there's anything that can be done to help. That bank manager is Britain, and that means all of us.

Now imagine that someone comes to bank manager Bert, a friend of his. Bill, please step forward. The friend says, 'There is a better way forward. My way is to tear up the contract and start again.' 'Can you do that?' asks Bert? 'Won't the whole system collapse if people don't pay back their loans?' 'My way,' says Bert's friend, surprisingly forcefully, 'is different. My way is to build a system in which loans are always cancelled eventually. Cancel the debt. You can do it. Just cancel it.'

Bert goes off to his accountant. David, come on down! Bert the bank manager asks David the accountant 'What about cancelling the debt on Bill's house in Sutton. What will happen if I do that?' The accountant frowns and shakes his head. 'You just can't do it. I know that you'd like to do that, but you mustn't let your heart rule your head. If you let this man off his debt, it'll be setting a terrible precedent. All sorts of people will act irresponsibly. In the end no one will want to give a loan again, and then where will we be? Not to mention that, if you don't have that interest coming in, you may well have to cut back a bit as well. But the most important thing is that people keep to the rules, and the rules are quite clear. Debts must be repaid, even Bill's debt.'

Bert goes back to his friend. 'My accountant says it can't be done.' 'That's a pity,' says Bill, 'what will you do about your own debts then? What will happen to you when you can't repay?' 'What debts? Me? I can handle all my debts, thank you, and anyway, we're not talking about my debts but poor Percy's?' Bert points at Percy huddled up in the cold eating potatoes again.

'My way,' says Bert's friend, 'is to cancel your debt for you.' 'Don't be so stupid,' says Bert 'that's nothing to do with you. I can handle that; it's Percy we're talking about, and David says there's nothing that can be done. Rules are rules and that's that.'

'Who made the rules? My way is to cancel debts, to forgive. Then Percy can have a great new start, he can rent out a room or two, he can help you grow potatoes - he knows a thing or two about potatoes by now. I like rules, but I love mercy. I like tidiness, but I love generosity. Don't you too?

Don't you love mercy? Don't you love generosity? Don't be afraid, do it my way. Cancel the debt.'

Bert was in a dilemma. Who was he going to listen to? His accountant or his friend?

That is the dilemma Britain is facing now. This year we have the invitation and the opportunity to cancel debt, to be generous and extravagant once in 2000 years. This is what Jesus is calling us to do. But His enemy, who dresses so respectably, and speaks so seriously, is calling us the other way. Who are we going to listen to? This is today's Battle of Britain. Who is going to win? Or are we going to try to keep both happy, cancelling just a little debt and no more? (Thank you, gentlemen, please sit down again.)

Today's Battle of Britain is a crucial battle. It is another phase of the same old battle: are we going to follow Jesus' way, or his enemy's? Unfortunately at the moment it looks like we in this nation have made the decision to listen to our devilish accountant, with a little concession to our friend Jesus. A little debt has been cancelled, but there has been no true mercy, no generosity, no love.

Sixty-one years ago this country decided to go to war, the war that would involve the Battle of Britain in which some of you fought. To start with, though, it wasn't the Battle of Britain at all. It was the Battle of Poland. We went to war, not because we were attacked, but because Poland was attacked. We didn't leave them to sort out their own problems. With great generosity and courage we took their problem on ourselves and joined the fight. Now I'm not saying that we should always, or even ever, fight a war like that again, but we should be involved like that again. Where there are nations like

Poland, fighting against an overwhelming enemy, we should be on the side of the victim. In 1939 we didn't keep apart in our comfortable little island; nor should we today. We knew than that the enemy would come for us one day and we had to do something about it.

The enemy today isn't Nazism, it's the debt-collector. The debt collector is knocking at the door of the poorest countries in the world. One day he'll come knocking on our door too. If we are on the side of the debt collector now, who will help us when he comes knocking on our door? We have to see that it's not just their problem, any more than it was just Poland's problem. It's our problem too. For Jesus said, 'If you do not cancel other people's debts, neither will your Father cancel your debts.'

'Our debts?' we think. 'What debts?' We think the world owes a debt to us for all the good we have done to other countries. We don't recognise that before God we owe the world a huge debt. 'If we say we have no sin we deceive ourselves,' says the Bible. If we say that the good we have done outweighs our sin, we deceive ourselves too. When this nation is judged by God, there will be an overwhelming debt to pay. To take just one example: there will be millions of slaves, who gave their freedom and their lives to build up the wealth of Britain, and whom we cannot repay. That is why we need to listen to Jesus now and cancel debt now, so that our debt will in turn be cancelled. But will we lay down our pride and admit that we are debtors ourselves?

This is the Battle of Britain today. On one side we have Jesus, and His ways of faith, hope and love. On the other side we have Jesus' enemy, and his ways of selfishness, greed, and pride. Two ways are set before us: which one shall we choose? To go Jesus' way we have to give up what seems like a lot, for the promise of true life. To go the other way is easier now, but it is the way of judgement and death. If we go the other way we can't complain when the lightning of disaster strikes, as it surely will, mark my words.

There is a choice set before us a nation. Will we finally allow Jesus to be in front of us rather than just alongside us? Will we allow Jesus to live His life through us, or will we live our own life? Will we allow Jesus to send us on His way or will we go to Hell singing 'I did it my way?'

The same choice is set before us as individuals. Maybe you've counted Jesus for years as a useful distant friend, someone whom you visit maybe once a year, maybe at Christmas, but there to call upon in an emergency. Maybe you've thought that you don't really need Jesus, you're not really in debt to anyone, and, on balance, you've lived a decent life, doing good where you could. You don't see much need to be forgiven; you don't see much need for Jesus, except occasionally.

Jesus doesn't want to be just a distant friend, He wants to be closer to you than anyone else. Jesus doesn't want you to face your judgement alone. When you are called to pay your debts, Jesus wants to be there with you, paying for you through His death on the cross. Jesus wants you to die with Him and to live with Him, not your way but His way. Your way, your life, can, only end in death and in a mountain of debt that you cannot pay. His way, His life, can only end in life, in a new beginning for everyone that is completely and utterly free. Which way will you choose? Which life will you choose? Which death will you choose?

The chief obstacle to living with Jesus, living his way, is probably pride. You don't think you need Jesus, you don't think you have any debts that you can't handle. I'm going to ask you now to put this to the test and simply to ask God, now, to show you something of the debt you owe. If all I've been saying this morning is rubbish, you've only lost half an hour in a pleasant warm building. If I'm right, then one day you will find yourself facing a mountain of debt with no one to help you. Why not take a chance now to put it right? Let's all simply ask God to show us something of our debt.

Those of us who have been Christians a long time now, need this too. We know we haven't always allowed Jesus to influence every part of us. As God shows us something of our debt, we will realise again exactly how much we need Jesus. Let's pray.

'Father God, we know that you want the best for us as a nation and as individuals. Thank you for all the good there is in Britain, and in our own lives. Thank you above all for Jesus who has been friend to so many of us over the years.

But, Father, as we think of Jesus, we think again of His death on the cross. He suffered much and it was all somehow necessary. We hear that there on the cross Jesus died for our forgiveness, to pay the debts that we all owe. But, Father, we don't find this easy to understand, how he could pay for us, what debts we have.

Father God, please will you show to us something of our debt that meant that Jesus had to die for us. Father, please send your Spirit to us now. Not to condemn us, not to make us feel hopeless, but to show us something of our debts, so that we can understand Jesus forgiving us. Father, show us the pain we have caused to others, show us the opportunities we have missed. Show us now, and show us when we are on our own with you, maybe at night. Show us something of the debts we owe.

Then show us Jesus too, Father. Show us His forgiveness, and lead us to live His way now and always. Amen.'

Monday

The sun was shining around and almost through our heavy blue bedroom curtains as I woke up. I had a pleasant moment looking gratefully at the glow before the questions charged at me. Should I phone Mohammed? What would I say to him? Wasn't it better to leave things for the police to sort out? Wasn't it a bit ridiculous me playing private detective? And why was I now vicar's assistant too? What on earth was going to be said at Patricia's and how could I stop it all becoming a sharp argument? Who did I think I was? Wasn't bed so wonderfully comfortable?

Jane was still and asleep beside me and the rest of the house seemed quiet. The red numbers on the alarm clock read '6.42' so, if I did manage to push myself out of bed, I would only have 15 minutes before the other various alarms sounded and there was the usual scrum for the bathroom and then the toaster.

This Monday I felt I really did need to pray first, so I dragged myself downstairs and found my Bible and Bible notes. We were in a series about receiving more of the grace of God, and this morning it was Jesus coming to the disciples, especially Peter at Galilee after the resurrection. The writer said again how Jesus' three questions to Peter would have reminded him of his three denials and given him an opportunity to put things right. That has never seemed very kind to me. Would Jesus really have wanted to bring up something in the past that was forgiven by then? Could Peter saying the right thing this time make any difference to what he had said before? Or was Jesus making a different point entirely? I thought I'd ask Jane later. I just felt some sympathy for Peter saying to his mates, 'I'm going fishing.' His life had been turned around and upside down and all he wanted to do was get back to his familiar boat, to something he felt secure in. I knew just how he felt.

Breakfast came and went and everyone seemed to know what they were doing, although they didn't communicate much. I did some washing up and picked up the paper and felt very distant from the busy children. The front door had a hectic few minutes as friends came and then went with our lot in various groupings, and suddenly it was peaceful. This was a moment that I rarely experience, the contrast of the emptiness after the bustle. I made my lazy way up to the bathroom and the questions came back. Should I phone Mohammed? Was I poking my nose into things that were too complicated for me? What really had happened to poor Lizzie? Why on earth would anyone want to kill her? All I wanted to do was to go back to a normal day at the office. I didn't even know what to wear; what do you wear on a funeral visit? I decided to wear my best court suit just in case.

'You look ready for work.' said Jane cheerfully. 'I was thinking of going to see Patricia to give her her keys back and see how she got on over the weekend. I don't suppose you want to come with me, as you're going officially later. Are you off to the office then?'

I couldn't see why not, and I wasn't looking forward to a
morning in the house on my own, so I simply said 'Yes,' making
it seem that I had it all decided a long time ago.

'Say hello to Rose. I hope her dog's better.' I had forgotten
that Rose's poodle had begun to have bad eyes. Keeping a
poodle was Rose's one weakness, or, to me, madness, especially
when she went out on Friday lunchtimes to buy him his special
fillet of fish.

The Rover seemed pleased to be going on a very familiar
journey, and I enjoyed the slightly emptier roads later in the
morning. 'Good morning, David,' smiled Rose with a mixture
of pleasure and concern which I had seen often. The attitude
reflected years of Sunday School teaching. 'Are you all right?
Everything's quite quiet here.'

I wondered what 'quite quiet' meant, probably a reference
to the Press people who had long ago found something more
topical to rush off to.

'We're fine, thank you. Jane was wondering how Fliss was?'

'Oh he's a bit sorry for himself.' Rose smiled sweetly. She
didn't exactly say 'Good Boy!' but it felt like she was. 'But he's
enjoying the extra titbits he has since he's not been too well.
Are you here for the day?'

'Only for the morning. I have to help with arrangements for
the funeral this afternoon.' I paused, wondering why I was
there, and quickly realised I needed to play the part of the
decisive manager. 'I thought it would be good to come and read
some post and clear the desk a little. You can put calls through
to me as well. That'll be fine.'

I went through to the familiar dark wood desk sitting rather
oddly next to the bright pine computer table. The new high-

backed chair that Jane had bought me the previous Christmas seemed somehow to keep the peace between the wise old desk and the brash new computer. I wasn't sure whether to switch on the computer and see if I had any e-mail or whether to pick up the paper contents of my in tray. The e-mail would either be too demanding or junk so I decided to settle for the old familiar routine of the post.

On top of my filing cabinet was a rough plywood box, with 'DJ' marked on the front in even rougher chisel marks. This was the pride of my office and the embarrassment of all Peter's visits, an in-tray which was his second achievement in woodwork, or 'Resistant Materials Technology' at school. Before this he had produced a set of coat hooks, which, being much simpler, looked considerably better and were still in use in his bedroom.

The contents of this box were engrossing for a while. There were several offers to supply us with a new photocopier, with a sheet that Rose had done, tabulating the various options. She had even helpfully added on the bottom that she would be happy to talk about this more with me when I was ready. It seemed that she was on the verge of making a recommendation - a helpful development, that I did not want to discourage.

Taking the bull, of the American waffle and flannel variety, by the horns, I asked Rose to come in and talk with me about the photocopier. She managed to say something nice about all the offers, with something especially nice about the offer from the company who supplied our last copier. I took the cue and said how I did believe in loyalty unless there was a very good reason to go elsewhere, that I was thinking of staying with the same firm, and what did she think? Unsurprisingly she thought it was an excellent choice if I was happy with that, although I think we both knew that it was her choice first.

The surprise of the box was a letter from a friend of Mohammed asking me if I would act for him in buying a new shop to add to his chain. I wasn't sure what this was about, and wondered who he had been using before. It was quite exciting to have new business, especially as it was what I had hoped would happen from the work with Mohammed, but I didn't feel able to say 'yes' immediately. I wanted to leave it to one side, but decided it was better to acknowledge the request at least, and dictated a non-committal reply.

Mrs. Bright had written me a long and involved letter explaining all her current dilemma about what to do with her divorce proceedings, including much detail of what her friends had said and experienced in their divorces. The upshot of this was that she was quite unsure what to do, and would I advise her. I thought I already had advised her quite clearly to accept what her husband was offering, but she wanted me to advise her another way. I was wondering how blunt to be with her when the telephone rang. It was Mohammed.

'Good morning, Mr. Man of the Law. I trust that you are in peace at work this morning. Please convey to your lovely wife our thanks for her kind gift of cake. We have enjoyed it very much.' Mohammed's tone was brightly crisp, contrasting with my sludgy mind.

'Good morning Mr. Khan.' I wished I had had another cup of coffee. 'Your bottle is a delight to savour for a special day.'

Mohammed carried on with hardly a pause. 'It was good to see you on Saturday morning and to talk about our tragedy again. You said that you might be able to find out some more detail of Tariq's friends, who you thought might have some part in all this. I hope that you have managed to find some hard information, as it is important to clear these things up soon.'

'Thank you, Mohammed. It is good to talk with you too.' I was more awake at last, spurred by the prospect of responding to Mohammed's challenge not to make vague unfounded accusations. 'Yes, it was good to see you too, and yes, I have managed to find out some names. When are you free to meet? Perhaps tomorrow some time?'

We arranged to meet on Tuesday morning, and I put the phone down with relief. Mohammed was still on friendly terms and had not insisted on hearing the names immediately. Rose came in with a coffee and a couple of digestive biscuits. As before, she timed it to perfection and knew when a coffee was not substantial enough without a biscuit.

The rest of the morning continued quiet. I decided I couldn't do with pussy-footing around Mrs. Bright, whose dilemma wasn't a matter of life or death, more a matter of wealth or more wealth. I dictated a brief letter thanking her for asking for my advice, and saying that my advice had been, for some time, that she accept her husband's offer. Part of me wanted to suggest an addition: 'P.S. Get a life!' but I didn't think Rose would think it funny.

I was beginning to wonder what to concentrate on next, when I remembered Will. He hadn't been at church and I remembered how Dr. Rahid had said that Jason would probably be discharged early this week. I wondered how Will would react to me phoning him, and thought it would be best to talk with Jennifer first. Phoning their home, I had at least a half chance of catching her. I took a deep breath and dialled.

'Jennifer, it's David. I thought I'd just phone and see how Jason is doing now.'

'He's stable and looking better. I'll fetch Will.' My heart sank.

'David. You're phoning at last. Where are you?' When Will heard I was at the office, he asked if we could meet. I couldn't see why not, and, as he was going to be on his way to the hospital, we agreed he would come to me. He didn't seem cross with me, but I did think that it would be harder for him to lay into me as my guest.

It wasn't long before Rose was showing him into the room, and I asked her for coffee for both of us. 'Not for me thanks, David. I've had too much liquid today as it is.' We sat away from my desk on the functional little armchairs.

Will leaned back. 'David, I'm sorry I was cross with you. Jennifer's been having a go at me for being cross about you going to see Jason on Saturday. Of course you wanted to see him. It was just that the doctors had been pushing us out ...'

'That's O.K. Will.' I smiled inside as my back felt lighter. 'I could have tried to talk with you first. I didn't think about it. Jason's stable now, Jennifer said?'

'The doctors say he's stable. Seems anything but. Still wants to do himself in. Still bent on talking to the police. Won't talk to me or to his mother.'

I nodded slowly, as if I could say with authority that this was normal behaviour in the circumstances.

Will continued, gathering pace. 'And he keeps flying off the handle. Not what I call stable. But the doctors want to chuck him out anyway. Is there anything we can do? Can't you lock up people who want to top themselves?' Will looked at me with an intense mixture of challenge and pleading.

I took a deep breath. 'I see. He's not changed and you think he might be a danger to himself.' I nodded slowly again to keep up the impression of competence as my mind paddled frantically under the surface.

'For God's sake, David, he's done it once already!' The bull-like Will was showing through again.

I tried to keep up my 'trust me, I know what I'm talking about' act. 'When I talked with Jason on Saturday, he said he wanted to talk with the police. But he was talking, which he wasn't doing before, as far as I can see.' I paused to see if Will would challenge me, before I took another step. 'So.., it does look as though he's moved on from where he was when he went to the woods.'

Will frowned but said nothing, like a bull that finds itself in a slightly strange field.

I carried on more quickly and confidently. 'Of course, you can ask the doctor to keep him in under a section of the Mental Health Act, but that would need a doctor who had had nothing to do with him before, and a social worker, both to agree. It's an enormous step in civil liberties, and people have to be very certain of it. You could try, but, to be honest, I wouldn't advise it.'

'What do we do then?' Will looked at his hands.

'You have him home and you make him know how much you want him.' I relaxed as I could see a happy end in sight. 'You keep an eye on him, but not too closely.'

'Don't be naïve David.' Will looked up again, piercingly 'He'll be arrested as soon as he leaves the hospital. We won't have him home!'

My heart sank, but I felt I had to continue the upbeat patter. 'He'll be questioned and probably not charged. They need to gather evidence before they can charge him. He'll probably be with you, needing all the support he can get.' I wasn't at all sure that this was what would happen.

'That's what you think.' said Will gloomily. 'John Strutt isn't so sure. He says we have to be ready for Jason to be charged straight away and kept in custody.'

I felt sick, at having been led into a trap. John did have more experience with murders, or at least he had dealt with one before, which, despite what the television dramas portray, is pretty unusual.

I looked Will in the eye, as I half retreated. 'We'll just have to see, won't we? But it doesn't do to be always thinking the worst. If Jason is charged and kept in, he'll be safe in one way. He won't be able to harm himself there.'

Will just raised his eyebrow meaningfully and looked pointedly at the ceiling. He said no more and I kept quiet along with him, searching for something to say that might redeem things for me. 'Will, you know Jason didn't do it. I know Jason didn't do it. God knows Jason didn't do it. He won't let Jason or you down now.'

'Hmm,' was all that came out of Will at first. 'Who the bloody hell did do it then? God knows that; but he doesn't seem to be doing much about it.'

I tried to lighten the mood. 'God and I are doing what we can. A new team of detectives. If we can keep together, we should be able to crack even this one.'

Will didn't look either amused or impressed. 'What does your policeman friend say then?'

'I haven't talked with him for a while.' I could no longer feign competence. 'I'm sorry I can't help you more, but I am trying.'

'So who can have done it, then?' Will looked at me more gently than before. 'You thought mad Meg. She's wacky, but not vindictive like that. Wouldn't have the know-how to fix Tariq's car, not even her airy-fairy friends.'

Now it was my turn simply to say 'Hmm.'

'And who else is there? The paper said you suspected some sort of Moslem plot. That's a bit far-fetched too, David. It's a bloody mess.'

'Jason didn't do it. I'm more sure of that than nearly anything.' I wished I could give a reason. 'I don't know who did fix that car as you say, but it's far too simple to have been Jason. But maybe somebody wanted Jason to get the blame. Maybe someone knew that he would be the obvious suspect. He didn't have any enemies, did he?'

'O for goodness sake, David! This is for real.' Will fell into silence again, a silence which I didn't dare break. I looked at the table and the old red carpet, and over to my desk with the window behind.

Will shuffled and looked at me. 'David.' Another pause. 'David, what makes you so certain it wasn't Jason?'

'You know Jason, Will. He doesn't have it in him.' I hardly had to think before the words were out. Then I just carried on in the same vein, with a conviction that felt different from my recent play acting. 'He just doesn't. I've met some villainous people at work, and the odd one in church too. But he's not one of them. He isn't. You know him.'

'I thought he'd never do a stupid thing like trying to kill himself. But he did that didn't he? Perhaps we don't know him so well.' I had never seen Will speak so slowly and heavily. His shoulders were bowed down and he looked defeated. 'Jason told me what you had been asking on Saturday. About those Moslem lads. He'd kept most of it from us before, we didn't know it was as bad as that...'

'Look Will. I know it looks bad, and I have thought about Jason being guilty, believe me I have. But I still can't believe that he could do that. He couldn't plan it and carry it through. He couldn't misuse his gifts like that.' I was leaning forward earnestly as Will remained slumped. 'I know he's in a strange mood at the moment. He wouldn't tell me that much on Saturday and he did seem too keen to talk to the police. But we have to trust that he's still the same Jason.' Once I had said it, that seemed like the right place to end, the main point. 'Go and tell him my Rover needs a bit of extra attention, so he'd better stop flirting with nurses and get his hands dirty again. Except don't put it like that – you know what I mean.'

Will took my verbal dig in the ribs, and looked up. 'Yes. See how the loafer's doing. Thanks, David.' He tried to smile and stood up. I gave him a brief hug, our first, and then led him to the door.

I wondered if he saw me as naïve or positively dishonest. It was clearly too much for him to keep believing Jason's innocence against the odds. I wondered why the thought of Jason being guilty had never really penetrated my mind.

That was more than enough for one morning, and I was happy to leave. Rose looked at me, concerned. 'You haven't had a quiet morning have you? Don't worry about us. And I'll be praying for you, David.'

'Thanks, Rose.' I didn't have anything left to say, and did feel grateful for her meaning so well.

Jane had bought some carrot and coriander soup and fresh rolls, which were already warm when I came in. I told her about Will starting to doubt Jason, and felt heavy inside.

'Poor Will. He can't help thinking like that,' said Jane and fell silent herself. Neither of us wanted to say any more, neither wanted to upset or offend the other by not being able to see things exactly the same. I felt even heavier inside. I asked how Patricia was.

'Looking tense. Her weekend hadn't been as restful as she had hoped.' Jane explained that her car had broken down when they were nearly there and the AA had taken ages to arrive. The woman at the bed and breakfast had had to wait up for her, which made her feel awful, and then she hadn't sleep much, worrying about how she'd get home. It turned out all right, as one of Meg's friends had come and got the car going – something to do with leads or something – but Patricia still hadn't sleep much the second night either. And the weather there was damp and cloudy, enough to give any English woman a cough. And Meg had had some kind of big meeting so hadn't been able to see her mother much.

'All in all, she's had a hard time, and she's worried about you and Paul going this afternoon.' Jane gave me a 'you'd better behave' look. 'She thinks you've got her down as an atheist, after the hospital. I told her that Paul was very understanding and that I'd warn you not to be awkward.'

'Me?' I lifted my eyebrows innocently. 'I'm just there to help with practicalities.'

'Well, let Paul ask the questions. You're not a lawyer there, you know.' Jane smiled warmly, or else I would made a retort. 'Patricia's exhausted. I tried to get her to drink some camomile tea and go to bed for a couple of hours before you came, but she was waiting for her brother, and she had washing to do for Meg, would you believe it?'

I just smiled. I was wondering about Meg, and her expert car mechanic friend. I wondered if it was the same one who she had in tow at the hospital. 'It does seem a bit much for Patricia still to be doing Meg's washing. Has she just sent it home with her mother then?'

'No. Meg's come back with Patricia to be ready for the funeral, and her dirty clothes have come with her. Patricia feels she has to do them as Meg won't use her washing machine and she wants Meg's clothes washed 'properly' as she puts it.'

'So Meg will be there this afternoon, and she'll be around for a while.'

'Yes,' said Jane gently, quickly adding in a far more serious tone, 'And don't you go asking her awkward questions. That girl has enough to bear without you being suspicious around her. Allow her to bury her sister in peace.'

'Hmm. Yes. I won't push it, believe me.' I was wondering how long Meg would be around after the funeral, and how I could find out more from her and from her friends. Then it occurred to me that there would bound to be some of them at the funeral, and I thought that would be an ideal way of getting a foot in the door. I wondered how I could be interested in them, interested enough to make it worth my while making a visit there. Maybe I could say that I was interested in the legal aspect of communal living because a Christian I knew (well, me) had thought of trying to establish a Christian community. (The idea had been around a lot in the 70's and I had wondered about it then, so this wasn't exactly a lie.) Or maybe I could be interested in their spiritual life, hinting that I found Christianity's ties with the armed forces rather repellent. Or maybe I could say that I was thinking of writing a book which included a commune like theirs, and could I come and find out more about their life? This last option seemed risky, as I wasn't exactly planning on writing a book, although the story I was in was intriguing enough to make into a good book. But then I couldn't exactly explain the plot to them either.

Although I wasn't concentrating, I knew that Jane was talking about Patricia and what a kind woman she was. I just went 'Hmm' until she stopped me and said 'Isn't it time you went?' It was nearly a quarter past two.

I jumped up from the table, ran to the toilet, straightened my tie, combed my hair and headed for the door. Jane was standing there ready. She handed me a note book and pen, smiled encouragingly, and kissed me as I passed. 'Thanks. I love you,' I shouted back to her from the drive.

Paul was waiting in his car on the road outside Patricia's house, and was just opening his door when I opened the passenger door and jumped in. He looked at me quizzically. 'Paul, I know you said you weren't worried yesterday, but I thought I just wanted to say that if you need me to be lawyer-like and say that some things aren't possible in a Church of England service, I will. Just give me a nod if you want me to be the one who says 'No.' I'll be very understanding with them, believe me.'

Paul laughed again. 'It really isn't a problem. The worst that can happen is that we fall back on Canon Law, and I can handle that, thank you. Relax, David.' He looked at the note book I my hand. 'If you can just take some notes about the practicalities and look after those things, that would be great. I've talked with the Diocesan Press Officer, and she says that we need to have transcripts of everything in the service, sermon, prayers, etc., to hand to the Press on Thursday, before the service. If you could handle that side of things, and where the Press are going to go, I'd be very grateful.'

'Yes, of course, Paul,' I said, thinking that I hoped that man from the *Daily News* wasn't going to be there, although I couldn't see why he shouldn't be.

Paul was dressed in a dark green jumper with a tie showing at the top, and navy trousers. He looked like the assistant to my official suit. We walked quietly to the front door and Paul rang the bell. This time the response was quiet, and I wondered where the dogs were. Patricia came to the door with a big smile, looking remarkably cheerful. Behind her, Bill was walking from the kitchen to the lounge carrying a tray with cups and saucers and a plate of biscuits. We followed them into the warm lounge and sat down.

Patricia sat quietly as Bill handed drinks round for everyone. The biscuits stayed on the table until late into our conversation, when Meg went and picked one up and Patricia motioned to her to pass them round. Meg was sitting with her legs up in the same armchair as last time, with a book open and face down on the arm. Patricia was in another armchair, Paul and I on the long sofa and Bill on a dining chair brought in to complete the number. Paul began simply. 'I know this is usually such a busy time, so many things to sort out at once. How's it been?'

Patricia looked at Bill who replied. 'We managed to do all the paperwork last week, and we've been apart over the weekend. It's very hard on Pattie. We'll just be glad when Thursday's over.'

'It must be hard for you, Mrs Edwards.' Paul paused and then spoke with surprising liveliness. 'Lizzie was such a bright character. I can remember her in church a couple of years ago. She did stand out, her hair swaying as she enjoyed the band. You're going to miss her a lot.'

Patricia looked at Paul this time and eventually took a breath and decided to speak. 'She always enjoyed music, right from when she was born. It was the Olympics, and I sometimes had it on in the night when I was feeding her. Whenever the theme music or a national anthem was playing she always stopped and turned her head. She always wanted music on, whatever she was doing the radio had to be on.'

'Did she play an instrument as well?'

'She learnt the recorder when she was young, and she wanted to play the violin then. But there were no free violins in school and by the time she went to senior school she was too involved in sport to have time for anything else.'

Paul and Patricia were so engaged in their conversation that the rest of us simply sat, sipped and listened.

'She was keen on sports, then.'

'Netball, rounders, cricket even. She was in the school team for all of them, and played for Birmingham Schools a few times too. She always enjoyed her sport. Basketball was what she really loved. She would have loved to have had a game with the Bullets. She was almost good enough. She played for Lancaster in the national championships.'

'That was at University?'

'Yes. They reached the semi-finals and lost very narrowly to Keele. She didn't mind too much. They had a great time in London – an extra day of partying was how she saw it.'

'But she became a journalist and not a sports teacher. How did she take that up?'

'A boy friend of hers, a really nice young man, was on the University paper. She went along with him and loved it. All the meeting with people. At first she just wrote a bit about sport, but got interested in news too. She wasn't a good speller, but she said it didn't matter as the computer checked all that for her. She could certainly talk and she just wrote as she talked. People wanted to talk to her too. I think she would have loved to work in television. She certainly had the looks for it.'

'Yes, she was attractive.' The way Paul said this sounded so final that everyone else almost drew breath together, but Paul carried on. 'She was interested in animal welfare too, wasn't she?'

'That was a recent thing. She had this thing about turtles and she wanted to save them all. I'm not sure where that came from. But she was serious and she put her whole heart into it. That's why I would like to sing "All things bright and beautiful" on Thursday. Lizzie did love nature, and she was bright in her own way.'

Patricia sobbed a little and reached for a tissue from the box on the table. Paul pushed it closer to her. 'And you want to sing "Lord of the Dance" too?' he asked. I wondered how he knew.

Patricia nodded, with her tissue held comfortingly to her nose. 'She loved that one. I can remember her singing it in the house, the Easter before last. She woke me up with the sound of it. I don't know if we'll be able to sing it,' she looked round at Meg and Bill, 'but we have to have it for her.' She sat up and dried her tears. She smiled a little again. I wrote a note of the two songs mentioned so far.

Paul carried on in business like fashion. 'We have both an organ and a band on Sundays. I've had a word with our organist and some of our young people from the band. They're all able to come on Thursday. May I suggest we have "All things bright and beautiful" on the organ and "Lord of the dance" by the band?'

Patricia nodded again. 'Yes. She loved the band at your church. She once said it was a pity they only play at church.' Patricia smiled again, and seemed more relaxed with Paul.

'Is there any other music you would like to play, perhaps on tape or CD? Or we could sing another song if you wish? There's also the music as we come in and go out. Sometimes people like to choose something personal for then, sometimes they leave it to the organist to play something suitable.'

I steeled myself inside, as I wondered what mad Meg might want us to sing to complete the 'freeing' or whatever. Paul seemed unconcerned to be taking a risk, or maybe he was trying to keep the initiative instead of waiting for them to make the first move.

Patricia looked at Meg. 'Meg has a CD she gave to Lizzie which she would quite like to play. I don't know if it's suitable though.'

Paul leant a little towards Meg, and said very gently 'Oh, what's that then?'

'It's one of those nature CDs for relaxing – you know all floaty strings, and streams or beaches for people locked in towns. This one has dolphin calls on. It's the closest I could get to turtles.' Meg looked straight at Paul, with wide, clear, unblinking eyes.

I grimaced just a little in case Paul needed support, but he said brightly. 'That sounds great. We could have a wonderful quiet moment in the middle of the service for people to remember Lizzie and maybe think of the turtles. You're collecting for them aren't you?'

Bill joined in. He too seemed a bit more relaxed now. 'It seemed the obvious thing to ask people to contribute to.'

Paul was now in the flow. 'Perhaps you could let David have the CD and he'll bring it to church on Thursday. And I understand you'd like to have the coffin open during the service.' I blinked at the sudden addressing of the pagan intrusion and wondered how Paul was going to head it off. 'That's something West Indians and others do more than we English, but it can be good to be more open about what's happening. How did you see this working? Would we bring the coffin into church before the service, or would you want to come in with the coffin as usual and then have the lid lifted. I assume you don't have the lid off in the hearse?'

Patricia looked at Meg again. Meg replied boldly. 'I don't care how she gets there or when. We just want to see her properly so we can send her off properly.'

Paul now leaned forward. 'It is possible, as I mentioned, for the coffin to be brought in church on the night before. We can then have a simple service of symbols and prayers that evening. With the funeral on Thursday being such a public event, it might be quite nice for the family and close friends to be together by yourselves on the Wednesday evening. It would be more personal then.'

Patricia looked up as she pondered this new idea. I wondered what Paul meant by a service of symbols.

'I'm not sure about that,' Patricia said slowly. 'We were thinking of going to the chapel of rest on Wednesday. Do you think that will be enough, Bill?'

Bill nodded rather too definitely. He was already over his limit for the unconventional.

'That's fine.' said Paul. 'You can make the most of your private time at the chapel of rest. Then, what were you thinking of during the service, at what point do you expect the lid to be closed?'

Patricia looked up with kindly determination. 'Meg and her friends have this lovely idea. I didn't know what to think of it at first but I quite like the idea now. You know how people put roses into a grave on top of the coffin? Well … we'd rather like to put rose petals into Lizzie's coffin instead.'

Patricia looked at Paul and at me to gauge our reaction. 'It would be so much better than just leaving a rose on top of the coffin, it really would feel that we were sending her on with our love close to her, don't you think?' This sounded a bit like how

Meg might have put it. 'And anyone who was there could join in, like they do at a burial, but they wouldn't have to. And we could play something lively at the time.'

'I've never come across that idea before, but I can see the value of all being involved like that' said Paul quickly, smiling. 'It's good for me to have some fresh thinking.' He looked at Meg. 'I think we could do that – perhaps after the prayer and before "Lord of the Dance." We could put the lid on, which would be like burying Jesus' body. You remember the line: "They buried my body and they thought I'd gone?" But with Jesus life does go on, which is one aspect of what we're remembering on Thursday. You'll need some rose petals of course, and something to put them in.' Paul looked at me again. I made a note, not wanting to say that I hadn't a clue where to buy that quantity of rose petals.

'Meg's friends can bring the petals. They'll each collect some. They've thought all about it. It's rather nice of them, isn't it?' said Patricia. I had a suspicious unmerited thought about gangs of New Agers denuding rose bushes in front gardens all over Braydon.

'That's fine then,' said Paul brightly. 'David, perhaps you can work out on Wednesday where the rose petals are going to be. We'll also need a couple of sidespeople to show people where to go.' Paul turned back to the family. 'You realise that the Press will be at this funeral? Lizzie was in quite a prominent place, working for the *Birmingham Express*, and the national press might be there as well. We've been asked by the local television if they can film as well. I expect you've thought about that. What do you think?'

Meg jerked her head up and stared at Paul. 'We don't want voyeurs gawping at our Liz's body while they wait for the next adverts. Huh!'

'Lizzie loved working for the Post, and we'll be very happy for them to come, and maybe take some photos? But I think we'd all find it a lot easier if we weren't being filmed,' added Patricia in a conciliatory tone.

'Absolutely,' said Paul. 'It would make things easier for me too. Thank you. What about sound recording? We could try to record the main parts of the service on tape. But maybe local radio would like to record it for their news? Either way you'd have a record of the service if you wanted.'

Patricia, Meg and Bill looked at each other, clearly not knowing what to say. 'Well, we'll make a tape,' said Paul, 'and if the radio ask for a copy, we'll let them have one. OK? We have to give the newspapers a written transcript anyway, so it's not very different. I think we've just about covered everything. Have you any thoughts about music as we come in and as we leave.'

'Well...' said Patricia tentatively, 'Lizzie did have a couple of other songs which she used to sing a lot. I don't know if they're suitable. One I can remember her singing was "Somewhere", you know, from West Side Story. I don't know where she got that from, but she sang it a lot.'

Meg raised her eyebrows and rolled her eyes. Patricia didn't see, but spoke to her daughter. 'Do you think you could find a copy of that song, Meg? I bet Lizzie has it somewhere among her things.'

'No,' said Meg with force.

'Oh,' said Patricia taken aback. 'I... er... I don't know then.'

'I'm sure we can find that song for you,' I intervened. 'One of my friends is a musicals' fan. It shouldn't be a problem.' Meg raised her eyebrows again and I smiled at her. I wasn't doing very well at making friends with her so that I could investigate her more.

'Let's make that the song as we go out, shall we?' said Paul. 'Then if you have any thoughts about coming in, do have a word with David or myself and we'll arrange it for you.'

'If your band is going to be there, perhaps they could play a couple of songs as people arrive. If they could just play what they thought was suitable, I'm sure Lizzie would like that.' Patricia was taking more initiative than I thought she would at first.

'Well, I think we have pretty much all the details. Are Bentons doing an order of service? Do ask them to give me a ring to check the details. OK? And you do realise that this is a public service, for the whole community, as are all funerals in the Church of England, and that everyone is able to come?' I thought he might be referring to Jason, if the police allowed him to come, and maybe some of Tariq's friends, but I wasn't sure how he knew about them. 'We'll reserve some seats for your family, and friends you want included. Perhaps you could let David know on Wednesday how many seats to reserve?' I made yet another note in Jane's note book.

'Now I've heard quite a lot about Lizzie and it's great that I knew her, even if only a little. But often it's good for someone who knows the person better to talk about them, and I can then talk about the Bible reading, making the connection between the reading and the event. Can you think of one or two people who might briefly share their memories of Lizzie?'

'Yeah, that reminds me,' cut in Meg. 'Readings. We can have what we want, right?'

I couldn't help coughing as a prelude to some gentle legal objection to any attempt to hijack a Christian funeral, but Paul was quicker.

'You have something in mind? There's room for other things as well as the Bible reading.'

'Um, yeah. That one about the policemen, like, wearing black gloves.' Meg spoke vaguely. 'The rest is…'

' "Stop all the clocks, cut of the telephone," that's it, isn't it?' Paul surprised me with his knowledge.

'Yeah, I think so.' Meg was pleased. 'Yeah, that's it.'

'Is there someone who you'd like to read that?' No one spoke. 'Perhaps you could think about who would do that reading and about who might speak about Lizzie?'

Meg settled back with a satisfied smile, almost smug. 'Yes.., yes,' said Patricia with increasing brightness, 'there'll be someone, I'm sure. Thank you.' She smiled at Paul, grateful, it seemed, that he wasn't hogging all the speaking to himself.

Paul smiled back, with restraint. This was a funeral discussion after all. 'Is there anything else that you think needs to be said or done on Thursday?'

'You could say that she shouldn't have been getting involved with that Tariq and his friends,' said Meg in a low voice with half a smile on her face. Everyone else was startled.

I jumped in. 'I'm afraid we have to be very careful not to say anything which might affect the court case in any way at all. The best thing is not to mention anything to do with the suspicion of foul play.'

Paul cut in. 'I don't think Meg was being serious. I know Lizzie was a bright, athletic, sociable, caring and committed girl. I just don't want to misrepresent her on Thursday.'

Patricia smiled at him. 'I think you describe her well. She's just lovely.' Patricia looked at Paul with moist eyes.

'Thanks,' said Paul. 'Now I wonder if you'd perhaps like to pray? Some people do, it helps to know God close at a time like this. Some people would rather pray by themselves. Some prefer to wait for the service itself.'

'No, I'd like a prayer now, I really would,' said Patricia definitely. She looked around at the others, and no-one objected. Meg stepped out of her chair and took the tray into the kitchen.

Paul prayed a wide-ranging prayer, thanking God for Lizzie, praying for Patricia and Meg and asking God to make his grace and truth known in the service on Thursday. Patricia took another tissue as Paul finished praying, and blew her nose. 'Thank you,' she said. 'That was lovely.'

Paul stood up and handed Patricia a little booklet. 'It's some readings and thoughts which other people have found helpful at these times,' he said.

Patricia accepted the booklet graciously and we all made our farewells, calling to Meg at the kitchen sink as we went through the hall. It was bright outside, which was a bit of a shock to our eyes. Paul kept me back a while to check that I knew what I was to be doing. Suddenly I seemed to have a long list of things to organise and I had hardly made a start on the original things like the P.A. Paul seemed happy with how things had gone.

'You see, it was fine wasn't it? It's a bit different from what I'm used to, but nothing of the devil there, David.' I had to admit that it all seemed harmless. I just hoped that it would turn out like that when Mad Meg's friends were all there. 'Do go easy on the sister, David,' said Paul, almost reading my mind. 'She's putting on a brave face but she needs comforting too.'

'She seems a pretty hard nut, if you ask me. But I won't have a go at her on Thursday, trust me.'

Both Jane and now Paul were trying to curb my suspicion of Meg. I drove home eager to tell Jane all about my first, and no doubt last, funeral visit.

Jane was busy with school governor papers and left me to twiddle my thumbs. I had always before appreciated her relaxed but welcoming attitude to my day. If I wanted to tell her something, that was fine. But she didn't sit me down and interrogate me. She had enough going on in her own life, without having to live second-hand off my experiences. But today I would have appreciated a little more interest, a few more questions. This juvenile whining inside didn't match up in my head with the experienced lawyer I was. I went through my notes and worked out what I needed to do. It didn't add up to very much, and none of it needed to be done today.

Emily was watching television, so I thought I would relax by joining her, interested in what she was watching. It was mesmerising, and left me more tired and irritable.

'Sit still!' Em said with kindly annoyance. 'This is my thing, not yours.' I couldn't imagine ever saying that to my father at her age. Mostly I was grateful that the gap between my children and myself was closer than between my parents and myself, but there were times when I just felt I was being what they call a 'wuss.'

Jane came in and insisted the television went off for dinner, *Neighbours* or no *Neighbours*. She was firmer than I felt I could be. There are advantages to living with a schoolteacher.

Peter and Nicola bounced down the stairs for dinner – fish fingers with plenty of tomato ketchup for them. Peter and Emily had a yoghourt for pudding while I was allowed a slice of date and walnut cake. 'Not that you need it,' Jane said, 'seeing as you've probably been on the tea and biscuits all afternoon.'

'Eh? When...' was all I could manage

'When you were being the funeral assistant of course! It's all more tea, vicar, more biscuits, more cake. But you can have it here, you know.'

Thankfully the children all had things to do, mostly worthwhile homework things, so it wasn't too hard to dismiss them without the gory details they were craving. Jane then listened sympathetically and asked about my plans for the morning. When I told her about seeing Mohammed again she frowned.

'Go carefully, won't you, David? He's not someone you want to upset.'

'What makes you think I'm likely to upset him anyway?'

'You're in uncharted waters, for you, aren't you? You might hit a rock you didn't know was there.' Jane spoke softly, trying to be kind, but still stinging.

'It's not exactly water that you've ever navigated either, is it?' I countered more grumpily.

'But others have. Plenty of others. Christians and Moslems do seem to rub each other up the wrong way, without even meaning to.'

I pointed with both hands towards myself. Could she have been meaning mild mannered me?

Jane nodded with a little smile. 'But there are those who have gone ahead and learnt how not to offend. Don't you think it would be worth at least asking for some general advice?'

'About…?' I wafted my hands about.

'Just about things not to say, gestures not to make.' Jane turned on her stern stare and directed it to my hands. 'Don't you remember that Alex Indor from the Diocese?'

The Revd Canon Alexander Indor, Interfaith Officer, had come to talk to a Deanery event at our church which Jane had dragged me along to. Most of St. Luke's wouldn't want to go near what they suspected was a woolly liberal telling us how all religions are perfectly valid ways, and we should stop making such a big deal of Jesus. But Jane was not keen on prejudice, wherever it came from, and wanted to show some hospitality to a badly needed peacemaker. Possible future Moslem clients were enough of a spur to make me agree to go with her. It had been a good informative evening, with no sense that we were being urged to give up anything.

Alex Indor had spoken warmly of the Moslems he had come to know, some quite well, and how they had been able to talk of their differences. Someone even asked him what he saw as distinctive about Jesus, probably testing to see if he saw anything at all that distinguished Jesus. Alex's reply was as swift and brief as a times table answer: 'Forgiveness.' I warmed to the man, even if he was, it seemed, in the wrong camp. He was certainly intelligent, likeable and unflustered, unlike the blunt and wound-up speakers we had from some evangelical organisations.

Jane suggested I give him a ring, reminding me that he had offered to talk at any time. I could not think of a good reason to refuse, and hoped that he would be out at another Deanery pep-talk. Alex's posh-sounding wife answered the phone, but explained that he was in and would be happy to ring me back in five minutes.

True to her word, he phoned back, sounding relaxed and cheerful.

'Thanks for phoning. It's just that I find myself quite intimately involved with a Moslem client and I thought it would be good to just find out what pitfalls to avoid.'

'This man – I assume it is a man – is quite a Westernised Moslem is he?'

'Oh yes. Successful businessman, seems very comfortable in Birmingham circles.'

'Then the important thing is for you to be comfortable with him. Don't think of him as some strange foreigner when he isn't. You probably have more in common with him than many other clients.'

'It's just that I'm becoming involved in some quite personal areas, to do with his family. It's all quite unusual.'

'Let me simply reassure you that he almost certainly has a moral code that will mean that he is restrained and understanding towards you. And even if you do put your foot in it he will have been taught to be merciful. There really is no need to worry.'

I wondered if this short conversation would satisfy Jane, and decided to carry on. 'I can keep going as I have been doing, but it would reassure me to know something more specific about things not to say or do.'

'Yes, I know,' said Alex warmly. 'You're not the first person to talk to me like this. But the most important thing is not what you do or say, it's what you think. If you begin by thinking of hidden dangers, you'll come across as fearful at best, defensive at worst. For your defensiveness can look to others, no matter who they are, like aggressiveness. Just relax, and know that you are dealing with a man who has probably been formed in ways of politeness and integrity that many British people sorely need.'

'So I just carry on without thinking?'

'Carry on as you would with any other client – but maybe expecting that this one will be more considerate towards you as an outsider.'

'But that's what I am – to him I am more or less an outsider.'

'It's normal and natural to be friendly with people from one's own background, from the tribe or clan. Then you see people from other tribes as outsiders to compete with and be wary of.'

'You make it sound like the jungle.'

'Most British people have their own clan they belong too: public school, Black Country, that sort of thing. They don't trust people outside the clan. It is a bit jungle-like. If you don't mind me saying it, your hesitation sounds similar. You're seeing him as an outsider, while he may well not be thinking like that at all.'

'But they're well known for being wary of other people, quick to take offence.'

'Moslems are taught that restraint is a great thing and blessing is more important than personal justice. They have a sense of belonging to the whole of humanity – partly though the brotherhood of all Moslems, partly through knowing Allah as creator of all. They have to do good to all humanity, not just to their own tribe. Or else they'll be judged.'

I was quiet.

'I don't know this man, of course, but I have found it invariably true that a man like this is more trusting and understanding than you give him credit for. Moslems are taught to be kind to animals. I'm sure they can be kind to solicitors too!'

'Now you're going too far!' I responded cheerily.

'Look, if you're worried about anything you have said, then just ring me again and we'll talk about it. But trust me, the most important thing is that you let go of your wariness. Then you'll be fine. Think of St Francis. Just be simple, straightforward, peaceful and you'll enjoy a good relationship. OK?'

Alex really didn't want to continue the conversation. I thanked him, wondering how much help he had been. It's all very well to say 'Don't worry, don't panic,' but what else do you do? Still, he had reassured me a little, and Jane was reassured too. Sleep came easily that night.

Tuesday

Low cloud muffled the world outside our bedroom curtains even more than usual, and took the force out of the light, so that it hardly showed up the chest of drawers next to our bed. As my eyes opened into this half light, I assumed it was early and, with some determination, turned over, pulled the duvet round me and lay still, looking forward to more sleep. After what seemed like nearly ten minutes I was relaxing nicely, and the alarm buzzed impatiently.

I was cross for having missed the quiet before everyone else launched into the day, causing their own ripples and waves, which sometimes smashed into each other and splashed those around. Sometimes I found this morning mayhem exhilarating, sometimes intensely annoying. Today I didn't want to risk it and decided that bed was a good shelter from the storm.

'Aren't you getting up?' Jane asked, more surprised than anything, but concerned as well.

'I'm not seeing Mohammed until half past ten, so I'm looking forward to a quiet time when they've all gone, and then I'll get washed and dressed.'

'Quiet Time? You are taking this vicar's assistant thing seriously!' Jane sounded pleased despite her mocking. I carried on in the same vein, although I had not been thinking of a 'Quiet Time', beloved of evangelical preachers, just a few more snug minutes away from the hurly burly. 'Amen, sister! I have seen the light. I am going to spend precious moments with my Lord, indeed I am. As long as there's some good coffee to see me through.'

'Amen to that. Go for it, brother. And then I thought we might go off to the florist and order some flowers for Thursday. I think we know them well enough to do that and I do want something bright for Lizzie.'

Once again something I simply hadn't thought of, and felt acutely that I should have done, was slapping me gently in the face. 'Yes, you're right.' We do need to do that, and the sooner the better, I suppose. I'll get going now.' This suddenly seemed far more important than wasting time in bed.

'No, that's fine. You stay there and I'll bring you a coffee and your Bible. Where is it?' I couldn't get out of it now.

My Bible was on the top banister of the stairs, half covered by Nicola's green jumper, but Jane managed to find it and bring it, along with a large cup of milky coffee which had been my breakfast drink since our first French holiday as a family four years ago. The theme of receiving grace continued in my Bible notes. I remembered that I had intended to ask Jane about Jesus' questions of Peter, and made a mental note to try and ask today. This time it was Bartimaeus the blind beggar, and Jesus asking what Bartimaeus wanted Jesus to do for him. The writer of the notes stressed how important it is to be clear with Jesus exactly what we are asking him to do for us, even if that does seem impertinent. I didn't have a problem with that in theory; Jesus had made it plain that he likes to be given straight requests. It was harder actually to do it, to be bold enough to give Jesus his orders for the day. I asked Him to guide what I said, to stop me saying stupid things, and to cover up my mistakes when I did make them.

Concerns of enough bus fare, lunch and permission to go shopping after school were voiced loudly downstairs as I enjoyed a leisurely shave and shower. I walked down to a quiet house, with muesli, milk and a bowl ready on the table for me. 'Can you manage to make your own toast, dear?' asked Jane in her shrill, old-motherly, voice. I was tempted to rise to the bait and try to make her do it instead, but was too grateful to her to tease her. 'Thanks for thinking about the flowers. It hadn't crossed my mind at all.'

'You have plenty of other things to worry about, and flowers aren't your strong point. Even if we are going to have to drown poor Lizzie in rose petals, we need a traditional wreath as well. Nothing huge. I imagine a little basket of yellows, reds and oranges with some fresh green something that might last for a few days outside.'

If I hadn't been at home, Jane would just have bought the flowers on her own, but it was good to go together. It was one more way of saying to Lizzie and to her family what she had meant to us. That kind of things isn't easy to say, so any help expressing it is worthwhile. I surprised my self by having some sympathy with people who order enormous 'GRANDAD' letters, packed with the old man's football team colours. I couldn't really criticise them for doing extravagantly for someone very close to them what I was doing for someone I hardly knew. I did still tell Jane that when I die I definitely want "family flowers only".'

'You'll have something out of the garden with maybe a few extras from one of your favourite walks. That'll do for you!'

'Sounds perfect. Do you think I'll ever know?'

We walked back home quickly, as it was beginning to rain, and I then drove off to Mohammed's once again. This time I strode boldly into the front entrance and was immediately awed by the thick carpet and the panelling. Philippa was busy, giving me a brilliant smile, before asking me to wait, and then going to and fro in front of me with various coloured files. Her perfume was like a shower of musky mist coming at me again and again, and I couldn't help looking at her bobbing hair and sleek legs each time she swayed past. I had expected to wait a while, so was surprised when at 10.28 Mohammed came out and greeted me as warmly as ever.

'Mr. David. Thank you for coming. It is good of you to give me more of your precious time. Come in, come in. Two coffees please, Philippa, and no calls, except the one. Please, after you.'

I walked through into the spacious office and waited for Mohammed to beckon me to sit on the gold settee by the low coffee table.

'Mohammed, you are being very good to me, giving me all this time, and putting in good words for me to Mr. Anpal. I was very pleased to receive his letter and hope to be able to be of service to him, as well as continuing to serve you and your family.'

'David, you know that we do trust you and want to continue our partnership in all these matters.' The words flowed from him with no apparent effort, but always with a purpose. 'We have so many links now, and we are involved in so much. It is a pleasure to make a good name known a little more widely. If my friend Mr. Anpal, as you call him, is pleased with the service you give to him, then I will be very pleased too. A talent scout is not a great role, but there is satisfaction in knowing that other people will come to see what I see. You are looking well. Your capable wife is well too, and your children?'

My heart plummeted from my chest as I realised that I hadn't asked after Tariq. 'Yes we are fine. I am the one who should be asking you. How is Tariq now?'

Mohammed waved his hand over his shoulder. 'He is stable and almost out of danger. We will talk about that later. I'm so glad you've come, David. Your presence is reassuring. You are involved in this so much; you know a lot of people. And you have said that you know some names of people who are supposed to have been friends of Tariq.'

Mohammed paused deliberately; he didn't need to say any more. He had already commanded me to come out with the names.

'I do, surprisingly, know quite a few people involved in this tragedy with your son, Mohammed, but there's much that I don't know.' Mohammed smiled politely tapping his right fingers over his left hand. 'I don't know much at all about the young Moslems. I have just been given some names, which don't mean anything to me at all. They could be quiet people who have never had anything to do with extremists. They could be made up completely just to keep me happy. All I can say is that someone who knows Lizzie quite well reckons he has seen her with Tariq and Yusuf Iqbal, Fahid Masoof and, this is the odd one, - Peter Strang. Except that he doesn't call himself Peter Strang any more but Yusuf Maloud. Do those names mean anything to you?'

Mohammed had jerked his head forward when I spoke of Peter Strang. 'The first two are quite common names, and I do know that Tariq had one friend, Fahid. He's a strong-minded young man, but not without some gentleness too.' He moved his head from side to side a little. Then he looked more serious. 'Peter Strang I have heard about but I haven't met. I will have to find out more about this man. I understand that he has had a "Moslem phase", like many young men have different kinds of phases. But it could have passed already. We'll see. Thank you for being open with me, David. I know that you haven't held anything back from me. Let me know if you hear of any other names will you?'

'Yes, of course, Mohammed. And I trust that it will be in order to ask in a little while if you have found out anything more about this Strang boy. He seems to evoke quite a strong reaction in people.' I wanted to let Mohammed know that I hadn't been fooled by the smooth recovery after his original involuntary jerk. I was taking quite a risk. Later I wondered where my boldness had come from.

'Yes, of course,' said Mohammed quickly, waving his hand in the air again. 'How are the arrangements for the funeral? If I can be frank, I never really understand why it takes so long to arrange an English funeral. It is one of the most noticeable differences of living in a cool climate!'

Mohammed was trying to lighten the atmosphere again and knew that I enjoy the differences between our cultures. 'Yes, we have no need to rush, and as we have only one funeral event usually we need to take a bit of time to plan it all out.' I became more serious, respecting Mohammed's genuine personal concern, but for some reason not wanting to reveal my full role.

'I understand it's all in hand. My vicar seems to know what he's doing. It'll be quite a public affair with the *Birmingham Express* making so much of it. I have heard that it'll be unusual in one way: the coffin will be open and everyone will be invited to come and sprinkle rose petals at some point in the service.'

Mohammed raised his eyebrows. 'Yes that is unusual. It is almost Eastern in an odd sort of way. Will many English people take part in this?'

'I've no idea I'm afraid. If they're all like me they'll stay in their seats and then half wish at the end they had gone up.' Mohammed smiled with understanding. 'There will be some people who'll do it, no doubt. I do hope Tariq will be able to be there too. I'm sure that's what you would want too. He's still in hospital but stable, you say?'

'The doctors are confident of him making a full recovery, and they are allowing him plenty of visitors too now. Tariq is a strong man, so thankfully there is little to worry about now.' Mohammed paused after what could have been a rehearsed answer. 'My wife would like to talk with you, though, something to do with praying for Tariq. She is a little concerned and I trust that you or your priest can reassure her. She will be calling shortly.'

'I'm a solicitor, Mohammed!' I protested lightly. 'I can draft contracts so that no one gets the wrong end of the stick, but communicating with God is beyond my remit. I'll happily see if Paul, our vicar, can help.'

'I was somehow under the impression,' said Mohammed with the closest to a cheeky smile that I had ever seen, 'that you Protestants believe that there are no special holy men? Are you not famous for your equality before your God, equally able to pray?'

'Hmm.., yes, that's true in theory,' I floundered. 'But we also believe in gifts and talents.' Mohammed nodded sagely to acknowledge a decent riposte, and I hurried on.

'Raisa's a lovely warm-hearted woman, it has been good to come to know her a little. And how is your aunt now? I trust that she is able to appreciate the good points of the places the estate agent is sending her now. Perhaps she isn't as suspicious as the rest of us of anything written by an estate agent?'

Mohammed laughed. 'You should hear how properties are described in India – except that it is often not written down so carefully. Everything with a brick in it is such a mansion that one wonders why anyone ever leaves the country!' We laughed and drank coffee.

Mohammed carried on the friendly tone. 'You understand these things so well, David, and you understand how important it is to have the truth. Many exaggerated things can be said about people as well.'

'Yes, indeed. We do need to look at things carefully and not go by first impressions, which are coloured so much by prejudice.' I blushed as I realised how pompous and even racist I could appear to be. Mohammed carried on without apparently noticing.

'Yes, there is so much prejudice. You think that everyone is very friendly, but when you cross a certain line, such as with a nice English girl becoming very friendly with an Asian boy, people act as though they have been most offended. It is all about knowing the rules of the game. Find out what the rules are first, that is the thing.'

The telephone rang and Mohammed said quickly 'That will be Raisa. Please answer it David, I'll go and talk with Philippa.'

I dashed for the phone too quickly, knocking it onto the floor, and was kneeling on the carpet when Mohammed turned round in the door and, smiling, held up his hands together, palms facing each other.

Philippa said crisply 'Mrs Khan for you, Mr. Jeffery.' I stood up quickly.

'Hello, David here.'

'Ah yes, Mr. Jeffery. I am so glad that Mohammed has arranged to see you.' Raisa spoke with charming fluency. 'You must be a busy man. Thank you for all you have been doing, and for your prayer for Tariq. It is good to have friends in times like these.'

'It's good also to make the acquaintance of a charming woman,' I crooned, slightly embarrassed at myself.

'Mohammed has told me how glad he is that you are involved in our struggles. And now I would like to ask you something about praying, because you seemed to be able to pray very well, and I need to ask someone.'

'You do understand that I'm a lawyer,' I replied a little too abruptly. 'But if you tell me what's on your mind, and if I can't help, which is most likely, I'll pass it on to Paul, our vicar, who with us at the hospital.' First a funeral visit, then a question about prayer. I would be glad when it was time to go back to being a jobbing solicitor and not a vicar's assistant. 'Fire away!'

Raisa poured out her story, with encouraging promptings from me. 'You remember how we prayed when we were together in the hospital and how Tariq's leg moved. He really hasn't looked back since then and we think he could soon be in an ordinary ward. I'm so grateful to you both for what you did for him then. If only things could have been different for poor Elizabeth and her family. Well, I was thanking Allah for all this and then I tried to pray the same way at home last night. I was thinking of how feverish he is still sometimes. I thought that maybe he could do with a fan blowing by his head to cool him down (he has always been a bit of a hot head at times).

'Anyway I asked Allah to send him a fan to be blowing a cool breeze on his head, or perhaps one of the nurses to wipe his head with a cool cloth when he needed it. I sat back and enjoyed that idea. I could see Tariq in my mind and the kind Philipino nurse sitting by him. It was a good feeling, but then I saw something little hovering over Tariq's head. I couldn't see what it was at first, but when I looked closer I could see that it was a humming bird. It was bright and colourful and just hovering over Tariq's head. I could not see the nurse now, just Tariq.

'I was not afraid, but I did think that maybe my mind was imagining strange things, so I opened my eyes briefly and then shut then again. When I shut them I could still see Tariq and I could see the humming bird too. But this time it was not over his head, it was coming over his forehead and then hovering in front of his eyes. Then it came in very close to his eyes, just underneath them. I could see that there were tears on Tariq's cheeks and the humming bird was drinking the tears. It seemed so gentle. Just hovering there, and Tariq not even noticing it.

'Then it crossed my mind that this bird was taking something out of Tariq. It was taking away the fluid from his body. What if he needed that fluid? Could this have been a picture of strength being taken away from Tariq? There was no breeze and no coolness. The fever was still there and my Tariq was in pain and this bird was living off his pain. I wondered if someone had put a curse on him, or on our family, and I was being shown how the strength is being taken from him. It could be so awful. I thought it was good at first, but I just don't know now. What am I to make of this? I have been thinking of it all night and not sleeping at all. Is something taking away the healing that your priest gave to Tariq? I felt that I had to ask you. Can you help?'

It all sounded distinctly dodgy to me. Thankfully I have some experience in not answering questions and being reassuring at the same time. 'Raisa, thank you for telling me about this. I'm sure that we can help you in some way. Tariq is in good hands now, and it sounds as though he is making good progress. I can understand you being worried about this kind of thing, but the important thing is that he is stable. With the care that he is receiving, he must have a great chance of making a good recovery. I'll certainly have a word with Paul, but I'm sure he won't be worried about this. Our imagination can play tricks on us, you know.'

Raisa was quiet and then she seemed to be crying. 'Please will you talk with your priest, David? Please could you talk with him today? I am sure he will understand. Oh…' She caught her breath, and there was another pause. 'Could you ask him today? I will give you my mobile telephone number so that you can call me directly. Will you do that for me, David, please?'

Raisa didn't seem at all reassured and I didn't feel I had any alternative. I wrote down her number quickly, explained that Paul was a busy man and I couldn't promise when I'd talk with her again, and I then sat quietly on the sofa, taking a few deep breaths. It did all sound dodgy. Somehow it reminded me of

pictures of Indian gods with six arms and fierce eyes. Did one of
them have humming birds at their command? No doubt Paul
would be able to put her right, but I wondered what experience
he had of hysterical Asian women seeing visions. There weren't
many Asians living in his parish - yet. Mastering the school-boy
temptation to sit at Mohammed's desk and open a few of his
drawers, I walked the length of the office and opened the heavy
oak doors.

It was brighter outside in the reception area, the electric
lights glaring after the clouded daylight of Mohammed's office
with its three tall windows. Mohammed was standing by
Philippa's desk talking with a telephone in hand, which surprised
me a little; I still think of single telephone lines. Frank Gatley
was sitting on the sofa again.

Frank looked at me with some surprise, frowned briefly and
then smiled his jagged smile, showing off browned uneven teeth
with glints of gold inside his mouth. I smiled, although my heart
was sinking a little. It would have been good to be able to leave
quickly without the risk of being drawn into conversation with
this lonely old bigot.

Philippa was out of the room although her perfume still
made her presence felt. The scent was quite distinctive, both
flowery and spicy; I wondered if she mixed her own. Do women
ever do that? You could have a National Trust flowery perfume
with a dash of something strong and French - or would that be
expensive sacrilege? *The Body Shop* used to sell fragrances to put
in bath oil, and no doubt you could have a mixture of those, but
I think it never caught on somehow. But then I could try it with
aftershave maybe? I was beginning to feel nervous of where my
train of thought was taking me, when Mohammed finished his

conversation and Philippa strode smoothly back to her desk. She had probably been waiting tactfully for Mohammed to finish.

'Thank you, David,' said Mohammed quickly and privately to me. 'Our faithful Mr. Gatley is here again, enquiring after our Tariq. I have reassured him that he is receiving the best possible care, both from men and from heaven. But I don't think that Mr. Gatley thinks that heaven has much influence here. Is that not right Frank?'

Mohammed was making sure that there was no opportunity for Frank to question what I had been doing alone in Mohammed's office.

'Never done any harm as far as I know,' said Frank trying to be pleasant about something which he clearly found distasteful. 'As long as you don't rely on that too much. I've seen too many people waiting for God and allowing things to just get worse. Sometimes you have to take matters into your own hands.' Frank was surprisingly definite.

Mohammed smiled paternalistically. It seemed that this was a subject they had talked about often before. 'We do both, Frank, so you can be reassured about that. It is a partnership of heaven and earth, although sometimes we never quite know who is helping out who. David here is more knowledgeable about these things than I am.' He turned to me. 'Perhaps you could help Mr. Gatley to see some light? He seems to have lost the faith of his ancestors, which is a great pity. Perhaps you would like to have a drink now and see what you can do for Mr. Gatley too?'

It was an invitation, technically, but it would have been rebellious to refuse. No wonder Mohammed seemed to have his own way in his business deals. 'Umm, well, I could spare, er, some time… Yes. Thank you.' Did he know that it was almost a crime worthy of hell for an evangelical Christian like me to turn down an invitation to talk with someone about their faith? At the time I would rather have been driving home, and I wasn't exactly gracious.

Mohammed retired in victory. 'I am sorry I have to attend to more business, so I will leave you to enjoy each other's company. Thank you again for your visits and your concern for us all. With good friends we can pull through.' He smiled again and turned energetically back through the oak doors.

Philippa took our coffee order and I sat down by Frank. 'He's a good man,' I said, 'and a born leader, I think. But maybe he doesn't understand how we feel about talking about politics and religion. Do you want to take a risk and talk about Christianity?' I was trying to be light and friendly. I did want to evangelise if I could – we hear so much about it in church and hardly ever do it. But it wouldn't do to be pushy. This may be the most important message the world has ever received, but it doesn't do to be pushy. Not if you're English, of course.

'Course he's a good man – with some funny ideas.' Frank sounded gloomy after the lively congeniality of Mohammed. 'Seems to think all religion's harmless. With where his father came from, that's ridiculous. A funny thing, religion. It either makes people sit back and do nothing. Or it makes them primitive and violent. The old C of E's harmless enough, mind you.' Frank looked down at his sleeves. Did he realise how rude he sounded?

'Yes. Um … You said before that Mohammed's father turned away from the religion he was brought up with. You seem to have done the same?'

'Oh we saw eye to eye on a lot of things. Religion's a parasite. What has religion ever given us? It's science and hard work that make the world a better place. Religion just lives off the wealth.' Frank coughed and fumbled in his pocket for a handkerchief.

I waited politely for him, not wanting to shout back asking where he thought science came from. 'You're not a fan of religion, then,' I said lamely.

'It's something for people to indulge in. How many mouths has religion ever fed?' He spat into his handkerchief. 'People should recognise where it all comes from, and not go off with these strange religious ideas.'

'But in terms of world history, it's strange not to believe in something out there.' This was a tentative challenge, which Frank simply ignored.

'The young should know better. If they get infected with this religion thing again, then we're all for it. It'll just end up in more fighting. Giving people excuses for fighting each other. Pash knew what he was talking about.'

I hadn't expected such antagonism all at once. 'Well, Frank, a lot of terrible things have been done in the name of religion,' I suggested rather lamely. 'As a Christian, I can't help remembering how it was the religious people who had Jesus killed. I think he'd agree with you in some way. What do you make of Jesus, Frank? I mean he did upset a lot of religious people.'

Frank turned to lean close to me. His breath smelt of old cigars and kippers. 'People just wanting their own little kingdom. That Paul. He was looking for a fight. Blew it all up out of proportion.' Frank coughed angrily. 'Jesus was a failure, and Paul knew it. But he thought that in making Jesus out to be this great Messiah type, he could get his own followers. What did it make?' Frank coughed and spat again into his handkerchief. He carried on insistently and loudly. 'Trouble and fighting. That's all. Another new religion for people to fight over. As if there weren't enough religions and enough fighting already. That's all there's ever been through religion. It's a nasty infection and it's time that people got rid of it.' He put his handkerchief back in his pocket, breathing wheezily.

No wonder Mohammed was smiling, almost laughing, when he went back into his office. He had probably heard all this many times before from Frank and from his father. I could tell a brick wall when I came up against one, but the stubborn streak in me found it a challenge. Thankfully the coffee arriving gave me a little time to think.

'You're painting rather a black picture, aren't you? Isn't religion just a natural part of human life, which can be turned either to bad or to good? Look at the Millennium Dome. That's all about people and science, but there's the faith zone too. And it shows that the church has done a lot of good in Britain, as well as the worse things. Where would we be today without the influence of Christianity?' I hesitated to talk positively about the Dome, but couldn't think of anything better.

'A lot better off!' said Frank quickly. 'Not held back by mumbo-jumbo for a start. The people who got rid of smallpox didn't say it was just a natural part of life did they? Just because it's around a lot doesn't mean to say we want to hang on to it. It's fighting back, as these things do. But they'll appreciate it when it's gone, even if it takes some getting rid of.'

This was unremittingly obstinate. The brick wall could be shooting arrows soon. Frank seemed a little old to belong to the John Lennon '*Imagine*' school of philosophy, but perhaps it wasn't such a new school after all. It was time for a change of subject.

'Mohammed seems fairly comfortable with religious people, although he's not a man of strong convictions, I guess. I gather that Tariq is more of a Moslem than his father?'

Frank smiled wryly, sensing that I had given up and left him winning the argument. 'Yes. Got himself mixed up with some dangerous young men. Sad. Very sad.'

'Someone told me that some of his friends are strong Moslems. The odd thing is that one of them is apparently English. Someone called Peter Strang. I don't suppose you've heard of him?'

Frank snorted a little. 'He was seeing a lot of young Tariq. Mohammed didn't know. The worst sort. A gentleman and a traitor. Old Pash used to say that if it ever got into our young people we should watch out.' Frank took a deep rasping breath. With new strength and eyes wide open he whispered as loud as he could. 'Look, these people can do anything, anything. They thought Tariq was on their side but he was having cold feet. They're not going to just allow him to walk away are they? Mohammed can't see it, though.' Frank looked at his sleeves again, suddenly saddened.

'Are you talking about the car accident? You think it wasn't an accident, don't you?'

'Mohammed won't listen. He needs to tell the police. He doesn't even want to recognise who Tariq was associating with.

These people need investigating, but Mohammed doesn't want to know…'

Now I could see why it was important for me to find out who Tariq's friends were. I sat up, my mind suddenly alert. Jason was being taken to prison today. The police didn't seem to be looking anywhere else. It all seemed so clear, thank God. I had to somehow point them to this Peter Strang and his friends. If they were extremists and Tariq was pulling away from them, they wouldn't want him telling their secrets. Doing something to frighten him, to show him the 'or else' if he didn't keep his mouth shut, was natural for that sort. Mohammed might inform the police eventually, but I didn't want to take the risk, and I didn't want Jason in prison.

'Frank, what you're saying is really important.' He nodded and his cheeks went red. 'I can see that it's hard for Mohammed to take in what you're saying. But I do have a few contacts with the police myself. I'll do what I can to point them in the right direction. What do they need to know?'

'Just find out about that Strang boy and the others. Ask them what they needed his money for. I'll talk to them if they want. Tariq talked with me about it all, more than with his father. There's probably a standing order that's been cancelled recently. That'll point them in the right direction.' Frank sat quietly nodding his head, his eyes darting from me to the wall, to Philippa and back to me briefly.

My heart was beating fast and I suddenly saw Frank in a different light. Once again I just happened to be in the right place at the right time. Here was a key which might just unlock Jason's future and lock up the real murderers. I thanked Frank, making sure I smiled as warmly as I could to make up for my lack of grace before, drank up my coffee and walked out to see if Phil Wittle was in his office at West Midlands Police

Getting to see a police officer at work is not easy, unless you are an officer yourself of course. They are friendly to a fault with each other, but highly suspicious of anyone outside the force. The English are a suspicious nation now, thanks to so many critics and watchdogs in the ever-present media, and the police reflect the nation in that way too. Thankfully I have done some work with the Police Association so I can be counted as almost one of them.

My most important case was defending an officer who had been accused of raping a woman in custody, a black woman no less. The officer was himself black, which meant that the Press were gleefully talking about the jungle rape case. It had not been too hard to show up the inconsistencies in the woman's story. She was meant to have been held down with one hand over her mouth to stop her screaming. I got several of the witnesses, including her friends, to describe how she looked before the attack, making them think that I was going to accuse her of dressing like a tart, which is neither here nor there, in fact. They all said that she was wearing lipstick. I then asked all those who had seen the policeman as he had come out of the cell looking very flushed about his hands, and there were again, thank God, three credible witnesses to the complete absence of lipstick on any of his hands. It was only a small detail in a mass of details, but it seemed to have stuck in the minds of the jury; there was a short but significant pause as the penny dropped and they began to look at things from a different point of view. Since that time, those who knew me, especially the black officers, counted me definitely as one of them.

Carl Trestin was on the desk that morning, and he gave me one of his broadest gentle smiles. He didn't ask me what I had come for, although he should have done, he just enquired who I would like to see today and pointed me to the second floor, third door on the left for Phil Wittle CID.

'Praise the Lord and pass me the hymn book. It's my friendly Anglican solicitor,' Phil beamed at me. 'Who let you in here? You can charm your way in anywhere, you silver-tongued master of conviction you.'

'The Lord parted the waters and we walked through on dry land.' Those were the first words that came to mind, and as I was already panicking at how to respond to Phil's challenge, I happily spoke them out hoping that it would show that I had a little bit of wit in me too.

'We are honoured to have the presence of Moses himself! Oh you man of God you! Would this man of God stoop to taste some bitter black water with us mere mortals? You can always put wood in it if sugar's not sweet enough for you.'

I laughed and said that I was beginning to feel like a vicar with all the tea and coffee that was being offered to me everywhere I went.

'Take a seat, then,' said Phil, pointing me to an old upright dining chair to the right of his desk. He sat on his swivel chair behind the desk and scooted himself round the desk until he was sitting with me. 'What can we do for you then?'

'How's the investigation about the reporter's death going? Any nearer a conclusion?' Phil just looked at me, assuming, rightly, that this was just a soft flannel opening. I decided to harden up, a bit more like a lawyer and less like a friend. 'I know it's early days, but it's not unusual for the suspicions to be narrowing down already. You may have a good idea of who you'll end up charging when the evidence has been gathered? I don't know how you do it but you certainly impress me with the speed with which you come to the heart of the matter.'

'Flattery will get you nowhere, David. You're not here to ask questions any more than I am here to answer them. What's your information?' Thankfully Phil was smiling as he said this.

'It's always worth knowing what someone's thinking is before you offer them your own thoughts. You may well have been aware of this of course, but I wanted to offer you a few thoughts on an alternative way of looking at the whole business. I take it that by now you are clear that the car was tampered with, and you know exactly how. There are too many resources being put into this for something that might turn out to be a nasty accident.' I didn't know this at all. It was just likely. And I did want Pail to think that I was more clued up than maybe I had given the impression up until now.

'The question then is, who had reason to kill Tariq Khan? You know that I know the family of Jason Jennings, so I have a personal interest. It has made me look for an alternative motive.' Phil raised his eyebrows but he was no longer smiling. I steamed on in lawyer mode. 'I grant that this was the reason why I started looking in places I would not have been looking otherwise, but it does not mean that my vision was necessarily distorted as I looked. If you are looking for the source of a smell and you find something nasty, it doesn't mean that you are only seeing what you want to see. I have been looking, as you know, and what I have seen has given me enough concern to want to bring it to your attention too. You can make a full record of this conversation if you wish.'

Phil just sat looking at me with his sober expression, leaning back in his chair with both hands supporting his head. He wasn't dismissing what I had to say, but he wasn't rushing to take notes either.

'I have been looking for other places where Tariq might have enemies. I have looked among his English friends and those of his girl friend. I have treated them with a high degree of suspicion and been reprimanded, by my own vicar no less, for my excess of suspicion. While retaining my concerns about certain of the English friends, but encouraged by others to be at least even-handed in my suspicions, I also looked among Tariq's Asian friends.

'There I found that he had been closely associated with a group of young Islamic radicals. He seemed to have been important to them not least because of his wealth. Recently he seems to have distanced himself from them in a remarkable way. Among people who perceive themselves to be at war, traitors and not treated lightly. It may well be that there was no intention to kill Tariq, but just to frighten. It constitutes a possibility that merits investigation – among others of course. Thank you.'

It all sounded far too much like a court speech, but it is hard for a lawyer in such a situation to do anything else.

'Thank you, my Lud.' said Phil. 'Yes thanks. We'll make sure that we include that part of the jigsaw too. Now are you going to Spring Harvest next year? Our church rep says that places are going fast?'

Such a rapid closure of the subject was breathtaking. I blinked for a second or two and carried on regardless.

'Thanks for listening Phil. I know that it's not the most politically popular train of investigation, but it does have to be considered along with everything else. I sometimes wish the police force was not under the control of local politicians. At times it must put you under pressures which are not helpful.' Again I was guessing, fishing, and Phil knew it. He smiled.

'Yes indeed, yes indeed-ee-oh. No stone unturned. That's the good old thorough police way, no stone unturned no matter what you or anyone else may say. Rest assured that we are investigating the matter fully, and I look forward to seeing you again in the pool at Minehead.'

This time there was no way I could continue talking. The best way now was to go along cheerfully with what he wanted and to look for an opportunity to drop in a little something else before I left. 'How many of you are going then?' We relaxed and talked happily about Butlins and what degree of crudeness we rated it, and why Baptists were so much better organised than Anglicans, who believed much more in church order.

'Thanks for your time, Phil,' I said warmly. 'And thanks for listening. It's good to know that I'm leaving it in the hands of a friend who will look in all the dark corners, however crude they may be, or however they may be out of the accepted English order of doing things.' I was quite proud of my being able to sum it all up so neatly. Phil seemed to not to notice.

'Thanks for coming, David. I expect you'll find your way out just as you found your way in. Give my love to the family. Especially your exciting free-thinking wife!'

I was still thinking about whether this remark had any implications for what we had been talking about as I walked into the rain outside. I wanted to get home quickly, and I wanted a trip to the lavatory. I didn't know where the nearest toilet was and didn't want to risk it, so I turned round and went back into the police station. Phil was in the reception area for some reason. As I came back in, he took me to one side and whispered. 'We are looking into those Moslem friends of course. You think it was his money they were after?'

I nodded quickly. 'You might find a standing order has been cancelled not long ago.' Phil patted me warmly on the shoulder, thanked me and told me where the toilet was.

Back at home I was overwhelmed by the complexity of it all. Here I was suggesting that a radical Moslem group had attempted to murder a former member, while at the same time I was still wondering how I could find out more about Mad Meg and her pagan friends. The New Agers were no doubt implacable enemies of Islam – at least that's how the Moslems would see them, even worse than the 'people of the book' who at least didn't worship idols like earth goddesses. I wondered why Mohammed had been so accepting about the pagan petals. Then there was all the arranging to do for the funeral, finding out about handling the Press, and working out the parking and seating for this extraordinary spectacle. Where would I find time to sleuth around, protecting Jason's innocence, and arrange the most complicated funeral the parish had ever seen?

I began to wish that Paul had not been so good at 'enabling the laity' and done the work himself like a good old-fashioned vicar should. Why on earth was I up to my neck in all this, with no idea of what I was really doing or how it was all going to work out? What was Paul doing anyway? Preparing yet another sermon that half of us wouldn't remember half an hour later and the rest would have forgotten in a couple of days? My uncharitable thoughts rumbled on. He couldn't pray all day, and he was pretty sharp at dishing out jobs for everyone else, so what did he do all day? Was he out in his immaculate garden with his bees?

'Hummingbirds!' I suddenly remembered Raisa and her weird ideas. Jill, at the parish office, said Paul was with the Archdeacon, and could he phone me back in a few minutes? There was nothing to do but wait and see what there was for a late lunch. Over a satisfyingly thick slice of bread the telephone went again.

'David. I'm glad you rang. I've just been talking with the Archdeacon because he had a funeral something similar to ours in his last parish, except worse - a child abducted. He's available later today. I think it would be a good idea for you to ring him and get some advice about the practicalities of the day. Or would you like me to do that? You may be finding that you have enough to do without that.'

'Thanks. Yes, that sounds really helpful. I'll ring him later. Did he say a time?'

'He'll be back in around 4. Are you sure that's OK? I expect you're used to dealing with people far more weighty than an Archdeacon.'

'The only weight on most of my contacts is their criminal records. It'll be the first time I've talked with anyone so exalted and close to the Almighty. But if for some reason I have to go out, would it be OK if Jane rang him? I'm thinking of doing this more with her if that's OK with you.'

'Brilliant idea. Just right for Jane. A woman's touch will be great.' Already bemused by the thought which had emerged suddenly, I was almost overwhelmed by Paul's enthusiasm. Did he not trust me as much as he said he did?

'Paul, there's something I need to ask you. You remember Tariq's mother at the hospital, the one you put on the spot when she asked us to pray?'

'Yes...'

'I was round at Tariq's father's today and she wanted to have word with me. She's been praying like you said, imagining all sorts of things and now she's worked up. Mohammed is worried abut her, thinking her imagination is running away with her. Could you advise us what to say to her? We can't just get her back to something safe like the Lord's Prayer. I don't think that would go down well with a Moslem.'

'You say she's anxious and been imagining things. What did she say to you herself? What has she been imagining?'

'Well she was praying for Tariq and saw this hummingbird flying in front of his face, drinking the tears that were coming from Tariq's eyes. She thought it meant there was something nasty going on. She wanted to know what I thought and I just said I'd have a word with you. She was talking about being cursed or something. The weird birds were taking strength and goodness out of her son. How do you calm down a hysterical Moslem mother?'

'Calm down, David! ' Paul was gentle but firm. 'Let me tell you a story. In my last parish there was a small group of us who met to pray every week. We were learning to meditate using pictures, asking the Holy Spirit to show us a picture of Jesus. One of the men, a salesman for bathroom equipment and not at all hysterical by nature, once said that he could see Jesus, a bit away from him. Around Jesus' head was a bright crown that was shimmering, vibrating. As he drew closer, he could see the crown more closely. It was made of hummingbirds and it was brilliant, a great picture. So I think hummingbirds are good. Whoever heard of a poisonous hummingbird?'

'But what were they up to with Tariq? They didn't seem to be bringing him any blessing or anything?'

'They were taking his tears away weren't they? Doesn't that remind you of Jesus too – the one who one day will take away every tear from every eye?'

'Oh.' I was relieved, and a little disappointed, to find that he did have an answer, and a pretty good one at that. There was nothing more to say.

'I'll tell Tariq's Mum what you said. Thanks Paul. It's not a curse then?'

'Why do people always think that something a little out of the ordinary is suspicious? The Holy Spirit enjoys being creative like this, and we just throw it back in his face. Please reassure her and encourage her to keep praying. If she's praying like that it must be good and her prayers are being answered.'

As I thought about ringing Raisa, I realised that I wanted to ask Frank a few more questions about these radical Moslems. How did he know about them and in such detail? What was their relationship with Tariq? Was there any evidence that there was a serious argument between them? If the police were taking all this seriously, would Frank really agree to talk to them? The sooner I had a word with him the better.

Philippa was warm and friendly. She laughed when I asked for Frank's mobile. 'He's determined never to have one, too afraid of boiling his old brains, poor man. That's just one of the many ways in which our brilliant Western civilization is under attack, I'm afraid. He really does get worked up about it all. So please don't mention the words 'mobile phones'. Here's his home phone number.'

Raisa was delighted to hear from me. 'Mr Jeffery, thank you for telephoning so soon. Have you been able to talk with your priest already? This is good news. Can he help us with this problem of prayer?'

'It is good news, Raisa. Paul thinks there's nothing to be worried about and it might well be something good that's happening with Tariq.' I told her what Paul had said about the hummingbirds around Jesus. She was enthralled and wanted to know where it said that about the tears being wiped from the eyes. 'We have a little Christian Bible which Tariq was given at school one day by some Christians. Would I be able to find it in there do you think?'

Once again I was out of my depth and had to explain hurriedly that this was not my sphere of expertise. I know that it was in the Bible, in the New Testament even, but couldn't possibly say where. I said I would have to get back to her on that one and wondered who I could ask. I would feel too foolish ringing Paul up again so soon.

Frank was in, barking out his number like an order for a firing squad. He was suspicious at first and I thought he was going to hang up on me but then he suddenly agreed to meet for tea to talk more about Tariq and his Moslem lads. All I needed now was for Jane to come in from wherever she had been. She was probably over at Patricia's again. No wonder it seemed like a good idea for her to be organising the funeral with me. She was seeing a lot of them.

The door slammed and Peter walked in. 'How's the heroic investigating lawyer doing today? Almost ready to announce to the waiting world how the car was maliciously mucked around with before pleading for forgiveness as the best Christian lawyer always has to do?'

I said I was well but confused, and even admitted to being in some pretty deep water with unknown currents, - without, of course, being out of my depth at all. 'Dad, you're still in the papers you know. They're making a huge thing of this whole "our golden girl" thing, inviting people to bring flowers to the park opposite their offices. And whenever they mention the investigation, you get a little mention too. Here, look.'

He swung his rucksack onto the kitchen table and took out a battered copy of the *Birmingham Express*, open at page 2. 'The police have still not released details of the car. Mr Khan hotly denies that his son had been drinking. "The car must have been tampered with. If the police do not bring out the truth, I and my lawyer, David Jeffery, will make sure that justice prevails."' Mr Jeffery's office said that he was unavailable for comment.' Dad, what's all this about the drinking? They must know by now mustn't they? The driver was taken to hospital, right? Whatever they'll have done it means using his blood, OK? So they just test it for alcohol. End of problem.'

'In this country permission has to be given for every blood test. Tariq was unconscious on arrival at hospital, so he couldn't give consent then, nor could anyone give it for him at that stage, even if anyone had thought of it. His treatment involved blood transfusions, naturally, so after a few hours, his blood was very different. I believe alcohol washes through the system fairly quickly.' I smiled cheekily. 'You might know more about that than I do…'

'You mean no one will ever know? That he can't prove his innocence?'

'The law is quite clear. Without permission, there can be no testing, and now it's too late. There may be other ways of determining whether or not he was drinking that evening, but it won't be through a simple blood test.'

'Grief. So if they can't pin it on him, that makes poor Jason more exposed.' Peter sat down 'Wow. What a mess.'

My heart moaned as Peter rubbed in the hopelessness. Rather than cry, I put the kettle on. It was not looking good for Jason. My own worry about my name still being in the newspaper, was a little relief from the great abyss facing Jason. I would have to ask Mohammed to stop the publicity. My name had been given enough of a push, and I wasn't sure that I wanted everyone thinking I was just Mohammed's tame lawyer. Later I realised that at least part of this was being afraid closet racists would steer clear of me, and didn't feel good about my pandering to that kind of fear. I also didn't know whether to say anything about the radical Moslems Frank had mentioned. But there was no one else there and Peter was old enough.

'There's another aspect to this all. I heard today that Tariq had contacts with a radical Moslem group who may have considered him a traitor.'

'Wo, Dad. Hang on there!' Peter looked at me wide-eyed with a hint of disdain. 'That's even more way out than the fruit loop of a sister. I know you want to help Jason, but don't you think the dark menace of Islam is going a bit too far? They're not all barbaric cut-throats with curvy swords and bad breath you know?'

'Do you want some tea or not?' I asked, a little sharply, stung by Peter's rejection of my sharing my riskier thoughts. 'This whole business is just getting more complicated by the day and I don't know what to think. We just have to be open to every possibility.'

Peter just looked at me, stood up, swung his bag off the table and went to sit down in the front room. It was time for me to leave to meet up with Frank. Where was Jane? I wrote her a long note explaining that I would like her to help with organising the funeral and asking her to ring the Archdeacon and note what advice he had to give us. I mentioned that I had already recruited Bill and Bert and had a few ideas about where people were going to sit. Thinking that it sounded too much like a memo for a secretary, I added 'Thank you. I love you' on the bottom. But would she think I was just trying to soften her up?

Frank was waiting for me at the Queen's Arms in Hockley where he had suggested we meet, an old-style pub proclaiming that it was Open All Day – Food. This always suggests to me that the brewery managers have been on holiday to France and are trying to coerce their landlords into imitating a café in Bordeaux. But we don't have the weather for café culture and we all know that boozers are for booze. Unless there's a new market of divorced Dads who would rather eat a pie watching the lads play pool than beans on toast in front of the telly in their compact maisonettes.

Frank was alone, on a stool by the bar, and he gave me a wary glimpse of grimy teeth as his lips curled up in greeting. He seemed to be looking behind me as much as at me, but was affable enough.

'What are you having then, err, David, isn't it? A good Welsh Crusader's name.'

I felt a bit reckless having a half a Guinness before tea time, like a teenager enjoying adult pleasures a little early. I had never been called a Welsh Crusader before, but then this strange week many people seemed to have their own ideas of what I was for them.

'This is very kind of you. Thanks.' I suggested we move to a table, not feeling enough of a regular to be at the bar, nor wanting the barmaid to pick up bits of our conversation.

Making an effort to treat him as a kind friend and not an old bigot, I thanked him again for the Irish sustenance. 'Frank, I was very interested in what you said this morning about Tariq's friends. That's a whole new area that I know nothing about and I just thought I'd like to know more.'

Frank looked around himself warily, touched his collar, and said nothing.

'You know that Mohammed wants me to find out all I can to prove that Tariq is innocent, and I also happen to know the family of that lad who is being suspected of tampering with the car. It seems I know rather a lot of the people in this business, but not much about the background to it all. You said Tariq was connected with some radical group or something and they could have thought he was betraying them?'

'It's not just what I thought, I heard it from the lad himself. He's always done what his grandfather told him. Pash made him promise that after he died he would treat me like a grandfather.

So I heard all about those lunatics. Too much.' Frank swigged his beer defiantly.

'What did Tariq tell you about them?'

'That they were true Moslems, free from the yoke of the Crusader West. It made your blood go cold. Pash had always said 'God help us if they start their religious fanaticism here.' Here it was, the works, the whole shooting match, the religion of the desert gone mad.'

This seemed an extreme way of describing people who held to their faith more strongly than he would have liked. I remembered he seemed to count us Christians as dangerously deluded too.

'What were these people saying, then?' I asked as calmly as I could, hoping he would not pick up how unbalanced I found him.

'The usual stuff and nonsense about God needing a pure way of life, about the evil of our way of life sucking blood out of the poor Moslems. How it was time for them to overthrow the armies of Satan and establish the pure way of Islam in the only way they know how, from a gun.' Frank coughed, retched a little and swallowed as though even speaking was distasteful. 'These religious people always find it easy to criticise others, they are always saying what decent ordinary people should do and shouldn't do. They just want to be in charge and treat us like slaves. They can't run a country, they just make life miserable for everyone.'

It was my turn now to look wide-eyed at the older man, Frank. Remembering Peter, I tried not to let any disdain show in my face. 'It sounds like young people who want to put the world to rights,' I said with an avuncular smile. 'Hotheads they used to call them.'

'Have you seen what these hotheads have done in Iran, in Afghanistan? They bleed the country dry of anything that's remotely enjoyable, turning the whole place into a desert. You think they don't want to try it here?'

'I'd like to see them try making a desert in our soggy land!' I said, as good-naturedly as I could.

'It's not just talk, they have guns and bombs and our ridiculous government, who probably listen too much to that closet Moslem who can't wait to be King, just welcomes them with open arms. "Come in, come in. Come and talk about how evil and rotten we are. Come and make your home here and let us show you how tolerant we are. Come and fill this country with your children, with your indoctrination. We won't say a word against you. Do what you like!" ' He took a long drink.

It was going to be hard to get some sense out of Frank. I wondered if he had been drinking before I arrived, and for how long. He was beginning to burst like a volcano, his face red and his thin lips oozing white saliva at the corners.

'Most people don't understand it, although the high-ups know. They have a plan. It's all set out. Pash explained it. They begin by just being here, nice and friendly, making us all think they're easy-going peace-loving, just like us. They despise us really but you wouldn't see it unless you're looking.'

It was my turn to raise my eyebrows in questioning disbelief. 'That's rather sweeping...' I said feebly.

Frank snorted. 'They begin to establish themselves and when the time is right they just attack. They target the centres of our life, the oil supply, the money supply, and when it's all falling apart they take over. They're only doing what their religion says, doing what their great leader Mohammed did and told them to do. And because they think they'll get a great reward in heaven for it, they don't care how many people they kill in the process.'

Frank took another drink and I looked at him, so old, so full of fear and hate. But did he have a point? What would Jane have said to him? 'Frank, don't you think you're exaggerating? Didn't most of them come here simply to have a better life?'

'Pash knew what they were about – he grew up among them. His aim in life was to warn the rest of us. They got to him before he could publish. But I know, and I'm not afraid to speak out.'

Frank looked around warily. Why was he telling me all this? 'You said that Tariq was tied up with a few extremists like this?'

'Extremists? They got one thing right, they say they are just being true to their religion and they are. I've gone into this, the Koran, there's a chilling read if ever you want one.'

'Frank, you do seem to have heard just one very extreme view.'

'I know what happened in Egypt, in Armenia, in Ethiopia. There's never been a peaceful take-over yet. They just keep attacking until there's no option.'

'But you can't just say "they" as if they were all the same – any more than you can for the extremists in Northern Ireland.'

'The only way to stop them is to fight them. That's all they understand. Draw a line. Tell them they'll be blown to pieces if they pass it and hold the line. That's all you can do. That's what stopped them in Spain and in India. Nothing else is any use. And what are our pansies in government doing? "Come in, come in. Come as far as you want!" '

Part of me wanted to shout, 'For God's sake, stop being so paranoid!' But this was a battle that Frank would never let me win, and It was Tariq I wanted to talk about.

'You said he left this group?'

'He tried to, poor idiot. Do you think they ever let people just walk away? That's the great crime, apostasy. Traitors deserve to die.'

Frank looked me in the eye. He had made his point. I kept quiet, letting him know I understood the significance of what he had said. As I focused on this insight, all around me seemed to go quieter. I spoke softly.

'What did Tariq tell you about all this?'

'He said he had found a better way. He'd been thinking about some of the things his father had taught him. There was another way. So he wanted to stop funding the group and let them go their own way while he went his.'

'You mentioned a standing order that he had cancelled.'

'There's probably something like that somewhere. That's what he did though, I'm sure. He had his better way and they didn't like it.'

I stared at Frank, not quite believing what he had just said. Was his evidence was just a wild surmise, as wild as his vitriolic diatribes? 'You're not sure about the standing order? You haven't seen anything?'

Frank didn't respond to my hardly veiled incredulity. He wagged at me with his finger and carried on insistently. 'I just know how that family operate, they don't like to do things in an underhand way, never have done. He was giving money, so it must have gone through the bank.'

How much of Frank's tirade was just him adding up strangely, two plus two in his eyes making nine, with no hard evidence to go by? No wonder Phil Wittle treated me with caution. I had to challenge him.

'If you're serious about this, Frank, and you seem to be very serious, you know what you're doing is making an allegation of attempted murder? It's the police you should be talking to, not me.'

'And do you think they'd pay any attention to an old crackpot like me with a bee in his bonnet? They'll charge me with disturbing the peace, saying all these hard truths about the Moslems. You make sure they're looking in the right direction, that's enough. Mohammed trusts you so I think you must be OK. He knows people well enough.'

'I might need to take you along with me. They aren't likely to listen to second-hand information either.'

'They'll trust you more than me. They don't want the likes of me messing up their community relations. They really wouldn't be too comfortable interviewing me. They'd just want me to go home and leave them to their cosy ideas, multiethnic I think they call it now.' Frank shivered and looked round. He seemed to be afraid someone was listening, even here, and would report him for political uncorrectness.

This was another brick wall. 'If I wanted to check these things out, Frank, what could I do? Is there anyone I could talk to about this?'

Frank raised an eyebrow and looked at me with a faint sneering kind of smile. 'It's true enough. Just look at the Koran and you'll see it all. I don't suppose you've ever read that have you?'

'My wife knows it better than I do, and she's quite impressed how similar it is to the Bible.' This was an exaggeration but I had to make a point somehow.

Frank leaned forward and raised his fist. 'Listen! The Germans ban *Mein Kampf* - too dangerous. This is Mohammed's version, but because it's been around for years people think it's just a nice religious book.'

I shook my head, but couldn't think of anything more to say. Frank carried on, like a sneering rat with a platform. 'Religion! It pretends to be nice, but it ends up trying to take over, by force, whenever it can. If you don't care about what's really going on here, I'll just have to find someone else to help.'

Something erupted inside me. Heat flared in my chest and the words boiled out. 'Frank! This whole business has torn my heart in goodness knows how many pieces. There's a lad I've known since he was a toddler, the kindest, gentlest boy I've ever known, and he's the prime suspect for murder. He didn't do it, he can't have done it, he can't possibly have. Somehow, God knows how, I'm in the middle of it all and everyone's talking to me and there's no one who knows what to think, least of all me. But I am not going to see Jason's life ruined because some people can't be bothered to think further than they can see and some people are too afraid to speak up, Frank!'

I slapped my hands on the table, pushed myself upright and walked out without looking back. If I was confused before, now it was worse. If Frank was refusing to talk to the police, it must mean that he was afraid they would see through him for the old bigot he was. I felt embarrassed for having listened to him at

Mohammed's and shouted at myself in the car for rushing in too quickly again. I just wanted to get away from Frank and his bilious ranting so I could think clearly again. The drive home was slow and wet. Jane's car was on the drive and, on balance, I was grateful, for if I kept thinking about all this by myself I would just spiral with every wind of suspicion and fear.

Jane was kindness itself when I walked through the door. Her bright voice called from the kitchen. 'Dinner will ready in half an hour. Why don't you go and have a bath while you're waiting?' I went in to hug her waist as she stood at the cooker. 'I'd rather have a drink and talk with you.' I looked out a bottle of Côtes du Rhone from our holiday stock-up, poured two glasses and explained where I had been. As I recounted Frank's venomous attitude Jane was looking worried. 'He's no right to be saying those things. Mohammed's been very good to him, keeping him in the family and respecting him like that.' We agreed that he was so caught up in his own world of enemies and threats that he was at least unreliable as a witness to anything. Jane reassured me that Phil would overlook my hasty attempt to tell the police how to do their job.

'I talked with the Archdeacon. He has a lovely voice; he ought to be doing radio plays or adverts. All fruity and warm with bass notes that vibrate inside you – well maybe not inside you David!'

I blasted a few bars of deep bass humming and Jane winced with a smile. Singing is not my strength.

Jane carried on with enthusiasm. 'Anyway, he was very helpful too. He said that the most important thing is to handle the press. They will need copies of everything we can give them, the order of service, the address, the prayers.' She noticed my face reacting as if to a whiff of manure. 'Don't worry. I'll have a word with everyone this evening or tomorrow morning and make sure that they know. Paul won't mind; he's so organised.'

'You're doing a great job.' My mind wasn't really able to take in the details.

'Then there just have to be agreements about where the press sit, where they stand outside church. He said it's a good idea to keep them on one side of the path into church so that Patricia and the family don't feel surrounded as they have to walk through the barrage of cameras. Then there's parking, but I expect you can sort that out with the men as usual.'

'Thanks, Jane. That's brilliant – a weight off my mind.' I was more than happy to let her take charge of the arrangements for the press, and realised that there was enough time tomorrow to set up the parking arrangements. 'What about the petals, though, what's happening with that?'

'I've been with Patricia to a couple of florists and there's really no problem. We want some good flowers in the church, so when they come and set those up, they'll bring the petals and a big glass bowl and even some rose scent to add in.'

'Easy when you know how!'

'Then it's up to Paul to work out how people drop the petals into the coffin. The only thing that would be a bit tasteless, to say the least, would be any filming of the body itself. We'll just make sure they know that that's off limits. You wouldn't think that most people needed telling, but nowadays you never know.'

I felt knots release inside me - it was all working out so smoothly, and I felt foolish again for worrying.

'You've seen Patricia today?'

'Yes, I told you I would call round there again in case there was anything I could help with. There's something I need to tell you about that, but I don't want you to take it the wrong way, now David.' This was indeed a warning. I tried to perk up and look alert, but I was wondering if my brain could take anything else.

'It's just that Meg is now saying that she doesn't think she'll come to the funeral. Patricia's distraught of course, but Meg's just gone off back to Wales.'

'What? The blooming petals, pardon the pun, were all her idea. What's her excuse? Why doesn't she want to see her sister's body now?'

'Calm down, David. She'll probably change her mind again. You just have to let her be dramatic for a day or so, that's all.'

'What did she tell her mother? Or did she just walk off without an explanation saying "see you when I see you"?'

'She's just not sure she can cope with all the media razzmatazz. They lead quite a simple life in the commune, and she doesn't want to feed the media empire any more private scenes to make a profit for the likes of Murdoch.'

I shook my head in exasperation. 'Excuses!'

Jane looked at me sternly. 'Well, I can't help sympathising with her, David.' She then softened a little. 'I wonder too if she thinks that she would just row with her mother about what to wear and how to behave and thinks that it would just be a lot better for everyone if she kept a distance. They'll have some sort of celebration at the commune, burning a symbolic body or something like that.'

I didn't know what to think. It seemed like another example of the mad selfishness of the girl, but I couldn't help also wondering if she was avoiding something. There could be other reasons why it would be too difficult for her to attend her own sister's funeral. Guilt would certainly make her pretty uncomfortable. But Jane had warned me not to jump to conclusions, so this would have to be kept to myself. What would be the motive for Meg to have such a violent go at her sister, or at her sister's boyfriend? If someone had tampered with the car, they must have known how dangerous it was. Why would Meg want to do something so extreme? But then she was the most impulsive person I had ever met, and she did hate what her sister was doing, the world she was becoming part of. I was too tired to work it out any more.

Dinner was quiet. The children had theirs in front of the television and Jane and I sat in the kitchen not saying much. Suddenly there was a shout from the front room. 'Dad, it's *Midlands News* and it's Jason.' I rushed through in time to hear the reporter say 'Charges are expected to be brought tomorrow before the funeral on Thursday.' The picture was of Jason looking dazed as he was led into the back door of a police station. I hung my head in my hands and stared at the screen. If Meg was an unlikely murderer and Frank was wildly exaggerating, had Jason really found a jealous anger inside himself which was more powerful than I had wanted to imagine?

Thinking like this I didn't know if I ought to talk with Will and Jennifer but I couldn't help wanting to commiserate with them. Their phone was either engaged or on the answering machine constantly, in between Jane making her calls to alert people to the need to provide a copy of what they were to say so it could be duplicated on Thursday morning. In the end Jane decided that we had better just go round again. 'They need to see us, not just have a few words tossed at them through the telephone.'

The drive was looking more untidy than I had ever seen it, with leaves in soggy clumps and the roses showing mostly dead heads. We stood at the door, waiting, until Jennifer peered out of a side window, gave an attempt at a smile and then came to open the door. Jane simply reached out her arms and hugged her, as I stood for a while wondering what to do. Sometimes its easier being a woman. I wasn't American enough to imagine doing the same thing with Will, however much I wanted to. There was no need to be worried as Will was settled firmly in his blue armchair and hardly looked up as we came in. Jennifer wiped her eyes and, snuffling, picked up tissues from a box on the settee. Will had a glass in his hand, nearly empty. We stood still for a while, waiting. It seemed that they were waiting for us to say something.

Jane looked at me. 'We just wanted to see how you were. You must be... Jason is... It's not looking good I'm... I 'm sorry I don't know what to say.'

'Oh, just sit down,' said Will with some exasperation. 'We know it's bloody awful and there doesn't seem anything anyone can do about it.'

Jennifer shook herself a little and offered us a drink. She took Will's glass and I asked for whatever he was drinking, which looked like bitter. The least I could do was to keep him company. Jane went with Jennifer into the kitchen.

'It's not the end yet, Will. They'll find out who really did it eventually.' I so much wanted to reassure Will.

'Oh yeah? They won't even be looking now that they've pinned it on Jason. Too much like hard work to think beyond their noses. Bloody stupid for even thinking they would make an effort.'

'I know they're making charges but that's mostly just to keep people happy. They're still investigating. Believe me.'

'You really think they would face all the hassle of being accused of bringing false charges unless they were damned sure?' Will looked at me as though I was telling him he had won a fortune in a spurious prize draw. 'Dream on.'

My stomach lurched again. It wasn't an easy thing to do to bring charges. Will was right. Had Phil just been humouring me at the police station? Where would we go from here? We sat in silence for a while, looking at the same black storm cloud.

'Who do you have acting for Jason?'

'Paul Feeny. Do you know him?'

'Don't know him but I've heard of him. A bit if a bruiser they say. Probably a good man to take on a fight like this.' Feeny had worked in London for a while before joining a Birmingham firm, something to do with his wife's family who are well established here. He had a good degree from Bristol, but he hid it by being unsophisticated, especially with his criminal clients. He was doing well, they said.

'Blunt and to the point. Doesn't think we have a cat's chance. But says he'll fight it all the way. I'd drop him tomorrow. What's the point of having someone who's heart isn't in it?'

'He can still put up a good fight.'

'Jason likes him and won't drop him. That's probably gloom. He's just resigned to his fate. That's all he says, poor lad.'

'Feeny's not told you outright that there's no chance has he? I can't believe any solicitor, certainly not him, would throw in the towel at the beginning.'

'He's just made it very plain that Jason's the prime suspect and he'll do what he can, but he's not promising anything. In other words, there's no chance. He doesn't care. He'll have a fee whatever happens. Lazy bastard.'

I let the last comment go as the sort of 'Will-ism' that I might expect. 'You'll have a barrister for the actual case, and he'll have more impact on the outcome than anyone.' My heart wouldn't let me throw in the towel yet, either. 'Believe me there are people working on this still, looking into it from all angles. Jason's going to be OK.'

Will looked at me aghast. 'Believe you! Who do you think you are, God almighty!' He leapt to his feet and clenched his fists as he leant towards me, spitting out angry words. 'What the hell have you done, you and all the fucking lawyers? No wonder Jesus couldn't stand you lot. Always a smooth explanation, always an excuse, always a bland word that means bloody nothing and doesn't commit you to anything. You just stand at a distance and make money out of other people's misery.' Will looked over his shoulder at Jennifer and Jane coming quickly in from the kitchen. 'We'd be better off without bloody lawyers. Sorry David.' He collapsed back into his chair and went quiet.

Jennifer looked at him angrily, like a mother who has told her toddler that they have had their last chance. 'I'll just fetch the drinks, then.'

Once again, I had no idea what to say. Will and I sat in morbid silence while the women talked. Jason was going to be charged tomorrow, after which he might well be able to come home. This seemed unlikely to me but it was what Feeny had said and I couldn't take this bit of hope away from them.

Jason still wasn't saying much, just that he knew Lizzie and had loved her very deeply and couldn't quite face life without her. He had always hoped that she would return to him, that they would regain the simple joy of being together, like when they had first met. That was all. Most of the questions he didn't answer. He just said he couldn't remember and he was sure it would all come back one day. But he just couldn't think now. He couldn't remember why he had driven to the woods that day. He couldn't remember if he had seen Tariq's car before. He couldn't remember where he had been earlier on the day of the accident. He just sat dazed, still, saying that he couldn't remember. When Will pleaded with him, shouted at him that he had to remember as he was digging himself a hole in prison, Jason looked blankly again and said that he just couldn't remember. All he could think about was Lizzie, and that was all he wanted to think about.

It did all sound like denial, no doubt about that. Jason almost seemed to be doing his best to convince people that he really had done it. But why? He couldn't have. Not Jason. He was so soft and always had been. At camp he would never sleep outside the tent. He was vegetarian and frightened of spiders. Jason couldn't have done this. The more I heard, the more my head understood what other people were thinking, but the more certain I was that they were wrong. Jason just couldn't have attacked anyone, not even 'only' interfering with a car. He was a lazy wimp sometimes, but this kind of calculating malice just wasn't in him. Who did have it in him though? The more it went on, the more the police would find evidence to back up what they were thinking. 'Building a case' was what they called it. Phil may have been genuine when he said that he was looking elsewhere, but there were many others whose job now was simply to make a case against Jason, and they would all want to earn their bonuses. Perhaps Will's depression was catching.

The women managed to talk until the drinks were finished. Then, as Will and I still sat in morose silence, they told us that we were no good for anything and needed to be tucked up. I nodded in cheerful resignation and was glad soon to be driving home with Jane.

'What's the sleuth been thinking now?' Jane asked me unexpectedly.

'How do you know I've been thinking anything?'

'It's when you're just quiet, nodding, then shaking your head from time to time, pursing your lips. Pretty obvious that there's some electrical activity going on under your beautifully thinning hair.'

'You have a lovely way with words sometimes.'

'Flattery doesn't get you out of answering the question. What have you been thinking? From the preponderance of shaking over nodding, I surmise that you still don't think Jason did it?'

'Nope. I just can't take that in. Other people seem to have it firmly in their heads, but my mind just won't take it. No. He can't have done it.'

'I think you have a rather nice mind – for a lawyer.' Jane grinned as she turned the corner into our street. 'Keep going as you are. It won't do anyone any harm, and it might do some good. Who knows?'

This faintly reassuring thought was still with me as I went to sleep, wondering how I was going to find out more about Tariq's connections with unlikely Moslem terrorists in Birmingham. Who would know more about all this? And have access to his bank records? Mohammed had seen far too much of me with nothing to show for it, but I couldn't think of who else to talk to.

Wednesday

I woke up early with a strange dream on my mind, even weirder than usual. I was looking at a big old Austin Cambridge, when another one drove up all by itself. There was no driver in either so I went to investigate the second car. I climbed into the passenger seat and found that I was in the engine, with cables and metal parts all around me. There were two of everything. Fuel was dripping from a grimy part with red and blue leads, presumably a fuel pump. Overhead were two giant spark plugs which had become free and were shooting sparks over my head, falling all around me. I suddenly realised that a spark was going to land in the dripping petrol and I would be a goner.

Desperately I looked round for something, anything, to stop the fuel in time. The sparks were arcing closer and closer. Then a firework appeared. I almost went berserk, seeing that in there with sparks falling all around it, but, as I was about to throw it away, I saw that the label said 'emits cloud'. I put it to one side and carried on looking for something to stop the leaking petrol. Suddenly the engine started, and the parts all around me began to whirl. A strange monkey-like hand reached down and took hold of the spark plugs, moving them closer to me and to the leaking fuel pump. I had no idea who this strange hand belonged to. The sparks were still falling, coming closer and closer, and there was nothing I could do to stop them. I tried to go over to the fuel pump, but I was stuck in the whirring engine. A couple of sparks looked as though they were going to hit the fuel pump, but they passed by on the far side of me. One or two hit the leads. It was only a matter of time. The monkey's hand pushed the spark plugs closer still. Just as I was losing all hope that something could be done, there was a sudden burst of sparks, falling all through the engine. One hit the firework and I knew that that was it.

The firework fizzed and spluttered. Smoke started pouring out of the top of it, more and more smoke, denser and denser. A think cloud spread under me. It covered the floor of the engine, and everything began to quieten down. Chains and cables disappeared under the cloud. The fuel pump was engulfed. The sparks were still falling but the cloud absorbed them and took the power from them. They were lost in the damp cloud and could do no damage. A huge relief swept over me and I crumpled and fell backwards.

The cloud reached up to me and I found to my surprise that it was warm, like a warm bed rising up from underneath me. I was lifted up, higher and higher. As the cloud came close to the spark plugs, the monkey's hand drew back smartly. The spark plugs themselves were engulfed in cloud, and I was still being lifted up above it all. Soon all I could see was cloud underneath me, while I was resting in sunshine. It was bright and calm, like in an aeroplane above the clouds. I thought I could stay and rest there forever. I promptly woke up, wanting only to return to the sunshine above the cloud.

I stretched and wondered where Jane was. It was unusual for her to be up before me, especially as it was still early. Soon she came in and smiled, asking me if I would like a cup of tea. I accepted this unusual offer and sat and mused with my hands warmed by the familiar cup. Going to see Mohammed, or at least talking with him, seemed the only thing I could do.

My Bible reading was familiar, Psalm 23 again. The commentator did manage to say something new though, that the first mark of God being our Shepherd is that we find ourselves having to lie down. Often we rush through the first verse and think that he makes us lie down in green pastures. But it says that he leads us in green pastures. Before that, it says simply that he makes us lie down. This was a new and strange thought. 'Let him make you lie down and rest. It was a command of Jesus that people who are tired and carrying heavy burdens should come to him and rest – a command, not an invitation. So we need to obey this command and let him lead us to rest, to lying down. When you have the opportunity, lie down and let Jesus be your shepherd, just being with you and giving you rest.'

I have never been a go-getting type, and lying in bed, savouring the tea I had just drunk, I wasn't in any mood to leap out of bed. This was an excuse too good to miss. I lay there, thinking again of the cloud that I had seen in my dream, and wondering what the engine was all about. It didn't seem to matter much, as the cloud had made it all safe again.

As I lay there I could just about picture that cloud, spreading itself all around under me, as far as I could see, while I was in the bright sunshine. The cloud rose in little tufts and peaks, like whisked egg white from which someone has pulled a spoon. In one place the cloud seemed to be separating, thinning out by itself, and then a stage rose up through the cloud with a band playing on it. It was a lament, a sad, sad song which made your heart weep. I found that there were tears trailing down my cheeks, not many but a few. Yet I knew that the sad powerful music was all right, it was meant to be. The musicians stopped and took a bow and then sat down again. Suddenly in the middle of them I could see Frank and he was crying too, crying freely, tears streaming out of his face, but with a kind of peaceful smile which I had never seen on him. He looked relaxed and reassured, as though everything was now going to be all right. The music had released something in him and he was now fine.

I wondered if I was somehow meant to go and see Frank again. But I couldn't exactly take an orchestra with me, and I had no desire to bear the brunt of another of his rants about religion. He wasn't so important anyway. The important thing was to find out what had happened to Tariq and poor Lizzie. The thought of Jason trapped in prison, wasting his life in misery and constantly picked on by the real thugs, was just too much for me. The only lead I could think of was with those fundamentalist friends of Tariq. If I could somehow get closer to them, then maybe I could get closer to the truth of it all. I stirred myself, kicked off the duvet, knocked my cup and saucer onto the floor, and headed for a swift shave and shower. Facing people like this felt like going into uncharted territory, or even, - I thought with some excitement - walking on water, as Peter did in the storm with Jesus. There was certainly a storm blowing and this was no time to be sitting snugly in the boat when there was danger around. I was going to step out, and do something brave.

Jane was downstairs sitting with her Bible for a change. I didn't think she did this much. 'I was just thinking about the funeral. It seems such an important day, and I don't know how Paul copes. He has to get this just right or else the media will slap him for it so publicly. Could we just spend some time in prayer for it all? To be honest we don't have to say anything, but if we could just sit quietly together and each pray for the funeral, I think it would somehow make me feel better.'

'That's a nice idea, Jane, and I am really grateful you have taken on organising that end of things. Paul's more competent than you think – years of experience of funerals. He's a professional. I don't think you need to worry about that! Could we do this later? I need to get out as soon as I can as I think I can see what to do next.'

'Maybe it's just me, David, but this feels like.., quite important. It's certainly the most important thing I've been involved in for a while and it is what Paul asked for help with. Look, why don't I ask Beryl and a few others to come round this morning and pray for tomorrow? You can join us if you're around, but if you're busy with other things we'll manage without you.'

The thought of having to sit while Beryl came up with more sweet nothings made going out to Mohammed's and picking up a trail from there quite attractive. I was beginning to enjoy this walking on water business. I had no idea where it would all lead, but I was now up and moving and that in itself felt hugely better than sitting with some old biddies worrying about a funeral service.

'That's a good idea. I'll join you if I can, but do give them my apologies. You could also pray for me as I go ahead with my investigations.' If only I hadn't been so quick to put down my Bible.

Jane raised an eyebrow at me and smiled. Soon I was out of the house and on my way to Mohammed's.

He wasn't in and Philippa had no idea where he was or what he was doing. I sat defeated on the settee in Philippa's office. On another day I would probably have felt too deflated and come back home to wait for a phone call from Mohammed. But today I was determined that I was going to get to the bottom of whatever was in Frank's mind. It could be all nonsense, of course, but somehow I didn't think so. And the only person apart from Mohammed who knew anything about these Moslem warriors was Tariq. And the only person who could give me the key to getting in to talk with Tariq was Philippa. This walking on water business was more exciting than I had thought.

There was more urgency in me as I tackled Philippa. The thought flashed in my mind of Philippa enjoying a fast ride on her horse. I thought I could give her a good ride myself! Sexy thoughts like this didn't come to me too often, and I was always half ashamed of them and half excited by them. I smiled and looked to see where I could get with her. It was amazing how quickly all this went through my head, far more quickly than it takes to write it down.

There she was, surrounded by maroon walls, sitting behind the large dark desk with the long brass lamp making her papers glow and shining back up towards me. She had dark tights on her firm legs and her hair shone smoothly like a television advert. Taking an interest in women, I thought, has often been a good way of softening them up.

'What do you have on today then?'

Philippa raised her eyebrows at me and put down her pen. She put her hand on the front of her cream blouse. 'Not a lot,' she said huskily. She smiled. 'What about you? Are you after me, or something else?'

This was either much faster and looser than I had expected, or I had met someone who just enjoyed turning the tables on me. I was supposed to be the one asking the questions and being interested, so as to get her to tell me what I wanted to know: how to get to see Tariq again so he could point me to his old buddies.

'Mohammed's been asking me to follow up some leads on what might have happened to Tariq's car. That's the main thing, but it is a pretty big thing. There's a lot at stake here. I could do with an assistant.'

'You make it sound very exciting, David. Are you some sort of free detective masquerading as a stodgy lawyer?'

'Not so much a detective – certainly not like in the films or on TV!' I paused a little so that the connection I had just denied wanting to make could indeed be made. 'It's more like being a crusading French lawyer, an investigating magistrate who has to actively seek out the criminals instead of just sitting back and waiting for someone else to bring them before him.' This was a new thought to me too but I was grateful for it.

'So I would be the glamorous and faithful assistant to a handsome Gauloises-smoking official sleuth? I would smooth his brow and maybe more?' She opened her eyes wide at me and pushed her lips forward tentatively.

'I could certainly use some help in what would be a very important matter for Mohammed and maybe for all of us.' I was beginning to feel a little flustered and at the time couldn't think why.

'Well, I didn't have much in the way of breakfast – it doesn't appeal when you're eating on your own every day. Why don't we pop round to the Victoria for a coffee and croissant and you could fill me in?' I felt flattered that this rather exciting woman wanted to spend time with me. It made me feel bigger than Mohammed, taking his woman out from under him.

I simply stood up and said 'Sounds good to me.'

It was warm enough for us not to be wearing coats as we went into the dining room of the Victoria hotel. The waiter looked at us and asked what room number we were in. Philippa smiled a conspiratorial smile at me before turning back to him and telling him that we were just there for breakfast.

We sat down at a small round table tucked into the back of the dining room, with a thick cotton tablecloth and gleaming cutlery. Just as I was about to thank her for agreeing to help me with my concerns, Philippa spoke out appealingly.

'David, you don't know what a pleasure this is, the beginning of many I hope. Breakfast in intelligent company. I have thought for a while that I would like to get to know you better.'

'I don't know quite how much we'll be seeing of each other after all this is over. Mohammed may well decide that he needs a sharper lawyer.'

'Now, David, don't put yourself down.' Philippa looked me in the face, pouting her lips a little. 'You have many good strong points I'm sure. You're not the sort of man who dawdles through the morning in his dressing gown eating porridge. Here you are making me work with you first thing in the morning. If he ever finds out, I think Mohammed will actually be rather impressed.'

'It's kind of you to say so, Philippa, although I do have to admit to being rather partial to porridge.'

She briefly pulled a gently mocking face. 'But I know you can handle a good strong cup of coffee. What are you having with me? A good large juicy sausage with a couple of plump mushrooms would fill me up nicely.'

'Scrambled eggs with some grilled tomato are more close to how I feel now.'

We ordered and the waiter brought us some juice and coffee. Neither of us wanted cereal, going straight to the main course. I thought I had better try Plan A again, taking an interest to help her to be open to what I wanted.

'You're an experienced equestrian, aren't you?'

She laughed. 'It's only posh commentators who use that word now. Yes I'm into horses, have been since childhood. It's a good way to relax. Working with a large animal, making it go along under you while you know that it has the power to throw you on your back. It's pleasing and vaguely thrilling at the same time. How about you? How do you get your kicks?'

'Badminton for exercise. The family keep me pretty busy and occupied otherwise, and they've been known to kick me from time to time. And there's church. That can be er... stretching shall we say.'

Philippa grimaced again a little. 'Families are wonderful sometimes. They're like the British weather. All that cloud and rain is necessary and useful, but we all need the occasional break somewhere warm and hot. Don't you think so?'

I wasn't sure where this was going but carried on merrily. 'A break in the sunshine might just dry things up nicely. These last days I've been feeling that I'm in a kind of fog. Some bright sunshine would be very welcome!'

Philippa looked seriously at me and smiled. 'I'll see what I can do to give you an atmosphere to have a break in.' She raised her eyebrows. 'We don't have much time now, but I could make myself available for you later too. See how we get on now.'

'There's really just one thing I need at the moment. My role seems to be to investigate what really happened in that car crash. It certainly wasn't just an accident, and it wasn't a lover's jealous revenge either, I'm pretty sure of that.'

Philippa nodded trustingly. I carried on. 'Now Mohammed mentioned that some friends of Tariq had recently had a disagreement with him, rather a serious disagreement it seems. I think that needs investigating. But the police seem stuck on their loony lover theory and, to be honest, I think they're scared stiff of inflaming the radical Moslems. They think that if they start hinting that they have suspicions about those people, someone will just cry foul and have them up before the race relations board or whoever.'

Philippa sighed and shook her head sympathetically. 'So you just have to do it.'

'No one else is going to do anything now! Time's running out. There doesn't seem to be anyone else doing anything useful about this whole business. Not wanting to be dramatic about it all, but it does seem to be up to me, and I need to act soon or it will be too late.'

'Yes, I can see. What do you need to know?'

'These friends of Tariq's. How can I get hold of them? I just want to meet them and ask a couple of pertinent questions.

Somehow I think that I'll be able to tell if this is where the spotlight needs shining. All those trials listening to criminals squirming give you a pretty good idea of who's guilty and who isn't. So if there is something there to be investigated, I'll make jolly sure that it really is uncovered.'

Philippa smiled again. 'I'm really glad you're taking this on, David. It's Peter Strang and his mob you're talking about isn't it?'

I nodded with surprised vigour and took a good swig of coffee.

Philippa leant towards me, putting her hand on the white tablecloth near my saucer. 'It's time these people came under proper scrutiny. They've needed checking out for a while now. I think I can help you there.'

I put down my cup near Philippa's hand and kept hold of it, fingering the rim. 'You're an angel in disguise!' I said warmly.

Philippa looked coyly at me and paused. 'You go and see what you think. But it's not a straightforward matter. I wouldn't want you to go jumping to wrong conclusions from lack of experience with these guys.'

I tapped the top of my cup. 'Experience comes in all shapes and sizes,' I said, a little incoherently.

'You need to meet them for yourself. You'll also need to talk about it afterwards with someone with some experience. I've known these guys for longer. So if I tell you how to contact them, you'll agree to come and talk it through with me before you do anything else. OK?' She raised the fingers of her hand towards me.

At the time it seemed like an excellent idea, more than I had been looking for. Not only did I get straight to the suspects without bothering Tariq, but I had someone with whom I could talk it all through. Without Philippa all I had was Jane and she was taken up with arranging the funeral. At the time…

'You want us to debrief together, as the Americans say? You've got yourself a deal, baby!' I clasped her hand.

Philippa smiled and slid her hand out of mine. 'It'll have to be back at my place.' She raised her eyebrows again. 'Debriefing at 6.30. With us together we'll turn up the heat. On those guys of course! Thanks for having me on board, captain.'

Early evening was probably going to cause all sorts of problems with Jane and the family, but there were more important things on offer here. I assured Philippa that I would see her at her canalside flat. She told me in remarkable detail where I could find Peter Strang, and we finished off our breakfast in the thrill of being new companions on an adventure. I did feel pretty warm inside, neck tingling with the heat, and a headache beginning to appear at the back of my head.

The walk to the car cooled me down but the headache kept nagging. I felt that time was short and sped off to the first place she had said I could track down Peter Strang, a shop selling electric musical equipment in which he was apparently a partner. As luck would have it, there were a couple of parking spaces free 150 yards from the shop, by a parking meter that was out of action. Not only did I not have to circle for ages looking for a free space, I didn't have to pay!

A wide sliding door led into a room with rows of guitars on the wall and keyboards standing waiting for someone to try chopsticks on them. To the left of the door was a payment counter enclosed in glass. I asked the young Asian man behind the glass if Peter Strang was in and could I see him please. He thought for a while and then a penny seemed to drop. He seemed surprised that anyone was asking after Peter, and said that he didn't know if he was there or not. He phoned someone else, spoke in Gujarati, and then smiled back at me. 'He should be coming in very much shortly. Please look at our store while you are waiting.'

There weren't any chairs visible so I wandered around looking for one. The shop smelt of new plastic and packaging which didn't do my headache any good. I went down a narrow staircase to a basement full of amplifiers and various black electrical boxes. The basement seemed bigger than the shop upstairs, several areas half divided by brick walls with a low brick ceiling curved in places. There was a chair here, a dining chair type in black plastic so, after nipping upstairs to tell the man in the kiosk where I was, I sat down for a while. I tapped my feet and pushed my tongue around my teeth. I remembered reading a column in the *Observer* a while ago in which the writer lamented the waste of waiting, while saying that the only people who don't mind waiting must be vicars, who can just catch up on their praying. 'I'm no vicar, I'll just have to sit it out,' I told myself ruefully. Solicitors have a fair amount of waiting to do in court, waiting for cases, waiting for reports and judgements, but I have never mastered the art of waiting patiently.

I wanted to get up and wander around. The electric lights made a perfect greenhouse for my headache to grow. A few more people came into the basement, looking knowledgeable and excited. I hoped they would stay away from me. Rap music started filling the air, not too loud at first. I tried to work out what the words were, but failed. My throat was becoming dry and my stomach rumbling from trying to digest an unaccustomed second breakfast. I was no hobbit! The pain kept clawing at the back of my head, even louder now. I looked at my watch for the fifth time. I had been there twenty-five minutes. Suddenly an amplified voice joined in raucously with whatever the rap was. I winced as the pain in my head shouted for the noise to stop. I left my torture chair swiftly to remind the lad upstairs that I had not gone away.

Walking up the steps now jarred my head. It was beginning to look like aspirin was needed. Upstairs was brighter, with sunshine streaming through the wide doors. I screwed up my eyes, wincing again. The kiosk was empty and there was no sign of the young man. A girl was putting out a new guitar.

'Where's that lad who was sitting in there?' I asked abruptly.

'Samjay? He's not meant to be here, got his shift wrong. Can I help you?'

'He told me categorically that Peter Strang would be coming in half an hour ago. I need to see him rather urgently.'

'I'm new here, I don't know many people's names. Ask in the office if you like.'

'And where is this mysterious office? Three stories up a winding staircase?'

The girl was surprisingly accepting of my rudeness. 'Oh no, it's just next to the stock room downstairs. Ask anyone down there, they'll show you.'

That hi tech dungeon was the last place I wanted to go to. I thought of going outside, at least for a break, but I had wasted enough time.

My head jarred even more with each step back down into the infernal rap music, the fluorescent lights and the smell of plastic. I looked round to see an office door or a stockroom. There were three different ante-rooms off the main area, and I couldn't see a door out of any of them. There was a man in a black polo shirt with the company logo standing with a customer looking at an amplifier. I hung around waiting to catch him. They were standing under one of the loudspeakers. The beat thumped inside my head and I had to butt in.

'Excuse me! Where's the office?'

The customer looked back sharply at me and I just caught the salesman raise his eyebrows at him. 'Through there,' he said pointing behind his left shoulder. 'Turn right and it's straight ahead.'

I charged out, hoping that the so-called music would be quieter in the next area. It wasn't, of course. A shop selling PA equipment had the whole floor wired up perfectly. But round to the right there was a single door next to a double door. I knocked at the single door and went through.

It opened out to another door. The second one was heavy glass and the walls were suddenly no longer bare brick, but covered with polystyrene sound insulation. It was quiet, so quiet that you could think you had stepped into a church. But it was bright, the white walls glaring over a shocking orange carpet. My head thumped its pain into the stillness, beating with my heart beat.

This room seemed empty at first, but I then realised that ahead there was a turning to the right. Sure enough, there was a desk with a large spiky green plant standing next to it, a chair pushed back, a few papers, a telephone and a laptop. I stood by the chair waiting again. This was not going to be my day for quickly getting through anything. I tapped on the desk and rubbed my head and looked around. Eventually a prim older woman with a thin sharp face and heavy glasses, wearing a grey trouser suit, came out of a door behind the desk.

'What do you want? This is a private area, you know.' She scowled. 'The salesmen outside can deal with any request you care to give them.'

'Look, I'm sorry. It's not a shopping request I have. I was told that I could come here and find Peter Strang? Can I see him, please?'

'Peter is not available at the moment. He is a very busy man, with much to do.' She spoke in a rush, like a harassed schoolteacher. 'He has a full schedule for this morning. I suggest that you ring his PA at the other office and see if you can arrange a meeting another day.'

I bit my tongue. 'Could you just take him a message, now?' I paused to check that this request was not completely against the local rulebook. 'It's not to do with business, more personal, and I do think he will want to talk. Can you just say that Mohammed Khan's solicitor wants to se him concerning Tariq?'

Slowly the woman wrote down, in long hand, speaking out each word as she wrote 'Mr. Mohammed Khan's solicitor wants to see you concerning Tariq. That's it. That's what I am supposed to take to him now? Are you sure this can't wait for another time?' She held the paper in her hand, hesitating.

'Today, now. I need to talk with him today.' At the time I was aware that I was exaggerating a bit. The only reason I needed to talk today was to satisfy my own need to be doing something, and so that I could have something to report when I saw Philippa later. There was not much point in being a crusading investigator if I was not willing to be pushy from time to time. Today was a day to be very pushy, or so I thought.

She looked hard at me. 'I think it would better if I gave him this message after he has finished the meeting he is in now. Could you give me a telephone number where he can contact you to arrange a meeting?'

'For God's sake, just go and take him the message! I've been waiting for over an hour already. This is important. More important than you realise. Just give him the message, won't you?'

The woman jerked back her head, breathed out sharply and lectured, 'There's no need to bring God onto your side! Wait here.'

She turned and went back through the door. A few seconds later she reappeared and silently handed me the piece of paper. It looked just like it had when she was writing it, but as I looked more closely someone had scribbled '3.15' to one side. 'He will fit you in this afternoon, Mr. Jeffery. Until then…'

'Thank you!' I barked abruptly, turned and stalked out. It was only when I was outside in the grey drizzle that I realised that she knew my name. It was unsettling. James Bond is always the one to pronounce his name when he wants to, which gives him power over the enemy. If they knew my name, what else did they know about me? I could imagine my Peter telling me not to be so ridiculously melodramatic, and I suddenly felt very small and very stupid. What did I think I was playing at here? I dragged myself to the car and found a plastic bag attached to the windscreen. With a sick feeling inside I pulled it off and sat in the car reading my sentence. £45 for using a parking meter that was out of use. I almost wanted to cry. At least I could get this dealt with at the office and Jane need never know.

That thought made the office seem more attractive than going home. Part of me very much wanted some tea and sympathy from Jane, but I was afraid she would not understand what I had been up to. Rose's tea and sympathy would be more sickly sweet, but it felt better for me now. I drove off to join the comfortably familiar route to the office.

'David, you look in need of more than tea,' was Rose's reaction when I played the sympathy card. 'Don't you think you'd be better off at home having a proper rest?' Did she know somehow that I was trying to avoid home? She seems so innocuous but has a knack for discerning little boys' games.

'I've not been in here for a couple of days. It would be irresponsible to leave it all and let it go to pot. Put a couple of sugars in that tea, please, and if you could find a couple of aspirin too that would help. I have a touch of headache and don't want it getting any worse. I'll go through the post and look at what needs doing.'

Rose looked at me in her motherly way, shook her head and let me go through to my familiar office. I sat down heavily at my desk, admitting at least to myself that my headache was now thumping. The photos of the children on the bookshelf next to my desk were appealing, in bright sunshine in France two years ago. Today, though, they were a bit disturbing, making me a touch cross. I turned away and looked out of the window. The horse-chestnut tree outside was beginning to turn golden. Sunshine caught the leaves and made them shine with a last glow of health and strength before the quiet slumber of winter came upon the branches and they let go of the leaves. Letting go of the leaves. That phrase stuck in my mind for a while, but I couldn't make sense of it with my headache.

I stood up and walked around the room, looking for where Rose had put the post. There should at least have been something to do with the purchase of the flat for Mohammed's aunt, but she had clearly hidden it somewhere. There was another copy of the Law Society Journal, to add to the three or four which I had not yet read, but I wasn't desperate enough to sit and read that with my head hammering. As I stood there a bit forlorn, there was another gentle knock on the door and Rose came in with tea, two aspirin and a plate of digestive biscuits. I was, to my shame, more pleased to see the biscuits than I was to see her.

'Where have you hidden the post? We're well behind now with that flat purchase for Mr Khan's aunt and there must be other matters to deal with as well?'

Rose put the tea and biscuits on the coffee table and looked at me with a slightly wounded air. 'Mohammed phoned to say that with the current crisis in the family, no progress will be made on the flat for Mrs. Shingar. I think we have the Press to thank for the lack of business otherwise. They have left us alone now, thank God, but I expect that most people had some idea that this is not a good time to trouble you with more mundane matters. At least I guess that's what has happened. We've just been very quiet for a couple of days.'

Once again I felt stupid, expecting that Mohammed could still buy flats as though nothing else had happened. 'Oh. OK then. It's good to know that you're not exactly overwhelmed!' I was trying to make light of it.

'The only thing I am concerned about, now that you are here, David, is you. You look troubled. I know that what you are doing for those poor people is very important and we all want to support you as much as we can. Enjoy your tea in the peace and quiet and then you'll be able to go home with a clear conscience. We are fine here, we really are, and if there is anything urgent that you need to attend to, I'll let you know. That's all right, isn't it?' She put on a broad smile.

There wasn't much I could do about that at all. I just thanked her, sat down by the coffee table, picked up a biscuit and held it in the tea briefly. Knowing that this was a MacVities rather than a Sainsbury's, I also knew, from years of practice, exactly how long to hold it in the tea to dunk it to perfection. As I picked it up again half of the soggy part fell away disappearing into the tea. Even my timing for dunking was all wrong; things were pretty bad. What was worse was that Rose would know I had lost my touch. I couldn't admit to getting a parking ticket today as well, so I kept that nasty plastic envelope in my jacket pocket.

There really did seem to be no point in staying to read the Journal with a headache. I thanked Rose for her tea and told her that I would be at home if anyone wanted me.

'Bill and Bert have been after you, something about car parking for tomorrow? Where have you been?' Jane was annoyed but trying to be gentle with me. I hadn't taken my coat off before she was at me.

'Hello, dear, how are you too? Are you all right? Have you had a hard morning?' The heavy sarcasm in my voice gave my wounded anger some satisfaction. 'Yes, it's been a right pain. Trying to find out information from people who won't see you and getting a nasty headache in the process.' Somehow it didn't seem wise to mention breakfast with Philippa just now.

'Come on, David. You're the one who's supposed to be looking after the practical side of things for Paul. It's tomorrow, you know. Your investigations can wait a bit, and they're not going to put off the biggest funeral in Birmingham just for you.'

'OK, tell me what's been going on.' There had been plenty going on. Beryl had come to pray and they had managed ten minutes before the phone went and it was the Archdeacon ringing to check up and see if he could help in some way. A strange but immediate answer to prayer? Or was the Archdeacon actually sabotaging the whole spiritual side of the day, as some people seem believe is the mission of Archdeacons, by terminating the prayer with his excessive concern on the practicalities? At least he had phoned here and not Paul. 'Bet you enjoyed that.' I goaded nastily. 'The man with the fruity voice!'

Jane gave me a hard stare. 'Where have you been? Please could you give him a ring and let him know if there is anything for him to do. If you know that is.'

'Careful. I have a terrible head and I don't need you making nasty comments.'

'Look, why don't we sit down and go through what needs to be done. I think we're both getting too wound up about this thing. Go and sit in the sitting room. I'll make a cup of tea and we'll go through it together calmly. Coffee for you?'

I guessed she was thinking in her healthy ecological way that caffeine would not be the best treatment for a headache and one of her herbal tea bags would be more soothing, but I have never come to terms with the cat wee smell of camomile and that sort of thing. 'Yes please, a strong milky one.'

As I sat down my head was thumping again, already. I wished I knew where the aspirin was kept so I wouldn't have to ask Jane and wouldn't have to wait the prescribed time. It was peaceful, though, looking out onto the leaf- and apple-strewn lawn. It was a good year for apples. I wished I could have some time just to be at home, tidy the garden and pick the apples properly, instead of half of them rotting on the ground. Apart from the pulse of blunt pain in my head, all was quiet. I took my shoes off and stretched out my legs, closing my eyes to sink into the peace a bit more.

The door opened gently and Jane came in with a tray. She had found some malted milk biscuits. After two breakfasts and some digestives I wasn't at all hungry, but couldn't refuse her kindness. I just restrained myself from dunking.

'Not a good day to have a headache,' Jane commented gently. 'Can I get you anything for that?'

'Rose gave me a couple of aspirin. I'll be fine in a bit.'

'There have been a few people worrying about details for tomorrow. I expect it's all in hand really, but if I can help with anything, I've made sure I have time this afternoon. Perhaps we could just make a list of what still needs to be done?'

Jane was being very kind and calm today. Most probably she knew that very little was in hand but was sparing me the full glare of the truth.

'Well, there's the car parking. That's what Bill and Bert would be on about.' We needed a couple more people and Jane agreed to ring round for them. She also suggested talking to the police to see what they were planning in terms of bollards on the road or whatever. She was happy to do that as well, although she did look at me a little quizzically as though she would like to know more about why I couldn't do it myself.

'Then there's the press packs,' continued Jane. 'The Archdeacon said that we need to give each member of the press a copy of everything that is being said – Paul's sermon and prayers especially, plus a running order. We need to agree where the reporters will be and where the television cameras will be as well.' Once again Jane was quite happy to talk with Paul about this and arrange for a couple of people to be at the church to steward. It was looking like I was being made redundant. I wondered how much I could portray this as my superior delegation skills.

'What's happening about those ridiculous rose petals? Or have they seen some sense and decided not to make everyone feel awkward like that?'

'That's more than just a headache,' said Jane quickly but gently. 'Just because you think you'll feel awkward doesn't mean that everyone is the same. Most people actually like a funeral to have a distinctive personal element to it. And no-one's going to be forced to do anything.' Jane was forceful, but kindly still, thank God.

'So? There won't now be a net of petals suspended over the coffin to fall down like tears while we all sing "Where have all the flowers gone?" ' Somehow her kindness was just making me more antagonistic.

'There will just be a couple of large bowls next to the coffin and people will be able to come and throw a few petals in, with their own thoughts and prayers, and, no doubt, a few tears as well. It'll be just right for Liz. We all need something to do to express our grief – other than making nasty comments that is.'

This time I just kept quiet.

'There's one more thing, which looks like it will need you to handle.' Jane continued cautiously. It began to dawn on me that there was a reason she was being so nice to me. I looked up and raised my eyebrows with exaggeration. 'Jennifer phoned while you were out and wanted to talk to you. In the end she agreed to tell me what it was about, but she really wanted to talk with you. It's about Jason. He wants to come to the funeral.'

'Well he can want what he likes, but there's no way the chief murder suspect will be allowed at the funeral. He must be crazier than I thought.'

'He's desperate. He'll have a police escort, and Jennifer and Will really want him to have someone else, someone he trusts, someone who believes in him, with him also.'

I looked wide-eyed. 'So it's all been set up while I was out? That's what you're telling me. My job for the day is to be Jason's minder.'

'You seem to have taken on the job of being Jason's champion – and this is just a part of it. You do want to help him, don't you?' Jane could be determined and persuasive if she wanted to. Maybe she should be a lawyer. That would put me in the shade. The only thing I could do was laugh.

'Yes m'lady. I will happily go as Jason's minder. Can't think why I didn't think of that before. Thanks for doing all the arranging. It looks like it might be my last chance to see the lad before it has to be in a prison visiting room.'

Jane was looking at me with great tenderness. 'It's not looking good for him?'

I shook my head. 'Chief and only suspect in the eyes of the law.'

'Even this practitioner of the law?'

I sighed heavily. 'I don't know. Logically it doesn't make sense. That old grouch who hangs around with Mohammed thinks it was something to do with Tariq's more extreme Moslem friends.' Jane now raised her eyebrows. 'It's probably an old man's deranged mind putting two and two together and coming up with eight and a half. But I can't let it go. I'm pursuing that one for now, before I throw in the towel and trust the courts to expose the truth about Jason. I just wish I had more confidence that they really want the truth and not just a verdict.'

Jane shook her head gently side to side. 'I wasn't going to say this after you've been so impossible since you came in, but although we didn't pray for long, Beryl did think she had something about you. She had this picture of you walking up a steep hill with a big rucksack on your back, just passing a black signpost that was pointing in the same direction you were going. She thought it meant that you were on the right track. I don't know quite what to make if it, especially now you are giving the impression you have something to hide. But that's what she saw anyway.'

The picture did feel encouraging, but there was something wrong there too. Why was I on my own? Was it more likely a warning that I was heading off on my own track into the hills? 'Thanks dear. I'll think about that. There's nothing more to get ready for the big day then?'

Jane shook her head, and smiled at me. I looked away from her and closed my eyes. My head was still throbbing. She picked up the tray and went back into the kitchen. I felt sad and out of sorts. Part of me wanted to talk with her some more, but I didn't think she would understand, or, if I was honest, approve, and I didn't want that battle. She had just shown that she was in a strong frame of mind. I would have needed more than a clear head to take her on, so I just let her go.

Sitting quietly in the chair was nice, and I thought about going off to bed for a snooze. But I knew I would only feel worse, like my tongue had been replaced with that of a dead cow. Someone was moving about upstairs and I was convinced that Jane was still in the kitchen. Who was this intruder? Jane assured me that it was only Nicola who had not gone to school, having woken up with a nasty cough. 'Why don't you go and see if she wants something? She'd be happy to have someone to talk to.'

Not knowing why Jane was being so kindly towards me, I happily went to see the invalid. Nicola was just climbing back into bed, looking pale but contented. I fetched the apple juice she requested, together with another mug of coffee for me.

'How's your throat?' I asked dutifully.

'It's sore,' she croaked, before a lengthy bout of coughing ended up with a retching of phlegm. 'How's your case? You talk.'

'Bad.' I said with mock gloom trying to disguise the real despair. 'Jason's the suspect and there's not a lot I can do about that.'

Nicola sipped and looked at me. She shook her head. 'Not him.'

'Yeah, it's sad. A fine lad, but maybe this is what they call in France a *crime passionel*. Jealousy is a powerful thing.'

Nicola shook her head more vigorously. 'No. He couldn't have done. Knows too much about cars.'

'He does know rather too much about cars. That's what the police see. Cutting a power steering tube is not something you or I could do.'

Nicola looked at me with a hard stare. 'You couldn't. But I could if I was daft enough.' She forced herself to continue between coughs. 'Jason would have done it better. It was an amateur job not a professional.'

'How on earth do you know so much about it all of a sudden?' I was taken aback.

Nicola pulled out yesterday's Birmingham Express and handed it to me. She pointed to a couple of paragraphs near the end of the report. 'The police have confirmed that the car was tampered with. Sources close to the investigators have said that cutting a power steering fluid tube would have caused the steering to fail, not immediately, but after a while. The car could have been driven safely and only when it went into the underpass at speed, did the damage become apparent.'

I sighed deeply. 'Yes. That's what they're saying apparently. And it would take someone who knew what they were doing to work out which tube to cut.'

Nicola took another swig from her glass. 'Jason knew too much. Could have done it without cutting. Just loosening the connection. That's all it needed. For those who really know… An amateur.' She couldn't say another word.

That was enough, though. I was alert now, but not yet convinced. 'How come you know this?'

Nicola gave me a withering look and pointed to the pile of copies of Autocar on her floor. I had thought she was only interested in the glamour of Formula One, not in the intricacies of car intestines.

I had to press on. 'Are you sure? This wasn't a flash sports car, just a rather old Nissan.'

Again she gave the impression that she would be better off talking with a cockatoo than her thick father. Impatiently she gesticulated again in the direction of the magazines. This time I could see, leaning up against the back of the pile, a Haynes Workshop Manual for a Nissan Sunny. 'Not just you. I think he couldn't. Not Jason. Does know too much.' Nicola doubled up, coughing loudly, and then blew her nose hard.

I didn't know what to say. Part of me was feeling an ignorant fool, humbled by a young girl who had more sense than her flighty father. Part of me was proud and exhilarated to know that I had such an intelligent daughter who thought the same way as I did. 'Thanks Nic. You're amazing,' I said quickly, feeling that it wasn't quite enough.

I picked up the manual and she showed me the relevant pages. She did know what she was talking about, or at least she convinced me. She even said I could have the book to take away with me, she just had to return it to the father of a friend of a friend at school sometime. I would happily have paid them £50 for it, or at least bought them a new one. It wasn't proof, but it was a pointer to Jason's innocence, even if it was the only one so far. I gave her a hug and left her to recover in peace with her Guns and Roses CDs and Polky the teddy bear.

Coming downstairs I met Peter coming in for lunch. I had forgotten that he had two free periods on Wednesday afternoon, and had convinced us that he would do more work at home than hanging around at school chatting to his mates. When I had said that the TV must stay off, he insisted that he couldn't work without something on in the background. I wasn't sure how much work was actually done, but his teachers were not complaining.

We sat round the kitchen table over bowls of home made soup and bread. My headache had calmed down, just a snare drum beat in the middle distance rather than six kettle drums all around me. We heard about the new lads who had just arrived at school, one of whom was too good-looking and had set up instant and vicious competition among all the girls, and about the plan by the Headteacher to have 18 months career break in Australia, which, apparently, some teachers were discussing with Peter and his friends.

'That's enough of my riveting life. How's the sleuth saviour shaping up? Got Jason off the hook yet – or should I say off the noose?'

'Peter!' that's horrible' blurted Jane.

'I wish I could take it so light-heartedly,' I said. 'Jason is still the number one suspect, but your sister has just given me the best argument so far for his innocence.' They eagerly wanted to know what good could come from a teenage girl, and were impressed into silence when I explained. Peter could not keep quiet for long.

'So if our Jason didn't do it, who did? You must have an idea of that, Dad. Surely you need another suspect, or else they'll just say that Jason was all hot and jealous and not thinking straight.'

'There's an old Englishman who knows the family of Tariq Khan well. He thinks Tariq had enemies among the radical

Moslems, people who saw him as a traitor, people who would have wanted to get rid of him.'

'Hang on Dad! You know what you're saying here? A bunch of Moslems, who are all as peace-loving as the rest of us. They couldn't possibly do things like that. They're religious.'

'Unfortunately, Peter, there are violent extremists in Islam, as in many other religions.'

'Yes I know that,' said Peter impatiently. 'But you can't go round saying it can you? Blaming the darkies for a white man's crime, that's what they do in America.'

'I'm just trying to find out the truth here, Peter!' I snapped.

'Just be careful, won't you Dad? It's how it's going to appear to the politically correct people with power. You need to be very sure of what you're saying, that's all.'

Jane was also concerned. 'Don't charge ahead on your own, David. Have you talked with anyone else about this?' It was my turn to give her what I hoped was a hard and off-putting stare – quite unmerited.

'How are you going to find out about radical Moslems anyway?' Peter was too interested to stop.

'Actually I have an appointment this afternoon with another Englishman who is a Moslem himself.' I looked hard at Jane again to say that I was indeed talking with other people.

'And what sort is he, a gentle moderate or one of your suspects?' Peter was determined to know. It never occurred to me, in a family discussion, that I could have just said 'No comment.'

'He has a reputation of being close to the radicals.'

'And you're just going to walk up to him and say, "You killed Tariq Khan, didn't you?" There's libel laws for people like you, you know.' I still wasn't sure if Peter was exaggerating for fun or being serious.

'What are you going to say to this man, David?' Jane had not been silenced, as usual.

'I'll simply ask him what he knows about Tariq's connections with the radical Moslems,' I said, beginning to feel on the defensive.

'A real policeman plod way to begin. You might as well say "You are under suspicion of being involved in the suspicious circumstances surrounding the road traffic accident on Saturday last." Can't you think of anything better than that?' There is something about the cheerful way that Peter talks that enables him to get away with disrespectful questions, at least with me.

'I am only seeing if there is any truth in what Frank was saying. I'm not an investigating magistrate or anything like that, I just want to check out something I've been told.' This was less than honest, but how were they to know?

'Yeah, right,' was simply Peter's dry response. 'Tell you what, why don't you say that MI6 are accusing Tariq of committing suicide because he was being hounded by these fanatical Moslems, and that you have been asked by his family to protect them and the whole Moslem community against this pernicious slander! That should make them more likely to talk to you. At least you'll be trying to be on their side, even if it is a load of codswallop.' Peter was enjoying himself, probably never expecting to be taken seriously.

'That's an interesting idea, Peter. Thanks.' I wasn't going to get anywhere, so I said to myself that the best way to end it was to agree with him.

'No David, No.' Jane thought I was taking him seriously.

'Just trust me, dear. I know what I'm doing.' I didn't want to talk about this any more.

'Just don't start saying anything that's not true. That's no way to find out the truth about anything.'

'Look, I'm walking in the right direction, remember? Don't worry. Anyway, it's time I was off. Thanks for a great lunch. I don't know when I'll be back, sorry.'

Jane came out to the hall with me. She looked at me with loving concern. 'Please be sensible.' 'When have you known me any different?' was my flippant reply as I walked out without a kiss, quite glad that I had managed not to say anything about Philippa.

As I turned into the road by the music shop I remembered with a sickening lurch that I had failed to bring any change for the parking meter. I looked round for a shop where I could buy something small for the change, couldn't see one, decided to find a car park instead, turned the wrong way, only seeing the car park in the mirror as I sped along. By the time I had turned round, parked and walked to the shop it was ten minutes after the time Peter had said. I was flustered and my infernal headache was coming back with a vengeance. The music downstairs was again loud, and Peter's secretary's desk was again eerily empty.

The astringent woman walked in wiping her hands on a paper towel. She looked at me. 'Mr Jeffery. Mr Strang is waiting for you. Please carry on through.' She made it sound like I was a naughty schoolboy from whom nothing better could be expected.

Peter was standing with his back to the door, a short man with short black shiny hair. He turned round and formally offered me his hand. 'Mr David Jeffery. Welcome.' His grip was fierce and after the shock I tried to return him muscle for muscle.

'It's good to have a proper handshake for a change. These Asian handshakes are so limp.' As Peter talked, he smiled collusively. I did not return his smile, more from shock than from principled opposition.

'You look a bit surprised – perhaps that we know your name?'

'Well yes. That's part of it.'

'David Jeffery is famous all over Birmingham now. The friend of Mohammed Khan is someone we must treat with respect.' Peter spoke quickly, almost curtly, and I could not tell if he was mocking or not.

'Thank you for seeing me, Mr Strang.'

'Call me Peter, that's the correct English thing to do. Just don't call it my Christian name. I'm not interested in feeble titles. Have a seat.'

He pulled a high-backed leather chair from behind his desk and waved me to a black plastic upright chair to his left, the other side of the desk. The room smelt of pine air freshener. It was long and fairly narrow, with a mat along the opposite side to me and a motif on the wall which I took to be the direction to Mecca.

'The best exercise in the world,' Peter said, noticing my interest in the mat. 'Building up spiritual muscle. And the spirit gives strength to the mind and body. Even your Bible says that. Just a pity that your Church never gets people to do it. Why do Christians want people to be feeble? They are easier to control as sheep, but they don't grow up properly. Anyway you haven't come to learn about the strength of Islam you've come to learn about Tariq Khan?'

'You are well prepared!' I was trying to regain my balance after being knocked off guard. My preparation, such as it was, was almost in tatters. 'Mohammed Khan has asked me to do what I can to find out the truth about the terrible car crash. This means me talking to as many people as I possibly can, who have had any connection with Tariq at all. And a couple of people mentioned you, so here I am.'

'Yes?' Peter peered at me like a housewife allowing a fishmonger to try to sell her something other than her usual haddock.

'So here I am, yes, interested in Tariq Khan and the people he hung around with. What can you tell me about his friends?'

'Nothing that you can't learn from them. Tariq is a fine Moslem, an upright member of the community who has been the victim of some nasty attempt to discredit us all.'

'You mean the suggestion that he had been drinking?'

'That and more. They are many ways to skin a rabbit.' Peter stopped firmly and enigmatically. I wanted him to continue but couldn't think of any way forward. The headache didn't help. We kept an awkward silence while I blinked and tried to recover my preparation.

'Are you sure you want to have this conversation now? You could just wait for Tariq to recover and talk with him then?' Peter was being more kindly now. I didn't like being treated like an elderly man who needed help crossing the road.

'Yes, as I said, Mohammed is keen that the truth comes out as soon as possible and the police are unfortunately not looking at this as dispassionately as they could do. What it would be helpful to know is the connections Tariq had with people who might have wanted to harm him in some way.'

'You do want to continue…' Peter leant forward, looking more stern and determined. 'Right. What makes you think that I can tell you things about Tariq that his own father doesn't know? And the most likely people behind this are people who have a prejudiced fear of Moslems, especially Moslems who take over great British institutions like fish and chip shops. Why go poking around among Tariq's friends for goodness sake? And why don't you just wait until he recovers properly and ask him himself?'

It all hit home like a swarm of wasps had stung my mind in several places at once, leaving a string of sore doubts. I felt foolish. I felt like slinking away to find some soothing cream for my poor head. But I couldn't think of a way out that would not make me look even more foolish. Regaining a bit of credibility seemed more important. I wanted to make this work. I wanted to be the sort of investigator that Philippa wanted me to be. A short pause was enough to register or half register these thoughts. I took a deep breath and carried on regardless.

'I can see the point of what you say, and, yes, this does have as much to do with me as with Mohammed. Let me explain things a bit more.' I adopted my most serious confidential expression and my slow courtroom manner which gave me a little time to think as I went along. 'As well as knowing Mohammed, I know a senior police officer involved in this case. At the moment the police have several theories. For the public they are talking about one suspect – a so called jealous lover – but they know that the evidence against him is very weak. They have also been told from a reliable source that Tariq had connections with a radical Moslem group, connections which he broke recently. There is evidence that this group made threats to Tariq which he was finding very hard to live with.' I paused to see if this caused any reaction in Peter, but he just sat sternly.

'The police have a habit of getting a bee in their bonnet. Once they are set on one direction they will keep on and on, ignoring the warning signs that this is a dead end road, until they hit a barrier. Often, on the way, they cause considerable damage to others, and to their own reputation, about which they seem to have minimal concern.'

Peter leant back and looked up at the ceiling. I felt I had to notch up the urgency in my spiel. 'The police therefore seem ready to haul a few people in for some unpleasant questioning. No-one knows how long it will be before Tariq will be fit to be interviewed and there is intense pressure from above to make progress on this matter. I need hardly say, also, that there are elements in the force who would be very happy if this investigation showed some sections of the Moslem community in a bad light.'

Peter looked back at me nodding gently. Encouraged, I continued. 'It seems to me that if I could help avert this blundering about, and worse, by giving my officer friend some information to reassure him, that would be a service to Mohammed and to others.' I thought I had probably said enough, without carrying on into a definite request for Peter to tell me everything he knew about Tariq and his contacts with the radical Moslems. I was feeling drained and a little sick. Lying does me no good.

Peter peered at me intently for a couple of seconds and then sat back looking towards the ceiling again. 'You just want to be of service? You have no interest of your own to pursue here? We tend to be wary of Christians who use talk of being of service as a cloak for advancing their own interests. Of course you may not be infected by this particular hypocrisy.' He paused. I resisted the impulse to defend the Christians and waited for him to continue.

'You want to serve Mohammed and to serve us. Let us think how you could best do this. The truth does need to come out and it is our duty to shine a light so that the truth does come out. There is indeed sin in the world, as you are so fond of talking about. But it is not for us to sit back and leave it to Christ or anyone else to take care of, we have to expose it, fight it, cleanse people of the cancer that is eating away at our society. We attack the cancer aggressively, knowing that the treatment may make the body weak for a while but it will live on without the cancer instead of dying with it.' Peter seemed to check himself a little.

'So it seems clear that your duty is to go back to the police, let them know that if they are not careful you will expose their racist prejudice – shout it from the rooftops, I believe someone once said. You can tell them that from us too if you like. If they continue to act in intimidatory ways, justifying their violence with exaggerated fears of the Moslem community, they will be exposed, they will be brought to justice, one way or another. Tell 'them' that. That'll do.' Peter looked me in the eyes. He was challenging me to continue if I dared.

I felt very weak and very foolish. What I had said had been less than the truth and not convincing. Peter had just taken it and thrown it back at me, and I wished I had never tried to talk with him. Part of me wanted to rise to his challenge and provoke him into talking more about Tariq's friends. But it was too much effort. My brain felt like a battered sponge. I threw in the towel.

'I will do what I can to warn those in authority of the consequences of acting on prejudice instead of rational evidence, of course I will. And if you do come across anything which might help me to convince them of the futility of their actions, please contact me. Thank you for your time, Mr. Strang.' As I took out my diary and fumbled for a business card, Peter stood up and started walking to the door. I had to get up quickly and scurry after him. 'My secretary will take that. Good day Mr. Jeffery.' Peter dismissed me as if I was a pesky photocopier salesman.

Outside it was a heavy grey drizzly day. I walked slowly to the car park with my head down. I was at a loss for what to do next, after hitting a strangely Islamic British brick wall. My headache was thumping again and I felt cold inside, like a damp log left outside too long. I just wanted to be inside and warm. But home seemed a long way away. Jane would want to know exactly what I had been up to and I didn't want to tell her. I looked up to the car park ahead on my right which was stark, more grey, like a prison. On my left was a pub, with a warm light and surprisingly gentle music. A good red wine or maybe a brandy would warm me, I thought. I had had a hard time and I deserved something to cheer me up. Looking again at the car park and where it would lead to, I was glad that I was not on a parking meter but could just pay whenever I left. There was no reason not to stop and have a break over a glass.

The wine was a little rough, like the pub itself. Warm air, with an edge of cigarette smoke. Plush golden seats frayed at the edges. I gratefully took my coat off and settled by a window.

The last time I had been in a pub in the afternoon, or by myself, had probably been when I was a student. I smiled at how I was drifting back to my old ways. Perhaps we never really change at all? The setting was familiar. The range of draft beers was more international, and it was more normal to be drinking wine than before. The television screens were new, but turned off. There were only two other people in the bar, both men in jeans, each with a bottle in front of them. It struck me that in my student days this place would have been closed at this time. The thrill of doing something that had once been forbidden made me smile.

As I thought back about my encounter with Peter Strang I made myself smile again. His small stature was at odds with his reputation as a bully boy, but I had to admit that he had seen me off pretty effectively. He was probably smirking to himself about an easy victory over a silly old man, if he gave me a second thought. His reasoned hostility to Christianity was something new to me. None of the Moslems I had met before had been so openly aggressive. I wondered how I could have responded to his comments about our weakness and hypocrisy. There didn't seem to be anything to say and I was hardly on solid ground taking up Peter's wild suggestion about how to proceed. I smiled to myself but soon the smile had sunk into a rising gloom within me. Why had I been so stupid? What had I thought I could achieve? I finished my glass of wine too quickly.

Making myself think about the following day, it seemed so odd that Jason would be at the funeral. Phil would know about this and I decided on impulse to give him a ring. The public phone was in a draughty toilet corridor. 'Phil, it's David. How are things with you?'   'Good afternoon to you too. And how is the life of fame treating you now?'

'I'm looking forward to a bit more normality, thank you. Can I ask you what seems to me a fairly big detail to do with the funeral tomorrow?'

'You can ask me anything you want and I'll tell you everything I know about funerals. Should be a quick phone call.'

'I've been told that Jason Jennings is going to be at the funeral accompanied by a police officer.' There was no response. 'Can this be true? It seems most bizarre.'

'I was hoping you were going to ask me about hymns or coffins. This I do actually know about and I can assure you that it is true.' I wasn't sure if Phil wanted to say any more or not.

'Good grief! You lot think it's wise?' I vaguely noticed that this maybe wasn't the sort of thing I normally said.

'There has been some discussion, shall we say, about this here.' Phil's tone of voice was professionally neutral. 'As far as we are concerned, he is on bail without any specific funeral restrictions. Whether he would be well advised to go is another matter. I'm not sure exactly who the police escort is for.'

'What a mess it could all end up in!' I said gloomily.

'And I hear that he may have another escort too?' The cheery Phil was back. 'A world famous solicitor to guide him through this particular minefield?'

Perhaps it wasn't so surprising that he had been talking with Will or someone who knew the plans for tomorrow, but it still took me aback. I thanked him for his insider knowledge, glad that this time he had been able to answer my question.

The wine had warmed me but the draughts and the cold-shower realisation that I was indeed being dragged into a minefield chilled me down again. The headache, which a little earlier had been tapping in the background, was now bashing away more fervently. A brandy would soothe and warm me up, although it was a while since I had driven with that much alcohol in me. A cup of tea at home would be the insipid alternative, but I wasn't keen on dropping in there quickly before going out again to see Philippa. Somehow I knew that if I went home I wouldn't go on to Philippa's.

On the tattered gold plush with my brandy in front of me, I suddenly felt like a sad old man. I had wondered about lonely men sitting in pubs in the afternoon – didn't they have anything brighter in their life? Now here I was, sad and hypocritical, good for nothing. I banished the thought with the fact that this was very much the exception for me. I was more like a teenager again trying new pleasures. A good sip of brandy lit up my throat and chest and I settled down to think of not very much, watching the three people in this bar and the barman talking with a couple of others away in the other bar. It was good to be out of the windy damp of Birmingham. I remembered what Philippa had said about marriage being like a chilly damp climate from which a break in the sunshine was welcome. I didn't think Paul would have liked it, and thought I probably shouldn't think much of it as a Christian, but it was a good picture that would ring bells with a lot of people. Why shouldn't Christians appreciate *bon mots* like this? We need to avoid appearing straight-laced and condemning.

I was relaxing into the new role of man-of-the-world, and thought about having another brandy to celebrate and seal my freedom from dusty old convention. Looking at my watch I knew it would have to be a quick one if I was not to be late at Philippa's and the miserly part of me wondered if it would be worth spending that much on alcohol too quickly swallowed and not savoured. I was pushing against this thought, telling myself not to be so cowardly and conventional, when I noticed that that *Millennium* song was playing again in the background. I pricked up my ears to see if I could make out the words this time. What was it that Peter had said? '*We know we're falling from grace, and we're praying it's not too late, Millennium, Millennium.*' It still seemed a cash-in song, but it had distracted me from thinking about the second brandy, which I no longer wanted. I thought about where we would be on December 31st, which we hadn't decided finally yet. Being together as a family would be best, with some friends from church as our extended family. I certainly didn't want to spend £50 or more a head on some posh do in a hotel. Thinking of Jane and the children made me think of going home for a cup of tea. But I had an appointment with Philippa who would mind less about the brandy on my breath.

A slightly wobbly car ride, wet nose to wet tail to begin with, enlivened by singing along to *BRMB*, brought me sooner that I had expected to Philippa's dark blue door. 'What are you doing here? What are you looking for?' came rather clearly to mind as I just sat and waited for the clock to catch up. With the help of the car mirror I straightened my tie, and ran comb-like fingers through my hair, with a touch of American film star swagger, beautifully understated of course. I hadn't brought anything for Philippa. Should I have done or would that have been taken the wrong way? I wondered where the nearest petrol station or corner shop was, but checked myself. This was just a business meeting, a little unusual but just business. Life was unusual at the moment to say the least.

There was no response at first from the metal speaker grille above the six bell pushes by the door. I rang again, remembering the instructions my mother had given me – one firm ring, wait ten seconds, another short ring then, if no answer, walk away. I thought I could just walk away now, but after some indecision rang again. As I rang, the door opened.

'Hold on, tiger, I am here for you!' Philippa sounded playful. I was surprised to see her in a pale blue towelling dressing gown and tried not to show it. 'You're a serious man, aren't you, bang on time. And here I am all flustered because I'm not ready. Come in!' She took hold of my arm gently with her right hand and led me inside, keeping her touch on mine as she closed the door behind me with the left hand. 'It's good to see you. Thank you for coming.' She rubbed my arm gently as she welcomed me and then let go. Whether it was the wine and brandy or what, I was flustered. 'Come on up,' Philippa called cheerfully as she walked quickly up the stairs, her bare legs smooth under the soft blue cloth.

I followed her into her flat, warm and softly lit, dark red and black colours, with a passionately sad blues singer in the background. 'Make yourself at home. You can take that tie off for a start. I'll just throw something on so that it doesn't stop what we're here for.' Philippa stood smiling at me in the open door of her bedroom, a fine gold chain around her neck, with a curly almost snake-like pendant emphasising the deep white V of her neck and cleavage. She turned slowly and I could see the double bed with its covers turned down ready for the night.

I sat down on her soft black leather armchair and fingered my tie, loosening it but leaving it on. The flat smelt of coffee and expensive perfume, exotic spice with a touch of treacle. I closed my eyes and breathed in. This was better than a tawdry pub. Feeling even warmer I pulled off my tie and laid it on the arm of the chair. There were few books on show, unlike with most of my friends. Just one small bookcase dominated by a deep red table lamp. There was no clutter. Tasteful space framed with expensive ornaments. There were no floral patterns or country scenes. Lush long red curtains and a couple of abstract pictures, strokes of black and red piled on top of each other. I wondered if I could get used to this. For now it was a welcome break.

Philippa came marching into the room dressed in an orange jumper, soft wool with strands of fibre reaching out from the surface, and black trousers, her feet bare. The jumper was loose fitting hanging low from her bare shoulders. She came and stood by me picking up my tie and stroking it in her hands. 'I'm glad you're here, David. A nice change for me too.' She stood close, leaning forward slightly so that the bottom of her jumper fell away from her body. There didn't seem to be any clothes underneath it. The same smell of spice and treacle came more strongly from her freshly showered body.

'Thanks for the invitation, and thanks for the information about Peter.' I sat up a bit stiffly. 'That was a good way to introduce me to the chief suspect!' Philippa raised her eyebrows in a question. 'At least in my mind he is the chief suspect, although God knows how anyone else can have any confidence in what I'm thinking.' I wanted for some reason to keep talking, fill up the space, take a step or two back to normality. 'There's no way that the police will ever see him as a threat, not as the threat he really is, and… and he's not one to give anything away either. Just a hard man wanting to keep me at bay. So, thanks for the lead, Philippa, but it doesn't look like we're going to get very far, I'm afraid.' I sat glumly, my head sunk.

'Call me Philly, David.' She said, softly shaking her hair a little letting it fly fragrantly to draw my attention. She smiled a warm smile. 'I think you're going to get farther than you ever thought possible, David.' She raised an eyebrow, beamed briefly and then looked at me with calm wide eyes. 'What can I get you to console you to begin with, before we get to work together?'

I felt like reaching out to touch her hand. I could have drawn her down to sit on my lap and breathed in deeply the warm softness of her jumper. Surprised by this rogue thought, I blinked and mentally shook myself. 'A good cup of tea would be a treat, er.. Philly. I'm still an English gentleman at heart.'

'And I know that that's only half true. There's something more fiery in you than the usual damp male of the Anglo-Saxon species, all timid and proper and keeping to convention.' She laughed as she said this. 'So I think a spot of Italian sunshine distilled into the red wine of Chianti would appeal to that other side of you. You could be setting this side free so that the world can see it and admire it more. There's a side like that to all of us, believe me, and this Philly is looking forward to getting to know that burning passion a bit more. So do you really want tea and sympathy?'

This was the point at which I should have held back and gone for the tea. She wasn't being subtle and a little shudder down my left shoulder told me that there was danger ahead. But lower down something was indeed stirring. The thought of Philippa on my lap raising her jumper over her bare breasts would not go away. The taste of pub-priced cheap wine and brandy was calling out to be joined by more, the more sophisticated and smooth, the better. That would just be enough to slake the thirst, something finer would not leave me wanting more, I thought. And it would be rude to turn down such a generous offer, of course. I looked at Philippa and raised my eyebrows too. 'You're a good saleswoman, Philly. I'm seeing sides to you that I didn't know were there. Some liquid sunshine would be nice, thank you.' This felt like a bit of a feeble response but my fuzzy head would not allow me to come up with anything better at the moment.

As Philippa went she let her hand stroke across my shoulders. I tensed up briefly at first and then, thinking how stupid I was being, relaxed and settled back, comfortable in the chair with my eyes closed. There she was again in my mind, sitting bare breasted on my lap leaning her head over mine so that her hair fell down brushing my ears. I told myself that this was so unlikely to happen, that it was harmless to play with the idea. From somewhere I remembered that it was a good Christian practice to lie and be still and let your thoughts wander a bit, not trying too hard but accepting whatever comes from the Spirit. What I had in my head was a bit unusual, but I thought that if God didn't want it there, it was up to him to take it away. Warmth pulsed round my chest pleasantly, although my neck was still a touch cold.

'So you don't think you're going to get anywhere with Peter Strang at the moment?' Philippa handed me a very large wine glass half filled with red wine. Once again she stood next to my armchair looking down at me with her glass in her hand.

'Thanks for your help, Philly. I wish I had more people like you around me to encourage me. Everyone else thinks I'm barking up the wrong tree. But I'll keep barking for a bit longer. Another day the dog will try again, but this day has been a dead end.' I wasn't making much sense and took a gulp of wine to clear my head. Philippa just stayed where she was looking down at me with sympathy.

'There's more to you than meets the eyes David. You have an animal side like the rest of us!' Philippa laughed and swung her head again so that her hair flew free. 'It's going to be interesting getting to know you more. I don't want to feel like I'm abandoning you to your misery. Could I just perch on the arm of your chair while you tell me more?'

I patted the arm of the chair and lifted my hand to hers. I pulled her gently downwards and as she was lowering herself on to the chair increased the force and took her across onto my lap. 'The chair's a bit hard,' I said as calmly as I could. My heart was beating strongly and my head felt hot. I rubbed her back briefly in a friendly way.

Philippa smiled and had another sip. She turned to look at me. 'So? You want to tell me about it, or is just sitting here enough?'

I suddenly felt uncomfortable, almost trapped. I knew that I had gone too far. I pulled my hand away from her back and thought that if I just said a little, then when it was over I could make some excuse and get back to a safe distance.

'Yes. Frustrating more than anything I suppose.' Keep going, I thought to myself. Just keep talking and then you can work out how to move out from under her without offending her. 'It took an age to eventually see him. I thought he would be a tall athletic sort or maybe a Lawrence of Arabia figure, a young Peter O'Toole, making friends with the Arabs.' Philippa smiled. 'But he was short with oily hair and a nervous manner and pale skin. He doesn't look like he'd survive long in the desert. He was bright though, I give him that. Bright enough to stop me getting anywhere. But it doesn't matter. I'll try again and actually there are more pressing things to attend to now, things that I should have been looking into before now. So I just wanted to thank you very much and leave you to it. You remember it's the funeral tomorrow and there are a number of things I need to attend to this evening at home.' I finished the glass off looked at Philippa for her to stand up.

She leaned a bit further towards me, nudging her body against mine. She spoke softly. 'Thanks for coming, David. I know you have a lot on your mind and it's good of you to come and see me here when you didn't need to.' Still feeling trapped, I let out a deep breath and leant forward a little. 'Home's a strange place isn't it?' She continued silkily. 'Sometimes it seems like it's the only place where you fit, at other times it's more like a prison of expectation. I just hope that being here with me will help you unwind so that you can be yourself more fully.'

I wanted to make some effort towards getting out politely. 'Look Philly I do like you but…'

'And I rather like you! Watching you coming and going in the office made me think. There's an interesting man. Kind and good but interesting, someone who it would be good to get to know a bit more for a while.' She smiled and raised her eyebrows.

'Well, that's very kind of you, but maybe I should be going.'

'I'm used to men coming and going. That's fine by me. That's the nice part of the freedom I have, not shackled to any one master, bit free to enjoy different rides. This morning I was even thinking how nice it would be to see you again, and then you walked in. Strange. So you could stay a while and we could begin to know each other, better that is.' She raised her eyebrows as she said 'know' and reached out to touch the hair over my forehead.

My hand went to touch her back again, and I held it there lightly, still. Lie back and enjoy it, you'll regret passing up an offer like this you have dreamed of all your life. I remembered as a teenager reading a friend's pornographic magazine with a story of a lad who had had been seduced by an older woman. It had seemed at the time too good to be true, sex on a plate from an experienced and accepting woman who wasn't looking for anything more. I had wondered, off and on over the years, whether this sort of thing really did happen or whether it was all made up by an imaginative editor who knew teenage boys and their fantasies. I had recklessly kept that memory alive, an intriguing private puzzle. Paralysed, I stayed where I was. I felt stupid. Why couldn't I just get on with it and enjoy it healthily or be brave enough to push her away properly? I was just a weak ditherer getting hot, bothered and nowhere.

'God help me,' I thought. Between my legs I was thick and throbbing. A prickly dry heat had hold of my body. My hands were still on Philippa's back, not leaving, but not moving, not yet. The song suddenly made sense. '*We know we're falling from grace...*' Falling but not able to stop, having breezed past the point of no return. Even Jesus can't help you now. The resigned thought was calmly placed before me like a trump card.

Thinking of Jesus did stiffen my back a little. Had the point of no return passed? I had already committed adultery in my imagination, so surely there was no point in holding back from the reality, the soft, inviting, free reality? This was temptation and I was sunk in it. I imagined again the sheer thrill of lifting

Philippa's jumper and nuzzling her soft breasts. I imagined her nipples firm in my mouth. I just wanted it so much. Somehow I also remembered someone once saying that the only power stronger than temptation was the cross. That can't help now. What can an ancient execution do when your body is crying out to be satisfied now?

Maybe it's not too late, I thought. 'When you're really tempted, imagine Jesus on the cross.' That's what the man had said. It was at a Men's Group in the old hall before it was refurbished. He seemed to know what he was talking about. What a pathetic wimp, I thought, going all religious at a time like this. Come on get on with it.

But I could try it. It probably won't work, but there's no harm trying. Quickly I closed my eyes and thought of Jesus, his hand nailed to a rough piece of wood, blood shooting as the nails went in. The picture was surprisingly vivid. It was graphic, arresting. What agony that must have been. How vivid it all seemed at that moment. The picture of Philippa's breasts faded. I felt strangely cool, as though water was flowing from my shoulders.

I stretched my body up and breathed a deep breath. 'I'm not used to this kind of heat,' I said jokingly.

'Relax, it's good for you,' Philippa crooned. She took my hand in hers and patted it. It was the worst thing she could have done. Nicola does that sometimes, even when she is sitting on my lap. I saw myself with my daughter on my lap and felt cold and sick. What would she think of me now? I trembled and stiffened all over. My head felt suddenly clearer than it had for hours. What was I doing here with this woman? Yes, what exactly was I doing, and what was I going to do? How could I look my family in the face again?

'Sorry, Philippa,' I said quietly, wondering why I had to be so apologetic. 'This kind of heat burns up too many things I want to keep. Sorry. It's just not me.' I took her hand and firmly put it on her lap. I shuffled back and stiffened my back. 'I'm an Englishman who prefers the climate he's been given, with everything that's growing there.' I found that I could lift her up. Before she tumbled to the floor she steadied herself. 'Sorry Philippa. I feel like I've led you on and now I have to disappoint you.'

She stood up quickly in front of me and put her hands up to push back her flowing hair. Her breasts bulged against the front of her sweater in front of me. 'I thought you were more of a stallion than you seem to think you are. I don't want to think of you as just as another gelding but if that's how you want it, David?' She stood, challenging me and offering me still.

I smiled. This time the game seemed clearer. 'You keep looking Philippa, just not here. I think I'll go home now. Thanks anyway.' She whisked her head round and strode over to the bottle of wine. I stood up. She poured a full glass, gulped it straight down and turned to face me.

'It's a nice way to treat a lady, David. Turning up the heat and then throwing a wet blanket all over her. You could at least keep me company for a while and not let me down so roughly.' She was wheedling a little, cleverly and with sophistication, but it was, at root, a wheedle. Thank God I could now see it.

'I don't think that prolonging this any more is going to do either of us any good, Philippa.' I said and moved off to where she had hung up my coat.

At first it was just good to be out of there, in the cool evening air. I breathed deeply, thought briefly about going for a walk but knew that I had to sit down. Back in the Rover I collapsed inside. The car felt so ordinary and clean compared with me. With my shoulders down I screwed up my face and kept shaking my head. 'Stupid, stupid, stupid. O God, O God.' I just wanted to go away somewhere where no one knew me. It was a long time, it seemed, that I just sat, not knowing what to do next. Thoughts about facing Philippa again at Mohammed's office were unbearable but insistent. It looked like the end of this client.

Worse than these, were the thoughts about going home. It was asking too much to walk in there without showing that anything unusual had happened. I was not a good enough actor for that. I would have to say something, but what? I didn't want to go through the whole stupid story, but I knew that one day I would probably have to. I shuddered.

I ran through in my head what to say when I arrived home. 'Jane, love…' Even using her name felt wrong now, and it certainly felt false with any mark of affection. How could I say that sincerely after this evening? Maybe I could just avoid using her name at all, as I usually found surprisingly easy with clients whose names I could not remember. But that felt too cold and distant. I needed to make contact with her even though I couldn't be a proper husband again. Perhaps I should just creep in late when they had all gone to sleep and lie on the sofa downstairs? I was beginning to feel cold inside, but a night on my own somewhere sounded like the best option.

Getting away from Philippa's was the first step. I parked round a few corners and pulled my coat tighter around me.

Where could I get a strong coffee at this time of night? Perhaps one of the places around Broad Street would sell coffee. I told myself that more wine, or even brandy, were out of the question. I would have to keep searching until I found somewhere. At least the drive would warm up the car and me a little. I switched on the car radio.

Not again! Not that awful song again. Don't they have anything else to play? '*We're praying it's not too late.*' Not too late, too late. The words kept driving through my head, not too late? Too late?

Today had been a stupid day. Charging round making a dangerous fool of myself. Why hadn't I just stayed in and had a quiet day before tomorrow? I grunted loudly at myself in anger.

Tomorrow. The funeral. Paul's big day. God, he wouldn't want people like me backing him up. Look what a mess I had made of today! Who knows what disaster I could bring on at Lizzie's funeral? It was better to bow out. Jane was a much more capable assistant than me. She would make sure it all went smoothly. They would all be better off without me. I was a liability, worse than a waste of space.

It all seemed grimly clear. I would just go and find a hotel. I could phone from a pay phone to say I was OK. If I kept out of the way, no-one else would get hurt. I felt dejected and despicable, but I could tell myself I was doing the honourable thing.

It wasn't that I had worked all this out. It was more a train of thought which rumbled inexorably through my head. All I had to do was see what the next carriage was.

I turned towards a cheap chain hotel, not far away, looking for a phone box. Did I really have to phone? Would they miss me so much? Maybe I could just say I was running late. Jane would go to bed without me and never know I was out all night. Wouldn't that be kinder? She would probably be glad of a quiet, snoreless, night. She wouldn't want to have to talk to me with tomorrow on her mind.

I pulled into the hotel car park. The train of thought kept coming. Once I was settled by my crisp white sheets, I could phone Philippa and make up for rejecting her. No point in making two women miserable in one night.

Where did that thought come from? Before I slid too far back into my sensual imagination, I pulled myself up in the car seat. Yes, where had that thought come from? It was clear where it was heading, and it was too soon for me to go there. It made the whole train look like it was heading back into outlaw country. Who was driving the train? It didn't feel like it was me.

'God, I need some help!' This time I really was turning to heaven. I closed my eyes and tried again to picture Jesus' hand on the cross, bright red blood dripping from his palm, his arm muscles tensed and rigid. I groaned and held my head in both hands. The weight felt like a helmet.

Yes, where had all my thinking since leaving Philippa's come from? Would I really not be missed? Wasn't it more likely that Jane would sit up waiting for me and call the police when I didn't return? I could imagine her sitting downstairs with a book, waiting in the dark. Another train was appearing, on another track.

Wouldn't it make tomorrow worse if I wasn't there, if people had to spend time and energy worrying about me instead of the funeral? Wasn't it better and braver to face up to the people who knew and loved me, rather than go away and hide among strangers?

Again, in a different way, it seemed clear. I still felt dejected, but a little more hopeful. But I would have to explain about today and this evening. That, I was not looking forward to. And I had tried to convince myself that it was all for Jane's sake that I was keeping away!

I thought of her looking at me as I charged out of the house, her eyes wide and calm, like a pair of turquoise candles. Keeping away could blow something out. Going home would mean stepping into light, but not a glare. I could cope with that. I too a deep breath, turned the key and turned the car towards home again. Maybe, again, I wasn't man enough to go it alone. 'So be it,' I sighed, remembering old struggles when I used to think other boys saw me as a bit of wimp.

At a traffic light I put my hand under my chin and in front of my face to direct my breath straight to my nostrils, something else I had not done for years. Thinking I should be adult enough to be honest about my drinking, at least, I stopped for some petrol which I did not need and picked up a packet of Polos.

By the time I was home, I knew what to say. 'Jane, I've been an idiot. Had a terrible day. I should have just stayed with you instead of rushing off on wild goose chases and worse. I'm sorry. Just tell me what needs to be done now and I'll do it first thing in the morning.' Plunging into placing plastic bollards or clearing litter from the churchyard was a welcome picture. I didn't know if I would sleep much, but at least there would be something to occupy me in the morning. That thought made me want to head for the sofa. 'I'm in no fit state to sleep properly. I'll probably toss and turn. Just let me spend the night on the sofa.' That felt comfortable. I could get through the night like that and then work my way back into the family again in some way.

There was a reassuring light on by the front door. I stayed in the car on the drive sucking my second Polo and gathering strength. Suddenly I felt tired, more than I expected, and part of me wanted just to snuggle up to Jane. Did I have the energy to go through with this? The light by the door seemed very bright. I couldn't pretend that everything was all right because Jane would see my twisted face. She could read me like the expert in Italian which she had been. Yet looking at the light I felt that I had to go towards it, like a moth. Mentally I was trying to dance round it, even escape from its orbit, but I knew that I would always end up moving to that light by the front door.

Remembering again what to say, I turned the key gently. I had hardly pushed when the door opened and more light flooded out towards me. I screwed up my eyes, focusing in Jane's chest and neck in front of me. 'Jane, I've been an idiot.'

'No you haven't. You've come home. Come in, come in!' Jane grabbed my right shoulder and dragged me through the front door. She gave me a hug and a kiss. 'Yes David, it's good to see you too! Come on.'

Jane grabbed my hand and led me into the kitchen. She had been baking again, a spiced apple cake. She cut me a generous slice to go with the last of the French drinking chocolate. That had been supposed to be being kept for a special occasion. She fetched my slippers from by the bed.

I tried again to say my piece but she was more interested in telling me how everything was arranged for tomorrow, how helpful people had been, how pleased they were to be doing something for me. 'I didn't know you were so popular! I could understand it if they were happy to do things for Paul, or even God. But they really did say you. You're more highly rated than you think you are.'

I sat there shaking my head slowly, wondering whether to tell her the truth about the day. 'They might have had a different attitude if they had seen…'

'Oh shut up and just accept a compliment when you have one thrown at you.' Jane was smiling. 'It's not exactly as if you have them every day here, is it?'

'Yes, but…'

'Yes, but that's all there is to it for today. And we still have things to do, like choosing some words to go on the flowers we're sending. And having a proper pray together for Paul, who needs as much as he can get.'

The agenda for the rest of the evening was set. Eventually I relaxed and our time of prayer began with a really heartfelt 'Thank you for being there and guiding us, despite our stupidity,' at which Jane squeezed my hand.

Eventually Jane was satisfied that there was nothing more to do. The children had been watching a film in Nicola's room. Emily then went to bed, as Peter came charging in.

'Wow. You're going to enjoy tomorrow Dad. Your name before the national news hounds and all that.' I couldn't tell, again, if he was being serious.

'Like a hedgehog in the headlights, you reckon?' I smiled, surprised at the metaphor.

'Go, Dad!' Peter put his hand up to slap mine.

'Since when were we on American TV?' I said shaking his hand vigorously. He turned round, waggled his finger in front of his nose and ran off. Some life was normal, no, somehow better than normal. And it certainly wasn't cold and damp.

'I'll make some Ovaltine while you get ready for bed.' I looked at Jane blankly, still not being able to take in the warm goodness from everybody. 'Come on! We need to settle down in bed together. Do you want sugar or honey?'

There was no arguing with that. Meekly I climbed the stairs. The Ovaltine settled my stomach and my head and Jane warmed my body, so sleep came easily.

Thursday

Bright light pierced around the edge of the curtains as I woke up. My head was heavy. Even though the alarm clock said it was already 8.15 I had no real desire to be out of bed, as I knew I should be. The memories of yesterday crept up on me and I headed for the toilet. Jane must have been listening for my movement for she was soon in with a cup of tea.

I tried to be cheerful and direct. 'I think I've lost the plot. Today's a very important day, I know that. But I have no idea what I'm supposed to be doing.'

'The funeral's not until 2.30 so there's plenty of time for everything. You could even go back to sleep for a little. Or do you want your Bible and notes again? Thanks for last night.' Jane smiled.

Her last comment took me aback. 'Well, thank you. And I think it's high time I got going. How's Nicola?'

'She's a bit better this morning. She'll be up soon. Do you want your Bible?' Jane seemed to be acting as guardian of my soul.

'Have you read it then? Is it particularly worth reading today?' I wanted to know what was behind her matronly interest in my spiritual life.

'I've no idea, that's your business. I just think that once you're up properly you'll never settle again today. There's a football match on tonight.' She gave me a longsuffering look, softened by her lips rising in a smile.

'Go on then. I'll be a good boy. Vicar's assistants are meant to do this sort of thing. Or maybe you should do it instead, now that you know more of what's happening than I do?'

'I'll fetch it for you. Then we can talk about your duties for the day. Stay there!' She thrust out her hand to emphasise her command and left.

It was another Psalm, a less familiar one, Psalm 141. It was not easy reading about needing to be kept safe from the company of the wicked, from the temptation of eating their delicacies. I felt ashamed again but safe, well away from the siren voices and safely in harbour again. I knew that I had more to learn about this but today was not the day. 'Let the righteous strike me, let the faithful correct me.' I don't generally like asking masochistically for anyone to strike or correct me, but today I could pray those words. I needed to talk it through with someone, with Paul probably, so that he could show me where I went wrong and what to do about it.

Thankfully the writer of the notes wasn't concerned about sin as much as I was. He focused on the first few verses, where we ask that our prayer is counted as a sacrifice. Once again what he wrote was new to me, about how revolutionary this idea was and is for religious people. Imagine getting away with not giving anything, no sacrifices or offerings, but instead just asking to be given what you want. Religion keeps asking people for commitment, for offering their lives, their hearts, their money. People are suspicious, rightly so, of such religion. It is a parasite on good-living hard-working people. Strong words which I had not expected from a religious writer! Instead of the sacrifices people are asked to make, God is actually happiest when we just bring our requests to him, not thinking that we will have to pay for them, but just because we know that he is more than ready to help us. Instead of holding back and thinking whether we'll ever be able to pay for what we want, we just ask. Let the lifting up of my hands, let my pleading for my needs, be counted as a sacrifice. Let my asking be counted as my giving. How many churches would dare to tell people that when the collection plate comes round they could put in a request instead? Now that would be revolutionary. Part of me liked it and smiled. The Church council member in me was worried though and I couldn't see it catching on. However, the writer seemed to know what he was talking about, and encouraged us to ask, simply ask, and think that, because you have asked, your account is actually in credit! It was certainly an odd way of thinking.

It made me think about what I needed to ask today. Bewildered was how I felt. I knew I had responsibilities to see to today, but I wasn't sure what they were or how to carry them out. Jason was uppermost on my mind. Was it really true that he had been cleared to come to the funeral and I was to chaperone him? How on earth was that going to work? What I really wanted was for everything to work out well for the funeral, for Paul to say the right things and everything to go smoothly. I didn't want my first funeral as a vicar's assistant (and I hoped fervently my last) to dissolve into chaos. 'Please, Lord, sort it all out. Take charge, make sure that everything happens just right. Please. Partly for my sake, I admit it, but also for the family's sake too, for Patricia and Meg especially. Lord bless

Meg especially. Thank you for her strange contribution. Please make sure that the thing with the roses works out OK. Please keep her under control. Just as I am with Jason, please will you keep someone with Meg, just to keep an eye on her and a restraining hand as well, if necessary. Keep the influence of her wacky friends weak, Lord, and the influence of your Spirit strong.'

I wondered why I was praying for Meg, and stopped. Why was I thinking of her more than anyone else? She was a good girl at heart, I suspected, and I smiled when I thought of her. Her mother would need her around more now, and I hoped that they would get on well, better than it seemed they had so far. I prayed for Jane and the family, especially for Nic, and felt stronger, more settled, ready for breakfast.

Downstairs Jane had already made a list. I could see it on the table but I wasn't allowed to look at it until I had eaten. Black pudding was frying on the cooker, to which Jane added a couple of eggs and plenty of toast. 'You need a hearty breakfast today. It's the sort of day when you don't know if you'll be stopping for lunch or not. There'll be food after the service so you may just have to wait until them, poor man. Come on and let's be having you!'

It was good black pudding, crisp on the outside and fragrantly light and soft on the inside. I wondered why none of the rest of the family would touch it. Being put off by the idea of something without ever tasting the reality. I smiled. Christianity was just like that to some people. All that talk of blood from the cross, it seemed crude, primitive. They couldn't bring themselves to taste it. Such a shame. With egg and toast, a piece of black pudding was a wonderful feast.

'I must be getting into this role as vicar's assistant,' I thought, ' thinking theological thoughts over breakfast.' I smiled again and wondered about my smiling. Last night I had thought I would be sleeping rough and not be allowed to smile for a while. In fact for most of yesterday I couldn't remember smiling. It had been a tense, frustrating, almost disastrous day, and I was glad that it felt like a month ago already.

Jane put her hand on her list and I was eager to see what was in it. 'This is all taken care of. Remember that your main job is to look after Jason. You're the only one who can do that, so just leave the rest of it to us.' Jane was firm. It seemed that she had thought it all through and there was no arguing with her.

'Are you sure that they'll really let Jason come to the funeral? It seems so odd. I can't remember a precedent. What do the family think? Patricia has enough to cope with without having to see him.' Murder suspects at their victims' funerals might happen in Hollywood but not Birmingham.

'You know the family enough, David, to know that there's an unconventional element in them? If something strange comes out of that family where do you think it comes from?'

That was an easy question. 'Mad Meg? Is this one of her crazy ideas? Does she want to make Jason throw petals into Lizzie's coffin, forcing him to look at her? Does she think that'll somehow make him confess? Good grief! If that's what it's about, I think I'll keep him away.'

'Calm down, David. Why do you get so aggravated whenever her name is mentioned? I'm sure that she's thinking of nothing like that. Actually she's as mad as you are in one way. She thinks Jason is innocent too.'

'Meg?' This was hard to believe.

'She said that he was such a nice part of Lizzie's life and all of theirs, that it would be unthinkable for him not to be there now. It was she, and Patricia of course, who actually took the lead and asked for Jason to be present.'

'Did anyone think of asking poor Paul?'

Jane looked at me with controlled exasperation. 'Paul had no idea what to do about it when they asked him, but he contacted the police who checked with Patricia and it's all arranged. She's an amazing woman really, not at all the conventional housewife everyone thinks she is. If she had been born thirty years later she might have been madder than Meg.' Jane, it seemed, was finding a new friend. She spoke with admiration and joy at having seen the unconventional in someone else.

I paused to take all this in. 'So you can reassure Jason that they don't think he was the one. At least they'll be able to trust each other for the day then. But don't let him off the hook completely. While you're with him you could see if he'll tell you what led him to be so stupid.'

'What? You mean the suicide attempt? He was desperate, grief-stricken, wishing that it all could have been different, wanting to be with Lizzie still, not knowing how he could live without her. I don't know. I think he's over that now. What's the point of talking about it?' I was beginning to become angry, but didn't want to be. Not today.

'David. It's time you allowed yourself to see what everyone else sees.' Jane was trying to be kind to me, but she reverted a little too much to patronising teacher mode. I gritted my teeth for what I thought was coming.

'There's no point in pretending. Jason was obsessed, we all knew it but we didn't do more to help him. We didn't want to interfere. But he was obsessed, more than was healthy.'

'Oh for goodness sake, he was heartbroken. He was young and in love!'

Jane carried on, unmoved by the interruption. 'He should have at least started getting over losing her, but he didn't. It just grew worse and worse. Hearing Jennifer talk about these last months – it was awful for them.'

'He moped a lot, that's all.'

'You heard more of it than most of us, but that was only half. He was taken over, obsessed, by grief.' I was glad I had not heard this depressing view before, and couldn't quite believe I was hearing it now. Jane carried on, crisply. 'In the end he snapped and did something very stupid for which he'll be paying for a long time.'

'Rubbish,' was all I could manage

'You could at last try to help him come to terms with reality now, David? This may be the last time that any of us have with him properly for years. Can't you just help him come to terms with what he's done?'

I stared at Jane, shaking my head resolutely.

Jane pleaded. 'Reassure him that we'll still be here for him when he comes out, that sort of thing. Just be a friend and hold his hand and help him come to his senses. That'll make life so much easier for him in the end, and for all of us.' Jane was in earnest. I wanted to throw cold water over her.

I kept my head down, fighting with the anger inside me. 'You build me up by saying that I'm not the only one who thinks Jason's innocent and then slap me down again. No Jane.' I lifted my head and looked at her, made bolder by a new thought. 'What about Patricia? If she's such a good woman, why can't you go along with her?'

Jane shook her hand warily like a teacher who has already explained to a naughty boy exactly what the school rules say about uniform. I snapped.

'How do you know?' I was louder now, losing control. 'How on earth do you know that Jason did such a horrible thing? For God's sake, Jane! Innocent until proved guilty! Isn't that true for Jason as much as anyone else? The court will decide – and even they can get it wrong, God knows. Just leave it to them, won't you? Oh, for God's sake!'

I paused and checked myself. Jane stood quietly waiting for her pupil's tantrum to subside. She wasn't listening. 'Look I'll go and clean my teeth and then we can talk some more about the day. And I am not going to tell Jason to accept responsibility for a crime he did not commit. I'm just not.'

As I stomped up the stairs, I was surprised by Nicola sitting just round the corner. She smiled at me. 'Go Daddy, go!'

Before I could say anything, she was up and running downstairs. 'Mum! How could you?' It was my turn to sit down and eavesdrop. If Jane was going to treat me like a schoolboy I might as well act like one. 'Well how could you? Can't you answer me?'

Jane had her arms crossed and sounded as patient and long-suffering as she knew how. 'Nicky, dear, this is between your father and me.'

'This isn't a private little joke you know! We know Jason too. He's our friend, and he's innocent.' Nicola was furious.

'Nicky, it's not worth getting so upset about. The courts will decide anyway, not us.' Jane was remarkably restrained.

'Dad knows Jason didn't do it. I know too. He knew too much about cars. Why won't you listen to us?' Nicola was in tears.

'Nicky…' cooed Jane motheringly.

'Don't Nicky me. Just listen to me, for God's sake! If you want to kick Jason now he's down, don't get Dad to do it for you, and don't talk about it when I can hear. OK?' There was a pause as, I imagine, Nicola stared through her tears at Jane. There was no response and Nicola stomped up the stairs past me, slamming the door of her bedroom.

Once I was dressed, it didn't seem sensible to raise with Jane again what I was going to say to Jason. She was not ready to apologise, and I was not ready to give in, especially not with Nicola backing me up. 'That feels better, a fresh body for a fresh day. Thanks for doing the list, dear.' I was as cheerful as I could be.

'And I suppose you want to know what's in it? It really is taken care of you know.' Jane was slightly mocking my anxiety that she wouldn't have remembered everything.

Trying not to rise to her mockery and resisting a temptation simply to grab the list, I continued in good cheer: 'I'm no expert either, but two heads are always better than one. What needs to be done today?'

Jane picked up the list and read it out. 'Check car parking arrangements with Bill and Bert. That means that there are reserved places for a few invited people and the press, and plenty of space at front of church for the hearse and cars.' She looked at me gently challenging me to find a fault with this.

'Great. Thanks.' I smiled gratefully.

'Check service contributions and collect them at 12. That means I'll ring Jill at the office and make sure that she has received the sermon, prayers and tributes so that they can be photocopied and given to the Press before the service. I'll be the one actually handing them out.' Jane paused again.

'Very efficient. Wouldn't have thought of that.' I was mostly preoccupied with wondering how I would handle Jason, but now that I had begun I needed graciously to play the part of funeral arrangements supervisor.

'Meet television crew at 10.30. Although they're not filming inside we still want to keep them in their place outside.' Jane paused again, looking at me only briefly before carrying on.

'Church at 1.30. I should have time for a bite of lunch before being there early to make sure the orders of service and petals are in place. I really don't think it's going to be a problem. Not like having to get thirty seven-year-olds all dressed, ready and quiet at the same time.' Jane smiled again, challenging me to belittle her experience if I dared.

She had won. I could only move on. 'Good. I might be able to join you for lunch then, depending on when and where I meet with Jason. Any idea?'

Now the smile was more relaxed, assured. 'The police will escort him from the bail hostel home to Will and Jennifer's. You'll then go together to the Church. They'll tell you more when you see them. Sorry. That's all I could find out.'

'So I'll go now and see how they are, and if they know any more.' I was quite pleased that I could just concentrate on the one thing, however odd it seemed.

'Give them my love. I'll be thinking of them – and of you of course.' Jane came close and kissed me on the cheek. It felt like a kiss of peace, a gentle drawing of a line under all that had gone on, both today and yesterday. I relaxed and put my arms round her. We hugged.

I put on my jacket, picked up the keys to the Rover, looked at it and decided to walk. It was a bright day with a hint of chill in the air. A few dead leaves had collected on the lawn but the roses were bright. I was glad we had inherited such a variety of bold yellows and reds, not the pale pinks which seem so popular. There was no sign of the press. They had withdrawn, knowing they would have their grandstand view at the service.

Will opened the door warily. He didn't have the chain on, but looked as though this was only because he didn't want to advertise his insecurity. He greeted me in a matter-of-fact way and stepped back to let me in. The house smelt as clean and fragrant as ever. The memory of Meg's aversion to air freshener almost made me smile. I didn't know how Will would react so I squashed it.

'Jennifer's got a blooming migraine again. So she says. Taken herself to bed. Come through.' Underneath Will's grumpiness he seemed pleased to have some company. We stood in the kitchen while he made coffees and then just carried on standing. I eventually sat down on a stool by the worktop and Will leaned over by me.

'It's a strange day, Will. You must be pleased to be seeing Jason though. Have you seen much of him the last few days?' I realised with shame how out of touch I was.

'Nope. Jen's talked on the phone. That's all.' Will rolled his eyes and shook his head with a brief forced grimace. We kept an awkward quiet.

'Do you think Jennifer'll be all right for this afternoon? She does want to come, does she?' As I spoke I realised that maybe it was all too much for her.

Will shrugged his shoulders, opened out his hands briefly and breathed out heavily with bemused resignation. More silence.

'It's good of the family to want Jason around. Meg was the main mover, I understand.' I wasn't sure how mad Will thought Meg was.

He rolled his eyes again. 'Used to stick up for him she did.' A tear came to his eye which he brushed away quickly. There didn't seem to be much else to say. We drank coffee and looked straight ahead at nothing.

Eventually I gave up trying to be interested or sympathetic and became practical. 'I understand that Jason's coming here with a policeman. Have they given you a time?'

At first Will didn't seem to have heard the question. I drank another gulp of coffee and wondered what to say next. 'Two o'clock Jason said. Doesn't want time here with us. It's hard on Jen. Hard on both of us really.' Will wiped his eye again and kept looking ahead.

'Yes. Not easy for either of you. Sorry, Will.' I had clumsily trodden on a painful toe and was trying to make amends. We were quiet together again. I tried and failed to imagine what it would be like to be in Will's shoes. I now had what I had come for, but it would be callous just to leave. What on earth to say though?

Will turned to me with a smile. 'Thanks for coming, David. Good of you to take the time.'

All I was aware of was how little help I had been to them and this made me even more guilty. 'No one makes a stronger coffee than you Will. Sometimes I just need to escape from the ladies and their dishwater decaff.'

Will smiled and raised his mug. 'Cheers, David. Bugger the sleep eh?' He drained his mug and turned to me again. 'There's not much more to say. Jason's not decided what to plead yet. His lawyer's on at him to make life 'easy for all concerned.' Wish we'd never had the smooth bastard.'

This was an invitation for a professional opinion. 'Good. He's sticking up for himself at last. Between us we'll get that Strutt to do his job properly. Or I could find you someone else?' I was glad to have something I could talk about more freely. 'It's not so unusual you know. It's a very personal relationship, a lawyer and his client. Often it doesn't work at first.'

'Jason's decision,' said Will with resignation.

'OK. I'll try and talk with him about it. He'll expect me to be interested in the legal side of things anyway. How did Jennifer think he seemed?' It was unnerving to think that I might have to persuade him one way or another when it was only me, it seemed, who wanted him to plead not guilty. If everyone, including Jane, was right, and he did plead not guilty, his sentence would be a lot worse. I didn't want to condemn him to years more in prison, but I still couldn't see that he had done it.

Will shrugged again and kept quiet. I told him about young Nicola and her theory. He looked up brightly at first but then down at his empty mug, shaking his head. 'Do you want another?'

'Not now, thanks. I'll see you later, after it's all over, and we can chew it over then. We may need something more though, one of your famous liqueurs?' We both smiled.

'They're ready and waiting,' said Will, seeming more relaxed than he had been for a while. 'Thanks, David.'

'Give my love to Jennifer, and I'll see you at a quarter to two.' It seemed that I hadn't made a complete pig's ear of my visit.

I walked home with a lighter back, even carrying my jacket, for the sun had warmed the air and the ground. Half way home there was a man on a sit-on lawnmower weaving round the trees, spraying natural fragrance for us all. A buddleia in a corner garden was shimmering with red admirals. I stopped and looked, wanting to enjoy this slow time before the strangeness of the afternoon. Maybe I could divert to the park for a few minutes? But the strangeness was already lapping at me and I couldn't stand and enjoy the sunshine. Normal life had been suspended. Jason might never again enjoy these manicured gardens, each a different variety of shapes of green with splashes of mauve and yellow and red. Even the pale orange and pink snap dragons seemed charming rather than sickly and artificial. The birds were still singing, starlings gathering together on the telephone wire across the road. It all seemed somehow exhilarating and yet out of tune. Even the late ivy above our front door in rich maroon seemed too vibrant for this day.

Nicola came downstairs as soon as I stepped inside, wanting to know the latest. 'Mum sent these round for you.' She handed me a brown A4 envelope and stayed to watch me open it.

The envelope wasn't sealed, and I was impressed that Nicola had obviously not opened it. Her upbringing had been far more religious than mine, so maybe those temptations didn't nag at her as strongly as they had done me. I smiled at her as I pulled out a sheet of papers.

It was a pile of photocopies of newspaper cuttings from the last few days, with a note from Jane. 'David, dear, Jason might have read these so I thought you would find them useful too. See you soon, love Jane.'

'Come on,' I said, beckoning Nicola to the sitting room sofa and coffee table we could see from the hall. 'You can help me see what's being said about Jason. You're on the team now, on his side I mean.'

We settled down in silence and read. There was the speculation about Tariq's drinking on the night of the crash and features about both families. Stern denials that Tariq could have been drunk were printed without question. Jason was mentioned in write-up about Lizzie as an early love whom she had outgrown. One article from the *Birmingham Express* went into his background as a car mechanic at some length, leaving the readers to draw their own conclusions. Jason's suicide attempt was headlined, although 'murder suspect' had replaced his name. As soon as Jason had been held, the papers could say nothing more without interfering with the court proceedings. Yet there were a number of people quoted pointing out that to see this as the work of any group, when none had claimed responsibility, was diabolical scaremongering. The implication was that this was a simple '*crime passionel*.' I wondered crossly if Jane was here trying to tell me something along the lines of what she said earlier.

There was a variety of touching photos of Patricia and Meg walking their dog, from a photo shoot which had passed me by.

Mohammed looked sad and not too angry by a headline 'Father Frustrated'. A sympathetic report explained that he was fed up with the rumours making his son out to be the perpetrator and not the victim. Nicola found an old picture of me in my court suit of six years ago next to an article explaining that Mohammed had hired me to defend his son. I wasn't sure if my refusal to talk more with the Press had been a good move or not. I could have given them a more accurate view, but were they so interested in accuracy?

Nicola enjoyed summarising stories for me and was remarkably good at it. Standards of English comprehension in schools have not plummeted despite the scaremongering. I thanked her, and told her about Will and Jennifer. She was concerned to know if Jason would have to be photographed at church. 'I hope not. I don't want my balding hair in the papers,' I laughed. 'I hope they'll not recognise him until it's too late, but it might be worth going in through the vestry just in case.'

Jane found us at the coffee table. She threw me a plastic wallet with more A4 papers. 'Paul's not holding back, as if he ever would. See what you think. I'll just have to make my own lunch.'

'Cheese and pickle, please dear.' I smiled cheekily at Jane who wagged her finger at me. 'Just this once…' Nicola kept quiet.

The papers were what had been prepared for the service: prayers, readings, a couple of tributes to Lizzie from the newspaper and a University friend, and Paul's sermon.

Paul Cooper's Sermon at the Funeral of Lizzie

Since the day I heard of Lizzie and Tariq's car accident, one Bible verse has kept recurring to me. At first I thought it was just me being pessimistic, but then when Lizzie died, it seemed more accurate. I have tried to dismiss it as melodramatic, but gently and persistently it keeps coming back, often when I am praying and have been thinking of something else completely. It is one of the famous verses in the Bible about mourning, coming in both the Old and New Testaments, so perhaps, I thought, it might be appropriate to speak on it today. Patricia was quite happy for me to make this verse the centre of what I want to say today. Other people have spoken more eloquently than I could do about Lizzie herself. My role is to take something from the Bible and hold it before you in the hope that it will shine a light for you in what must be a dark and confusing time. The verse for today is Matthew chapter 2 and verse 18: 'A voice was heard in Ramah, wailing and loud lamentation. Rachel weeping for her children; she refused to be consoled for they are no more.'

These are sad words for a sad and painful time. They are firstly Jeremiah's words, but Matthew takes them to help make sense of what is known as the Slaughter of the Innocents, King Herod killing all the little boys in and around Bethlehem so that he could kill Jesus before he grew to become a threat to his kingship. I think we can then take these words to help us make sense of Lizzie's tragic death.

Lizzie was an innocent victim. Let us say that boldly and clearly. Like those hundreds of children slaughtered by Herod for his own selfish purposes, Lizzie was killed by someone for their own selfish purposes. It is her innocence which makes this so hard to bear. Innocent, trusting, likeable, uncomplicated – these are the words that have been used again and again in describing Lizzie. The cards and letters you have written to Patricia and Meg witness repeatedly to the innocence of Lizzie's character. What does the Bible have to say to us mourning the slaughter of a young innocent?

'A voice was heard in Ramah…' Ramah was five miles north of Jerusalem, not the political centre of the nation but certainly in its heartland. Birmingham is the heartland of England and, through what happened twelve days ago, Birmingham voices have been heard. So be it. Let our voices be heard for what has happened here is a tragedy indeed and the whole country needs to take notice.

'…wailing and loud lamentation. Rachel weeping for her children…' Today is a day for tears, for coming together and crying together. Let no one say that they did well today because they did not cry. This is too important a day and Lizzie was too important a part of your life. She has been violently taken away from you. Don't mark this with 'stiff upper lip, life carries on as usual' nonsense. Let this be a day for wailing and loud weeping. How else can we respond to this wonderfully beautiful but dead girl?

Let this be a day for shouting that anguished question, 'Why?' Let this not be a day for shrugging and saying, 'Well, these sorts of things happen in our day and age…' Let this be a day for declaring to everyone that this slaughter is unacceptable. We are not going to just take this. We need to know why this happened – which will mean, of course, knowing who caused this to happen. So we pray earnestly for our police force and our courts that they will be led to the person who caused this ungodly death. And let me take this opportunity, in this public service, and, more importantly, through the media, to address whoever was behind this devastating death.

Why? For goodness sake, why? Why would you, whoever you are, deliberately set out to damage a car knowing that this could easily cause death? You may think you had your reasons. Herod thought he had very good reasons. He thought he could see a power struggle ahead between himself or his successor and this new king that the so-called wise men had told him about. Herod maybe imagined a new civil war between his supporters and the supporters of the new king. A civil war would leave thousands dead. Much better to kill a few hundred and avoid more deaths in future. So Herod and his advisers would have thought. It is better for a few hundred to die for the sake of the whole nation.

Is that the kind of thinking you have been led into, whoever you are? Did you somehow think that what you were doing would make life better, safer, for you or for other people? Know that Herod is now exposed as a selfish and cruel murderer. Your thinking may not have been so grandiose. Maybe it was simply that someone had hurt you badly and you needed to make some kind of balancing. You may have thought you had your reasons, but we tell you that whatever you thought, it was not worth killing Lizzie. If you think you had to do this, speak up and tell us your reasons. Admit what you have done and stand by your intentions. Don't skulk and hide. Come out and let us hear you. We need to know why Lizzie had to die and you, whoever you are, are the only one who can tell us.

'A voice was heard in Ramah, wailing and loud lamentation. Rachel weeping for her children.' Encouraged by Scripture, we weep and we let our voice be heard. This verse goes on:

'Rachel weeping for her children, she refused to be consoled for they are no more.' That's how it feels in the sharp pain of loss. Nothing will bring Lizzie back, nothing and no one can comfort us.

But left there, this is a strange message for the Bible to be giving. Is there really no comfort? If there is comfort are we to refuse it? When we look at this verse not on its own but in its original place in the words of Jeremiah, we see more clearly. Two verses before, Jeremiah records words that came to him from God. 'I will turn their mourning into joy, I will comfort them and give them gladness for sorrow.' And Immediately after the description of Rachel refusing to be comforted, God commands: 'Keep your voice from weeping and your eyes from tears...' Although Rachel refuses to be comforted God is still close to her, offering comfort, and warning her of problems to come if she keeps refusing.

This, of course, fits in with the general message of the Bible, from God saying through Isaiah 'Comfort ye, comfort ye my people,' to Jesus saying 'Do not let your hearts be troubled. Believe in God. Believe also in me.' There is comfort for God's people. He Himself is the Shepherd who has been through death. His tears have flowed at the death of those close to Him. With God, with Jesus, there is comfort. Through His Spirit and through the people He sends you, there will be comfort offered to you. Please do not refuse it. However hard and hopeless life may seem, don't shrug off what people want to do for you, don't dismiss the words of the Bible. Allow yourself to weep and allow yourself to be comforted.

For grief comes as a wave, sometimes quite unexpectedly. It washes through with almost overwhelming force, and then it ebbs away. Let the grief come and let the grief go. That is the essence of what the Bible tells us to do with grief. Let it come, with the tears and the gloom. Let it go, expecting that there will be comfort and peace, at least for a while. Don't hang onto grief. Blessed are those who mourn, who know both tears and comfort.

Part of this comfort is knowing that other people, including Jesus, have been through this dark valley before you and can accompany you if you will let them. Part of this comfort is knowing that the valley does have an end. The valley of the shadow of death ends in a broad place where there is a full table, abundant oil, a cup overflowing, a room in the house of the Lord, the house of Jesus' Father, for ever. Even if we never come fully through this valley in this life, we know that there is an end and that Jesus will take us there. We cannot find this place, this room in the Father's house, without Jesus. We do not know where to look or how to reach there. But Jesus, our Shepherd if we will let him, will guide us there. He has promised to come and take us and He always keeps his promises. Lizzie looked to Jesus as her Shepherd, her friend and guide through life. So we know that as she continues to look to Jesus, He will bring her through to His Father's house. Comfort ye, comfort ye my people. Believe in God. Believe also in Jesus.

With this comfort, we can let grief go. And as we let our grief go, we can let our anger and desire for revenge go. The most beguiling, yet the most dangerous part of hanging onto grief, refusing to be comforted, is holding onto our anger. We rage against the walls of the valley of the shadow of death and we are stuck there in our rage, never moving through the valley. We rage against those who have thrown us into this dark valley and want desperately to drag them into the darkness too so they can know what it feels like, and worse. This, more than anything, keeps us trapped in the dark valley. If we let our grief turn into revenge, we will be dragging others into the dark valley of the shadow of death and we will be trapped there, possibly for ever. If we keep blaming ourselves too, for whatever reason, we will be locking ourselves in the deepest darkness.

This is why God seems so hard with Rachel, commanding her 'Keep your voice from weeping and your eyes from tears.' Jesus commands his followers 'Do not let your hearts be troubled.' When God issues a command it is not because he is a sergeant major who likes ordering people around. God's commands are the urgent call of a parent who sees their child about to step out in front of speeding lorry. 'Stop! Don't do that!'

God does not want us imprisoned in the valley of the shadow of death – that is the work of the devil. But there is a real possibility that if we hang onto our anger and desire for revenge, if we refuse to be comforted, we will be stuck there and never come through the valley to the Father's house.

So today let there be tears and let there be comfort too. Let us hold to each other in the darkness of the valley of the shadow of death, and let us assure each other of the forgiving light that is ahead of us, and that is even now shining on us like the first rays of the dawn. Let us be determined to live in the light and according to the light, the light of God's love, God's forgiveness, mercy, grace and truth. Let us be honest but let us never look for revenge. Let grief come and let it go. And let whoever caused this tragedy hear this. We want you to know and feel, not the darkness and anguish into which you have driven us, but the light and grace which comes from Jesus and is Jesus. As you explain what you have done, we will not hold it against you, however hard that might be for us, for to do that would be to lock ourselves into this dark valley.

Patricia, Meg, our hearts go out to you. Thank you for sharing Lizzie with us all. From what you have said, from what I have known of her myself, I know that, if this had happened to someone else, Lizzie would want to comfort you. Part of your pain is that she cannot now comfort you in this life. Do not ask her to, for that is not her role now. Your comfort will come from other people, and from Jesus. But know that Lizzie would want you to be comforted. She would not want you to refuse comfort. Let grief come, let it surge. Let grief go, let it ebb. Maybe grief won't ever leave you completely in this life, but know that as you look to Jesus, you will be comforted.

'A voice was heard in Ramah, wailing and loud lamentation. Rachel weeping for her children....' 'Do not let your hearts be troubled. Believe and trust in God. Believe and trust in Jesus also.' 'Blessed are those who mourn, for they shall be comforted.'

'Phew!' I exhaled slowly as Jane came in with the sandwiches.

'Nothing illegal there is there?' Jane challenged.

'No slander or incitement. But addressing the murderer? Why? It can't be usual?' Paul wasn't one for playing safe but this seemed unnecessary.

'Someone has to say what we're feeling. That's his job. Isn't that what you would want to say if you could talk to whoever it was?' Jane seemed pretty certain.

'Have you talked to him then?' Criticising Jane was one thing but criticising Paul himself was another.

'Paula said she had talked about it with him as he was preparing it. She said it took her a little while to understand but she's with him now. He really will be talking to the nation, including the poor person that did it.' Jane seemed confident that, although I might take some time, I would come to agree too.

'Does he know that Jason's going to be there?' My guess was that he didn't know or else he would be less direct. Or maybe he thought that the murderer was someone with more Herod-like motives that a jealous lover? As strange as the sermon seemed, I could see hope for Jason. Jane stared at me in response shrugging her shoulders a little to say that she had no idea and didn't want really to talk about it any more. She had made her point.

'O.K. He has the nation listening to him. Some people would preach the gospel. Where is the message of the cross? People will say he's been distracted by sensationalism into missing a golden opportunity.' I genuinely wasn't sure if I thought this or not, but I was certain that some people would. There was a small but influential group who took every opportunity to bemoan Paul's lack of 'gospel' preaching. Paul seemed very Biblical to me, but sometimes didn't say what I expected to hear. Like today.

'Let them play their own games!' Jane was surprisingly forceful. 'I think this is what people want to say and there's enough Scripture here to satisfy anyone, surely?'

'He's a braver man than I am, or a more foolhardy one.' We weren't going to agree, especially as I didn't know quite what to think. I filled Jane in on Will and Jennifer and she agreed to make sure that the vestry door would be open. She or someone would see us drive past and go and open it for us. I would have Peter's mobile phone as well just in case. Jane went out looking very smart and sober and, after changing, I followed suit, so to speak.

There was a strange car in the Jennings' drive. A quick look inside confirmed that it was an unmarked police car. I was impressed that the police were sensitive enough not to draw attention to Jason. I could imagine the vehement language the officers had used when they heard that permission had been given for this crazy stunt but they had, as ever, knuckled down and cooperated. This impression was confirmed when I was greeted by Simon Plant, a tall sergeant who had given evidence with me during the last speeding clampdown in the city. He was in plain clothes and, at the first opportunity when no one was looking, raised his eyebrows mockingly. I was glad that Jason was with someone I knew and trusted to be firm and sympathetic. Simon had been dismayed at the widely varying sentences handed out by Magistrates on different days, especially when licences were actually taken away from first-time speeders who depended on driving for their living.

Jason was sitting next to Simon, although in his own home there was no need. Another man whom I did not know, presumably the driver, was sitting by the door. Jennifer was sitting by the fireplace in a large dressing gown with what looked like a jumper underneath. She was clearly not well and was happy for us to know. At first no one talked. Will, who had shown me into the sitting room and then gone to make me a coffee, came in quite quickly. He was flustered and shaking as he handed me my mug. He was wearing a dark suit.

'Look Dad, you don't have to come. I'll be OK with Sergeant Plant.' Jason sounded calmer than his father. 'If you want to stay and look after Mum, that's fine.'

'Jason dearest, I'm so sorry I can't be with you today of all days. You will come and see me after the service though, won't you?' Jennifer looked more at Simon than at Jason.

Simon replied. 'We don't have to be too strict with time today. I know it's important to all of you to have time together. After it's all over might be easier.'

Jennifer smiled and settled down in her chair. Will stood beside her, dithering. 'Don't know what I'd do if I came anyway, Jase. You've got David and the sergeant with you already. You don't want your old man tagging along too.'

'Dad, it's up to you, your choice entirely. If you want to come because it's Lizzie and you knew her, come. If you want to stay here with Mum, stay here.' Jason was showing his annoyance a little. This conversation had probably been going on for a little while.

Will looked at me. 'You're welcome to come Will, it'll be fine to have you with us.' I glanced at Simon who didn't react. Will had responded to Jason's suggesting that he stay at home by talking about what would happen if he came. He was wearing his suit. This was Will's way of indicating that he wanted to come but preferred someone else to make the decision. I recognised this tactic as a practitioner of it.

Jason shrugged, Jennifer coughed ever so slightly and Will flashed a smile at me. I didn't see why I shouldn't be a friend to Will at the moment even if I was supposed to be there for Jason.

I did wonder if having Will with us was such a good idea, and hoped that we would find someone else for him to sit with. But then people might see that as strange? I was tense and confused already and we were nowhere near the church.

Like a group of athletes waiting for the gun, we kept quiet, trying not to look at each other. Simon was the most relaxed and fairly quickly put his hands decisively on his knees and raised himself forward. 'Well-,' he began. 'Well,' I continued, hoping he would see and continue the joke. 'Well!' he completed, 'said the policeman.' My stomach lurched as I realised that this was not the time for jokes about holes in the ground. 'Let's be having you then, mister Jennings.' Simon seemed to have seen the pitfall too, thank God.

We did move and slowly made our way outside, taking extra care not to brush into each other. Jennifer stayed by the door. It was bright outside and she was half lost in the shadows. Once in the car it occurred to me that I didn't know what my role was.

'It's good to be with you Simon. Thanks. What's the plan? I've arranged for us to be let in the back door of the church to avoid the photographers.'

'No worries, mister lawyer. We'll just keep a low profile, join in the service and go home at the end.' Simon was reassuring. 'I hope you know the hymns. You're more used to this kind of thing, aren't you?'

'Yes… There's just one thing. Do you know about the rose petals?' I explained Meg's fancy idea and Jason smiled fondly. He was still saying very little.

'We'll just have to take it as it comes and make an informed impromptu decision. If everyone's doing it, we could, I suppose?' Simon looked back at Jason from the front seat. Jason just looked at him and silence took over. Will was moving uncomfortably on the other side of Jason. I wondered who else would be there. Mohammed and family of course. Would they come in the funeral cars with Patricia and Meg, or would Patricia see that as making too much of the relationship between Lizzie and Tariq? Tariq himself was still in hospital, now in high dependency and almost off the critical list.

As we drove past the church, Jane put her hand in the air to acknowledge us, not waving but sedately still. Her white hand stood out above the mingling crowd. She looked the part in her smart black suit. Would undertaking be a second career for her to consider? The road at the back of the church had cars parked along it already. We had to turn into the next street which was also filling up. The driver reversed to the church and we stepped out into the road. Coming in at the front of the church would draw attention to ourselves in a different way and I wondered about how wise it had been to suggest we walk round the back. But there had been a lot of photographers near Jane.

The door opened and Trudy Bagshot welcomed us inside in her kind matronly way. Her tweed skirt and thick shoes were a welcome sight. She pointed out the 'conveniences', the organ music growing louder as we walked past Paul's office. Like a gathering flock of birds, the voices of the people already there simmered in our ears as Trudy opened the door, and we were on the carpet at the front of church looking out at the pews. The front four rows were empty, and after that the church was about half full, thicker at the back than at the front. Four champagne buckets stood guard around a coffin-shaped space.

Simon spotted some empty seats six rows from the front and went straight there. I was wondering how many people knew who Jason was. Was there a frisson among them as we walked up the church? I couldn't tell. Simon stood in the aisle and motioned to Will to go in first, followed by myself, then Jason, and, lastly, Simon sat by the aisle. He was reassuringly in charge. Trudy came back with some orders of service, with a photo of Lizzie on the front. Jason took his and went straight into a tight Anglican crouch, whether to pray or hide tears I could not tell. His back seemed calm. 'All things bright and beautiful' was to be our first hymn, followed by 'Lord of all hopefulness' and 'Praise my soul' to finish. The family intention seemed to be upbeat. I wasn't sure how Paul's words would fit with this 'look on the bright side' approach.

Jason sat up, wiping a tear from his eye, and looked at the order of service. 'She really liked that one,' he said, pointing at 'All things'.' 'Soppy, she called it, but it reminded her of a blind choir mistress at her village church. Apparently she had amazingly gained her sight, well 25%, after some healing prayer.' I raised my eyebrows, not understanding the connection. 'He gave us eyes to see them.' Jason started crying, and I offered him a handkerchief. 'Keep it,' I said, as kindly as I could. I might even need it later, but I expected that Simon would be resolute and probably had one he could pass my way.

Will was stiff and pale, and kept looking around the church. He was not used to sitting so close to the front, poor man. I followed his gaze and saw Pete Hardy helping out on the sound desk. Suddenly it seemed better for Will to have something to do at the back. It took me a couple of minutes to work out how to get Will there. I tore a page out of my filofax and scribbled.

'Mike, please can I have a copy of today's service on tape – and please can you keep Will with you if you can. I think he'll cope with it better if he has something else to think about. David.' Mike was going to make fun of me for months for landing him with the most dangerous assistant possible but I didn't care. Will brightened when I asked him to take a note about taping the service to Mike and was quickly up and pushing past us.

Not long after that the organ music became more sombre and we all stood up. The tune being played seemed familiar but I could not place it, as was my wont A quick look back confirmed that the church was still a quarter empty, not what I had expected. It didn't seem right to crane round, to see the coffin and the mourners, as we would at a wedding. We looked steadily at Jesus on the cross in stained glass as Paul's deep voice rang out with the opening Scripture verses. He seemed full of poise and confidence, thank God, quite the professional. He gave the impression that he really did believe that nothing could separate us from the love of God. I was proud of him.

The coffin followed behind Paul, a very light wood with green cushioning just under the edges. Various people started and stared. I was one of them, despite having been warned so long ago that Lizzie's coffin would be open. There was a kerfuffle a few rows behind us on the other side and I think someone was lifted from the floor and escorted out. Thank God we could see no more at the moment. I sympathised with Paul, who would have to look at us and speak to us without letting his eyes wander down to pale Lizzie. His shocking description of her – 'wonderfully beautiful but dead,' - made more sense.

Patricia followed behind the coffin in a neat black suit and hat. She was staring straight ahead, maybe at Lizzie, maybe beyond. Holding her right arm was Meg in a dark crimson skirt, a loose navy top and an improbable rainbow scarf. This flaunting of mourning convention shocked me and I must have shown it. Jason leaned towards me. 'Lizzie made it. Wanted to brighten her up,' he said, a brief smile showing on his lips. Other family members followed and stood in front of us. I picked up my hymn sheet, expecting to sing, but the organ music just kept playing, interspersed with more verses from Paul. It seemed that many people had been waiting outside the church and were now filing in and trying to find seats. 'Why didn't they come in before? Are people too afraid to come into a church building? Or has the crematorium procedure taken over?' I asked myself. It was obvious enough that there wasn't another service immediately preceding Lizzie's but still so many people held back, making what felt like an interminable wait before we could begin the service. Paul seemed comfortable, suggesting where people could sit. Finally, after an opening prayer, we sang.

Well, I sang, and Sergeant Plant sang a little. Jason just looked at the words. After the first verse and chorus I had a quick look round and guessed that half of the people were singing. Mohammed and Raisa, with Frank as ever, were one row back on the other side. Raisa was singing a bit but not the men. We had a flourish from the organ before the last verse – it seemed he had been told to lift us for what was to come. I was ready for a rest and glad to sit down.

The order of service said that there were to be the two tributes, with a reading from Kahlil Gibran in the middle. Not everyone on the PCC would be entirely happy with a Sufi Moslem reading in church, but it seemed appropriate. The first

University friend was a confident and dapper lad. He described first meeting Lizzie in the communal kitchen of the Hall of Residence, as she burst in after everyone else had arrived, dumped her bags in the middle of the floor, dropped to her knees to rummage, and handed round a tin of Marks and Spencer chocolate biscuits. For him this summed her up, scatty and impetuous, a bit classier than the average student and always generous. 'And she really only liked dark chocolate,' whispered Jason to me wryly. He seemed to be sitting calmly but one hand clutched the handkerchief I had given him and his order of service was creased all over from being squashed into a ball and then folded out again, three times I think.

After the first couple of sentences of the Gibran reading I wasn't at all sure what it was about, as my mind was already wondering how on earth the petal dropping would go. In the order of service it said, 'Quiet personal tributes to Lizzie' which I took to be the opportunity for people to come up and put a handful of rose petals in the coffin. I hoped that a few people would take up the offer, enough to make it not seem silly, but not so many that we would have to join in. Jason was more edgy than I had first thought.

The second friend, the one from the newspaper, turned out to be an older woman. She talked of the ease with which Lizzie could write, like her 'tinkling' voice which would never want to stop, and yet her ability to free people to talk with her. Some people make good listeners through their quiet gentle attentiveness. Others, like Lizzie, draw people into the flow and joy of talking. Never self-obsessed in her talking, it was as though Lizzie provided a bright frame of words into which other people were invited to draw their own picture. Her piece on the parents of the two lads arrested in Italy during the last World Cup was outstanding both in sympathy and acute observation. Lizzie's colleague was not expecting her to be in Birmingham long and was glad that the Second City had had a first rate journalist for a while.

There was a little ripple of applause from a few rows behind us. Paul immediately stood up. 'Yes, indeed. Let's applaud these two wonderful character sketches of Lizzie, and applaud both her and the God who made her.' The applause was deafening and my eyes filled with tears. We were giving her a good send off, bless her. She was special and everyone felt it together.

As the applause died down, Paul introduced another unusual part to our service. Applause did not normally happen at funerals, nor was the coffin left open in a normal English service. We were used to scattering earth onto the coffin which was somehow a good way of our saying farewell physically. Today we weren't going to wait to the end for this, there would be an opportunity now for everyone who wanted to make their own personal act of saying farewell to Lizzie. 'Lizzie's sister Meg is going to explain a little more.' I started with alarm and Jason jerked forward too. Simon looked quizzically at us. 'I just hope it'll be OK' I whispered lamely.

'Yeah, it's like the vicar has said. We're not going to stand back and watch all this from a distance. This is for real. Life's a bitch sometimes. Lizzie lived with people. Some of them were pretty scary people but she wanted them all involved. Involved with people, she always was. So here's some rose petals.' She moved over to the nearest champagne bucket, lifted out a handful of petals and let them drop from her hands. 'I'm going to take a handful and give them to my Lizzie. Life's a bloody bitch, but you were so beautiful. Live on in the roses Lizzie, live on my Lizzie.' Tears were streaming down her face and handkerchiefs were sought all round the church. Meg took a deep breath, shook herself and looked at us. 'Well, that may not be your thing. That's fine. But if you want to join us, just come and put some roses in with Lizzie for her final journey. You can put in what you like – we're not bothered. Choccy biccies if you want, just make sure they're plain chocolate. Newspaper cuttings, whatever. Roses are our thing for Lizzie and that's why they're here. Join us if you want. Feel free.' She turned back to Paul. 'OK?' Paul nodded. Meg went up to the coffin and stood there. Everyone watched her in silence. Then she grabbed two handfuls of rose petals and threw them angrily into the coffin. There was a shower of petals all around the coffin. Meg turned and ran back to Patricia, burying her face into her shoulder and sobbing.

All this time Jason was engrossed, like all of us. He stared ahead at Meg and whispered. 'Go, girl, go!' His eyes were bright with tears. When she pulled herself together so did he, wiping his eyes with the handkerchief again. He did seem more relaxed somehow.

No one knew what to do next. Paul later said that he knew that he had a choice. He could stand back, pause for a moment in case anyone else wanted to follow Meg and then carry on, for it was unlikely that anyone would break ranks with Patricia occupied with comforting Meg. Or he could encourage people more to join in, taking the lead himself. He said he was half aware that some people would criticise him for encouraging paganism in the church when he could easily have let it go. But he was more aware that he had promised Meg and Patricia to make sure that people did have a chance to take part. Paul spoke up. 'This is for those who want to express their grief in this way. Please come. If you want to be involved, come forward.' He himself went up to the coffin, took a handful of petals, dropped them simply, paused for a moment and then returned. A couple of family members from next to Patricia went forward as well, followed by four people from the other side at the front. Already a little queue was forming. Paul announced that we would sing 'Lord the dance' as people came forward. 'This is your opportunity. Take it if you want.' Years of evangelistic altar calls seemed to have rubbed off on him strangely. Patricia now joined the queue herself, unmistakably petite and black.

The band started a Celtic drumming, deep and slow and somehow wilder than in a normal Anglican service. It fitted with the strangeness of the petals, though. When the female singer sang out at half the normal speed 'I danced in the morning when the world was begun…' I knew it was all right. The connection with Jesus was the main thing, however it was expressed. Not many of us joined in. But that too was OK; a poignant solo accompaniment to the queuing mourners.

Jason was suddenly agitated. He looked around and returned to smooth out his squashed his order of service again. He moved forward slightly as though he wanted to go out but I was holding my order of service in front of me and he didn't seem to want to push past. I carried on singing, not sure of what to do. It would make life easier for all of us if he just stayed put. There was a steady flow now. Mohammed and Raisa came forward with Frank hesitantly in front. Mohammed's hand was firmly on Frank's shoulder. As they waited Frank was coughing loudly. Raisa looked at Mohammed, questioning what he was doing in guiding Frank to the front, but Mohammed just smiled at her and kept his hand on Frank's shoulder.

People were returning from the front, many with tears running down their faces. A few were looking up at the ceiling as people do when returning from Communion. Some were shaking their heads sadly. Others looked as angry as Meg had been. Frank just stared at the coffin perfectly still for a few moments. Having pushed him up there, Mohammed now had to drag him away. Frank look whiter than anyone and he was almost gasping for breath. He went out of the church with Mohammed while Raisa stayed in the pew singing.

Jason seemed to have calmed down and the hymn was coming to an end so I relaxed. 'Please keep coming, we do want to give an opportunity for those at the back. We'll sing again from the first verse, 'I danced in the morning…'

More people poured out from the back of the church. I stood firm, with my hymn sheet lifted high, and looked at Jason. 'OK?' I asked solicitously, but with a definite hard edge. He nodded and returned to fiddle with his sheet, still not singing. So many people were moving that even fewer were singing. Some in front of us sat down and hugged each other. Others just stood in the pew holding each other and sobbing. A young woman just behind us burst out into anguished tears. It was all I could do to keep up the singing. Hardly anyone else seemed bothered. I looked round to encourage those who were singing, nodding at them to keep going, and noticed Mohammed come in again with Frank who still looked listless and deathly white.

As I was turning over my right shoulder, Simon leant in front of me and nodded to Jason to go to the front. Jason dropped his paper on the floor and the first thing I knew he was pushing past me. I flashed an angry frown at Simon who was just stepping into the aisle as Jason followed him. The only thing I could do was follow.

It was as crowded as an Underground platform in rush hour, but more polite. Simon and Jason darted ahead while I had to let someone coming back pass by. A young couple pushed in between Jason and myself. I pushed up against the couple but they turned round and looked at me, not understanding my rudeness, and I had to hold back. 'O Lord, it's over to you now.' I whispered. 'You keep a hand on him now.'

Simon and Jason reached the coffin and Simon pulled out a few petals from the bottom of the urn. It seemed that there were not many left. Jason just stood there, tears running down his cheeks and his body shaking. I remembered times at Pathfinders when he had been the only one to cry at a video. He looked eleven years old again and lost.

It was too hard to watch. I reached forward with my arm, past the couple in front and put my hand heavily in his left shoulder, sort of pulling him away. Immediately he shook me off fiercely and started shouting. 'NO! NO! NO!' His scream filled the church. Even the organist stopped playing wondering what was happening. 'I'm sorry, I'm sorry, I'm sorry. I let you go. LIZZIE!' The whole church was looking at him. I wanted desperately to pull him away out of the focus. This was our worst nightmare. No doubt the papers and the television would be full of this tonight if they could.

Suddenly there was a movement behind me. A bright scarf weaved past at chest height, Meg charging through to Jason. She wrapped her arms round him and kissed his cheek. 'Jasey, Jasey. We all let her go. It was all of us. O Jasey. She was so lovely!'

Meg was only talking quietly. I had never seen or imagined her so motherly. Jason turned to Meg and buried his face down in her shoulder. Now he was crying seriously, sobbing with his whole body. I looked at Paul for reassurance and saw that he was smiling with tears rolling down his cheeks. He dabbed his face briefly, not enough to wipe away all the tears and, stuttering, announced that we would sing 'I danced on a Friday when the sky went black,' asking Jesus to be with us in the darkness of our grief.

Meg had her arms strongly round Jason now and pulled him with her, to sit by her. What were we to do now? Simon ushered me with him back to our seats. I knew that I had failed at the one task I had been given for today. Even for me, singing was hard now. I kept my eyes firmly on Jason which was all I could do, as Meg continued to hold him tight. Patricia put her arm round them both. The whole thing was so extraordinary. At the time I didn't think it through. How could the mother and sister of a murder victim embrace the man who had just confessed to the killing? Had they not heard what he had said? The rest of the church knew and there could be little doubt in anyone's mind. Still they hugged him like a son returning to the family.

If Meg somehow knew that Jason had not killed Lizzie, despite all appearances, was this because she knew more than anyone who had done? Why was she so angry with the rose petals which had been her chosen way of mourning? What had been going through her mind? It seemed that what she had thought was for the best turned out to be empty and meaningless? Had she somehow thought that Lizzie's dying was for the best? Meg seemed to know something that no-one else did. What was it?

Eventually the song finished and we all sat down for the reading. Unfortunately there was room for Jason at the front and there was nothing we could do but sit. The order of service said it was John 14, read by an Executive of the Newspaper Company. I wondered how he could keep his mind on the reading when he would be desperate to work out what to write about all this. After some half-familiar words about rooms in the Father's house I registered nothing else. Bitter recriminations were going through my head. Why had I allowed Jason to go forward? Why had I reached out to grab him? I looked gloomily at the floor as Paul started. 'Since the day I heard of Lizzie and Tariq's car accident...' was he really going to go through with what he had written?

Paul said afterwards that he had no choice. Enough people already had a copy of his words and he had enough experience to trust that his judgement sitting calmly in his study was more influenced by the Holy Spirit than his judgement in such a heated moment. As it turned out, the whole atmosphere had been so charged that his words, even about Lizzie's dead body, didn't seem odd, but right for the occasion. We had all seen her and felt that pang that he evoked. Moving on to address the person who had committed the crime did cause people to look up at what he was going to say. I thought he stressed heavily the Herod parallel rather than any other motive, probably to encourage Jason somehow. But it was a forlorn hope.

Paul proclaimed the Bible verses at the end of his sermon with a ringing confident voice. Later he told me that he was full of doubt about how it had all been received but knew he just had to stick to what he had prepared. There was a silence with people sniffing and coughing.

'We've sung together and listened together. We've expressed our grief together,' said Paul, glancing towards Patricia, Meg and Jason. 'Now we'll be quiet together, allowing our hearts and minds to mull over this day and what it means to us all. The music playing is music that Lizzie loved, helping her feel close to the sea and its inhabitants.'

I marvelled that he could be so calm. I hung my head in my hands. Not only was I a failed husband, I was a failed detective, a failed lawyer, a failed Christian. The music went on too long, but anything was too long for my torment.

Next in the Order of Service were the prayers, led by Susan Wardle, Lizzie's godmother. Susan was a plump woman in her 50s, a schoolteacher maybe, from her manner. She was more composed that Paul looked, now that he had finished preaching. She said some simple direct prayers, thanking God for Lizzie's love of life and asking for comfort for those who were going to miss her terribly over the months ahead. We joined in the modern Lord's Prayer which was printed on the sheet.

Paul seemed to have collected himself again as he announced 'Praise my soul', which I expected had been Patricia's choice. The undertakers placed the lid on the coffin quickly and neatly. Singing 'well our feeble frame he knows' brought some comfort to me and made me pray for Jason in his frailty again. It seemed I had been wrong all along. He did have it in him. Only God knows fully. I felt like walking out of the church and keeping walking. Thankfully Simon was still alert and when Paul had given the final blessing of some sort, Simon grabbed my arm and we moved up the aisle to the front. Meg stood up, her eyes flashing 'Hands Off!' but Simon bent down to her. 'We want to keep him away from the cameras, love. It will be better for him.' Meg nodded sharply, kissed Jason on the cheek and said 'See you soon. We love you too.' Patricia just waited patiently while all this was going on, happy for Meg to be showing this affection to her daughter's killer.

Simon stayed to one side with Jason as the family moved off behind the coffin. The organ struck up very softly and this time I did recognise the tune: 'Somewhere' from West Side Story. Jason crumpled into the seat and Simon sat next to him with a hand on his shoulder. I joined them, afraid to touch Jason this time. The familiar words sang out in my head, and, I expected in the heads of quite a few present. 'We'll find a new way of living. We'll find a way of forgiving. Somewhere. Someday. Somehow…' It seemed a forlorn hope. Jason would not be in this church or among his family again for a very long time.

I was vaguely aware of people leaving church and wondering when would be the best time to make a move, sooner probably rather than later, as the cameras were busy at the front now. 'David! How can I talk to your vicar? I need to see him, confidentially.' I had trouble at first placing the rough voice which barked in my ear with a smell of stale cigars. Frank Gatley wanted to see Paul? I snapped. 'For goodness sake, Frank, he's in the middle of a funeral, if you hadn't noticed! What all this about now?'

Frank beckoned me to one side. 'Look Frank. I'm sure this can wait. I need to stay here.' I looked to Simon for confirmation and he just waved his arm. 'We'll wait until it goes quieter,' he said confidently. Why was he so blooming accommodating? There was nothing for it but to go and have another earful from Frank.

'Look, Frank. If you want to have another go at religion, please don't take it out on Paul.' I looked at him with as much patience as I could drag up from inside me.

'David, you know what you said? You were livid with me then.' Frank paused, breathing heavily. He coughed and spoke in spurts, not stopping for me to respond. 'That lad. Doesn't deserve to die. That family have been through enough. I've had my life. Pash warned me. Even in one's own family. There was a reason. Maybe the best now is for *me* to tell the court.'

'Frank, I really don't understand what you're saying. What do you want to tell the court? If you insist on talking now, you can at least make sense.' Looking back I was astounded that Frank told me anything. In fact my anger seemed to spur him on.

'The court. Your honour.' Frank seemed to be raving now, losing touch with reality. He stared into the air, facing the front of the church. 'That lad is a dangerous man. Far more dangerous than you all realise. He and his lot will keep going until they collapse us all in a pile of dust. And he's the leader. O Pash. You warned us. You warned us.'

'Frank.' Suddenly I felt some compassion for this crazy old man. 'You're upset. You've just been to a very emotional funeral. It's all right. Who's dangerous? What lad is dangerous? Calm down.'

'Frank looked at me with tears in his eyes. 'Tariq. More dangerous than anyone. Seems a nice lad. But he wants to bring us all down. They all do. Bloody desert Arabs and their bloody desert mentality.'

'What? What's this to do with Tariq?' A chill went down my spine as a penny dropped. It was more like a ha'penny. Unsubstantial at first, not enough to make full sense. 'OK Frank, just tell me what you want to say. I'm listening.'

'That's all there is to it. Some of them want to blow us up literally. They're just crazy and they don't have enough support. That's what Pash said. God, he knew what he was talking about. "When they find more respectable ways of bringing you all down. That's the time to get worried. Stop them." He held my arm and looked me in the eye. He was dying and he could see things. Dreamt of the Natwest Tower, with a crescent on it, collapsing into rubble. That's it. That's what you need to be afraid of, God help you.'

'A dream of a big city building crumbling. What's that got to do with Tariq? Or with you talking to the judge?' There was a little sympathy in me for the raving old man, but not a lot. I hoped that it was nearly time to be taking Jason back home, poor lad.

'Listen to me! For God's sake! They target one big bank, fill it with their money. Then when there's a pretext, they pull all their money out to some purer bloody Islamic bank. Our bank collapses. Simple. Dominoes. England collapses. Mary bloody Poppins.'

'Mary Poppins, for crying out loud!' My sympathy ran out. 'What?' I put as much aggressive incredulity into that one word as I could. It wasn't hard to do.

'Banks! Bank falls, England falls. Good God he could see it happening. Can't you see it? O for God's sake.' Frank drooped his head, shaking it in despair.

'Are you saying that Moslems pulling their money out of a bank will make England fall? And why? I mean why say this now?' I also wanted to ask why he had suddenly become so religious, but it was more important to make some sense of his raving.

' "Stop them," Pash said. "Whoever they are. Whoever they are. Whoever ".' His bloodshot eyes tried to fix mine with urgency. 'That arrogant bastard Tariq couldn't help boasting. He was going to do it, God help us.' Frank calmed down at last and put his hand on my arm. 'That's why I had to stop him.' He paused briefly. 'I failed, God help me I failed. A bloody mess. Now I just need to have my say, whatever it costs. They'll turn this place into another bloody desert if we don't stop them.'

The penny finally clanged. I waved for Simon to come over to us. He stayed with Jason. 'Sergeant Plant,' I shouted, with urgency and relief. 'You need to hear a confession.' I couldn't quite believe that Frank was serious, but he was, as the court found out months later. Paranoid and unhinged maybe, but deadly serious.

Are you puzzled by praying in tongues?

Do you want to know more about praying in pictures – for angels or humming-birds? Are people really healed through this?

Would you like to read more about what Christians think God is saying to people in Britain today?

And how do Christians seriously think that they can hear God speaking to them today?

Ladder Media plan to publish another book by Roger Harper in which he addresses these questions and more:

The Holy Spirit in Britain Today

The Holy Spirit in Britain Today will include the best of Roger's articles from *Christianity* magazine, together with much new work, describing and analysing Christian faith in contemporary Britain.

Details will be available at <u>www.abritishcrash.co.uk</u>

Ladder Media Ltd. is a Christian Equitable Company (CEC) – a company where investors and workers love each other as they love themselves.

A CEC is a company limited by guarantee and without a shareholding. Those who invest in the company and those who work for the company are equal partners in running the company and in benefiting from profits.

In a normal shareholding company, the shareholders appoint directors to run the company on their behalf and in their interests. Shareholders take any profit which is not reinvested in the company. Workers receive a salary but normally do not benefit from any increased profit. For workers it has been described as 'working to make other people rich.'

In a normal shareholding company, the shareholders own the company as a piece of property which they can transfer, with continuing entitlement to profit, through generations. This has been the main mechanism through which the gap between the rich and the poor has widened considerably, especially in recent years. Overall, capital is rewarded more than labour. This arrangement is not 'loving your neighbour as you love yourself.'

A cooperative seeks to reverse the inequality, with the workers controlling the company and benefiting from profits. This too is not 'loving your neighbour as you love yourself.'

Christians believe that it is supremely important to love God and to love our neighbour as ourselves in every aspect of our life. Hence the recent formation of the model of a Christian Equitable Company.

Ladder Media Limited is pioneering the development of Christian Equitable companies in the UK.

It is hoped that a Venture Capital CEC, Jerusalem Developments, will soon be formed, to help set up further CECs in the UK and across the world.

For further details or to register an interest in helping with the development of CECs, please write to lad1@abritishcrash.co.uk

And did those feet, in ancient time,
Walk upon England's mountains green?
And was the holy lamb of God
In England's pleasant pastures seen?
And did the countenance divine
Shine forth upon our clouded hills?
And was Jerusalem builded here
Among those dark, satanic, mills?

Bring me my bow of burning gold,
Bring me my arrows of desire.
Bring me my spear: O clouds unfold,
Bring me my chariot of fire!
I shall not cease from mental fight,
Nor shall my sword sleep in my hand,
'Til we have built Jerusalem,
In England's green and pleasant land.

William Blake, c1804